DONNA ANDREWS PRESENTS

MYSTERY MOST HUMOROUS

DONNA ANDREWS PRESENTS

MYSTERY MOST HUMOROUS

A MALICE DOMESTIC ANTHOLOGY

EDITED BY JOHN BETANCOURT,
MICHAEL BRACKEN, AND CARLA COUPE

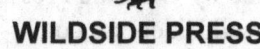

WILDSIDE PRESS

CONTENTS

MURDER MOST HUMOROUS

DONNA ANDREWS

Many years ago, when I was writing the first chapters of what eventually became *Murder with Peacocks* (my first published book), I was in a writing group with a feisty senior citizen named Leo. I never could figure out what, if anything, Leo actually read, and I tended to take his critique with more than a few grains of salt because I am prone to humorous exaggeration and he was astonishingly earnest and literal.

Still, I was delighted one week when he held up the pages I'd passed out to the group, shook them briskly, and exclaimed, "This is funny!"

"Thank you!" I said.

"But it can't possibly be funny," he said. "It's a murder mystery!" And he intoned those fateful words as if imitating Vincent Price doing a dramatic reading of "The Fall of the House of Usher."

Alas! Poor Leo! I don't think he ever became reconciled to the idea of a humorous murder mystery.

And he's not alone. We live, alas, in a culture in which a great many people think that you need to be serious to be taken seriously. That there's something vaguely disreputable about having humor and homicide between the same covers. That being earnest is not only important but somehow required if you're going to be a real writer.

Fortunately there are also a fair number of us who feel differently. Who appreciate the comic side of crime. Who understand that humor is often the best way to tackle a serious subject. Or who find that sometimes laughter is the only way to keep sane in this crazy world of ours.

And nobody ever called Will Shakespeare a hack for including some pretty hilarious comic relief to works like *Hamlet* and *Macbeth*.

So if like me you're one of that number, this book's for you.

DIRTY DEEDS

DONNA ANDREWS

I was still on my first cup of coffee when Mrs. Farwell called to give me a heads up.

"There's a truck in front of your aunt's house," she said. "From one of those junk hauling companies."

"Which one?" I pulled open the drawer in which I kept the files on all the projects I was doing for Aunt Josephine. The way things were going, I might need to clear out another drawer before too long. The files were packed so tightly that I had a hard time plucking out the file marked "Josephine: junk removal estimates."

"The truck says Dirty Deeds," Mrs. Farwell said. I could imagine her, sitting in her front window with her binoculars, and allowed myself a moment of satisfaction at how I'd turned the neighborhood nuisance into a useful ally,

"I don't recall getting an estimate from them," I said. I flipped through the file to make sure. I found my copies of the estimates I'd given Aunt Josephine—from 1-800-GOT-JUNK and College Hunks, along with a local outfit called It's Haul Good. No, my memory was correct. I hadn't gotten an estimate from Dirty Deeds.

"I've never heard of them." Mrs. Farwell said.

I hadn't either. But I did an online search and found their site. A small, local outfit. Amateurish photo of two scruffy young men playing guitars in front of an overflowing dumpster under the headline "Dirty Deeds Done Dirt Cheap!" A red banner proclaimed "Removals a Specialty!" According to the website, they offered not only junk hauling but also hoarded house cleanouts, crime scene cleanup, and biohazard remediation. I glanced again at the photo. Very unprepossessing young men. I had a hard time imagining them capable of anything as sophisticated as biohazard remediation. Then again, maybe that was just their way of indicating they'd tackle any cleanup job, no matter how nasty and disgusting.

"Thanks for letting me know," I said to Mrs. Farwell. "I'd better come over there to make sure it's going well."

After I hung up, I sat for a few minutes, fuming. I'd been trying for months now to get Aunt Josephine to agree to let me help her declutter her house. It wasn't quite as bad as those houses you saw on the TV shows about hoarding, but it was headed that way. And the older she got, the more danger-ous it was for her to live in a house with an ever-increasing number of things that could trip her or fall on her. I wasn't sure whether to feel vindicated that she'd finally admitted the need for some junk removal or exasperated that she'd ignored the estimates I'd given her. The time I'd spent checking out those companies! Weeding out the ones that had too many bad reviews or just seemed unprofessional. I looked regretfully at the estimate from Haul Good, which featured a cheerful cartoon character in a green uniform. Col-lege Hunks featured two clean-cut green-uniformed staff.

The Dirty Deeds pair didn't look like the sort of people I'd have hired, but this was Aunt Josephine, the aging hippie. She probably liked the way they looked.

And I could overlook their appearance as long as they hauled away a reasonable amount of Aunt Josephine's useless junk and didn't make off with anything valuable. But that last thought energized me. I needed to get over there to supervise. I could so easily imagine those two scruffy young men rifling through drawers. Opening up Aunt Josephine's jewelry chest. Waiting until her back was turned and then slipping out to their truck with the heavy wooden box in which she kept her silverware.

Although before leaving the house, I selected a few files to take with me. If she'd finally seen the wisdom of my advice on decluttering, perhaps she might be open to a few of the other recommendations I'd been pressing her to consider. It was high time she considered making a will—a real will, drawn up by a competent attorney, instead of the highly unprofessional handwritten one she kept waving at me. And a power of attorney, so I'd be better able to help her out. And…yes, perhaps I should also make another attempt to talk her into letting me rent a safe deposit box for her so she could stop leaving valuables lying unprotected all over the house.

That was probably enough for the time being. Truth be told, I was be-coming slightly frustrated at how resistant Aunt Josephine was to letting me help her. I'd even tried to consult Adult Protective Services to see if I could enlist their help. How was I supposed to know that the head social worker was such a good friend of my aunt? And that she would run straight to Aunt Josephine when I contacted them? I was still trying to undo the damage that caused to my plans for helping out.

I tucked the relevant files in my briefcase, noting with annoyance that all three of them were getting more than a little worn around the edges.

And just for a moment, my mind rebelled. Why was I bothering? Aunt Josephine would once again rebuff my efforts, as she had for the past four years, ever since I'd returned to my hometown and realized how much she needed my assistance. No doubt I'd spend a frustrating day, arguing not only with her but also with those unfortunate-looking young men. With luck I'd manage to keep them from robbing her blind, but I could already feel the beginnings of a tension headache. Actually, I'd started calling them Josephine headaches.

When I arrived at Aunt Josephine's I found a small, battered panel truck parked in her driveway. The small size was reassuring—they couldn't possibly make off with more than a few pieces of furniture. And apart from rather a lot of empty boxes, there were only two things in it: a dead lawn mower that I'd been trying to talk her into discarding for years, and a collection of old magazines. Maybe the Dirty Deeds crew weren't completely useless if they'd managed to convince her that there was no resale market for old issues of *TV Guide*, *Women's Day*, and *Southern Living*.

I checked the empty boxes, just in case—mostly cardboard ones, and a few sturdy wooden ones of various sizes. I wasn't sure I liked the look of those wooden boxes. They looked more suited to moving breakable valuables than hauling junk. I'd be keeping a close eye on what they put in those.

I strode up the front steps, knocked briskly on the front door, and tried the doorknob. It was unlocked, so I let myself in.

I found Aunt Josephine in the living room, having tea with the two young men from the ad. Actually, she was having tea. They were both sipping cold cans of Pepsi.

For once, Aunt Josephine looked almost glad to see me.

"This is my niece," she said. "The one I told you would probably show up. Justin and Zachary."

She didn't make it clear which one was which, and since I wasn't sure I'd be able to tell them apart anyway, I didn't ask for clarification. In person, they looked every bit as scruffy as they had in the ad, and I suspected they were brothers, if not twins. But I was encouraged by the way they looked at me. They seemed cheerful and expectant. Maybe they'd already figured out exactly how obstreperous their client could be and would be not only willing but eager to take direction from someone with more of her marbles intact.

"And I bet she already checked your truck to make sure you weren't making off with anything valuable," Aunt Josephine said.

"We're fine with that," Justin-or-Zachary said.

"In fact, we welcome it," Zachary-or-Justin added.

"We promise our customers that we'll remove anything and everything they want removed…and only what they want removed." Justin-or-Zachary made it sound like an aspirational saying, or maybe a corporate motto, like "We try harder" or "Just do it."

So began what I quickly realized was going to be one of the longest and most irritating days of my life. I set up my station on the front porch, where I could inspect each outgoing box, bag, or item. At the same time, I could also keep an eye on the driveway, to make sure nothing made it onto the truck without going past me.

To my surprise, though, it went rather smoothly. The first time they came out bearing an item I didn't think Aunt Josephine should be discarding—a box full of family genealogical papers—Zachary-or-Justin didn't protest when I told them to just tuck it in the backseat of my car instead of in their truck. For that matter, neither did Aunt Josephine when she realized it was happening.

"If you want to give house room to that junk, fine by me," she said.

At times, I found myself longing to be inside, where I could point out items for consideration. But I reminded myself of how contrary Aunt Josephine could be. My flagging an item as junk might inspire her to dig in her heels and keep it. And I realized that if I'd been inside, I'd have been driven crazy by the slow pace of the decluttering. At one point, they had a half-hour conversation about a single item of junk—a threadbare, broken-down velvet sofa. Aunt Josephine told them half a dozen stories about events that seemed to involve the sofa somehow before finally sighing and telling them to haul it away.

"I've loved it for a long time," she said. "But it's time to let it go."

I hoped she wasn't paying them by the hour.

And in their idle moments—Aunt Josephine's slow pace made for plenty of those—the two young men made a point of telling me that they didn't just dump everything in the landfill. They donated or recycled wherever possible. That, they claimed, was the purpose of the sturdy wooden boxes—to protect breakables that their clients wanted to have donated.

"Old china mostly," one of them said.

"Or small pieces of furniture," the other said, pointing to the largest of the boxes. "We can fit a grandfather clock in that one."

I refrained from pointing out that Aunt Josephine didn't own a grandfather clock. And I was disappointed not to see any of Aunt Josephine's gaudy china heading for their truck. A pity. That would have eased the headache that had set in after the first hour.

Still, by sunset their truck was mostly full. It was far from enough—the small load they were hauling off barely made a dent in the clutter. But at least it was a start. And they'd proved surprisingly good at gently coaxing her into giving up some of her junk. I'd have to figure out how to convince Aunt Josephine to have them back for more decluttering—I rather suspected complaining about them would work better than praising them.

"You want to take a last look at the truck?" Justin-or-Zachary asked me. "Just to make sure you're happy with what's leaving?"

It seemed like a good idea. So I waited until Zachary-or-Justin set up the ramp so I could walk up into the truck, and did a polite but cursory inspection. Annoyingly, the grandfather clock box stood empty in the middle of the truck with its lid to one side. Evidently they hadn't talked Aunt Josephine into donating any large but fragile items.

Just then Justin-or-Zachary appeared behind the truck, with Aunt Josephine at his side.

"We done?" he asked.

"As soon as you load that one last item," Aunt Josephine said.

"You're sure?"

"Positive."

Suddenly one of the scruffy young men grabbed my arms and held them behind my back. The other one raced up the ramp and stuck something into my hip. I felt faint, and although I tried to put up a fight, I began losing control of my muscles. I wasn't able to resist as they bound and gagged me and shut me up in the large wooden box. As I fought to stay awake, I could hear them talking through the lid of the box.

"Now remember," one of them said. "She drove off a few minutes after we left. Just do your best to act surprised when the police come to notify you about the accident."

"You're sure this is going to work?" Aunt Josephine asked.

"Absolutely," the young man said.

"We've done this plenty of times," the other said.

"And we've never had a problem. Remember—removals a specialty."

And that was the last thing I heard before I blacked out.

THE MASQUERADE BALL

GIGI PANDIAN

A JAVA JONES FLASH FICTION STORY

"Why did I agree to perform at this masquerade ball?" Sanjay's tuxedo jacket flapped in the crisp wind, but he didn't seem to notice the cold.

I wrapped my rented cloak more tightly around me, but the chill of the San Francisco night air still seeped in. "Simply because there's sure to be at least one other person dressed like an old school stage magician?"

"I don't care about copycat costumes, Jaya. I'll look all the better compared to them."

My friend's healthy ego could use a reality check, but I was too cold to quibble. Our ride had texted that he was only a block away, but I should have known better than to wait outside.

"There you go." I rubbed my arms to keep warm. "Nobody is going to confuse you with Timothy." Timothy Dixon had recommended Sanjay for tonight's handsomely paid gig as the entertainment at a Victorian-themed masquerade ball, and Sanjay had agreed *before* learning Timothy would be the opening act.

"What I care about," said Sanjay, "is guys who rent a costume and immediately think they'll be brilliant performing the coin tricks they learned at age ten. But they flub it so badly they reveal magicians' secrets."

A sporty silver car pulled up next to us and the window descended. Inside sat a man wearing exactly what Sanjay had feared. A tailcoat of flimsy, wrinkled fabric with garish pops of red. Only the shirt underneath fit properly. An ill-fitting top hat rested on his head, looking incongruous over his stylishly cut brown hair.

"Sorry I let you get cold while you waited, Jaya," Timothy said. He turned up the heat as I got into the car, which was more difficult than usual in the full skirt of my Victorian dress.

"You were cold?" Sanjay asked.

Timothy laughed. "This is why you're single, Sanj."

Sanjay's eyelids lowered. He avoided glaring at Timothy, but I knew his expressions well enough to know he was furious. He had no problem being single, but he hated it when people took the liberty of calling him "Sanj."

We were headed to a mansion north of the city, in Marin. According to Timothy, it couldn't be found via GPS, and only "insiders" had directions, which is why he picked us up.

Sanjay is a stage illusionist known as The Hindi Houdini. After his theater burned down, he started taking highly paid private gigs, like this masquerade ball at the home of a couple who'd made their fortune in tech. Timothy ran in tech circles, but he'd recently suffered a setback with a failed startup, so he was hoping to network at tonight's party.

I'm a history professor who has nothing to do with magic or tech. I received an invitation because I've become marginally famous for finding a few treasures, and I'm known to be a good friend of Sanjay's. I love a good party—especially one where a personal chef is cooking. You could say my healthy appetite matches Sanjay's healthy ego.

We arrived at the glass-clad mansion to find only two dozen guests, with half of them in masquerade-style masks in addition to their costumes. Among them were a king and queen introduced as our hosts, a jester in a velvet suit of green and black diamonds who'd invented an app on my phone, and a Sherlock Holmes halfway through a "digital detox" weekend without technology who was starved for conversation.

When the evening's entertainment began, I cringed as Timothy obviously pocketed a "disappearing" ball that bulged in the cheap jacket's pocket and palmed a coin that showed between his fingers. At least nobody booed him off the stage, so I didn't feel guilty about enjoying the exquisite canapes. Sanjay's follow-up was met with enthusiastic applause.

"That first magician wasn't very observant, was he?" Sherlock whispered while we sampled skewers of grilled red grapes after the performance.

I didn't have a chance to reply—or to finish my grapes, which were growing on me—because that's when the scream rang out.

"My sapphire ring is gone!" the queen cried.

Several guests rushed to the queen, but Timothy headed for Sanjay. I followed.

"Sanj," Timothy whispered. "I know you're hard up, but it's a very bad idea to mess with our hostess."

"What are you talking about?" Sanjay hissed. "I didn't take her ring. And why do you think I'm—"

"*Nobody else* could have done it. You're the only person here who knows sleight of hand. And we all know about your theater burning down."

I studied Timothy as he spoke. The precise haircut. The perfectly pressed shirt under the careless costume. But it *wasn't* careless. It achieved the hapless effect he wanted.

I thought of Sherlock's words about Timothy: *He wasn't very observant, was he?* Except Timothy *was* observant. He'd been the one to notice I was cold.

Tonight was an act. Just not the one we thought we were watching.

"Is this any way to treat your hosts?" the queen demanded of Sanjay.

"Search Houdini," the jester shouted.

"Sanjay was set up," I said, stepping between him and the irate guests.

"But it had to be him." The queen stared me down. "He's the magician."

"Not the only one." I locked eyes with Timothy.

"I know I'm *dressed* like one." Timothy gave a meek smile. "I tried my best—"

"To fool us," I said. "You only pretended to be an incompetent sleight-of-hand artist."

"You framed me?" Now Sanjay *did* glare at Timothy.

"Search this other magician, too," the green-suited jester said as he grabbed hold of Timothy.

Timothy's face turned a bit green then too.

The next day, Sanjay stopped by my university office to show me a newspaper headline. *Hindi Houdini Unmasks Masquerade Miscreant.*

I raised an eyebrow. "The Hindi Houdini solved the case, did he?"

My simultaneously brilliant and clueless friend grinned. "Masquerade balls are the best, aren't they?"

DEAD MAN'S CHEST

MARCIA TALLEY

It wasn't a long walk—just a short stroll on a street the locals call UpAlong—but it required effort, the last two hundred yards or so winding through the village's sprawling burial grounds and up a steep hill. I was relieved when we reached the top, where I paused to catch my breath and asked Jane, "So, where is it? Much farther?"

"You're looking at it," Jane said, and pointed toward a grove of twisted palms. "I warned you it was a fixer-upper, Annie."

I'd been hunting for a bargain-priced island retreat, but this? As we neared the cottage, I could see that plywood covered two of the windows, shingles clung to the roof in patches, and a two-by-four supported by a pair of cinder blocks served as a step leading up to the porch. A sign dangled by one corner from what remained of a picket fence. Its faded letters spelled out "Pineapple Cottage" in bright blue capitals.

And yet, compared to other homes I'd seen on Bonefish Cay, Pineapple Cottage remained relatively unscathed. Battered, for sure, but it stood solid and proud on a rocky promontory overlooking the Atlantic Ocean, where it had survived—against all odds—the wrath of a hurricane that had flattened most of its neighbors.

Like me after the divorce.

As Jane showed me around the property, I felt a growing kinship with the cottage. The gate hung crookedly, but a new hinge could fix that. Shingles and pieces of siding begged to be replaced, a missing windowpane in the bathroom called out for attention…but, it was easy to picture myself sprawled on a porch lounger, sipping a margarita while the sun split into a double yolk and bled into the horizon, slipping into a sea that spread out before me, painted by Mother Nature in inky blue and aquamarine, edged with foam.

For the second time that day, Jane apologized for the cottage's shabby exterior.

"Nothing a hammer and a few nails won't fix," I assured her.

Easier to repair than a shattered heart.

"I think you'll find the interior easier on the eyes," Jane said as she stepped onto the porch and opened the door, which wasn't locked. "C'mon in."

We stood in an airy rectangle, divided by white-painted walls into four equal rooms. The walls ended about a foot short of the ceiling—typical for historic Bahamian cottages—to allow the tropical breezes for which the islands were famous to circulate freely.

The living room was furnished with a sofa and two wicker armchairs upholstered in a nubby white fabric and artfully strewn with a rainbow of Androsia batik cushions. A bedroom was off to the right, where a double bed faced a dresser over which hung a mirror framed in seashells. "All the furniture conveys," Jane said as she led me through to the kitchen, equipped with dated but fully functional appliances.

I'd toured a lot of houses recently, and I appreciated the work that went into preparing them for sale. "You've done a great job of staging," I told her as I fingered the crisp dotted piqué curtains that hung at the window over the kitchen sink. "At this price point, I'm kinda surprised the cottage hasn't already sold."

Jane grinned. "Full disclosure, Annie. Pop Weatherford was quite the hoarder. Never threw anything away. After his family decided they wanted to sell, it took us months to clean the place out."

Moving clockwise through another door found us in a spacious bathroom. "You'll love this feature," Jane said as she pointed out the generous shower stall, equipped with both an inside and an outside door. "You come straight up from the beach and step directly into the shower." She reached in and twisted the tap to demonstrate how robustly the water cascaded out of the showerhead.

"Sold!" I said, surprising even myself.

Jane's eyebrows shot up under her bangs. "What? Really?"

"There'll be a ton of details to work out, I'm sure, but yes, really. I think Pineapple Cottage will do quite nicely."

The following day, Jane and I were sitting on the porch discussing details of what would be—thanks to a generous divorce settlement from an ex-husband with perfect white teeth who couldn't wait to get rid of me so he could marry his dental hygienist—an all-cash sale. As Jane explained the ins and outs of the deposit, closing costs, stamp taxes, and legal fees, clouds gathered on the far horizon and the wind picked up, fluttering the pages of the sales contract I was about to sign.

Oooh-woo-whoo!

Somewhere nearby, someone was moaning.

Startled and a bit spooked, I turned to Jane. "What's that?"

Jane chuckled. "Just Old Spindleshanks the Pirate, come looking for his lost treasure. You'll get used to it."

I laid the pen down and stared. "Stop it!"

Jane held up three fingers. "Scout's honor. His real name was Garrick Evans. Spindleshanks was the bane of commercial shipping back in the early seventeen hundreds. Harassed the Spanish practically nonstop in a frisky little sloop called the *Crimson Tide*.

"*Baja mar,*" she continued. "Shallow sea. The average depth of the water around here is ten feet. Before the Loyalists started arriving en masse from the US in the years immediately following the Revolutionary War, the Bahamas were a pirate's paradise. Blackbeard, Captain Kidd, Ann Bonny…they were all here at one time or another. Two hundred twenty-nine islands," she began, ticking them off on her fingers. "Six hundred sixty-one cays, over two thousand islets." She paused to let those numbers sink in. "So, when the Brits or the Spaniards came chasing after you in their deep draft ships, you could tuck in just about anywhere." She grinned. "Pirate sloops were nimble.

"According to my grandfather," Jane said, "Spindleshanks used Bonefish Cay as his base of operations. He'd hang lanterns high in the trees after dark to lure unsuspecting ships onto the reef, where he'd murder the crew and steal their cargo."

"Golly, what a sweetheart," I said.

Jane shrugged. "Wrecking was big business back then, but naturally, the authorities were unamused. One day in the spring of 1732, some Portuguese conquistadors were hot on his heels, so Spindleshanks nipped into that little cove down there"—she leaned forward and waved vaguely toward the sea—"rowed ashore with his treasure, and buried it somewhere. Grandfather claimed that as a boy, he'd even seen the hand-drawn map."

"A map? X marks the spot and all that?"

"Exactly. Spindleshanks planned to come back for the treasure later, of course, once the coast was clear, but then a hurricane happened. X or no X marking the spot, it's challenging to follow a map when all your reference points have blown away."

Whoo-whoo-whoosh!

"Listen," Jane said. "There he goes again, mourning his loss."

I picked up the pen, waved it in her face, and said good-naturedly, "I'm not going to sign anything until you tell me what's actually going on."

"Are you in a hurry?"

"No," I assured her. "I'm already operating on island time."

Jane anchored the documents to the table with a large conch shell and said, "Follow me." She led me out the gate and left along a well-worn path toward the sea. When I caught up with her, she stood balanced precariously on an outcropping of limestone that centuries of relentless waves had eroded into lacy but treacherous, razor-sharp edges, the "iron shore" on which so many sailing vessels had met their doom. She waved me over to join her. "Tide's about right."

Whoo-whoo-whoot!

Near her feet, a puff of steam shot sky-high, ruffling her hair.

I jumped back, nearly losing my balance on the rocks. Jane grabbed my arm, steadying me. "It's a blowhole," she explained once I'd regained my footing. "We've got three of them here."

As she spoke, the blowhole erupted again—*whoo, whoo, whoot!*—spouting vapor like a whale.

"There's a series of caves under this ledge," she told me. "When the wind and the tide are just right, the waves crash in, shooting water straight up through holes in the ceiling, and you get, wait for it..."

The blowhole erupted again, a gentle *whoo-poof!* of mist this time, and I began to laugh. "Old Spindleshanks's given up, I guess."

"For the time being, anyway," Jane said.

* * * *

A month later, sitting around a table down at the Thirsty 'Cuda with Jane and the lawyer representing the Weatherford family, papers were signed, money exchanged hands, and we sealed the deal with a round of Miss Dee's famous Bahama Mamas. Jane helped me find Leon, a contractor who worked wonders on the cottage, and a few days later, I moved in.

When you buy a hundred-year-old cottage, though, it's always something. Less than a week later, when the toilet backed up and a plunger didn't do the trick, Leon gave me the bad news. "The cess pit's failed, Miss Annie. Gonna need to replace it with a septic tank and dig a soakaway."

"Swell," I muttered, *ka-ching, ka-ching, ka-ching* echoing in my head. My divorce settlement had been generous, but it wasn't bottomless. I'd have to scratch a golf cart off my shopping list.

Leon must have read my mind. "I've got a secondhand septic tank I can lay my hands on—house blew away during Floyd, so they've got no use for it now. If it's okay with you, I'll get my crew here in the morning to start digging. Local boys from the mainland, Miss Annie. Won't cost you much."

Leon was as good as his word. Two days into the job, the hole was the size of a wading pool. It was late afternoon. I'd brought iced tea out to the laborers and was hanging around, watching them work, thinking they must be sweltering in the long-sleeve T-shirts and knitted caps they wore to protect themselves from the tropical sun.

"Hi," someone behind me said.

Startled, I turned. The voice belonged to a boy, nine or ten years old. His ice-blue eyes considered me seriously from behind a pair of Harry Potter eyeglasses.

"Hello to you, too."

"I'm Jackson."

"Pleased to meet you, Jackson. My name's Annie."

"I know," he said. "I was playing foosball at the Thirsty 'Cuda when you came in with Miss Jane. My mom works there." His eyes turned toward the pit the workers were digging. "What's going on? Why are they digging?"

I winked at him and said, "Looking for pirate treasure."

Jackson didn't smile back. "I found some treasure once. Want to see?"

I said that I did.

The boy reached into the back pocket of his shorts and pulled out a small drawstring pouch. "Hold out your hand."

He loosened the strings, upended the pouch over my palm, and dropped a coin into it. The coin was a dusty copper, about the size of a poker chip, and stamped with the profile of a ponytailed man: *Georgivs III D.G. Rex.*

"This is very cool," I told him as I carefully inspected the coin, softly worn, but the images clearly visible. Britannia herself was embossed on the verso, seated on a globe, holding a spear and carrying a shield.

Jackson beamed with pride. "It's from 1790."

"Wow," I said. "What's it worth?"

"Back then? A halfpenny. Today…" He shrugged. "Doesn't matter. It's not for sale."

Jackson held out the pouch and watched solemnly as I dropped the coin into it. He was stuffing his treasure back into his pocket when the rhythmic *scritch-scritch-scritch* of a shovel turned to a dull thud, and one of the workers shouted, "*Hey! Kisa sa ye?*"

The two others stopped digging to have a look. "*Sanble yon bwat,*" one of them said.

The men spoke Haitian Creole, but I knew enough French to get the gist of what they were saying. They'd discovered a box.

Leon grabbed a spare shovel, clambered down a short ladder, and joined them in the pit. A discussion ensued. With four men digging, it wasn't long before the box was uncovered, hauled out of the pit, and placed on my porch.

"*Pirat nan Karayib la,*" Leon said, and he and his crew shared a good laugh.

About the size of an old English steamer trunk, the chest was rectangular and had a domed lid. It appeared to be made of wood bound with sturdy iron straps. Faded letters stenciled on the side spelled out Signor Aiello—Palermo. Leon tested the lid, but because it was secured with three impressive padlocks, it didn't budge.

Leon checked his watch, clicked his tongue, and said, "We need to hurry or we'll miss the ferry." While his workers scrambled to put away their picks and shovels, Leon turned to me and said, "We'll be back in the morning, Miss Annie. I'll bring some tools and we'll get that sucker open."

"*Merci*, Leon," I said.

"*Pa dekwa*," he replied.

After they'd gone, Jackson—who'd spent the previous five minutes circling the chest and studying it closely—said, "I can tell you one thing for sure. There's no way this chest was buried nearly three hundred years ago. This isn't Spindleshanks's treasure."

Although I had reached the same conclusion myself, I said, "How can you tell, Jackson?"

Jackson wrapped his hand around one of the padlocks and gave it a tug. "You can buy big locks just like this down at Mr. Willard's hardware store."

I nodded. "I wonder what's inside?"

"Constable Fergus has some bolt cutters. Do you have a golf cart, Miss Annie?"

When I told Jackson I didn't, he said, "I'll go get him, then," and set off down the road at a trot.

While I waited for Jackson to return with the constable and his trusty bolt cutters, I attacked the locks with all the tools at my disposal—a screwdriver, a kitchen knife, a pry bar, even a rusty nail file, with no luck. I'd given up and was bent over, cleaning layers of dirt off the chest with a spray bottle of Windex and a damp rag when a bright yellow golf cart with a young man at the wheel pulled up next to the cottage and set the brake. He was tall and deeply tanned, around sixteen or seventeen, I guessed. The Orioles ball cap he wore barely contained a shock of unruly, sun-bleached hair. "I hear you dug up a treasure chest," he said.

I straightened, shook dirt off the rag, and said, "Here it is, but—"

"Is it heavy?" he asked.

"Not very," I replied. "Did Constable Fergus send you?"

The guy blinked. "Uh…yeah."

"Have at it, then," I said.

To my surprise, instead of whipping out a set of tools, the young man grabbed the chest by one of the iron handles and dragged it to the edge of the porch. Lifting it by both handles, he swung it the short distance onto the back seat of the golf cart, which had been folded down to create a flatbed. Figuring I was meant to accompany him, I said, "I'll just get my purse," and dashed into the cottage. I was gone only a few seconds, but when I returned, he'd already turned the golf cart around and was bumping away down the road. I ran a few yards, shouting, "Wait, wait," but apparently he didn't hear me.

The village was only a short distance away, and it was all downhill, so I sighed and set off down UpAlong on foot.

I'd already passed the Y in the road where UpAlong merged into Back Street when I ran into Jackson and Constable Fergus riding a golf cart, coming the other way. The constable pulled even with me, mashed on the brakes, and leaned out of the cart. "So, where's this treasure chest Jackson told me about?"

I gasped. "What? I thought you had it."

"Me? No. Jackson only told me about it ten minutes ago."

"Well, I gave it to that guy I thought you sent," I said. "Tall, dirty-blond hair. Driving a yellow golf cart."

Constable Fergus glanced heavenward and closed his eyes. When he opened them again, he said, "The Queen Bee?"

"Now that you mention it," I said, "it did have a bumblebee painted on the side."

"Manny's an idiot," Jackson piped up. "If you're going to steal something, you don't do it driving your aunt's duded-up golf cart."

Something wasn't making sense. "But, how did Manny know about the treasure chest, Jackson? We've only just found it."

"When he's not working," the constable explained, "my nephew hangs out at the ferry dock. Probably heard about it from Leon or one of the workers."

"I'm surprised he didn't pass you," I said.

"Must have taken Back Street, then," the constable said.

Jackson swiveled in his seat. "If he did, I think I know where we can find him. He's got a lean-to out by the airport where he keeps some things."

"What kind of things?" Constable Fergus wanted to know.

Jackson shrugged. "Car parts, old batteries, wood scraps, pieces of metal. Stuff like that."

Constable Fergus looked at me, clicked his tongue and said, "It's always something with that boy. Hop in."

The electrical power for Bonefish Cay was provided by a diesel generator the size of a boxcar. As we barreled down the airport road, the hum of its giant turbines grew gradually louder until we had to shout to be heard. We found Manny exactly where Jackson had said he would be. He'd parked his aunt's golf cart next to a primitive lean-to that was tucked away in the mangrove a short distance behind and well downwind from the noise and smell of the generator. My ears and nose were relieved.

"Stay here," the constable ordered as he parked his own golf cart under a flourishing Bismarck palm and climbed out.

Manny was facing away from us, kneeling in front of the chest, holding something long, narrow, and red, like a candle. "What's that in his hand?" I whispered to Jackson.

"It's a distress flare," Jackson whispered back. "I told you Manny was a doofus. I bet he's fixing to light it up and use it to melt the locks off."

"Sounds dangerous," I said.

Jackson nodded. "Molten magnesium is plenty hot, and if the flare's old, it can explode on you. I read an article in *Popular Mechanics*—"

Popular Mechanics? Most kids his age would be reading the *Goosebump* series or *Captain Underpants*. I reached out and squeezed the boy's arm. "Shhhh. I think Manny's uncle is about to handle the situation."

His footsteps dampened by the dull hum of the generator behind us, Constable Fergus crept up on his nephew from behind. "Up!" he shouted as he grabbed the teen by the back of his T-shirt and yanked him to his feet.

The distress flare went flying.

"I was just—"

"We'll talk about this later, young man. In the meantime..."

Constable Fergus whipped a pair of handcuffs off his belt, snapped one bracelet around Manny's wrist, and attached the other to the roll bar of the Queen Bee. With Manny under control, he returned to the cart where Jackson and I waited, reached into a rear compartment, and came out holding a pair of bolt cutters. "Let's see what all the fuss was about, shall we?"

Giving the Queen Bee a wide berth, and with Jackson scampering on ahead, the three of us converged on the chest.

"Are you going to turn him in to the police?" I asked as we walked, nodding in the hapless Manny's direction.

"I *am* the police."

In spite of the late afternoon chill, I felt my face grow red.

He frowned darkly. "Assuming you're not going to press charges, I've got something much worse in store for that young man. I'm turning him over to his aunt Dee."

Behind us, Manny groaned.

Ignoring us all, Jackson hovered over the chest. While the constable made quick work of the locks with his bolt cutter, Jackson waited, shifting excitedly from one foot to the other. After what remained of the last lock was tossed into the mangrove, the constable turned to me, bowed slightly, and said, "Will you do the honors, Miss Annie?"

I nodded and approached the chest, holding my breath.

I raised the lid.

The contents were made of metal, like coins, and round and flat like coins, too. They came in different denominations as well, so to speak. I recognized the distinctive silver and red of a Diet Coke can, the gold of

Schweppes tonic water, and the silver, red, and yellow of an island favorite, Bahamas Goombay Punch.

Constable Fergus sucked air in through his teeth. "There's hundreds of cans in there. A thousand, maybe."

Jackson selected one of the cans and turned it over in his hands, examining it closely. If he was disappointed, his face didn't show it. "Mr. Weatherford bought one of those fancy beer can smashers down at the hardware store." He dropped the can—neatly reduced to a disc by the crushing machine—back into the chest. "But, why…"

"He had a disorder," Constable Fergus explained. "Obsessive-compulsive disorder."

"OCD," Jackson agreed, nodding. "There was an article about it in *Reader's Digest*. Five things you should never say to someone with OCD, like, 'relax' or 'it's all in your head' or—"

Constable Fergus cut the boy off before he could recite the article in its entirety, which Jackson seemed intent on doing. "Pop Weatherford collected a lot of things," the constable said, turning to me. "Alarm clocks, antique glass bottles, Christmas decorations. Apparently he collected soda cans, too."

"But why go to all the trouble to *bury* them?" I asked.

"He had a ball of string as big as a watermelon," Jackson said, as if that explained everything.

* * * *

Manny began serving out his sentence on the eight-to-twelve shift at the island dump, keeping an eye on the rat traps and hosing out trash bins.

Once my plumbing was working again, I invited Jane over for dinner, a simple chicken casserole and a tossed salad. After she arrived, I whirred up a couple of frozen margaritas in the blender, then invited Jane to join me for cheese and crackers on the porch.

"Too bad there was nothing of value in that chest," Jane said as she settled into one of my new Adirondack chairs and adjusted a pillow behind her.

"I don't know about that," I said as I relaxed into the other chair. "How many soda cans do you think there were in that chest? Six, seven hundred?"

"At least," Jane said, stirring her drink with an index finger.

"Okay, consider this. They're worth five cents apiece in most states. Ten cents in Oregon, Connecticut, and Michigan. Do the math."

Jane laughed out loud.

Smiling, I reached for a cracker and topped it with a square of cheddar.

Whoo-whoo-whoot!

The tide was up, and so was Spindleshanks the Pirate.

I waved an arm, taking in the sea grape-covered dunes, the waves gently licking the pink sand beach, and beyond it, the vast expanse of the topaz sea. There was nothing between me—I'd looked it up—and the west coast of Africa. I took an appreciative sip of my margarita, licked salt off my lips, and sighed in contentment. "Spindleshanks may be doomed to search for his lost treasure for all eternity, Jane, but I got lucky. I've found a million-dollar view."

MAGGIE AND RICK

WILLIAM ADE

If you ever get lost driving in Vermont, there's a good chance you'll eventually pass through the quaint village of Pleasant Valley and discover Maggie's Bakery and Cat Café. Unless you're put off by cat hair floating in your herbal tea, I highly recommend you stop. There's nothing more Vermont than pulling apart a warm blueberry scone surrounded by a dozen meowing felines.

As a bonus, you'll meet the proprietor, Maggie Merriweather, one of those legendary small-town amateur sleuths who have kept Vermont's unsolved murder rate near zero for decades. Yup, Maggie is the total package; she bakes, neuters cats, and solves perplexing mysteries.

It's not that everyone in Pleasant Valley appreciates this talented woman. Rick Carlyle is not a big fan of Maggie, and if you sat for a minute in Duke's Tavern, Carlyle would happily share his reasons for disliking her.

"I'm a professional private eye, dang it. I'm licensed and bonded, and I've been beaten, shot, stabbed, and broken by cold-hearted women. But I can't make a decent living as a private investigator because that fool woman, Maggie Merriweather, solves crimes for free."

Now stay with me. This disagreement was more than a small-town kerfuffle. Life in this New England village grew dark when Maggie's beloved aunt, Miss Tippsy, was found head down in her backyard well. Not that it was something unusual for these parts. Many folks still drew water from a backyard well, and many toppled in. And it was no secret that local volunteer firefighters pulled Miss Tippsy from her well more than a few times in the past. What was so peculiar this time was that Miss Tippsy was dead.

It was afternoon when the siren of the village's only fire truck alerted me and everyone else in Pleasant Valley that something terrible had happened at Miss Tippsy's place. Folks quickly gathered, and we saw Jimmy Hoot and Pete Barkey, the only volunteer firefighters simultaneously out of work and sober, hop from the truck and spring into action.

Using a long rope and some fancy slip knot, Jimmy looped Miss Tippsy by her ankles, pulled her up, and laid her mangled body on the ground. Being a superstitious lot, no villager approached the corpse except for Maggie, who sobbed. "Oh, Auntie, what did they do to you?"

The county sheriff, Bobby Cantrell, blew into Pleasant Valley and, after a cursory examination of the remains, labeled Miss Tippsy's death as accidental. The fact that he spent little time examining the death scene didn't surprise me. I knew the Sheriff despised Maggie and would do her no favors. You see, Maggie had frequently embarrassed Cantrell. After the murder of a local citizen, Cantrell would claim it was the work of a drifter passing through the county and there was little he could do. Then Maggie would somehow find the guilty party living in the village, maybe running a roadside molasses stand or something equally innocent and bring the criminal to justice. Her success made Sheriff Cantrell look like a nincompoop. By now, folks believed the man couldn't solve a crossword puzzle if you spotted him all the consonants.

As you might expect, the exchange between the two antagonists as they stood over Miss Tippsy's corpse wasn't a pretty thing to witness.

"What, you're not going to start a murder investigation?" Maggie loudly said. "I don't believe it."

Cantrell, red-faced as a ripe Beefsteak tomato, explained through gritted teeth. "Dang it, Maggie. You can only fall into a well so often before you break your neck."

Hot words like poppycock and gee willikers streamed from Maggie's mouth, which didn't motivate Cantrell to do a thorough investigation. He instructed Jimmy and Pete to take Miss Tippsy's body to Montgomery's Funeral Parlor. He told Maggie, "I'll ask Mister Montgomery to prepare your aunt for burial at the county cemetery. You focus on baking some nice goods for the wake, and don't turn this unfortunate accident into some murder mystery."

Maggie huffed and loudly announced she'd not only bury her beloved relative in the family plot but find the scallywag who murdered her.

"Knock yourself out," Cantrell shouted as he crawled into his Sheriff's vehicle. "Plant your aunt in your vegetable garden with the carrots and radishes, for all I care."

That bit of conversation may shock you if you're one of those modern folks who pay others to bury your dead, but it's done differently in Pleasant Valley, Vermont. Kids are forced by inadequate internet service to grow up in tune with nature, and burying a relative is as natural as standing in a barn and watching your baby sister come screaming into this world.

However, the locals were stunned to hear Maggie Merriweather paid a visit to Rick Carlyle the next day. Now, I'm speculating about what was said, but I've known those folks all their lives, and I'm sure this is close to their actual conversation.

"Hello, Carlyle," Maggie said, the hand she'd typically offer in greeting stuffed in her sweater pocket. "Can we talk?"

"Sorry about your aunt turning up dead," Rick replied before taking a deep breath. "Now that I've acted all sensitive, what the heck do you want to talk about?"

"I know it might be hard for you to get this through your thick skull, but I'd like to hire you to find Tippsy's killer."

I suspect Carlyle was knocked back on his heels by Maggie's request, but the prospect of finally earning a legitimate day's wage as a private eye probably restored his sense of balance.

"Why me?" he asked.

"As they say, a lawyer who represents himself has a fool for a client, so I thought my mind might be too clouded with grief to do a good investigation."

Even a chowderhead like Carlyle realized Maggie had made an excellent point.

"If I take you on as a client, you gotta follow my lead. If heads have to be cracked to force answers, don't you slip behind my back with freshly baked cinnamon buns to convince the suspects to confess. You understand?"

"I'll keep quiet and defer to you, Rick."

Spoiler alert. Maggie had no intention of keeping her mouth shut.

"I'll be charging you my usual rate," Carlyle said, "and I don't want to be paid in kittens."

A handshake sealed the deal, and Rick invited Maggie into his house to discuss the who, what, when, and whys. Knowing Maggie as I do, as she entered Rick's domain, she had to wonder why male private eyes always lived in such dumps. They may get better decorating suggestions if they involve more practical-minded women in their lives and fewer femme fatales.

"Was Miss Tippsy involved in anything mildly illegal?" Carlyle asked. "Like harvesting maple syrup out of season?"

Maggie shook her head. "She was like everyone around here. She'd work a side hustle to make ends meet, but nothing that would prompt someone to kill her."

Carlyle set his cold blue eyes on Maggie and asked the uncomfortable questions that could quickly move a case along.

"More than a few locals are living out their lives at the big prison in Newport because of you," he said. "Maybe Miss Tippsy's death was payback."

I'm sure that comment resurrected painful memories of Maggie's mother saying, "Nobody likes a snoop, Magnolia Merriweather. You gotta stop picking through other people's personal business." But what could a naturally curious girl with a strong sense of right and wrong do? Birds gotta fly, and fish gotta swim.

"I suppose we should consider that," Maggie said, "knowing how my solving the Yuletide Yard Sale murder upset the Walker family."

"Don't forget the Tea Cozy Strangulation murder case that put Jo Cooper in prison for the rest of her natural life."

Maggie dropped her head and sighed. It must've greatly bothered her that maybe Miss Tippsy's death was her fault. I'm sure she gave that sense of guilt another second of life before her natural spunk snuffed it out. "I have to admit the shock of seeing Tippsy dead caused me not to do my usual thorough examination. We need to check out Tippsy's corpse ASAP, Rick. Let's hit the road."

Rick followed Maggie out the door, a notebook and pencil in his coat pocket and a .45 caliber pistol holstered under his arm. A pair of brass knuckles hung from his belt, and a switchblade was taped to his right ankle. Maggie carried a purse filled with old receipts and a peanut butter cheesecake recipe.

Maggie and Rick parked in front of Montgomery's funeral parlor fifteen minutes later. "That was fast," Rick said. "When there's no moose-on-car collisions on this road, traffic moves quickly." While Carlyle marveled at their excellent commuting fortune, Maggie was all business. "First, we'll examine the corpse and take detailed notes. Then we'll pack up Tippsy and take her home for burial in the family cemetery."

"I don't know about that," Rick said.

"Goodness gracious, you're right. We forgot the ice. Don't you think the temperatures are cool enough that Tippsy will stay fresh until we get home?"

Carlyle mumbled. "I can't do this."

"Okay, we'll get the ice first. Will that work for you?"

The man shook his head. "I'm not bothered transporting a dead body. I'm uncomfortable examining a naked one, especially someone I knew."

Okay, reader, buckle your seat belt. The rumor around Pleasant Valley is that our rough-and-tumble private eye, Rick Carlyle, is so modest that he showers in swimming trunks. I want to share how I know that, but I've only about three thousand words left, and Maggie and Rick need them to solve Miss Tippsy's murder.

Maggie left Rick and his modesty issues in his jeep and entered the funeral parlor basement. Approaching Tippsy's shrouded body, Maggie began at the feet, hoping to slowly adjust to the shock of seeing her dead aunt. She noted the rope marks around the victim's ankles. Those must've come from when Jimmy and Pete lassoed Tippsy's feet to pull her out of the well. Maggie's gaze was drawn to Tippsy's gnarly toes, a patchwork of varicose veins, and the pair of dice tattooed on the older woman's left calf. Nothing was out of the ordinary there, although the skin art looked recently inked.

The state of Miss Tippsy's body, from her knees up to her twisted neck, will not be further described. All I'll say is that decades of gravity had wreaked havoc on the woman's muscular tissues, leaving it at that.

Completely removing the sheet off Miss Tippsy was almost too much for Maggie. The face of her beloved auntie was smooched flat. It so resembled kneaded dough that Maggie made a mental note to call the supplier about her overdue bulk order of bread yeast.

Looking at Tippsy's hands for clues, Maggie noted that the woman's palms were as clean as a surgeon before an operation. Turning over the victim's hands, Maggie recoiled in horror. "Good Lord, Tippsy," Maggie cried out, "Why did you insist on buying your nail polish from Temu? Your nails look like crap." Moving past the chipped nail polish, Maggie saw the one thing that confirmed what she intuitively felt: someone had murdered Miss Tippsy.

"What the heck?" she said, "Why are there ligature marks on her wrists?"

Maggie made notes of her observations before taking ownership of the corpse. She intended to bury it in the family plot, about a mile north of the funeral home. As Maggie and Rick drove to the Merriweather family cemetery, he reminded her that he had a bad back and wouldn't be able to dig a grave if that were her expectation. It wasn't, she replied, because the grave was already dug and awaiting a corpse. You might read that line in a Stephen King short story, not one written by some hack from Pleasant Valley. But Steve King didn't know Maggie Merriweather as I did. When the local excavation company dug the grave for Maggie's Uncle Mortimer last year, Maggie, being a seasoned discount shopper, swung four open graves for the price of one.

Right before the internment of Miss Tippsy began, Maggie showed Rick the marks on her aunt's wrists. "I think she might've been bound when she went headfirst into that well."

"You were there on the scene when they lay Tippsy on the ground," Rick said. "Did you see her hands tied?"

Maggie shook her head and meekly replied. "No, I did not."

Carlyle had the sensitivity of a drunk walrus at a fraternity kegger, but even he could tell Maggie needed some empathy, for she was genuinely perplexed.

"How about after we bury Tippsy, we go to Duke's and see if Jimmy and Pete are there? They may have an explanation for the markings."

Maggie agreed, and following the last shovelful of dirt onto Tippsy's grave, they left for Duke's Tavern, but not before they stopped by Maggie's house so she could feed her cats. Her secondary motive was to arm herself in case of trouble at Duke's. She grabbed her weapon of choice, a loaf of a recently baked olive bread, and rejoined Carlyle.

Once our intrepid pair of investigators entered the tavern, they split up. Maggie approached Pete Barkey while Rick interviewed Jimmy Hoot.

"Hey Jimmy," Carlyle said, "I wanna chat about the condition of Miss Tippsy's body when you retrieved her from the well."

Jimmy rolled his head and stared blankly at Carlyle. "I'm still traumatized, man," he said, the smell of fermented hops riding on his breath. "I can't remember much, you know?"

"Perhaps hypnosis might help you recall what you're blocking out."

Jimmy smiled. "That might work."

"What will help you achieve that hypnotic state?" Rick asked. "A glass of ale or something dark and full-bodied?"

Jimmy's head bobbed in double time. "My brothers' Hooter Hoppy Hoedown is my beer of choice. After a glass, or two, my mind will be back at the well, remembering everything."

The popularity of brewpubs was strong in the Northeast, and Jimmy's more industrious siblings had opened Hooter Hoedown Brewery a year ago. The enterprise was struggling because, unfortunately, there were now as many brewpubs as beer drinkers in this part of Vermont.

"It's nice you're helping keep your brother's brewery in business," Rick said. "I bet they appreciate it."

The man let loose a juicy-sounding chuckle. "Yeah, they surely do."

Two tall servings of Hooter Hoppy Hoedown arrived, and the two men raised their glasses. "That's an interesting tattoo on your wrist," Rick said, pointing to Jimmy's hand holding his glass. "Why do you have a pair of dice without the dots?"

Jimmy gulped half his glass before answering. "I dunno. I guess that's all I had money for."

Across the room, Maggie had just served Pete Barkey a slice of her olive bread. Two bites of that tangy baked delight had Pete talking.

"I believe Miss Tippsy wore a long-sleeved blouse," he said. "Yeah, that I remember."

Maggie nodded. Her aunt preferred long sleeves, and because of her arthritis, the sleeves closed at the wrists with elastic, not buttons.

"Could you tell whether her hands were tied?"

"Truth be told, I didn't look that carefully because I didn't want to stare at a dead woman." Pete picked a breadcrumb off the tabletop and rolled it between his finger and thumb. "But I know her arms were floppin' when Jimmy laid her down. That I know for sure."

Maggie wouldn't waste another slice of olive bread on Pete, who appeared to have nothing else to add. If he saw Miss Tippsy's arms hanging by her side, maybe Maggie was doing precisely what Sheriff Cantrell always accused her of, thinking every village death was a murder.

Rick appeared at the table and waggled his head, signaling he was ready to go. Maggie wrapped up the loaf and stood. "Let me know if you recall anything else, Pete."

"Will you have any of that good tastin' bread for me if I do?"

"Sure, Pete, but you best not wait. The supply chain is all fouled up, and I might not be baking much bread for a long while."

Maggie and Rick climbed into Carlyle's jeep to return to her place. Rick broke the silence as he drove, unnerved, I suspect, by Maggie's failure to be her usual loquacious self.

"Jimmy Hoot is a slick fella," Rick said. "I bought him two beers and got nothing other than how his brothers' brewery is hurting for business. How'd you do with Pete?"

"My olive bread was only slightly more effective. Pete recalled Tippsy wearing a long-sleeved blouse with elastic bands at the wrists but nothing binding her hands."

Rick took his jeep onto the road berm and stopped. He looked Maggie in the eyes. "Maybe with Miss Tippsy being all butt-side up for an hour, the blood pooled in her arms and hands, pressing hard against the sleeve elastic. Maybe that caused what you thought were ligature marks?"

Maggie's professional competitiveness with Rick had cooled over the last few hours but having him explain away her suspicion with a clever insight was too much. She'd share her second observation about the state of Miss Tippsy's corpse. Even an idiot would be persuaded Tippsy was murdered.

"Okay, smart guy, here's something else that bothers me. Tippsy's well was pretty much dry because we haven't had much snow melt over the past two years to raise the water table. The last time she lost her balance and fell in, she was able to extend her hands to break the fall."

"Wow, she must've had some strong wrists."

"Tippsy tossed a sixteen-pound bowling ball down the alley every Wednesday and Saturday nights for decades, so, yes, she did have extraordinarily strong wrists. But when I examined the palms of her hands at the funeral parlor, there was no mud, bruising, or cuts on them."

Rick groaned. "Don't tell me her face took the impact."

"Yeah, the dear landed smack dab on the old schnozzle."

"Double ouch."

"Now, do you see why I think her hands were bound when she entered the well? No way would she not have gotten those hands in front of her face."

An intelligent man, maybe one who'd been married for decades to a spouse who freely pointed out his deficiencies, would've learned by now to say something like, "I hear you, dear." However, Rick Carlyle had never married, and most of his female relationships ended before lessons were taught.

"Maybe this was just her unlucky day?" he said, pulling the jeep back on the road. "You know, accidents do happen."

It was almost as if the Almighty decided Carlyle needed to learn from his mistakes because the traffic suddenly thickened, significantly increasing the time Maggie had to express her disappointment and hurt. She delivered enough proof of how he'd mishandled her emotions that even a knucklehead like Carlyle understood.

"I'm sorry," he said. "I totally missed how my comment might make you feel."

"Good Lord, you're a private investigator," she said. "You get paid to stitch together clues and solve mysteries. Why would understanding a woman be any different?"

Soon after Maggie finished unloading on Rick, the traffic thinned, and our two investigators were on their way. By then, Maggie's temper had cooled, and Rick's shame was compartmentalized enough for their conversation to restart.

"What were you saying to Pete back at the tavern?" Rick asked. "Something about supply chain issues shutting down your bread baking?"

"It's terrible. There is a major shortage of yeast here in New England. Prices have skyrocketed, and that's if you can find any for sale. I'll have to make more pies and a lot less bread."

"Although I won't take kittens in lieu of cash," Rick said, speaking in such a warm tone his vocal cords struggled to operate, "a nice apple pie would cover a couple of billed hours."

Maggie smiled at Rick's unexpected sensitivity, reached over, and patted his hand. The touch of her fingers on his skin didn't make him flinch. He thought it felt nice.

Okay, this is when you think I'm planting the seeds of a romance. Cozy and hard-boiled finding love despite a vast difference in temperament, history, and investigative techniques. We'd have peppermint tea versus eighteen-year-old single malt scotch, cats or pit bulls, manicures against bruised knuckles. If that's what you're thinking, go find a sappy romantic tale somewhere because Maggie Merriweather and Rick Carlyle were working on a murder case. There'll be no goo-goo eyes or smooching in this story.

Rick pulled his jeep in front of Maggie's place, and she climbed out. She said to Carlyle, "I can't figure out why Tippsy would get a tattoo at her age."

Rick lifted his shoulders. "Maybe she suddenly felt strongly about expressing herself."

"But why a pair of dice? Uncle Mortimer had a gambling addiction when he was alive, and she hated games of chance."

"Jimmy Hoot had a pair of dice tattooed on his wrist, as well," Rick said as a chuckle rose from his throat. "But the idiot ran out of money before the dots were added. I didn't know if it was supposed to be lucky seven or snake eyes."

Maggie gasped. "Oh my gosh, Rick. Tippsy's dice didn't have dots either. Do you think there's a connection?"

If there were a relationship between Jimmy Hoot and Miss Tippsy's tattoos, Carlyle would be the one to determine it. His world, after all, revolved around places where shady transactions dominated, like taverns, back alleys, and tattoo emporiums. He knew the person who might explain why people would pay to get an incomplete pair of dice inked into their skin.

"I gotta check out a source," Carlyle said. "I'll be back in an hour."

Rick sped off before Maggie could ask why she wasn't invited along, which greatly annoyed her. Hopefully, she thought, he was doing something that justified what she was paying him.

* * * *

She'd need not worry because, within minutes, Rick approached a tall, gaunt man sitting inside The Devil's Inkpot, smoking a cigarette. "Hey, Robert, how's it going?"

"It'd be better if you let me add some body art to your plump white flesh," the man answered.

Of course, knowing Rick's issues with someone touching his skin, Satan would be ice skating in hell when that happened, but you couldn't fault Robert for trying. It's tough making a living in this part of Vermont.

"I'm wondering if you've done many double-die tats over the past year?" Rick asked. "But the customer didn't want the dots as part of the design."

Robert looked away to hide the panic in his eyes, but he didn't move fast enough to fool an old pro like Rick Carlyle.

"Come on, Robert, I know your side hustle involves various illegal activities. Answer my question. Who's gotten such a tattoo?"

The skin artist shook his head. "I can't tell ya, man. I'd violate that hippa act."

Carlyle grabbed Robert's shirt collar and jerked it hard. "I don't think getting a skull and cross-bones tattoo is a medical procedure. Answer my question or I'll suggest to Bobby Cantrell where he might look for those stolen bags of goose down."

Robert groaned and fussed but finally gave Rick what he wanted. "It's a private design of two dice without the pips. It was specially ordered by the Hoot brothers, and only certain folks can get it."

"You telling me that Jimmy Hoot's smarter brothers, the owner-operators of the Hooter Hoedown brewery, have a unique tat design they control?"

Robert nodded, adding that the brothers send new employees for their customized body art once they pass their probation period.

"But why don't they want the dice to have the pips?"

If Robert wasn't suffering from emphysema, he might've sprinted out the door to avoid answering Rick. He took a deep drag on his cigarette instead. "Those aren't supposed to be dice, man. Them are supposed to be two cubes of dried yeast."

"What the heck?"

Most private eyes who charge by the hour instinctively fail to connect the disparate parts of a criminal investigation in the first hour. If they did, they'd never make any money. Rick Carlyle was no different.

* * * *

Luckily, Maggie Merriweather was back at her café waiting to assist him in understanding the importance of what he'd just learned.

"Why would the Hoot brothers insist upon dried yeast cubes as a secret symbol for their brewery?" Rick asked Maggie upon arriving at the bakery and cat café.

"Yeast is a key component in the beer brewing process," she answered. "And it's also critical to bread making."

"Didn't you say there was an unexplained shortage of yeast here in New England?"

"Yes, but I can't believe a couple of local yokels could be yeast kingpins. And why would it involve Tippsy? Who would murder my kindly gray-haired auntie who never harmed anyone?"

I have to give Carlyle credit. Maggie's comments must've triggered his mansplaining instincts, yet he resisted. As a cozy mystery maven, Maggie experienced the lighter side of murder, with no blood, guts, or gore. What did she know of the capabilities of genuinely evil men? Rick understood true wickedness because you don't get hard-boiled by solving murders at library used book sales.

"I gotta make a call at the firehouse," Rick told Maggie. "I think I can get us an answer."

Maggie shouted that she'd like to come along, but Carlyle again ignored her, quickly exiting Maggie's shop and hopping into his jeep. While irritated by his behavior, Maggie was impressed with how quickly Carlyle moved, considering the extra twenty he carried around his waist.

* * * *

"Hi, Jimmy," Carlyle said. He stood behind Jimmy Hoot as the man washed the village fire truck. "Got a sec?"

Jimmy claimed he didn't have the time, but having his right arm twisted behind his back convinced him otherwise. To keep this story within the submission guidelines prohibiting graphic violence, I'll just say the more Jimmy resisted, the greater his pain.

"Tell me what really happened at Miss Tippsy's well, or you'll be known as Lefty Hoot."

"Okay, okay, you brute, I'll talk," Jimmy cried. "When me and Pete were pullin' up Tippsy, and she was still top half in the well, I told Pete to stop because she'd gone sideways. I palmed a box cutter and reached in and cut the rope that was binding her hands. I knew Pete wasn't closely watchin' me, with him being all willy over dead bodies, so it was easy. But I didn't kill her, I swear. I was only cleanin' up my brother's dirty work."

Rick hustled Jimmy into his jeep and drove back to Maggie's place. He wanted her to have the opportunity to identify the scallywags that murdered her aunt, as she swore publicly to do so the other day.

* * * *

"Why did your brothers try to corner the yeast market?" Maggie asked Jimmy once Rick had sat the man hard onto a chair.

"Things were tough. My brothers had the idea they'd make more money stockpiling the yeast to create a shortage and then selling it when the price climbed."

"But why was Tippsy murdered? What'd she have to do with any of this?"

Jimmy wobbled his head. "The bulk yeast was wrapped in water-proof plastic and kept at the bottom of Tippsy's well. My brothers wanted to sell the yeast because they thought the price had topped out. Miss Tippsy swore the price would keep climbing and they argued and, well, Tippsy lost out."

If your jaw dropped with that information, you can only imagine how wide Maggie and Rick's mouths were.

"You telling me my sweet aunt was part of a criminal conspiracy?"

Jimmy snorted. "Who do you think came up with the idea? My brothers ain't that smart."

The arrests of the Hoot brothers and the recovery of three tons of dried yeast from Miss Tippsy's well were big news in Vermont and among the New England bread-baking community. Sheriff Cantrell hauled off the perps, delighted to appear doing his duty on the front page of the Pleasant Valley weekly circular. Maggie Merriweather didn't begrudge the Sheriff his glory grab. Since her sweet auntie was the criminal mastermind behind it all, how could she? Maggie was grateful that they'd solved the mystery so she could return to baking crusty bread.

Rick Carlyle enjoyed his day in the spotlight, further enhanced by the three-hundred-dollar check Maggie wrote him for services rendered. Two baked pies and the cutest darn kitten you ever saw were bonuses.

There you have it, folks. Next time you drive through a quaint village in Vermont and coo about how enchanting it looks, remember that some grandmother dressed in calico might be hustling drugs or that brewpub, with its fruity IPAs, could be a front for the Mob. Rest assured, however, knowing that a Maggie Merriweather type of woman also lives in that tiny burg. She may sell scented candles or wind chimes, but beneath that folksy New England charm is a strong sense of justice and the skills to bring evil people to heel.

THE LADDER RUNS BOTH WAYS

GREGORY MEECE

Mr. Huntington aimed his finger at the ground beside him and hollered, "Geoffrey, come here!" If he added the word "boy" to the end of that command, I would have expected a doggy biscuit for complying.

"I have something I need you to do, Geoffrey."

"It's George, sir. George Higgins."

"Yes…whatever. Put down that weedwhacker thing and meet me inside."

The day my boss, Mr. Huntington, asked me to pick up his sister at the train station changed my life—in more ways than one as it turned out. It was the catalyst that launched my business career, and the grungy "Highway to Hell" T-shirt I wore when I was the lowly groundskeeper at Huntington Manor had more to do with my success than my freshly printed diploma. In a few years, I had a penthouse office atop Huntington Trust and Finance, Inc., and an income bigger than I ever dreamed possible.

We baby boomers believed that a college degree could be cashed in for a high-paying job, so we did whatever was required to reach the finish line. I took any part-time work I could find to help pay for those fifteen credits each semester. If a shot at the American Dream meant schlepping some rich dude's Arnold Palmer Signature irons for eighteen holes, then so be it.

The competition for entry-level jobs in the early eighties was insane. I had a decent GPA. As it turned out, however, I would have done as well with a 0.0. When you are in the right place at the right time, you don't need to be on the dean's list.

After senior year, I was able to keep my efficiency apartment's lights turned on with my job as estate groundskeeper—a fancy title for someone who cuts grass and pulls weeds. At least I sat on my ass a good bit of the time. Tobias and Edith Huntington's estate had more acres than the college's campus, so I spent most days cruising around on their lawn tractor. Other duties included spraying the apple trees, weeding the flower beds, and feeding the fish—Huntington Manor had a Koi Pond the size of Lake Erie.

In addition to the generous minimum wage my millionaire employer paid me (too sarcastic?) the job came with a few perks: a suntan, all the produce I could eat while working in the vegetable garden…okay a *couple* of perks. You can't count my free fill-ups from the gas pump that Mr. Big

Bucks had installed on his property so he wouldn't risk being seen pulling into Rick's Fill 'n' Lube downtown. I stole the gas so, technically, it didn't qualify as a perk.

Until that day when Mr. Huntington asked me inside, the only time I ever crossed Huntington Manor's threshold was when I harvested beans and peppers from the garden and took them to the cook. She offered me a cool glass of iced tea, which was kind of her. When I left the kitchen, however, I could hear Mr. Huntington chiding her. "If the boy wants a drink, there's a hose by the barn," he told her. "You don't want him to take advantage of his situation." Oh—That was the third perk I was searching for—free hose water.

So, getting back to my story, Mr. Huntington summoned me with a voice that expected obedience. Beyond the mansion's opulent foyer, I saw what appeared to be the big man's study, so I walked that direction. Isn't that where men talk business? But Mr. Huntington stood his ground, blocking me from encroaching further into his domain. It wasn't like I planned to kick off my sneakers and nestle my sweaty feet on his oxblood leather Chesterfield.

"My sister Agatha is coming to visit us for a few days," he said. "She'll be taking the train from her home in Providence to Boston, and I need you to pick her up at the station. You can take my Mercedes instead of that, whatever that thing is that you drive."

"It's a seventy Challenger," I said proudly. "I installed the cassette deck myself." Mr. Huntington wasn't impressed by my accomplishment, so I didn't mention my muscle car's quadrophonic speakers, which I also installed.

Mrs. Huntington appeared at her husband's side. Somehow, she managed to look me over from head to toe while avoiding making eye contact. "Not dressed like *that*, I hope," she said.

I was wearing a souvenir T-shirt from AC-DC's 1979 USA tour. *Highway to Hell* had just been released, and the graphics showed the band members, some with devil's horns, standing against a wall of flames.

"I'm sorry, ma'am, but my chauffeur's uniform is at the cleaners," I said, hoping to disarm her with my charming wit, but there was not so much as a hairline crack in the makeup slathered on her cheeks.

Stone-faced, she said, "Tobias, give him one of your old blazers. I don't know why you refuse to donate them to charity." This made me wonder if: A) He couldn't fit into them anymore, or B) He never gave to charities. I guessed C) Both A and B are true.

They summoned Marian, their maid, and told her to fetch something appropriate for me to wear. Sizing me up, quite literally, Marian said, "You look like a forty-regular, tapered fit. Wait outside."

Since the boss was more portly than tapered, I assumed Marian would have to find something he wore in his much younger days. When she returned, she held a black blazer with an impressive crest embroidered on the pocket—a shield containing the word "Veritas" with an "X" beneath it.

"Mr. Huntington's old Harvard blazer," Marian said. "The Chairman was proud of it."

Mr. Huntington liked it when his staff referred to him as "The Chairman." It was in deference to his many years as Chairman of the Board and CEO of the world-renowned Huntington Trust and Finance, Inc.

"What's the 'X' for?"

"Those are crossed oars. The Chairman was captain of the Harvard Rowing Club."

The jacket fit me rather well. "Thanks, Maid Marian," I said, hoping my Robin Hood reference would elicit a laugh. Zero for two.

"The train will be arriving soon. Did anyone tell you about The Chairman's sister, Agatha?"

I retrieved a small photograph from my pocket. "Mr. Huntington gave me this so I can recognize her at the station."

Staring at the picture, Marian mused, "She will be older now. Did they tell you about her mental issues?"

"You mean she's…crazy?"

"I don't know the correct medical terminology. The last time she came, I believe they called it a 'mild cognitive impairment.' It affects her memory."

* * * *

Driving the Huntingtons' Mercedes felt like riding on a cloud, so quiet and silky smooth. In stark contrast, *my* car, with its rusted-out muffler and my Led Zeppelin tapes with the volume knob cranked to ten, could wake the dead.

At the station, I stood beneath the "Arrivals" sign and waited. I spotted Sister Agatha right away.

"Hello, ma'am. The Huntingtons sent me to get you." I took Agatha's suitcase and escorted her to the Mercedes. "Here's my car." I said it loud enough to impress a few girls who were thumbing through copies of *Seventeen* at a magazine stand. At first, they appeared blasé, but when they saw my Harvard Rowing Blazer the pretty redhead spoke up, "Nice wheels. Yours?"

"Of course," I replied. "I'd offer you a ride, but I'm due back at the estate. I don't want to miss our Rowing Club meeting. Toodle-oo, ladies." It felt nice to be looked at that way, even if only for a minute.

As it turned out, the trip with Agatha would be the most memorable car ride of my life.

"So, Toby, how is everything, my dear brother? It seems like ages since we've seen each other—what with you up at Harvard and me still at Brown."

"Sorry, ma'am, my name's George. I'm just the grounds—"

"Those girls were impressed with your car, Toby. Did Papa give it to you?"

"I'm not Mr. Huntington—"

"You're on break?"

"On break?"

"Summer break. I see you're wearing your rowing jacket. Did the Crimson win this year's Regatta? I'll bet you showed those Yale boys."

Yale boys? Marian wasn't kidding. The Old Bat had some cognitive issues all right. She was living in the past. She confused me with her brother Tobias. That I was wearing his old clothes and driving his car—one that I proudly announced was mine a few minutes earlier—likely contributed to her confusion. Setting her straight would be difficult—perhaps even dangerous—due to her condition. Better to go with the flow, I reasoned.

"Yes, Agatha, dear," I said, feigning an accent befitting the upper crust from "Hahvud." "We thrashed those Yalies. My chums even kidnapped their Bulldog mascot. Locked up the old boy in our frat house."

"Oh, Toby—how incredibly exciting! By the by, how is that delightful girlfriend of yours, Edith?"

"Simply peachy. And do you have a boyfriend yourself, Agatha?" I almost called her Aggie, but it might have been too hard to keep a straight face.

"Oh, Toby, we promised never to speak of that matter. Oh, heavens, never!"

"Remind me again, my dearest sibling. What matter?"

Agatha turned her head as if checking to make sure no one was in the back seat. She leaned over to me and whispered, "You know—how you killed Eduardo and sunk his body beneath the Koi pond. Toby! Watch where you're going!"

I slammed on the brakes, and the Mercedes skidded onto the shoulder of the road. "Excuse me?"

"Toby, you know how I loved you for defending my honor. My hero. That awful boy, Eduardo—forcing his way on me like that. I don't dare think what might have happened if you hadn't seen us together in the gazebo."

I calmed myself and eased the car back onto the road. "In the gazebo, of course. The cad! The coward ran off in shame." I impressed myself with how seamlessly I bridged the gaps in Agatha's tale, drawn from her confused thoughts.

"But, Toby, you know that he *didn't* run away," Agatha interjected. "After you struck him on the head with Papa's stone garden sculpture, you cracked off the head."

"Eduardo's?"

"The statue's. Honestly, Toby, you can be so droll at times. Wasn't it that replica of the Venus de Milo? No, that wasn't it. Oh, I can't remember things the way I used to. Oh, yes, it was one of those mythological creatures. I remember—a water nymph. My dress was so soiled I had to throw it away. I couldn't well ask the maid to scrub it clean without explaining how it got that way, collecting stones in the woods—you remember so that we could weigh down the body. I thought that old dinghy of yours was going to sink before you dumped the body in the deepest part of the pond. Toby, dear, please let's not talk about that dreadful day anymore. Tell me again about your plans for when you graduate?"

I saw the row of stately sycamores ahead. They lined the seemingly end-less stretch of driveway, building one's anticipation for the revelation of the Huntington mansion. Mr. and Mrs. Huntington stood beneath the portico, waiting to receive their guest. I could tell by Agatha's silence that the famil-iar surroundings were bringing about a change in her demeanor.

"I'll get your suitcase, ma'am," I said, holding the car door open for her. Agatha reached out her hand and spoke to me in a tone that differed markedly from our earlier conversation. Seeing her brother and sister-in-law in their seventies must have triggered something that shocked her out of her time-traveling state of mind.

"What did you say your name was, dear boy?"

"It's George, ma'am. George Higgins."

"Thank you for being my driver, George Higgins." Agatha reached into her purse and handed me a few dollar bills. If she had a clue about what she had told me just minutes earlier, her tip might have been a few thousand—to keep my mouth shut.

The week passed, and Agatha's visit to Huntington Manor seemed un-eventful. I heard nothing to suggest that any further conversations about the incident in the gazebo had occurred. Whatever happened many years ago remained locked in Agatha's addled mind—and perhaps carefully concealed in another's.

On one of the hottest days in August, I saw Mr. Huntington walking toward his car. Maybe it was from being out in the heat too long, but that's when the scheme first popped into my head.

"Can I help you, Gerald?"

"It's George. I was hoping for a sip of something cool, sir. Dehydration can cause someone to lose consciousness in this heat. On a big property like this, it could be years before anyone would find a dead body on Huntington Manor."

"What are you talking about, boy? If you're thirsty you can fill your water bottle at the hose."

"I'm not sure I like the idea of drinking hose water that bypasses your water filtration system. It may even come from the pond. You never know what someone might find at the bottom of a pond. Nothing you'd like to drink, I'm sure."

I tried to gauge Mr. Huntington's body language after I employed the phrases "dead body" and "at the bottom of a pond." The muscles in his jaw tightened and the creases around the corners of his eyes seemed to be carved deeper as he squinted at me.

"You know that gazebo, Mr. Huntington? I was out by your pond this morning, feeding the Koi, when I thought that a statuette between the gazebo and the pond would be a nice touch. Maybe a turtle or one of those frogs that spit water from its mouth."

"Mrs. Huntington and I will take your suggestion under advisement. Now, if you don't mind, will you please get back to work?"

"On second thought, maybe a frog's too gauche for a property as elegant as Huntington Manor. Perhaps one of those water gods from Greek mythology. I know—a nymph!"

Hook, line, sinker. It was time to reel in my catch. Mr. Huntington briskly escorted me inside the garage with his hand squeezing my elbow.

"Look, boy, if you have something to say to me, get on with it."

"I'm sorry if something I said upset you, Mr. Huntington—or would you rather I call you Mr. Chairman? But, since you asked, it did occur to me that I might request a favor. I've been trying to find a job where I can put my business degree to use. But the job market is really tight right now. There's one job for every twenty applicants. Do you think you could help me get my foot in the door at your company? Maybe something entry-level, of course—just to begin with, but with room for advancement—of course."

Before I knew it, I was filling out my W-4 form in the human resources office at Huntington Trust and Finance. The personnel director looked over my college transcript and then inserted it into a file with my name on it. He told me where to report for training as a junior financial analyst in the Analytical Products department and handed me my company-issued name badge, which read, "George Higgins—Anal. Prod." With an expectant smile, he said, "You'll be sure to give my regards to The Chairman, won't you?"

One thing I learned in college was that, in business dealings, you need a strategic plan to get ahead. Short-term goals lead to long-term goals. I also learned about networking and using contacts to get ahead. I had The Chairman's ear. More importantly, I had his balls.

In a short time, I moved up to banking associate. Then accountant, marketing manager, operations manager, and chief financial manager. All it took was a phone call to The Chairman every so often. We would discuss salary schedules, bonuses, and advancement opportunities. Of course, I would remind him of dead bodies, ponds, and nymphs to start our conversations. When he shouted things like, "That's impossible!" I would counter by reminding him that his name adorned the front of the building where we worked. "You know, Toby (Now that we had become close, I used the more familiar version of Tobias.), 'Trust'—as in Huntington Trust and Finance—is so important to your branding. I'd hate to think what would happen if your reputation, God forbid, was sullied by a scandal."

It wasn't as if I skipped steps. I just climbed them much faster than others. In time I became the youngest person ever to hold the title "Senior Vice President." Sure, there was office gossip about my meteoric rise, but that usually went underground after someone mentioned my close relationship with The Chairman.

The next year, I learned the sad news: Mr. Huntington's sister, Agatha, had passed away in her sleep. It wasn't surprising to me, considering that she was already old and auditioning for an internship at the funny farm when I first met her at the train station.

My final visit to Huntington Manor was at a gathering that followed Agatha's memorial services. Paying my respects was the least I could do for the woman who helped launch my successful career in business. As I sipped an excellent vintage port from Waterford crystal, I recalled the summer after college when I was offered the garden hose to quench my thirst. How far I had come.

My thoughts were interrupted by a hand firmly pressed into my lower back.

"The Chairman would appreciate your company in the study," said a man with a voice that seemed to be as polished as the rosewood sideboard.

Mr. Huntington sat behind his desk, which was only slightly smaller than the one I had seen pictured in the Oval Office. I half expected to see little John-John peeking out from its secret door panel.

"George Higgins, I'd like you to meet my attorney, Mr. John Galperin," The Chairman said.

With a gentlemanly nod, I acknowledged the man who had escorted me into the study. His navy pinstriped suit, paired with a maroon paisley bow tie, gave him an air of sophistication, which suggested his presence may have been more official than cordial. Turning to Mr. Huntington, I said, "I was sorry to hear about your sister. It was a long time ago that we met at the train station."

"And now that she is dead, it's time that you stopped using that car ride with my sibling to blackmail me."

I was stunned! It was the first time he used the "B"-word to describe what I simply viewed as our business relationship—my advancement in the company in exchange for my employer's good name and his luxurious lifestyle at Huntington Manor—instead of the state prison. Quid pro quo.

"Perhaps Mr. Galperin should leave us alone," I suggested.

"No. No. My attorney is here precisely to witness the end of you and your crooked dealings. George Higgins, you're fired."

Mr. Galperin's wry smile told me that he and Mr. Huntington had worked out everything in advance of the meeting. But why? It was the lawyer who provided the answer.

"You see, Mr. Higgins, Agatha's death means that The Chairman need not protect her any longer."

"Protect *her*?" I stammered.

"The Chairman had nothing to do with that man's alleged death."

"Alleged?"

"Officially, a missing person."

"Then, why—"

"Why did The Chairman give in to your demands? To protect his beloved and ailing sister from damning accusations. Now that she's gone, you're free to share your theories about the gazebo incident; not that anyone would take it seriously. You certainly have no evidence. There's no body. And poor Agatha is deceased."

"Oh no," I protested. "You're overlooking the body at the bottom of the Koi pond. I'll tell the police to drain it and uncover the remains of the man she was having an encounter with when Tobias Huntington struck his skull with the nymph statuette."

A smiling Mr. Huntington looked at his attorney and gave a little chuckle before he spoke. "Unfortunately, you have the facts mixed up. Not entirely surprising, considering my sister's mental state when she related the story to you. As you had become aware from your brief time with her, she tended to be confused about a few things. You can have my pond drained if you like. You'll find nothing at the bottom except muck and some irritated, flopping fish. I had that pond installed several years *after* Agatha's—altercation— with Eduardo."

"What are you implying? Are you saying that *Agatha* killed Eduardo?"

Mr. Galperin chimed in, "For the record, The Chairman is not saying, nor will he ever say, anything of the sort. But these are the facts: It was Agatha's property in Rhode Island. It was *her* Koi pond. *Her* gazebo. *Her* nymph statuette. Incidentally, when Agatha was placed into assisted living, her home was sold and developed into office buildings. Sadly, nothing remains of that pond of hers, I'm afraid."

Turning to my now-former employer, I spat out the last argument of my increasingly threadbare case against the defendant who had starred in my long-running drama: the motive for the crime. "But you—you were protecting her from Eduardo's unwanted advances."

"She was protecting *me* from what she assumed to be Eduardo's salacious behavior. Back then, any other possibility would have been unthinkable. Agatha feared it would have ruined the Huntington name. Thankfully, the times have changed. Eduardo and I were lovers."

* * * *

Sitting beside me in court, my lawyer explains that the Commonwealth frowns upon blackmail. *Now* he tells me. I watch as the skillful prosecutor seals my fate with the jury. It seems the career ladder runs both ways. Mine's going straight down, like a highway to hell. I wonder if the prison might need a groundskeeper.

BOSS CAT RULES

NIKKI KNIGHT

Hand over the tuna and nobody gets hurt.

From one of those cute little puffballs on the cover of Grandma's mystery books, it's an idle threat.

Not from me. Never mess with a big gray cat from the Bronx.

Wanna hear about the last fool who made that mistake?

Of course, the murder wasn't a good thing…but it sure was fun to help catch the killer.

By the way, I'm Neptune. My vet forms say Neptune Metz, gray domestic shorthair, and make some truly insulting comments about my weight. I don't use That Guy's name—he broke Ma's heart and let My Girl down, so he can go pound sand. Not to mention telling everybody he's not a cat person. Good for him. I'm not a That Guy cat.

Let's stay on a first-name basis.

I'm the Boss Cat of WSV Radio in Simpson, Vermont. Don't get me wrong. I don't know for radio stations, or Vermont, but I can't help hearing Ma say it when she starts the show every night:

"You're listening to your hometown station, WSV-AM 720, Simpson, Vermont. I'm Jaye Jordan with All-Request Love Songs at Night."

Apparently, people pay Ma to play that weird screeching you humans like—or they pay her to talk about where to buy groceries and get your car fixed, in between the screeching. I'm not a hundred percent sure. All I know is she keeps me in tuna and treats, so it must be working.

Which is good, because I was a little worried when she stuffed me in the car box and drove up here with My Girl after That Guy left. It turned out okay, though. Ma does her thing with the screeching in the basement and lives upstairs with My Girl and me, and I get to sit in the window and menace some interesting new birds.

It was all great until I saw a murder.

* * * *

The day started okay.

It hadn't snowed for a while, and the sun was shining, which felt nice on my fur as I hopped up in the window after shaking Ma down for a few extra treats when she returned from taking My Girl to school.

A bunch of chirpy birdies were in the tree out front. Most of them are these little gray and white things, and they bop around on the branches tweeting and chattering. They're fun to watch.

And then there's Nasty Bird.

Big dark thing, kinda shiny. With this cocky set to his head and smart-alecky twitch to his tail. Glares at me with these beady black eyes like he owns the place.

Of course I have to glare back.

Gotta tell him who's boss.

Be awfully fun to knock him out of the tree and jump on him.

So I was watching the snotty son of a bird bounce from branch to branch, wondering if he would taste like turkey pâté or chicken delight when I saw Cranky Lady.

She's a mean one. Face always squinched up like something smells bad, glares and snaps orders like she's the boss of the world.

Sorry, that job's already taken. By me.

For some reason, she doesn't like Ma, and she's always dropping by to complain.

Just yesterday, she came in and handed Ma some papers and told her not to announce the Yankee Daughters' Bazaar anywhere near the song dedications for Those People. I'm not sure what that meant, but Ma's face got all tight and she looked like she wanted to claw her.

I'd be glad to help her with that. Last time Cranky Lady came in, she nudged me out of the way of the door with her foot, and Ma had to pull me away before I got a chunk of her.

Ya don't touch the Boss Cat.

Anyhow, there I was sitting in the window, thinking about the best way to sneak out and get me a piece of Nasty Bird, when Cranky Lady walked out of the store across the street and held the door for a man.

He looked really old and kinda shaky, leaning on a cane. Shorter than Cranky Lady, pale and bald with a little fringe of white hair, wrapped up in a big thick coat. As he walked through the door, he smiled at her. One of those nice kind smiles you see from people who give their pets lots of treats.

Cranky Lady scowled back. Like she'd do anything else.

She looked around. The street was empty, like it usually is this time of day because everyone's at work.

Nasty Bird chirped at me and those beady eyes flashed.

Then movement. Not the bird.

The people.

It happened really fast, but not so fast I didn't see the whole thing. More than enough time for me to be sure what happened.

Cranky Lady knocked the old guy down. With a quick sweep of her foot, she took one of his legs out from under him. He flailed in the air for a moment, and she made fakey little motions like she was trying to catch him, and then he fell. His head hit the sidewalk with a thunk that made me wince all the way over here in the window.

Ouch.

Cranky Lady screamed.

The old guy wasn't moving.

I knew Cranky Lady was mean, but I didn't think she was that mean.

Wish there was some way to tell someone what I saw.

People were running toward them, and Nasty Bird gave me one more cocky chirp and flew off.

Not a damn thing I could do.

I'd had enough. I jumped down from the window and went into Ma's office, which she keeps nice and warm. I was curling up in my spot on her desk—I like to keep an eye on her while she does the business stuff—when the sirens started.

Ma looked out the window, sighed, and returned to work. We're from New York. Sirens aren't that big a deal.

But they're not nothing.

Ma reached out to pet me, and I let her.

Usually, I'm not the lap cat type. Never have been. I was a street kitty until the local precinct cops found me and my litter-mates huddled in the alley beside their house one cold night. Ma and My Girl walked into the shelter a few weeks later, and I knew the minute I saw them. I had to smack Ma on the arm to get her attention, but that was okay. Only fair for her to know what she's getting.

We have an understanding. Ma keeps the treats coming and I watch out for her and My Girl and tolerate a little attention. When I want some. It works.

Every once in a while, though, even a big tough cat from the Bronx needs a little love. And Ma does a good ear scratch.

"Everything's okay, big fella," she said in her warm, smooth voice.

Well, she was wrong there.

* * * *

I'd finally managed to get back to sleep when the doorbell rang. Ma headed to answer it, and I hopped down and followed her. Maybe it was Cranky Lady, and I could bite her ankle. Better than nothing.

"Chief George," Ma said as she opened the door for a big Black man in a black leather trench coat.

I leapt up on the reception desk. Chief is the local cop. He's former NYPD—a cat from the Bronx knows the look—and we have a man-to-man respect thing.

"Hey, big guy," he said, holding out a hand. "Bratton sends his best."

Bratton, as far as I can tell from the scent mark he left on his person, is a standup cat like me. I rubbed my head against Chief's hand, sending a little scent message back to Bratton, and accepted a pat.

"Coffee?" Ma asked. "Just made a pot."

"Sure."

I let Chief give me a good ear scratch while Ma went for the coffee. Everybody wins.

After he took a nice sip and complimented Ma on the brew, which she gets from a club—I know because I like to hide in the box every month—he got down to business.

"Checking around," he told her. "Mr. Grayson fell and hit his head in the street two hours ago and died on the way to the hospital."

"That's awful." Ma shook her head. "Mr. Grayson? That sweet older fella who used to run the gas station near the interstate?"

"Yep. State bought him out two years ago when they redid the exit. Apparently, he retired and moved in with the son and daughter-in-law. She was with him when he fell."

Cranky Lady!

"Who's the daughter-in-law?" Ma asked.

"Phyllis Recketts—works over at the gas company office."

I yowled. Cranky Lady's a killer!

They both looked at me.

"Need a treat, big guy?" asked Chief, nodding to Ma. "Maybe you ought to give him something."

I yowled again. Not the point. Not that I don't appreciate a treat.

Ma gave me a pat and I rubbed against her hand, trying to figure out what to do next. Even the smartest humans aren't up to cat level.

"You said Phyllis Recketts, right?" Ma asked, her face tightening into a scowl as she kept petting me. Normally, I'd be purring by now, but not with this kind of trouble.

"Yeah, she says they were walking together, and he just fell."

Like hell he did. I yowled again.

"Okay, okay." Ma patted me, reached for the packet of treats she keeps in the desk drawer, and put out a couple. "Here, buddy."

Well, everything's better with Tuna Crunchies.

I nibbled while the people kept talking.

"Do you know Phyllis Recketts?" Chief asked Ma.

"Yeah." The scowl again. "Secretary of the Yankee Daughters."

Yankee Daughters. That rang a bell.

I remembered Cranky Lady shoving the papers at Ma, saying something about not reading the Yankee Daughters announcement near her song dedications for Those People.

After she left, Ma tossed the papers down and stalked downstairs.

The papers were still on the desk.

First piece of good luck today.

I pounced on them and shoved them toward Chief.

"Neptune!" Ma said. "Why are you attacking the papers?"

"Cat gonna cat," Chief said, with a tiny bit of a smile. "What would we do without them?"

Ma smiled a little too.

Come *on*, people!

I yowled, pounced on the papers again. Tried shoving them at Ma this time.

She laughed. "Neptune, you're a real gift."

The door slammed.

Cranky Lady walked in.

I hissed.

Chief and Ma turned to me.

I hissed again.

"Control that cat!" Cranky Lady snapped. "He's always sitting in the window glaring at the street."

"Hello, Mrs. Recketts," Chief said, his voice cool and polite.

"Why aren't you at the police station?" she asked, pointing a finger at him. "They told me you were over here. Wasting time and drinking coffee with the DJ, I see."

"Ma'am," Chief began in a tense growl. Ya don't jump like that with former NYPD. "I'm speaking with Ms. Jordan."

"Well," huffed Cranky Lady, "I need to get the report on my father-in-law, Mr. Grayson's accident."

"I am still investigating."

"What?" The humans might not be able to smell fear on Cranky Lady, but I got a whiff as she looked at Chief. "What's to investigate?"

Ma looked at me. Obviously trying not to say what she was thinking. Something like, *the guy's been dead two hours, and this woman is worried about the paperwork?* I held Ma's gaze. C'mon. You're smart enough to buy the good treats. You can figure this out.

Nothing.

I'd had enough. I hopped off the desk. Headed for Cranky Lady, who was huffing at Chief, demanding to know why he was investigating.

Time for a little justice, boss cat style.

I padded over to her as she kept jawing.

"It was an ac—"

Cranky Lady broke off in a scream as I sank my fangs into her ankle.

"Get him off me!" she shrilled, kicking in my direction.

I'm faster. I backed up, hissing and moving into my fight stance. Claws out, ready to take her on. Somebody has to stop this rotten excuse for a person.

"Neptune!" Ma yelled.

Ma grabbed me from behind and picked me up. "Bad kitty."

I went limp and let her move me. No hard feelings, Ma.

"Control that animal!" Cranky Lady shrieked. "He bit me! I'm going to sue you and—"

"Ma'am, please calm down." Chief's voice suggested it wasn't a request. "We can sort that out later. Right now, I have a few questions about what happened to Mr. Grayson."

"Let's get you over to your window," Ma said to me. "Maybe you want to watch some birds…"

As she set me down, I had an idea. I banged on the window with my paw. Yowled.

"Neptune!" Ma sounded upset. "What is wrong with you today?"

I banged on the window again.

"Is it that bird?" she asked. She knew about Nasty Bird because she liked to watch me stalk him. Whatever. "What's up, Neptune?"

The tree was empty.

She looked at it. Then back at me.

Come on. Even my clueless human should get this. I yowled and batted at the window.

"It's okay, pal, the birds will be back."

I nudged her with my head.

Ma looked outside and kept looking.

"The window," she said.

Finally. I could see the realization hit.

About time.

Ma turned away from the window. "Chief, where exactly did it happen?"

"Outside the cable company office, right across from you."

I didn't need to watch for birds. The real show was Ma, Chief, and Cranky Lady.

"My doorbell security cam picks up movement across the way," Ma said.

Chief and Ma looked at each other and then turned to Cranky Lady.

"What are you—" she huffed.

"Mrs. Recketts, please wait a moment," Chief said. "Jaye, where do you have the doorbell video?"

"I didn't do anything!" Cranky Lady howled.

I hissed.

"Neptune."

Not Ma, but Chief.

I shut my mouth and waited.

"Here's the video," Ma said, handing Chief her phone. Ma's phone-crazy like all you humans—she uses hers to take pics of me and My Girl…and one time she let me watch a bird video. I think I need one, too.

"Please stay right there, Ma'am," Chief said to Cranky Lady.

She sniffed. Sounded like I do when I've got floor dust in my nose. Stood there glaring at us, arms crossed.

Chief watched the video, his eyes narrowing and hands tightening.

Then he looked up. His gaze burned into Cranky Lady. "Let's go."

"What— I— You can't…"

"You can come quietly, or I can drag you." If I hadn't known before that Chief was a former NYPD officer, the cool, deadly calm made it clear.

"I will be calling my lawyer."

"You can call your cat for all I care."

Of course, I hissed as he walked her out.

* * * *

That night, Chief stopped by the radio station during Ma's show.

He has the security codes and he's a friend, so when she's on, he comes downstairs and pours himself a cup of coffee.

I'd been dozing on this nice warm box behind Ma—she calls it the old turntable cabinet—and Ma had finished talking, when Chief knocked and walked in.

"Want to know how it came out?" he asked.

"Alicia told me it's a doozy," Ma said. She's friends with Chief's wife and sometimes goes to see them and Bratton. Of course, I have to re-scent her when she gets home.

"Oh, it is." He sat down and drank some coffee. "It was all about the gas station."

"What?"

"Well, remember, a few years ago, the state expanded the ramps for the interstate exit?"

"Happened before I came back, but I know it changed."

"The state bought some land for the work, and Grayson's gas station and the property around it was the biggest parcel. The business had been struggling because of all the environmental issues with old gas tanks, and the sale saved them. Since Mr. Grayson was the owner, the money went to him. And he moved in with his son and daughter-in-law."

Cranky Lady.

"Let's say it wasn't a happy family moment. He'd been diagnosed with dementia. They were going to have to spend some of that state money on home care—and eventually a memory facility."

"Not a cheap date."

"Not even a little." Chief gave a grim nod as he took a drink of his coffee. I'm not sure what the point of the coffee is, but they seem to enjoy it.

"And?" Ma asked. "Did she admit it?"

"No, but the video is pretty clear. Good thing you had that doorbell cam."

And good thing you had a smart kitty to remind you of it.

I purred. The super-loud, super-satisfied purr humans will do almost anything to hear. Both turned to me, and I gazed back at them.

Don't forget who's really in charge here.

Ma and Chief both slid their eyes back to each other.

"You don't think…" Chief said.

"Nah."

Fine by me. Let them believe they figured it out. Important to allow my minions to think they know what they're doing.

A few minutes later, Ma put on another request, Sinatra's "Summer Wind" for Charlene and Darla, and walked Chief up the stairs. After she closed the door, Ma and I stood in the foyer where I'd caught a killer earlier in the day, just listening to the music.

I love Sinatra. Huge, rich, knowing voice. And an old-school guy just like me.

Then, I rubbed against Ma's ankle. Gave her my best adorable-kitty look.

"C'mon, big fella, let's get you some more treats."

Now that's what I call a happy ending.

ASH TUESDAY

M.S. GREENE

The dead guy was on the kitchen counter for almost a week before anyone spoke up. If that surprises you, you've obviously never lived with roommates.

"Okay, is this *anyone's*?"

Colin dropped the day's mail next to the cardboard box in question. I could usually measure how pissed my old friend was by the octave of his voice. We were almost in soprano territory, and he leveled his gaze at me. "Trent?"

"Not mine," I muttered from behind an LSAT prep book. With the big test less than a week away, I'd gotten tacit permission to temporarily take over the dining room table. I say *tacit* because Colin couldn't quite hide his disgust at the fortress of textbooks and pizza boxes I'd built around myself. But it was *permission* nonetheless—we'd been friends for a decade, and he knew what law school meant to me.

Even so, this unclaimed package was about to send the poor guy over the edge. The box was simple, with yellowing tape and a shipping label addressed to "Current Resident." The return address had been scuffed, illegible when I discovered the delivery on the doorstep and almost gave myself a hernia hoisting it inside.

Okay, it wasn't *that* heavy. Maybe studying had made me soft.

"Lemme ask Ray," I offered, happy for an excuse to stand up. "He's always getting deliveries."

But Colin wasn't waiting another second. His voice reached new frequencies as he called our third roommate to an impromptu house meeting.

Ray emerged in a puff of smoke, like a magician on 4/20. He was pulling a tank top over his mop of sandy curls. "What's the problem, brother?" he crooned, meeting Colin in the kitchen.

Colin launched into a lecture about common spaces that I practically had memorized. I kept quiet, watching Ray's forearms flex as he slid the package from the wall and picked it up for a closer look.

I knew how this was gonna play out. Colin would dig in his heels, making the moment about *so much more* than a box on a counter. Pretty soon, we'd be revisiting the soaking dishes debate or re-litigating the case of the coffee table rings. Ray was all smiles, which I knew would only make things worse.

"How 'bout we open it?" I suggested in my best placating tone.

"That's a federal offense," Colin groused. "Shouldn't you know that from one of those...*books*?" He shot a hateful glare at my studying sanctum.

Ray slid the parcel across the counter until it thumped against Colin's chest. "Last I checked, *you're* the Current Resident here. Me and Trent are your loyal subjects."

"Subletters," I corrected.

"Whichever." Ray winked a slightly bloodshot eye in my direction.

Colin sliced the packing tape with surgical precision, and Ray sidled up next to me to watch the big reveal. I was still getting to know this newcomer to our apartment, still figuring out how he always managed to smell like the perfect blend of sandalwood and smoke. This might have been the closest we'd ever stood.

Colin wrestled the box open with a frown. "It's...is that a *bag* of something?"

Ray leaned over my shoulder. "It looks like..."

"It can't be." Colin had gone pale.

That's when I noticed the label on the side of the box. It must have been facing the wall, hidden from view for days on our counter. The bright orange of the sticker belied its macabre message in bold white letters...

Cremated Remains.

* * * *

It took a few minutes for Colin to stop dry heaving. He was hunched over the kitchen sink, waving me away as I followed Ray into the hallway.

"We've gotta ask the neighbors," he crowed, clearly enjoying this. "Anyone lose a dead guy?"

Jokes aside, Ray's reasoning made sense. Our unit at 4B could easily have been mistaken for anyone else on the fourth floor. So, we headed down the hallway and started knocking doors.

The elderly woman in 4C looked happy to see Ray, the two of them chatting like old friends until she saw the parcel in my arms. The poor lady's eyes flitted down, then back to mine with a grim shake of the head.

"Not one of your many boyfriends, Estelle?" Ray teased.

"Oh, they'd all end up home with their wives," she fired back. "Just where I want them."

The couple in 4D insisted we crack the plastic bag open to confirm this wasn't a prank. I extended the package right under their noses—the better to gaze at the dead—but the gray mass somehow didn't reveal its secrets.

Then came 4E and its middle-aged resident in a sweat-stained T-shirt and crocs. He knew at a glance what we were carrying, as if people regularly showed up on his doorstep with human remains. Like some kind of morbid Mormons.

"You're the boys from down the hall." The man leveled it at us like an accusation. "They say you might be able to get me some good reefer."

"*Who* says?" I asked.

"Estelle in 4C, for one."

I turned to Ray in disbelief. "Are you selling weed to the old lady?"

"Not *selling*," he contested. "But we chill sometimes."

It was a lot to unpack, but we had more urgent concerns. "So, to confirm…" I intoned, turning back to the neanderthal next door, "this package *doesn't* contain a friend or loved one of yours?"

The man shook his meaty head and went to close the door. Ray caught it with an outstretched foot. "Is that my wine?" He pointed at a package over the neighbor's shoulder. "I had a delivery go missing a couple days ago—"

"Well, your name isn't on it." The guy scratched his belly, avoiding eye contact with either of us.

Ray's foot didn't budge. "I had it shipped under an alias, dude. You wanna hand it over, or should I talk to the landlord?"

"Go ahead. Maybe I'll tell him there's a *drug dealer* in our midst."

Before Ray or I could respond, we heard Colin marching down the hall. "Oh, shut up, Christopher," he called out as he approached. "*Maybe* the landlord should know about your French bulldog that's *well* above the twenty-five-pound limit." Colin joined me and Ray in the doorway like an avenging angel of building bylaws. He crooked a thumb at me. "And my pal Trent here has the state cannabis regulations practically memorized."

It wasn't true, of course, but with my impending exam, maybe it should have been.

If looks could kill, our greasy neighbor would have landed us all in ashy packages of our own. But he knew we had him beat. Ray happily retrieved the clanging box of wine bottles from inside, muscling past its thief on his way out.

"Good day to you, sir."

Word of advice, if you ever plan to piss off a hostile neighbor while holding an open box of ashes: take a step back before he slams the door in your face. Unless you *want* to inhale a mouthful of dust.

And yes, "dust" is a euphemism.

I was hacking up bits of the dearly departed, Colin suppressing another gag as Ray resealed the bag with the solemnity of an undertaker. I barely noticed the crooked smile he shot me, or the way his fingers brushed against my arms when he scooped up the package to present to 4F.

"West Lawn Mortuary, that's their logo on the ribbon," the young woman pointed out. "They took care of one of my grandpas. He was a veteran, too. Yellow ribbon."

* * * *

The couple who ran the crematorium at West Lawn looked like something out of *American Gothic*. Gayle and Grant Gordon had gaunt faces and judgy eyes that bored into us like we were a trio of Gen-Z grave robbers. A scratchy speaker somewhere piped mournful organ chords into the chilly floral air. We tried to explain our side of the story, three grown adults cowering like kids in the principal's office.

"So. You weren't *expecting* a delivery?" Gayle's sinewy neck strained against a starched collar. "No recent *loss*?"

"Not even!" Ray clapped a firm hand on my shoulder and leaned closer to the couple. "To be honest with you two, I thought it might be a toaster. Kind of a Pop-Tarts nut myself. This guy knows what I'm talking about."

The Gordons weren't amused.

I cleared my throat. "Well, if there's nothing else, we'll leave this with you and be on our way."

"You misunderstand," Grant protested. "There are no *returns*."

Gayle couldn't agree more. "This isn't an Abercrombie and Fitch, boys."

It was all I could do not to laugh. "You guys aren't *serious*," I managed. "This was *your* mistake. You sent us a whole *person*, and somehow, *we're* responsible?"

"Trent..." Colin warned through gritted teeth. He always had an annoying deference to authority. Although, I couldn't see why a couple of disorganized morticians should have him so nervous.

But I wasn't giving up, even if it meant stretching the truth a tad. "I happen to be a law student, and I think the firm I'm interning at would *love* to tackle a little case of cemetery desecration. You didn't even label the box right; I looked it up. So, if you'd be so kind as to take back your ashes—"

"*We don't want him back!*" Gayle practically screeched.

I wondered if we'd wandered into the setup of a horror movie. By the way these two were talking, I could only assume these ashes were cursed, and we'd unleashed some unspeakable evil simply by checking our mail. Like Pandora at the post office.

With a curt nod from her husband, Gayle fired up an ancient computer. "Perhaps we can refresh your memories." Grant sneered at us. "Yours was the only address we managed to find. There must be *some* connection to the...to this...to the *deceased*."

"My god," Ray breathed. "Who *was* this guy?"

"He was what they call a 'John Doe,'" Gayle announced from behind the monitor, poking at the keyboard like an anemic T. rex. "Caucasian male, estimated seventy years old, no fingerprints or dental records to match. Remains were placed into storage, until a next-of-kin could be found."

Grant gazed at us expectantly, his horse-face melting a bit as we didn't immediately recall some long-lost white septuagenarian relative. Ray returned my shrug. Colin still looked clenched, but there wasn't a smidge of recognition on his face. "*No idea* who he was?" the old man pleaded.

Ray put his hands up. "We're as confused as you are."

"What about the ribbon?" I prompted, looking back at the box. "How'd you know this anonymous man was a veteran?"

Grant pointed a bony finger at the screen. "One of his tattoos. 'Semper Fi.' Although I didn't think they let his kind into the military back then."

I scooted forward in my chair. "His '*kind*?'"

"Another tattoo." The woman's lip curled up with distaste. "Of the *rainbow* variety."

So, that explained it. The looks of disgust, the desperation to keep this *kind* of man out of their facility. I'd seen my share of intolerance, but discriminating against a box of dust was on a whole new level. Were they worried he'd try to recruit the other corpses? Start an undead orgy in the ovens?

I took a deep breath of Glade plug-in air. Now was not the time to get on my soapbox. "That's all the information you had?"

It was Grant's turn to squint at the screen. "More tattoos, one bearing the name of 'Richard.' God knows who *he* was."

Gayle scoffed. "Or what those two got up to. While they were supposed to be defending our great nation."

"Not much else of interest on the body," Grant said with a smug purse of his thin lips. "Except for some obvious track marks on the arms. But no surprises there."

"I didn't ask for an autopsy," I seethed.

The couple stood up in unison. "We did our best under the circumstances," Gayle clucked. "This man was a vagrant who left no one behind to mourn him. He was a miserable case, but you can't hold us responsible for his poor choices."

Colin shook his head. "All right, easy Mrs. Gordon…"

"When we got *your address* from an anonymous call," she went on, "we were only too happy to be rid of this…*package*. It was taking up space for six months."

"*Six months?!*" I wanted to say more. I *needed* to say more, but the words caught in my throat, burning somewhere behind my eyes. My gaze flitted up to the crucifix on the wall.

Lord, forgive me for what I'm about to do.

In one swift motion, I snatched the box from Grant's cadaverous hands and cradled it to my chest as I backed away from the desk. I didn't know this man, this probably-gay-maybe-veteran who'd ended up on my front porch, but I wasn't letting him spend another minute in this chilly, frilly den of death and fluorescent lighting.

"Now, see here," Grant wheezed. "If you are not the rightful next of kin…"

"Then what?" I challenged. "You'll stick him on a shelf indefinitely? Not on my watch."

Colin may have looked scandalized, but he followed me to the exit, all the same. Ray hooted with laughter, turning around with a parting message.

"Ashes to ashes, dudes! Love is love!"

* * * *

Colin peeled out of the mortuary parking lot like a getaway driver. "You don't think they're calling the cops, do you?" His knuckles were white on the wheel.

"I think they're glad to be rid of us." I looked down at the box. "*All* of us. They probably mislabeled this package on purpose, probably *hoped* he got lost. The jerks."

Ray reached up from the backseat and tousled my unwashed hair, looking up directions to the Office of Veterans Affairs across town. A nagging voice in the back of my head reminded me I had a tower of flashcards to conquer by nightfall, but LSAT prep would have to wait. What's-his-name needed our help.

I tried not to think about what he must have felt like, alone at the end of a life that had been no picnic. My own quarter-life crisis paled in comparison. Sure, I was reeling from a bad breakup, wondering how I'd let a handsome face derail my five-year plan. But I'd had Colin to pick up the pieces and put a roof over my newly single head when it all went south. For all his faults and Type-A quirks, the guy had always been there for me. I only hoped the dead man in my lap had found a friend like that.

"You don't have to do this," I told Colin as he pulled into a parking spot. "I know you don't like getting in trouble."

He wrinkled his nose, finally releasing his grip on the steering wheel. "Come on, we're not kids anymore. We're not doing anything illegal, just asking some questions."

"That's the thing." I flashed an apologetic smile, "I may have a plan. And you might not like it."

The Veterans Affairs office was a sea of gray, dotted with faded posters and framed photos of heroes from days gone by. Ray and Colin followed my lead as the receptionist frowned at my made-up story and ushered us to a cubicle. She exchanged some hushed words with Deborah, a curly-haired lesbian. Or so I assumed.

"You boys are here on behalf of your…grandpa?" Deborah sank back into her desk chair and gave us an appraising look. Between Colin's chestnut skin and Ray's bone structure, none of us looked related.

"*My* grandpa," I clarified.

"We're here for moral support." Ray beamed.

Colin nodded in nervous solidarity.

The chair squeaked as Deborah rocked back. "What branch did ol' gramps serve in?"

"Well, that's the thing," I proceeded with caution. "He's not a veteran *himself*, at least I don't think…"

She raised her eyebrows. "Sounds like you two are close."

"His ex-boyfriend was a Marine," I said. "He told me all about it, very romantic stuff. And the guy lives nearby."

"Do you have a name?"

"Unfortunately not." Cracks were forming in my plan, but I doubled down. "Grandpa Richard can't even bring himself to say the guy's name. You know how it is for queer people in that boomer generation."

Deborah's chair rocked forward, her eyes narrowed. "Quite an assumption you're making."

"Oh no," Colin jumped in, defensive as ever, "my friend here would *never* presume to guess your sexual orientation." He glanced my way, hoping he was right.

But Deborah rolled her eyes. "Not *that*, I'm a big ol' lez. But I'm not a *boomer*. I'm forty-eight."

I barked out a nervous laugh. It had been a calculated risk asking to speak with the "LGBT+ Veteran Care Coordinator," a role I'd googled on the drive over. But if anyone was going to be sympathetic to our bizarre request it was her.

"I'll level with you, Deborah," I went on, "we know your office might not have any record of the guy we're looking for." I lowered my voice. "I think he may have been dishonorably discharged."

The thought had already occurred to me, though I'd hoped it wasn't true. Not that long ago, a gay serviceman caught outside the closet would have been booted out of the armed forces, a black mark forever next to their name. I was pretty sure the ghouls at the crematorium hadn't put those pieces together in their half-hearted search, but I knew better. And it seemed Deborah did too.

Not that it was an easy ask to make. Deborah shifted uncomfortably at the prospect of searching for ex-Marines in the area who hadn't been granted full veteran status. Her frown only deepened when I added, "Possibly deceased."

It was outside her purview, she explained, a search in a database she wasn't sure she had access to. But I wasn't giving up that easily.

"This man has been *erased*," I implored her, stepping on my soapbox at last. "Like so many others of his generation. And I know things are better now, and I know *you're* part of the solution. But this is our chance to make something right for a man who had his future stolen for the simple crime of being his true self. Are you gonna let them get away with that, Deborah?"

She looked impressed. "You make a hell of a case. You should be a lawyer."

* * * *

I wasn't sure how Deborah did it, but she managed to plumb the depths of the VA records until she tracked down a local man who matched our vague description. An ex-Marine, age 73, dishonorably discharged for "lewd behavior."

Frank Whitley deserved a little honor. At least in death.

We piled into Colin's car again, heading across town to Frank's last known address, all of us expecting the worst. I imagined a dingy motel with a flickering Vacancy sign, or maybe a basement apartment that had seen better days. But the luxury condo complex was a pleasant surprise.

White stucco walls and babbling fountains flanked the entrance, the tile-roofed dwelling units stretching out like something out of *Mamma Mia*.

"*This* is where our guy lived?" Ray asked as we walked the manicured path to the leasing office.

"Maybe he wasn't such a 'miserable case' after all." I winked at Ray, vindicated, wondering if it looked as effortless as I hoped.

The office was all white oak and polished leather. Two men with sleek suits and slicked-back hair greeted Colin as one of their own…then darkened a bit when they saw me and Ray bringing up the rear. At least I'd left the box in the car.

Frank. I'd left *Frank* in the car.

The photo attached to his USMC file was an old one, the quality degraded from the snap I'd taken on my phone. But recognition dawned on both of the realtors' faces as soon as they saw.

"Good ol' Frank," one of them said.

"Guy was a *legend*," added the other.

The older of the two shook my hand, introducing himself as Parker Wallace, the property manager and the person who had found Frank Whitley's body. We followed him outside, down another shrub-lined path as he went on.

"Frank knew he didn't have much time," Parker said as we trailed behind, "and no next of kin to leave his money to. So, Mr. Whitley decided to move into one of our finest units to, uh…run out the clock. Sorry to be blunt about it, but those *are* the words he used."

"Baller move," Ray murmured.

Parker seemed to agree. "Of course, Frank was a fighter, and he lived a year longer than the doctors expected. But what was I gonna do, kick him out?"

Colin's eyes went wide. "So, you let him live here for free?"

"For the last few months," Parker nodded. "Paid him a salary, too. Culture Director of the complex. He'd host movie nights, decorate for Christmas, tell stories about the shenanigans he got up to when he was younger. He made out with a Kennedy once, and *not* the one you're thinking." The smile faded on Parker's face as he pointed at a nearby unit. "It broke our hearts when he passed. Right in there."

I looked around the condo complex, trying to imagine the life Frank had made for himself in his dying days. But something didn't seem right.

"You didn't give them his information?" I probed. "Not the EMTs? Not the police?"

"There were no police," Parker said. "Guys like Frank just…slip through the cracks sometimes. And his arrangement here wasn't exactly *legal*, I wasn't gonna call any attention to his tenancy—"

"No one claimed him," I spat out. "If he meant so much to all of you, why didn't you take his ashes, do some kind of memorial?"

Parker blanched. "I didn't think it was our place. I told those folks at the mortuary to send his remains to the man he was always talking about. The one that got away, he always said."

"Richard?" I ventured.

"That's the one," Parker said. "Richard Kerrigan. We didn't have an address. Thought maybe they could track it down. But I still kept an eye out. Took a few months, but it finally came up in our database…"

"*Parker!*"

The younger man from the office came striding up behind us, calling out to his colleague with warning in his tone.

"That database is proprietary information," he went on.

"Relax, Alex." Parker turned back to us. "There's nothing illegal about it. We purchase contact information of discerning consumers in the area. It's all marketing, all above board. But to be safe I informed the mortuary *anonymously.*"

"But this doesn't make sense," Colin jumped in. "The address you found, the address West Lawn sent the cremains to…it wasn't Richard Kerrigan's."

"That's not true." Ray stepped forward.

Alex looked like he was at the end of his rope. "So, *who* is this Richard Kerrigan?"

Ray grimaced. "I am."

* * * *

Ray's wine delivery was a generous introductory offer—six bottles of the club's finest reds for free with a new membership. To hear him tell it, it was a pretty easy system to game. All he needed to do was sign up for a membership with a Visa gift card and a fake name.

What were the odds he'd come up with "Richard Kerrigan" and end up on a mailing list for local snobs? A mailing list Frank Whitley's old landlord was monitoring. A mailing list that would land his ashes smack dab on our doorstep.

"It must be destiny," Ray marveled as we stepped back inside the apartment. "Maybe that name was in the ether, you know? Maybe we were *supposed* to end up with Frank."

We were talking about the guy like an old friend now. And why not? As I shifted his package from one arm to the other, I realized he was the first man I'd touched since my breakup.

Not counting my affectionate new roommate, of course. Ray grabbed my arm as he pulled a bottle of Merlot from the crate. "What do you think, dude? We raise a glass to his memory?"

Colin got busy wiping down every conceivable surface in the kitchen, wielding antibacterial spray like holy water. He hadn't been happy to hear that his apartment was the site of Ray's legally ambiguous schemes, and I was sure he'd be checking the building bylaws before long. But there was a grudging respect budding between them.

As Ray disappeared into his bedroom to fetch the missing corkscrew, Colin fixed me in his gaze. "Well, you did it," he said. "Solved the mystery without getting us court-martialed."

"Yeah," I breathed, setting Frank on a barstool. "But now what happens to *him*?"

"I'm more concerned about what happens to *you*."

I'd seen this protective look in Colin's eyes before. It was there when I'd had a run-in with a nasty high school bully. It was there when my parents had cut me off after coming out. And it was there when Colin had given me the pep talk of my life and shoved an LSAT prep book in my hands.

Now he was smiling, dropping his washcloth in the sink. "Today was the most alive I've seen you in *months*. It was almost like having the old Trent back."

"The old Trent?"

"You know, the guy who was actually *excited* for law school."

"Who says I'm not excited?" I protested. "I'm just…"

"Scared you'll mess it up?" Colin raised his eyebrows. "Same reason you haven't been dating?"

I laughed. "Who died and made you my therapist?"

Colin's eyes drifted to the box. "Don't miss your chance to live your life. That's all I'm saying. You're gonna pass this test, you're gonna fall in love again"—he lowered his voice—"and you're gonna get over this ridiculous crush you have on our new roommate."

My cheeks burned. "It's that obvious?"

Ray emerged from his room, and I tried not to stare as he popped the cork. Colin was right, it had been a long time for me. But there was nothing like a glimpse at your own mortality to get you out of a rut.

Maybe Frank had inspired me. In spite of everything that had come his way, nothing seemed to have stopped the guy from loving and living fully. Until the very end.

The clinking of our glasses was underscored by the ringing of the doorbell. Estelle had come by to see if we'd identified our ashy acquaintance… and to check if Ray had any edibles lying around. He rummaged through his backpack as I offered our neighbor a glass.

Estelle looked curiously at the wine shipment, her soft white lashes fluttering at the shipping label. "How do you boys know Richard?"

Ray and Colin froze, the three of us sharing a single thought.

"No way," I muttered.

"It was…just a random name," Ray admitted. "For the free trial."

Estelle's earrings jangled as she shook her head. "Not random at all, young man. He's the sculptor I told you about."

Ray's cheeks dimpled with realization. "*That's* where I heard the name!"

Estelle nodded. "You were stoned, dear. But I told you all about him. Richard's the one I was mad for back in seventy-eight. But bless his heart, the fella was gay as the day is long. Still has his studio, though."

I rested one reverent hand on Frank's box.

"Do you know the address?"

* * * *

"Okay, next one," Ray called from the backseat.

"Haven't we done enough?" I groaned.

"Oh no," Colin scolded from behind the wheel. "You promised we'd study *all the way here*."

Ray clutched my test prep book as we rounded a corner. "You wanna stick with *Necessary Assumption* or move on to *Reasoning*?"

"I wanna know what we're gonna tell this Richard guy," I said, watching the industrial parks on either side of the street give way to rows of trendy galleries. "What if he doesn't even remember Frank? What if it didn't end well with them? What if we're dredging up some trauma this guy buried *years* ago."

"My god," Ray exhaled, his breath tickling the hairs on the back of my neck. "What must it be like in your head?"

The car came to a stop.

"We're here," Colin announced. "And I know the irony of this coming from me…but you're overthinking, Trent."

I looked out the car window at the address Estelle had given us, along with the assurance that the artist in residence would love a little blast from the past. Maybe Ray was right, maybe this was destiny.

Colin was out of the car before I could say another word. Still, I hesitated.

I felt Ray's hands on my shoulders. "Don't be nervous, man. You did good."

I nodded, unbuckling my seatbelt as Ray gave me a squeeze.

"It couldn't have been easy for these guys," he went on, "growing up when they did, facing what they had to face. Just to love who they wanted. We owe them a lot."

I twisted around in my seat, scanning Ray's face in surprise. The guileless eyes. The upturned lips.

"'*We?*'" I echoed. "You mean you're…gay?"

Ray scoffed. "Isn't it obvious?" He stroked my hair with one hand, throwing his door open with the other. "Come on, we have lovers to reunite!"

I looked at the box in my lap, then at the maddeningly confusing man following Colin inside.

"I dunno, Frank," I mused. "It's probably a bad idea. But he has a cute butt."

Frank was quiet. But I think he understood.

TAKE OUT

BECKY CLARK

Charlee Russo chased a recalcitrant morsel of chicken around a pool of vindaloo sauce in the sustainable, recyclable container she held, finally cornering and stabbing it hard with her plastic spork. "Isn't it neat that *take out* means food, dating, *and* murder?"

Her boyfriend Ozzi gave her the side-eye. "Neat?"

"Cool, awesome, delightful, jim-dandy, boss, keen."

"No."

"Party pooper."

"Not everyone is steeped in mysteries and wordplay like you. But"—he pointed his kabob at her—"I'm here on this stake-out with you, remember?"

"That's why I love you." Charlee shifted her weight in the low-to-the-ground folding beach chair she sat in and made a smoochy face at him.

"But remind me one more time why we're here." Ozzi swept his kabob around the cemetery. "I swear I'll get it this go 'round."

"Because of Fodor Glava."

Ozzi screwed up his face in an *I-know-you-told-me-and-I-should-remember-but-I'm-sorry-I-just-don't* expression.

Charlee sighed and sopped up her remaining vindaloo with a still-warm piece of naan. "Fodor Glava? Legendary vampire? That big article in *Westword*?"

Ozzi had the decency to look contrite as he shook his head.

She handed him her empty container and he packed up their trash. "He lived in Colorado and probably worked in one of the mines, but he died in 1918, during the flu pandemic. The townspeople were a bit spooked by a harmonic convergence of weirdnesses." Charlee held up fingers as she listed them. "I mean, *Dracula* had been published twenty or so years earlier. Poor ol' Fodor was from Transylvania, too. And three, their pandemic. Now we have firsthand knowledge about how spooky *that* was. Like during our pandemic, they wanted to find the cause, or at least someone to blame. And here's a guy from Dracula's hometown who seems like the perfect candidate."

"Transylvania isn't actually a town. It's a—" At Charlee's glare, Ozzi zipped it and gave a magnanimous sweep of his hand. "Please, go on, my love."

"So they dug him up and—"

"They dug him *up*?"

Charlee nodded. "And his fingernails were really long and there was what looked like blood in his mouth, and his teeth looked too big—"

"Because his skin had begun to shrink."

"Exactly. Now we know that's normal body decomposition, but they didn't. To be on the safe side, they pierced his heart with a stake and reburied him."

"As one does."

"And then later," Charlee dropped her voice and shined her flashlight under her chin. "They found a rose bush growing right above where his heart would have been. And ever since, people have claimed to see a tall man wearing a cloak and sporting long fingernails in the cemetery late at night. Haunting them for doing him wrong."

Ozzi clicked on his flashlight and swept it around the area. "So we're here in the middle of the night to catch a glimpse of Mr. Fodor Glava?"

"Oh, he's not buried here."

Ozzi stared at her, waiting for more of the explanation. When it didn't come, he sprayed her with the glow from his flashlight. "Then…why?"

"Seriously? I swear I've told you this…twice."

Ozzi pulled her close and kissed the side of her head. "Don't be mad, but I probably thought it was the plot for the book you're working on, and I tuned it out."

Charlee pulled away and her hand fluttered up, covering her mouth. Then she laughed and playfully swatted him. "I knew it."

"I would rather be surprised when I read your books after they launch."

"Good save, dude."

"Every word true. Scout's honor." Ozzi raised his right hand, fingers spread between his middle and ring finger, forming a V.

"That's the Vulcan salute."

"Whatever. I was never a Scout."

"I never was either, but I'm always prepared."

"Not if we're in the wrong cemetery."

Charlee blinked at him, three slow times, completely incredulous. "You really don't know what we're doing, but you're happy to tag along and eat Indian food in a cemetery in the middle of the night."

Ozzi shrugged. "I'm happy to do anything you tell me."

"Except listen to my stories."

"To be fair, I listen to most of your stories. And don't get all high and mighty, missy. When was the last time you listened to one of my work stories?"

Charlee grinned. "From the hack factory? I don't want to be arrested as an accessory after the fact."

"I'm not a hacker, I—never mind. You were telling me why we're in this cemetery if Mr. Fodor Whoever isn't even buried here."

"This is the cool part, so pay attention. It's not one of my plots, but it might be soon. Seems every cemetery in the Denver area is being visited by a tall furtive man in a long, dark coat. In the morning, a single grave has a piece of paper held down by a big rock." Again, Charlee flicked on the flashlight under her chin and dropped her voice. "It's a rubbing from Fodor Glava's grave marker."

Ozzi nodded. "And we're going to find him by sitting in random cemeteries and hope he meanders by. Of course."

"Ah, you misunderestimate me, boy. I have a plan and I'm going to win a thousand bucks."

"Color me intrigued."

"I knew you would be. A radio station offered a reward to anyone who figures out who this guy is."

"Then why isn't this place mobbed?" Ozzi flashed his light around again.

"Because I'm the smartest girl in Denver and I figured out that he's visiting cemeteries a certain way. He's using a geographic pattern in the shape of a set of vampire teeth. Like a great big W across the city." Charlee drew a large W in the air with her flashlight.

Ozzi stared at her. "You *are* the smartest girl in Denver, and I will help you win your thousand dollars. Unless I get scared and run away."

"Duly noted."

They sat in silence, flashlights turned off in their laps. They had positioned themselves near the middle of the smallish cemetery. They couldn't see the entire area, but it was flat, and Charlee trusted they could see enough. Certainly enough to notice a tall, cloaked figure.

Even though it was summertime, the hot day became a chilly night, and they covered up with a blanket Charlee brought. "Always prepared, remember?"

Ozzi dozed off and woke with a jolt when his head dropped forward. "You sure he's coming tonight?"

"Nope. Go back to sleep. I'll wake you if you need to run away."

"You're the best." Ozzi scooted closer and snuggled into Charlee's shoulder.

Charlee sat quietly, listening to Ozzi's deep breathing. Suddenly a twig snapped. She tensed, jabbing Ozzi in the ribs. He mumbled but she clamped her palm over his mouth. She felt him tense too. When she was sure he wasn't going to talk, she removed her hand. They both glanced around, trying to pierce further into the darkness.

Skittering nearby made them swing their heads left. Only a squirrel.

They held their breath, listening.

A rustling sound to their right caused them to snap their heads in that direction.

The rustling came closer.

Charlee shrunk backward into her chair and grabbed wildly for Ozzi's hand. They barely breathed. They had placed the beach chairs between two three-foot tall markers to be less conspicuous. Charlee hoped that was the case anyway.

The rustling came closer. Close enough that Charlee could see a long cloak brushing against the tall grass. Coming toward them. Whoever—or whatever—it was didn't need a flashlight to find their way through a cemetery.

Every muscle in Charlee's body was taut. This was a fight-or-flight situation, and she was fixin' for flight. She squeezed Ozzi's hand once, twice, and on three, they'd run.

She squeezed the last time, then leaped from her chair, scrambling backward, away from the rustling.

"Yeep!"

"Arrgghh!"

"Keep running," Charlee whispered to Ozzi. But the instant she did, she realized he was not with her. She skidded to a stop, surrounded by inky blackness, wondering if she should turn on her flashlight, simultaneously wondering why it wasn't in her hand.

The nearby noises—grunts and wheezes, with the occasional expletive—continued and she took a cautious step toward them.

Ozzi had to be tussling with the…whatever it was. Was she going to be more help to him if she stayed out of the way or if she leapt into the fray? She remembered that there was a reason she wrote mysteries instead of trying to solve them…she was a big, fat chicken.

But Ozzi needed her. She took a deep breath and flung herself toward the fray. She dove for the beach chair and felt around until her fingers grasped the flashlight.

She flipped it on and saw Ozzi going in circles with a figure in a long dark cloak wearing night vision goggles.

Charlee shined the light directly into the goggles. "Unhand my boyfriend!" she commanded.

The cloaked figure yelped and let go of Ozzi to cover its face. "Ow! Stop it!"

"You stop it!" Charlee's adrenaline surged and she moved forward to collect Ozzi. They shuffled away from the cloaked figure.

The figure pulled off the night vision goggles to reveal a woman at least eighty years old. "Why are you two trying to blind me?"

"We're not trying to— What are you doing out here?" Charlee asked.

"None of your beeswax, but if you're trying to win a thousand dollars, you can stop now. It's mine." And with that, the woman stomped away the direction she'd come. "And don't you dare follow me!" she hollered over her shoulder.

They stared after her. Finally, Charlee said, "I guess I'm the second smartest girl in Denver. Night vision goggles was a genius idea."

"Shall we call it a night?"

Charlee nodded. They gathered up their things and headed across the cemetery.

Ozzi lit up their path over the uneven grass.

Suddenly, Charlee grabbed his arm and swung the flashlight toward a grave. *Samuel Dransfeldt 1943–2004 Loving husband and father.*

On top of it was a large rock holding down a piece of paper. Charlee took a knee, then held the paper to the glow of Ozzi's light.

A rubbing of Fodor Glava's grave marker.

* * * *

Charlee and Ozzi sat on her couch and talked the rest of the night, speculating on what it all meant. They debated whether this apparition wanted to say something to modern people, and if so, what might it be? Was it a warning that vampires are reappearing? Are the people whose graves he marked actually vampires to beware of?

Charlee was spinning herself up, but Ozzi was a bit more circumspect. He wrapped his arms around her and said, "Remember Occam's razor. The simplest explanation is usually the correct one."

She narrowed her eyes. "Do you think Sir Know-It-All Occam ever ran into a vampire? Besides, what exactly is the simplest explanation here, hmm?"

Ozzi sighed and settled back in with her. "No idea." After a few moments he said, "What about that lady in the cloak? She was there. It had to be her. She's punking everyone."

"I've been going over and over that. First off, she was short."

"But remarkably strong." Ozzi rubbed his arms.

"Yes, dear. But she came from the opposite direction and after we saw her, she retraced her steps. She wasn't anywhere near that grave. Besides, she said she was after the reward too."

"I suppose."

"Whoever it was dropped that grave rubbing while we were sitting right there, not fifty feet away. And we didn't hear a thing. That's creepy." Charlee shivered and snuggled back into Ozzi's shoulder.

Over the next two days, Charlee did a deep dive into every person's grave that Fodor Glava had marked with the stone and his rubbing. She stretched and prodded her brain to make connections that would link them all. She cross-referenced birth and death dates. Hometowns. Employment history. Schools. Nothing overlapped. She branched out to their family trees and tried the same tactic. All she created was an elaborate Venn diagram with no overlap. So, really, just a bunch of circles.

Over the next two nights, Charlee and Ozzi went on more cemetery stake-outs, but they didn't even see any squirrels.

On the third night, after Charlee donned her long-sleeved black T-shirt and black yoga pants—what she referred to as her Vampire Vanquishing Out-fit—she knocked on Ozzi's apartment door.

When he opened it, he was wearing cargo shorts and a white polo.

"You're not ready yet? That's a first." Charlee laughed and pushed past him into the apartment.

"I'm not going. This is a wild goose chase, and I have better things to do."

Charlee put her hands on her hips. "Like what?"

"I haven't gotten that far yet, but I'll think of something." He scooped her up in an embrace. "Whatever it is, though, you can do it with me."

She struggled out of his arms. "I need to do this, Oz. I can't think of any-thing else except Fodor Glava and vampires and grave rubbings. It's going to drive me nuts until I figure it out. My publisher is waiting on my next book, but I can't concentrate on that stupid revision. Everything keeps coming out vampire-y!"

"But—"

"You don't have to come. Really. It's fine. To be honest, I've been feeling a tad guilty dragging you out every night. I mean, you have a real job to get to in the morning." She kissed the tip of his nose. "Want me to come by when I've unmasked the fiend?"

"I'll cry if you don't."

* * * *

Charlee sat in the driver's seat of her car, formulating her plan. She was sure her map of the Denver metro area's cemeteries was correct and that Fodor Glava was hitting them in the shape of fangs, but had she missed something? Why was no grave rubbing found at the cemetery she and Ozzi had parked themselves at the last two nights? Maybe she missed a post in the Fodor Glava Mystery forum. Or maybe it hadn't been reported for some reason.

She pulled out her phone and tapped until she was into the chat room. She scrolled until she grew exasperated by the ads, then clicked away. Instead, she found the phone number for the radio station offering the reward.

It was after hours, but she dialed the studio line and kept her fingers crossed. She doubted anyone would answer. She pictured a radio station as one enormous CD changer that someone pressed shuffle and play once every twelve hours or so. Or maybe it was a gigantic turntable with a bunch of those little records her mom still had in her attic. Forty-fives. She had shown Charlee how she would stack up five or ten of them and they would automatically drop to the turntable and play the song, then the next record would drop. It all seemed inefficient to Charlee, but her mom clearly enjoyed reminiscing about her Bobby Sherman, David Cassidy, and The Monkees records.

A voice on the phone startled her. "You're diggin' the Night Life."

"Um…hello, Mr. Nightlight—"

"Night *Life*…you know, like the life of the par-tay."

"Ah. My name is Charlee Russo—"

"Not *the* Charlee Russo?"

Charlee was flattered. Her name was well-known in crime fiction circles, but she didn't get much recognition out in the wild. "Um…yes, I suppose." She was about to ask him which of her books he'd read, but before she could, he interrupted with a laugh.

"Just kidding. What do you want from a radio station so late at night, Charlee Russo? Got a request? I ain't Casey Kasem, ya know."

"Who?" When she heard his loud sigh, she knew this was a piece of Americana she should research and made a mental note. "No request, but I have a question."

"Shoot."

"You know the Fodor Glava mystery?"

"You solved it? Well, I'll be a—"

"No, but I haven't heard of any grave rubbings left anywhere the last couple of nights."

"So?"

"I was wondering if I missed something or if there really haven't been any."

He was quiet for a moment then said, "I guess he's been busy with his day job."

"What? His day job?" Charlee held her breath for the massive clue Mr. Nightlight was going to shine on her.

Instead, she received another guffaw. "He's a vampire, isn't he? Surely there's paperwork involved. Maybe some *red* tape...get it?" He laughed at his own dumb joke.

"If he's a vampire, I think he only works at night."

"Oh. Yeah. Good point."

"So, you don't know if any more rubbings have been found since the one on Samuel Dransfeldt's grave?"

"Naw, I don't think so. I'd have heard."

Charlee thanked him and disconnected but didn't start her car yet. She turned on the dome light and unfolded her map of Denver where she'd drawn the vampire fangs bisecting, or at least coming near, all the cemeteries. She couldn't decide which to stakeout tonight. She waffled back and forth, mentally listing the pros and cons of each.

A tap on her window caused her to jump out of her seat.

Ozzi.

She rolled it down. "Cripes, you scared me!"

"What are you still doing here?"

"I've been trying to figure out which cemetery to go to. I think this one." She pointed to the map.

"Glad I could help." Ozzi flashed a grin that made Charlee wonder why she was going to drive away from him.

* * * *

This cemetery was different from all the others Charlee had staked out. For one thing, it had sidewalks and paved roads with actual signage, like a small town. Signs would have been quite convenient, had she any idea where she needed to be.

She still hadn't found a connection between the markers where Fodor Glava had left his grave rubbing under the rocks. The choices all seemed completely random to her, which, of course, didn't mean there *wasn't* a connection. It was as mysterious as Fodor Glava himself.

Charlee meandered up and down the sidewalks of the cemetery, keeping her eyes peeled for anything unusual. Strolling was pleasant in the comfortable summer night, but as soon as the thought formed in her brain, the clouds covered the moon and the wind blew through the fifty-year-old cottonwood trees and enormous blue spruces.

Charlee snapped the bottom two snaps on her jean jacket in an attempt to keep it from flapping in the steady breeze. Nervously glancing around at all the new sounds, she gave a small snort. *If I wrote this scene in one of my books, my editor would make me take it out, it's such a cliché. Perfectly lovely evening in a cemetery morphs just like that into a dark and eerie scene.* Charlee shook her head, but it did nothing to dispel her growing discomfort.

Why was this the night Ozzi chose to stay home? None of those other cemeteries were this spooky. Or were they not spooky because Ozzi was with her? Yet another question without an answer.

Charlee shook off her discomfort and forged ahead. The sooner she solved this mystery, the sooner she could return to writing her own mysteries…the ones she could control. She snapped one more snap on her jacket as she marched forward. If she had to walk every inch of these sidewalks, that's what she'd do. And if she saw nothing unusual, then she'd take it as a sign to give up this nonsense, reward be damned.

She mentally calculated she'd reached the center of the cemetery, mainly because she couldn't see lights from the parking lot any longer. It became darker and darker with every step.

A rustling noise off to her left stopped her in her tracks. She strained to hear and ideally, identify the sound. She squinted into the darkness, easing her phone from her back pocket. She assumed—wrongly, of course—that carrying the flashlight was too cumbersome since she had her phone. But she forgot that flashlights could double as weapons. That's simply Detective 101, she thought ruefully. Always prepared. Pfft.

She stepped off the sidewalk into the grass and tiptoed toward a big stone monument nearby. Hiding seemed like an excellent idea at the moment.

Hoping her silent steps allowed her to hide behind the tall granite marker without detection, she hugged the cool stone and peered around.

Nothing.

She hugged the other side, sidling to the next corner to peer around.

Nothing.

She listened for the rustling she'd been hearing, but felt silly when she heard the leaves all around her still moving in the wind. She was sure she'd heard something different, though.

Making her way to the next corner she peered around it, only to come face-to-face with dark eyes peering at her.

She yelped and jumped backward, losing her balance and falling to the ground. Her phone took a loud bounce.

Shadows from the monument fell across her and hid even the dim light from the cloudy sky. Scrambling on her hands and knees, she felt for her phone. Relief flooded her when her hand grazed it. She blazed up the flashlight app, frantically scanning the area, but saw nothing.

It suddenly rang and she nearly dropped it again, in her haste to silence it.

"Ozzi?" she whispered. "Why are you calling me?"

"I think I saw him," Ozzi whispered.

"Who?"

"Who do you think?"

"At your apartment?" Charlee squinched her face in confusion.

"No! I'm in the cemetery. Where are you?"

"In the cemetery, where do you think?"

"I'm near someone's grave with a tall metal spire," Ozzi whispered.

"I'm near"—Charlee shined her light upward then immediately turned it off when she saw how it spotlighted her position—"a big ol' thing with a horse at the top." Suddenly her phone went dark. "Ozzi? Oz?" She looked at her dark phone and barely whispered, "Where'd you go?"

A hand wrapped around her upper arm.

"I'm right here."

Charlee stared into Ozzi's dark eyes peering at her. "Oh for Pete's—it was you I saw."

Ozzi sighed. "And it was you I saw."

They giggled nervously and fell into each other's arms.

After a moment Charlee pulled from his embrace. "Let's get out of here. This entire escapade was a fiasco. Way too much work for that reward."

They both stowed their phones before gripping hands and heading back toward the parking lot.

Before they reached the sidewalk, Charlee yanked Ozzi's hand, using it to point. "Look! Fodor Glava!"

As one, they dashed behind a marker. Peeking around either side, they saw the cloaked figure moving away from them. They followed, zigzagging behind, hiding behind convenient markers and monuments, closing the distance between them.

Fodor Glava seemed unaware of their presence. He stopped before a grave and glanced from side to side before reaching into his cloak and pulling out a large rock and sheet of paper. He arranged the paper on the grave, then placed the rock on top. But instead of disappearing with a poof into the night, he again reached inside his cloak.

He pulled out a cellphone and took a photo of the grave.

"What the—?" Charlee rose from where she and Ozzi crouched.

Ozzi pulled her back down and pointed.

Beyond Fodor Glava, at least six apparitions floated toward them. Dark waves undulated in the breeze.

Fodor Glava saw the apparitions, and without pausing, turned, barreling directly toward Charlee and Ozzi. They barely had time to get to their feet before the three of them were in a human tangle, arms and legs twisting, pulling, punching, kicking to get free.

The apparitions continued to float toward them.

The human tangle continued to writhe.

Charlee quit fighting, sure the advancing ghosts were the bigger threat. Ozzi and Fodor Glava continued their struggle, but Charlee was mesmerized.

The figures were on the sidewalk, close enough she could see the dark clothing, the gaunt faces. One of the ghosts had extraordinarily long fingernails.

Suddenly Charlee scrambled backward in a frantic crab walk. "That's Fodor Glava and his…his dark minions! Look at his fingernails!"

Ozzi and the other Fodor Glava quit fighting and followed Charlee's pointing finger.

"And Dracula teeth!" Ozzi jumped to his feet and pulled Charlee to hers.

Before they could turn and run, Dracula popped out his teeth and in a heavy eastern European accent said, "Hello."

"You're Fodor Glava!" the fake Fodor Glava said breathlessly, eyes wide with admiration.

"We are!" Dracula beamed. "Who are you?"

"I'm your biggest fan!"

Dracula turned to Charlee and Ozzi huddling together. "And who are you?"

"You're Fodor Glava?" Charlee said tentatively, continuing to cling to Ozzi.

"We are." Dracula swept his arm to encompass all the apparitions, one of whom stepped off a hoverboard and with a quick kick of his foot, flipped it into his hand. The others did the same.

"Hoverboards?" Charlee stared in disbelief. "You're not ghosts?"

Dracula looked confused. "No. We are punk band from Romania." He stared at Charlee, Ozzi, and the cloaked figure with widening eyes. "You are ghosts?"

Charlee dragged Ozzi a giant step away from the cloaked figure. "We aren't ghosts. But I'm not so sure about him."

"I'm not a ghost! I told you, I'm Fodor Glava's biggest fan!" The cloaked figure did a giddy two-step, holding his hand out toward Dracula. "I'm Jimmy."

Dracula placed his vampire teeth in his other hand to shake Jimmy's. "I am good for meeting you."

"I saw you last month in Prague," Jimmy said excitedly, continuing to pump Dracula's hand. "Excellent concert."

Charlee loosened her grip on Ozzi's bicep. "Let me get this straight. You guys," she indicated Dracula and the other hoverboarding ghosts, "are a Romanian punk band named Fodor Glava? You named yourself after a Colorado miner who died from influenza?"

"He is big name where we come from. Left Transylvania to become cowboy. Very brave."

Jimmy finally released Dracula's hand and addressed Charlee. "Their US debut is at Red Rocks in a couple days." He turned back to Dracula. "I can't believe I'm actually meeting you!"

Charlee smacked her forehead. "Jimmy, was this some big guerilla marketing stunt to advertise their Red Rocks show?"

Dracula frowned. "Gorillas?"

"Why go to all this trouble?" Charlee asked. "Why not do a social media blitz or post flyers about the concert?"

Jimmy snorted. "You're in a cemetery in the middle of the night. Would you have put this much energy into a flyer you saw?"

She shrugged. "Good point."

* * * *

The next morning Charlee went to the radio station to pick up her reward. The same DJ she talked to on the phone met her in the lobby after his shift.

"Answer me this, Mr. Nightlight," she said. "Was the radio station in on all of this?"

"Night Life." He raised his palms. "You got me. Jimmy is one of our interns. It was his idea. He's their number one fan."

"So I hear."

He leaned toward Charlee. "If we give you tickets to the show, will you hold off telling anyone about this? We didn't think anyone would figure it out and we have this big reveal planned the day before the concert. Fog machine, all of Fodor Glava's music in a slow minor key wafting through the last cemetery, tons of costumed undead wandering around."

"Sure. I love a big reveal. Can I be one of the costumed undead?"

"Of course you can! You managed to take out the competition and solve the whole dang deal, didn't you?"

She laughed. "You'll appreciate this insight. Isn't it neat that *take out* means food, dating, *and* murder?"

He gave her the side-eye. "Neat?"

Charlee sighed, vowing to take out that word from her vernacular.

THE BOHR BROTHERS AND THE BOOTLEGGER'S MISTRESS

BRIAN COX

Sylvester Bohr in most, though certainly not all, concerns was an average fellow with normal perceptions, common appreciations, and reasonable appetites. He did, however, possess a singular mind, a passion for local history, and a particular penchant for putting off undesirable tasks for as long as possible—and sometimes even longer.

This last inclination included finding a job.

Mind you, Sylvester was not lazy; neither did he tote an aversion to manual or mental labor. Rather, Sylvester perceived himself to be a writer of potential import and simply lacked the time to make a living.

There were greater things afoot than toiling at a mundane job merely to buy bread and pay the mortgage.

Sylvester lived with his two younger brothers, Felix and Morris, in a grand old Victorian that their Great Aunt Kitty had left them at the time of her death some three years back. Felix and Morris were of much the same view as Sylvester, which is to say, they too had neither the time nor inclination to hold down regular jobs. As with Sylvester, it was not at all that they were lazy, but because they were also artists.

Morris sculpted in butters of all sort and was forced to spend long hours in the old house's cellar where it was cooler and the butter less likely to melt. He was yet to sell a piece, but if this revealed a lack of appreciation in the people of Freedom County—and perhaps many square miles beyond—it wavered Morris's confidence not in the least that one day Norse Gods sculpted in butter would become all the rage and he would know wealth and riches and fame as only a handful of men in world history have ever known them.

The youngest brother, Felix, had established his studio in the attic of Great Aunt Kitty's bequest where he pursued fame and fortune as a painter. The attic was dry, removed, and well-lit. Further, it provided a calming view of the surrounding unkempt grounds and the expansive home of their closest neighbor, old Miss Hackenburger.

In fifteen years of effort, Felix, too, had not sold a single piece of artwork. It was starting to wear on his belief that postcards depicting full-scale portions of landmark buildings such as the Empire State Building and the Eiffel Tower would ever be recognized in his lifetime as the products of genius they were.

Being a genius was not easy, as any one of the Bohr brothers could and would tell you, but being an unrecognized, unappreciated, and poor genius was insufferable.

On a sunny spring afternoon, Sylvester returned home from the library and hailed his brothers from their work in the attic and basement.

"Brothers," he said when they had gathered, "I have made the most fantastic discovery. Our money problems are soon to be solved."

If that were true, it was none too soon. The small sum Great Aunt Kitty had bequeathed them had been depleted to virtually nothing six months back, and with no other source of income, the brothers were in danger of losing heating, electricity, water, phone, and, most tragically, the house itself.

Daily now they worried about being evicted from their home. They had nowhere else to go. Where would they sleep? Where would they eat? Good God, where would they create!

"As you know," continued Sylvester, "my work on the sixth volume of the history of Freedom County is coming along quite nicely. I'm all the way up to the 1920s, and it was in the course of researching the era that I came across the name of Harry Puffpaff."

"Who is Harry Puffpaff?" asked Morris.

"He was Freedom County's most ruthless bootlegger," said Sylvester. "He smuggled Canadian liquor across Lake Erie and into the states. It's reported that he killed sixteen competitors with a shotgun."

"What a charming fellow," said Felix.

"Try as they might, the FBI couldn't get anything on him," went on Sylvester dramatically. "Then, in the spring of 1924, one of Puffpaff's right-hand men turned state's evidence and gave the FBI everything they needed to put Puffpaff away for the rest of his life. They caught up with Puffpaff one night out at the old Roberts' farm. Under a full moon there was a wild shoot-out. Two FBI agents and six of Puffpaff's men were killed. Puffpaff himself escaped out the back of the farmhouse and ran toward the lake where he had a boat moored. From the shore, the FBI fired off a barrage of gunfire as Puffpaff's boat slipped farther out into the rising lake mist. Suddenly, with a cry of anguish, Puffpaff stood up in the boat as if shot and tumbled into the water."

Sylvester paused, looked at each of his brothers in turn to determine the depth of their attention. Satisfied that he held them enthralled, he leaned forward and spoke in a low whisper. "They combed the shores and dragged the lake for days. They never found his body. And though they tore the Roberts' farmhouse apart and every other hideout Puffpaff was known to use, they never found the reputed half million dollars he had hoarded either. People have searched for the money for seventy-five years and not a dime has been found." Sylvester reached into his pocket and pulled out a photocopy of a news article dated October 11, 1922. He unfolded it on the coffee table and ran his hand over the creases.

"But I," said Sylvester, leaning back in his chair and smiling triumphantly, "know where it is."

Felix and Morris bent over the newspaper article. The headline read: "Opening Night at the Golden Crown Ballroom." Under the headline, a faded, black-and-white picture showed dozens of young couples smiling while they danced beneath ornate chandeliers.

Felix and Morris looked up at their brother in bewilderment.

"If you look closely at the photo, you'll notice a couple dancing in the background," said Sylvester. "The man is Harry Puffpaff. The woman, however, is not his wife, who rarely appeared with him in public. The question then, is who is the woman with whom Harry Puffpaff is dancing?"

"Who is she?" asked Felix, always disinclined to appreciate mounting suspense.

"For years," Sylvester went on, "it was rumored that Puffpaff had a mistress, but no one knew—or admitted they knew—who she was. His mistress, like his body and the half million dollars, was never located."

"So who is she?" asked Felix again.

"Few would be able to identify that woman after more than seventy years," boasted Sylvester, "but I, with my vast encyclopedic knowledge of the history of this county, had little difficulty in recognizing the woman as—"

"It looks like Miss Hackenburger," said Morris.

"Well," said Sylvester, clearly deflated, "as it so happens, it is indeed our neighbor Miss Hackenburger."

Morris sat back, pleased with himself.

"The point is," continued Sylvester, "I have solved a sixty-five-year-old mystery by identifying Puffpaff's mistress as Miss Hackenburger and have further deduced that his long-sought-after fortune is most likely within Miss Hackenburger's possession, somewhere inside her home."

There was a moment of silence.

"Are you suggesting," said Felix finally, his voice contemplative and no more than a whisper, "that we break into Miss Hackenburger's house and, assuming your deduction is correct, steal this dead bootlegger's money?"

"Desperate times call for desperate measures," quoted Sylvester, "and that is exactly what I'm suggesting."

* * * *

The brothers spent the remainder of the afternoon setting out the details of their plan. Sylvester removed from his briefcase a blueprint of Miss Hackenburger's house that he had procured from the county building and spread it out on the coffee table. The three of them studied the blueprint as though they were master thieves, identifying and marking with red Xs the most likely locations where the money may have been hidden. Ultimately, at Felix's suggestion, they determined to begin their search for treasure in the old woman's cellar.

They talked and debated until the parlor glowed yellow and orange with the rays of the setting sun. Finally, as dusk settled outside, Sylvester leaned back and contemplated his brothers as they sat across from him in shadows.

"All right," he said, "the only question left to be answered is when to do it."

"Tonight," said Felix.

"Before we lose our resolve," agreed Morris.

The three Bohr brothers nodded solemnly.

* * * *

At two in the morning, the Bohr men gathered at the hedge bordering Miss Hackenburger's property. Clouds obscured the moon, and her garden was black as if draped in cloth. The back of her house, where the brothers intended to make their entrance through the cellar doors, rose up like the dark side of a mountain. All was quiet.

Sylvester squatted beneath a green apple tree and waved for his brothers to join him. As they came running from the hedge and entered the overhang of the tree's branches, Felix rolled a fallen apple under his foot and tumbled backward. He cried out and the shovel and pick he carried clattered against one another.

"Shh," whispered Sylvester.

"I think I broke my back," groaned Felix.

In the cover of the apple tree, they huddled together and listened, but the disturbance did not appear to raise any attention from the house. All remained quiet.

"Okay," said Sylvester, "follow me." He turned on his flashlight and rose to his feet.

With little ado they located the double cellar doors, which were padlocked with an old and rusted chain.

"Fortunately," whispered Sylvester, "I had the forethought to plan for such an eventuality," and he raised the bolt cutter he had brought from the garden shed. "Planning is everything."

With some effort, they severed the ancient chain and raised one of the cellar doors, which groaned and grinded like the door to a centuries-old tomb.

They paused several times to listen for any sign of activity from the house, but there was none, and finally they had the door all the way back. Dark and damp cement steps led down into greater blackness.

"You go first," said Morris to Sylvester.

As they descended, with Morris trembling in the rear, cobwebs brushed Felix's face, and he shrieked in panic. In his haste to wipe the fine filament from his face, he lost his balance and stumbled forward into Sylvester, who in turn slammed his nose into the oak door at the bottom of the stairs. Felix then attempted to turn, which swung the shovel he hoisted on his shoulder directly into the side of Morris's bent head. Morris reeled from the assault and his legs gave way, collapsing him into Felix, who followed up by falling atop Sylvester. In the end, with groaning, squealing, and the racket of dropped digging tools, the three brothers were piled in a heap at the bottom of the cellar stairs.

"My nose is broken," said Sylvester.

"I think I have a concussion," said Morris.

"There are cobwebs in my hair," cried Felix.

After much scrambling and repositioning, they found themselves standing before the basement door, which was fortuitously unlocked. Sylvester turned the old wooden knob, and the door opened without so much as a squeak. They peered into the lightless cellar of Miss Hackenburger's historic home.

Sylvester slowly moved his flashlight around, revealing a packed dirt floor and shelves and shelves of canned jellies and jams. Opposite the door, a rickety wooden staircase led upward to the ground floor. Sylvester stepped inside the cellar. The air was damp and moldy, smelling of a swamp.

"Dear brothers," said Sylvester, his arms spread wide and his nose swollen, "let us begin."

* * * *

On the second floor, oblivious of the intrusion into her cellar, Miss Hackenburger awoke from a dream. The old woman took a moment to orient herself and then eased back the comforter and sat up. Putting on her flannel robe and fluffy slippers, she went downstairs for a glass of water. Unbeknownst to anyone, Miss Hackenburger rarely slept through the night.

* * * *

"There's a mound here, I think," called Morris softly. Far in the back corner under the staircase, he tapped the mound with his shovel.

Sylvester and Felix hurried over, playing their flashlights across the floor. It seemed clear that at one time someone had indeed buried something beneath the stairs.

"Could we be so fortunate so soon?" said Sylvester.

In perfect synchronization, the three brothers plunged their shovels into the dirt and began digging.

* * * *

Miss Hackenburger sat at the kitchen table with her glass of water. Feeling hungry, she stood up to make toast. It was then she realized that she had no jelly in the icebox.

* * * *

The flashlights cast beams of white light polluted with particles of floating dirt across the Bohr brothers' legs and over their sweaty faces. The slicing of the shovels into the dirt and the brothers' heavy breathing were the only sounds.

A few feet down, Felix's spade struck an object.

"I've hit something," he said. All three of them stopped digging and went to their knees. Breathlessly, they pushed the dirt aside and behind them.

Morris unearthed what he initially thought was a large, oddly shaped rock. "What's this?" he asked, wiping off encrusted dirt.

Sylvester grabbed a flashlight and turned it on Morris's find.

Instantly, revealed in the smoky white light, it became clear that what Morris held in his hands was neither a rock nor a dislodged foundation stone, but a human skull—and Morris dropped it immediately with a horrified gasp. It landed in the dug earth with its vacant sockets gaping back up at them.

They stared at it as if expecting it to speak.

"Who is it?" asked Felix in a whisper.

"I don't know," said Sylvester as he reached out to pick the skull up and raise it before his face.

The door at the top of the stairs opened. Quicker than any action the brothers had ever made before, they flicked off their flashlights.

"Shh," warned Sylvester.

They heard slow footfalls on the wooden steps, which creaked with age and marked the progress of the interloper. And then a light flared on, a bare bulb directly above Morris's head, which illuminated the cellar and captured the three brothers in their felonious act as if it were a searchlight on the high wall of the state penitentiary. Momentarily frozen with panic, Morris could only stand with shovel in hand and stare as Miss Hackenburger descended the steps. Sylvester and Felix crouched beneath the stairs, no more inspired to act than Morris. There was nowhere to hide, no corners in which to curl, no holes in which to burrow. They were caught. They were done for.

Then, as Morris glimpsed the wrinkled old face of Miss Hackenburger, he swung the shovel up toward the incriminating bulb with the intent of smashing it and taking temporary shelter in the darkness once again. Unfortunately, as fate would have it, the shovel caught on the shelf behind him and brought it shattering down on top of his already sore head. Morris ducked and thrashed to protect himself and in so doing shattered the light bulb and sent the cellar into total blackness.

Miss Hackenburger gave forth a garbled, surprised yelp and fell headlong down the stairs, landing at Morris's feet, where she lay silent and unmoving.

"Quickly," whispered Sylvester, rushing toward the cellar door to make his getaway.

"I think she's dead," moaned Morris.

Felix, who had been close on Sylvester's heels, turned back. He flicked on his flashlight and ran it over Miss Hackenburger's body. When he illuminated her red-smeared face, he gasped.

"Blood. My God, you've killed Miss Hackenburger," he said to Morris.

"I'm a murderer!" cried Morris, his face streaked with dirt and tears.

"Come on," called Sylvester from the cellar stairs. "There's nothing we can do for her now."

"We can't leave her here," said Felix.

"No," agreed Morris. "We must take her with us."

"And do what with her?" asked Sylvester.

There was a pause as Felix and Morris thought it over. They looked at one another. They looked down at the body of Miss Hackenburger.

"We'll bury her in the garden," said Felix.

"Yes," said Morris. "Under the lilac bush. It's the least we can do."

Between them, the brothers lifted Miss Hackenburger's limp body and carried her from the cellar. Felix and Sylvester each took a foot and Morris held Miss Hackenburger's shoulders. Across her backyard they trudged with their burden, the old woman's hand slapping Morris in the face every time Felix or Sylvester adjusted his load. They dropped Miss Hackenburger only once when Morris lost his footing by twisting an ankle on a fallen green apple. The poor woman's head thudded against the ground.

"Sorry," Morris apologized.

At last, after an arduous journey across dangerous terrain, the brothers lowered Miss Hackenburger beside the lilac bush in their untended and overgrown garden. Sylvester ordered Morris back for the shovels.

"Why me?" asked Morris.

"Because," said Felix, "you killed her."

Without further objection, Morris returned to the cellar. He was back momentarily with the picks and shovels and the brothers set to digging Miss Hackenburger a grave.

And just when each in his own mind thought matters could get no worse, matters of course did. The intended grave was a mere two feet deep when

Felix saw headlights coming up the drive. They saw a blue strobe light winking from the car's dash.

"My God, it's the sheriff," Felix cried, and but for the shovel that propped him up, he would have fallen in a dead faint headlong into the shallow grave.

"We're undone!" sobbed Morris.

The sheriff's patrol car came to a stop, and they heard the car door open and shut as the lawman climbed out.

"All right," said Sylvester, regaining his composure, "take Miss Hackenburger back to her cellar. I'll go talk to the sheriff. Hurry."

"Must we take her back?" whined Felix. "She's remarkably heavy for an old woman."

"Yes," said Sylvester. "In case the sheriff intends to search the grounds. Now go."

Morris and Felix once again hefted the body of Miss Hackenburger and started off back across the lawn.

"My back," said Felix, "is going to be killing me in the morning."

"I have a concussion," said Morris. "My vision is all blurry."

Their voices faded as they moved away into the darkness and Sylvester turned his back to them and headed toward the house to intercept the sheriff. He entered the house from the rear and greeted the sheriff at the front door.

"Sheriff Billingsby," he said in a carefully modulated tone, "what brings you out here at this hour?"

"Sylvester," said the sheriff. "Apologize for calling so late, but we had a report of somebody seeing lights around your place. Thought it best if I dropped by and checked on things. Can't be too careful with prowlers, you know."

"Certainly not," said Sylvester. "Not these days." And it was at this precise moment that Sylvester realized what a sight his appearance must be to the sheriff. His face and hands splotched with dirt, crabapple leaves in his hair, a scraped nose and swelling above his right eye where he'd slammed his head into Miss Hackenburger's cellar door. He thought quickly and said, "But I'm sure it was nothing. I've been working in the garden, and it was most likely my flashlight they saw."

"Kind of late at night for gardening, ain't it?" asked Sheriff Billingsby.

"Yes, well, it helps me sleep," said Sylvester. "I have horrible insomnia."

"I'm sorry to hear that," said the sheriff. "And I know you've got your worries and all. Sure am sorry about the house. I want you to know that when I come by next week, I'm just doing my job."

"Thank you, sheriff," said Sylvester, "that's kind of you. Now if you don't mind—" Sylvester stopped. His brow pulled down warily. "What do you mean, when you come by next week?"

"The eviction, of course. Ain't nothing I can do about it, Sylvester. Bank's making me do it."

"What eviction?" asked Sylvester, suddenly numb with horror at the prospect that the time had finally come.

"Don't tell me you ain't had notice from the bank? Why, Sylvester, they're foreclosing on this place tomorrow. You and your brothers are gonna have to leave."

And Sylvester, who had been so strong and rock-solid through all the trials and tribulations that fate had thrown in his path, now felt his knees give way beneath him. Everything it seemed came down upon him at once, and he surely would have collapsed at the feet of Sheriff Billingsby and succumbed to despair, if fate had not dealt yet one last, devastating blow.

A scream loud enough to be heard for miles around came from Miss Hackenburger's yard. Sylvester knew instantly it was Morris. In the same instant, he knew with complete certainty that the end was at hand and that all was lost. There was nothing to be done but follow the sheriff's lead and race toward the source of the scream, running with the resignation of a man all but condemned.

In little time, the two men came upon a site of such perplexing characteristics that both drew up short and gaped.

"Good lord," said Sheriff Billingsby.

All Sylvester could manage was an utterance the sheriff took to be concurrence.

Felix sat with his legs splayed out amongst a litter of green apples, Miss Hackenburger's head in his lap. At the moment the sheriff and Sylvester arrived, Felix was slapping the old woman's face vigorously and calling her name. As for Morris, he had fallen to his knees beside their neighbor's limp body and appeared to be engaged in an act of supplication, his hands clasped before his chest, his face lifted toward the dark sky. "Please be alive, please be alive, oh please be alive," he chanted.

Sheriff Billingsby, who had no cause to suspect foul play, came to the hasty conclusion that Miss Hackenburger had taken a fall and that her rescuers were now frantically working and praying to revive her. He further concluded that they might need professional assistance. "I'll call an ambulance," he said, and he turned back toward his patrol car.

Sylvester approached his brothers at a trot. "Is she alive?"

"We nearly had her back to the cellar when she suddenly raised her head and groaned," said Morris. "She's come back from the dead! It's a miracle!"

"It's jam," said Felix.

"Jam?" said Morris and Sylvester as one.

"Jam," said Felix, running a finger through the substance on Miss Hackenburger's robe and having a taste. "Blackberry. And quite good, too, I'd say. The perfect amount of tartness, not too sweet."

"Really?" said Morris, who now knelt beside Miss Hackenburger to sample the jam staining her robe. "I must say, that's excellent."

"Enough of this," said Sylvester. "We have but a few precious moments to get our story straight. Listen to me. We were working in the garden when we heard a scream from Miss Hackenburger's. We raced over, concerned that all was not well. We called and called and finally resorted to breaking into the cellar to gain access, whereupon we discovered Miss Hackenburger lying at the bottom of the steps, apparently having recently taken a nasty tumble. We dragged her out here and took emergency measures to revive her. Shortly thereafter Sheriff Billingsby arrived." Sylvester took a breath. "Is all that clear?"

"Yes, I think it's a splendid cover story," said Morris.

A groan came from Miss Hackenburger. She stirred and opened her eyes.

"Miss Hackenburger!" shouted Morris. "Are you all right?"

"I've hit my head," she murmured, raising a hand to her jelly-matted, gray hair.

"You fell down the cellar stairs," said Sylvester. "We carried you out. The sheriff is bringing help."

"The sheriff?" Miss Hackenburger struggled to rise. She fell back, exhausted and dazed. "You mustn't…" her voice faded, "you mustn't…let him…in the cellar." And she closed her eyes again, once more appearing as if she had gracefully forsaken this world for another.

"We must cover our tracks," said Felix.

"Indeed," said Sylvester. He pressed his hands together and tapped his fingertips against his lips and stared at the ground. After a moment, he looked up. "This, then, is how we shall proceed. Morris, you will go with Miss Hackenburger to the hospital to keep watch on her condition. Felix and I shall remain here to remove any evidence of this evening's illicit activities. We shall fill the grave in the garden and rebury the skull in the cellar. In the end, no one will be the wiser and we will finally be done with this entire affair."

"But I'm tired of digging," whined Felix. "Why can't I go to the hospital with Miss Hackenburger?"

"Because," said Morris, "you're not the one who killed her."

* * * *

When Morris returned from the hospital later that morning with news that Miss Hackenburger was fully recovered and would be released that same day, he found his brothers sprawled in overstuffed chairs in the parlor. Coated with dirt, leaves and twigs in their hair, crabapples scattered at their feet, Sylvester and Felix could not conceal their exhaustion. Morris, too, felt near collapse and he curled up on the carpet at his brothers' feet.

"It is done," mumbled Felix through a yawn.

"We have overcome against all odds," said Morris.

"We shall lose the house," said Sylvester, but the other two, having succumbed to sleep, did not hear their brother's lament and so Sylvester closed his eyes and followed his brothers into a well-deserved slumber.

* * * *

The knock at the door roused Sylvester. Groggy and aching, he sat up. It is the bank! he thought. Come to take it all away. He walked to the door like a brave man to the gallows, his chin out, his mouth set firm. He reminded himself over and over not to cry.

But it was not the bank. Imagine Sylvester's shock when he flung the door open only to find Miss Hackenburger on his doorstep.

"Good afternoon, Sylvester," said Miss Hackenburger. With her gray hair pulled back neatly in a bun and wearing a pink flowery dress that was cinched tightly around her narrow waist by a thin black sash, one would never have thought the elegant woman was nearly killed and buried alive beneath a lilac bush the night before.

"Why, Miss Hackenburger," stammered Sylvester. "How are you feeling?"

"Fine, fine," said Miss Hackenburger as she eased her way past the stunned Sylvester and into the house. "A little bump on the head was all. You look as if you've seen a ghost."

"I wasn't expecting you," said Sylvester.

"No, I imagine not," said Miss Hackenburger. "I imagine you were expecting someone from the bank." Sylvester nodded wordlessly. "Yes, well, you needn't worry about the bank anymore, Sylvester. I've taken care of your financial concerns with them."

"You—?"

"As a token of my appreciation for you and your brothers coming to my rescue. I had my accountant see to things. You now own your aunt's house free and clear."

Sylvester stumbled backward, his hand to his chest, his mouth gaping, his eyes wide.

"Why, Miss Hackenburger, that is generous of you. I am overwhelmed with emotion and gratitude."

"Nonsense," said Miss Hackenburger. "It is I who am grateful."

She sat in a straight-backed chair, crossed her legs, and considered Sylvester directly.

"Now. I would like to tell you a tragic story about a young woman who fell in love with a daring, rough, and reckless man," she said. "Theirs was a great and secret romance, very exciting. And then one night, the man came to her home in a horribly distressed state. This young woman, naïve and hopeful, thought the man had come to her for help. But she was mistaken. He had merely come for some of his belongings that he had kept in her cellar. A *large* amount of belongings," and Miss Hackenburger gave Sylvester a purposeful look. "And when the young woman realized that this man she adored had come only for his belongings so that he could make a hasty escape out of the country and had no intention of taking her with him, well—" Miss Hackenburger reached into her pocketbook and pulled out a small derringer. "The woman took a gun such as this one and shot the man twice in the back of the head. It turns out, this young naïve girl was not one to be trifled with."

"One should never trifle," said Sylvester, staring at the gun, his heart hammering, his teeth and tongue numb.

"She put him where he kept his belongings and he's been there ever since. The belongings, of course, she used herself to great advantage. Now then"—Miss Hackenburger stood replacing the derringer in her bag—"I hope we have an understanding. Nothing further need be said about last night's activities—I think we should all be better off living lives of quiet contemplation."

"Lives of quiet contemplation and artistic pursuit are all we ever wanted, Miss Hackenburger," said Sylvester.

"And now you have it," she said. "Your efforts would appear to have borne fruit."

CORPSE OF THE MONTH CLUB

MELINDA MULLET

FOR WHOM THE BELL TOLLS

It was all too much dying for Ellie's taste. She took a deep breath of the late evening air hoping to clear her head after the fourth glass of Sangria. Book of the month club had seemed like a good excuse for Longwood High School teachers to gather every couple of weeks and read a classic novel. But man, it was heavy going. Tonight was *For Whom the Bell Tolls*. Her friend Julia, who was hosting, had embraced the Spanish theme and added Sangria to the mix.

Now they were not only melancholy, but drunk. Not the ideal outcome. Ellie inhaled once more and headed for her car to retrieve the pan Vivian left at her place after *Brave New World*. She'd arrived late and was stuck parking half-way in the neighbor's shrubbery. Struggling to open the backdoor, she rummaged around on the floor amongst the discarded coffee cups and ungraded essays. *Damn, it must be in the trunk*.

Ellie wrenched open the stiff latch on her aging Ford Taurus and froze, staring at a balding, middle-aged man whose pasty face protruded from a white sheet. His eyes were tightly closed, his lips pressed into a thin line. She lowered the lid quickly then peeked again. *No. Not imagining this*. Slamming the trunk, Ellie scampered back to the safety of the house, ducking in through the rear door where she found Vivian sneaking a brownie.

"Calories consumed over the kitchen sink don't count," Viv mumbled through a mouthful of chocolate ganache.

"Forget the brownies. Come." Ellie dragged Viv back out the door, through the yard, and down the driveway to the street.

"I left my purse behind," Viv complained. "And we really should stay and help Julia clean up."

"We're not leaving," Ellie said, steering Viv round to the back of the car and clicking the trunk button. It rose with a jerk, revealing the same gruesome tableau that Ellie had just witnessed.

Viv let out a startled scream and Ellie clapped a hand over her mouth. "Shh."

Viv pulled away. "What have you done?"

"Twelve years of friendship and *that's* the first question that springs to mind?"

"Who is he?" Viv amended.

"Hell if I know. I came out to get your Bundt pan and there he was."

"You can keep the pan," Viv said, stepping back a few paces. "You need to call the police."

"Okay." Ellie glanced at the man then looked quickly away. "And how do I explain a stranger's body in the trunk of my car?"

"Tell them he mysteriously appeared during book club."

"You're hearing yourself, right? Nothing suspicious about that. What if they think I killed him?"

"But you didn't."

"*I* know that; *you* know that, but…" Ellie trailed off.

Viv turned away from the car and deposited a fair amount of Sangria and brownie into the gutter.

Ellie shut the trunk and led Viv to the house, where Julia was standing on the porch saying goodnight to her other guests.

"Thought you'd run off and left me with everything."

"Course not," Ellie said. "Is everyone else gone?"

"Donna's still pretending to help tidy up so she can drink more Sangria," Julia said, nodding over her shoulder.

Following Julia inside, Ellie grabbed a paper cup from the table next to the Nespresso machine. She drained the remaining Sangria from the pitcher into the cup. "Have a roadie," she said, handing over the drink and steering Donna toward the door.

"I was gonna stack the dishwasher."

"We've got it," Viv insisted. She waved Donna off down the street, then returned to the living room.

Looking pale and sweaty, Ellie had collapsed on the couch.

"What's going on?" Julia asked.

Viv sat next to Ellie and put an arm around her shoulder. "Something dreadful's happened."

"It wasn't the cheeriest of books, and there was a bit too much rum in the Sangria, but I wouldn't say it was dreadful."

Ellie looked up at Julia wide-eyed. "I hate dragging you into this, but I don't know what else to do."

"Don't be silly," Viv said. "What are friends for?"

Julia frowned. "What've I missed?"

Viv rose and pulled Ellie to her feet. "Show her."

Julia followed Ellie down the street, with Viv trailing behind at a safe distance.

When they reached the car, Ellie stopped and pushed the trunk button. "You look. I can't."

Julia peered into the trunk then back at Ellie. "What am I looking at?"

"You're the science teacher, surely you can figure it out."

Julia sniffed slightly and shrugged. "I see a Bundt pan, an ice scraper, and some reusable shopping bags. What am I supposed to glean from that?"

Ellie ran round the car and stared into the trunk. Julia was right—the body was gone.

Viv approached, peeking through her fingers. "Where is he?"

Julia frowned. "Who?"

"The dead man in my trunk," Ellie snapped.

"You've had too many Sangrias. There's no dead man in your trunk."

"We need to call the police," Viv insisted again.

"What do we say now?" Ellie demanded. "We've misplaced a dead body? If anything, that's worse."

Julia closed the trunk. "Come back inside, I'm going to make some fresh coffee. You two need to sober up."

* * * *

"I did *not* imagine it," Ellie insisted.

Julia added three scoops of coffee to the machine on the counter. "And you say he was wrapped in a sheet?"

"Or a bag, or something, I was too busy being horrified by his face to notice."

Viv had pulled out one of her healing crystals and was rolling it around in her palm. "It was disgusting," she confirmed.

"And you're sure you didn't recognize him?" Julia asked.

Ellie closed her eyes and sat silently for a moment. "All I can see is that pale face." She shuddered. "Beyond that he was a run of the mill, middle-aged, white man—pale, puffy, cold."

"That describes half of the living men around here, let alone the dead," Julia said.

Ellie turned to her. "Do *you* think we should call the police? I'm a thirty-five-year-old, divorced high school English teacher. I hardly fit the profile of a psychotic murderer."

"True." Julia strung the word out. "But I think your first instinct was right. There's nothing to report. You'll look delusional and that's the last thing you need while you're running for the school board. You're our best hope for some kind of sane representation and we can't mess that up."

"Oh God," Ellie said, collapsing back into the couch cushions. "I hadn't even thought about that. What if the papers get ahold of this? The bell really will be tolling for me."

"You're being melodramatic," Viv said. "Still, we can't ignore the sudden appearance of a corpse."

Julia poured the coffees. "No, but we can try to figure out why this happened before we go throwing Ellie to the wolves."

Ellie reached for the creamer. "Not throwing me to the wolves is good."

"A body doesn't appear and disappear on its own," Julia noted. "Someone put him there and then moved him."

"But why would someone put a body in my trunk?" Ellie demanded. "It has to be a horrible mistake."

"Exactly," Julia said. "If there's a dead man floating around town, someone will have reported him missing. Once we know who he is, maybe we can figure out how and why he wound up in your car. In the meantime, I think it's best this remains our little secret."

1984

Ellie hadn't even bothered to bring the book. She'd read Orwell's classic with every Freshman class for the past ten years and knew it by heart. The gathering at Donna's had been sparsely attended and wrapped up quickly. Now Ellie, Julia, and Viv were sitting in Julia's parked car warming up with caramel lattes from Starbucks while studying the new billboard across the street.

Avery Acton—Actons speak louder than words.

"It's awful," Julia groaned, "but the bubblewrap brigade will love it."

Julia called the parental contingent intent on shielding their teens from life the bubblewrappers. Each year their ranks swelled until they'd become a vocal segment of the Longwood PTA, and Avery Acton was their self-appointed general. Big Sister is watching you. She'd had more books banned from the school library on the grounds of indecency in the past twelve months than anyone else had managed in the entire forty-six-year history of the school district. As an English teacher, it grieved Ellie to see books being denigrated simply because they addressed basic human emotions and embraced marginalized members of the community. It was her disgust that had emboldened her to put her natural shyness aside and run for the Board.

The support of teachers like Julia and Viv, along with the more moderate parents, had given her hope that she might win; but looking at the billboard she felt what little confidence she possessed shriveling up like an old balloon. Not that it took much to undermine Ellie's confidence. After eight years of being married to a man whose favorite pastime was inflicting emotional abuse, she was an easy target.

"Anything in the papers today?" Viv asked, returning to the subject that had consumed their attention in the two weeks since *For Whom the Bell Tolls*.

Ellie shook her head.

"Nothing," Julia confirmed. "Not one mention of a dead or missing man."

"It's almost as if he never existed," Viv said. "Except he must've."

"Did you have any luck with your neighbor's Ring camera?" Ellie asked Julia.

"I told Dave a check was stolen from my mailbox, and he sent me the video." Julia retrieved her iPad and flipped through her files. "The footage is blurry, and unfortunately your car was parked off screen. The book club members were obvious enough, but there was one person I didn't recognize." Julia found the file and clicked forward to the segment she was looking for. "Here."

The grainy black-and-white footage showed a man walking down the street from the direction of Ellie's car before slipping into the bushes across the street from Julia's house. He was wearing jeans and a dark T-shirt with a baseball cap pulled low over his face. They watched Ellie come out and return to the house, then Viv and Ellie headed to the car and hurried back. At that point, the figure left the bushes and made his way down the street in the direction of Ellie's car.

"That must be our man," Ellie exclaimed. "He's on his way to remove the body."

"We can't prove that," Julia said. "Knowing what happened next, we can guess, but we don't see him actually move the body in or out."

Ellie leaned into the screen and pinched and pulled the image to get a closer look at the man's face. The hat shielded him from the camera, and even if it hadn't, the image was too blurry.

"Do we recognize the hat?" Viv said, leaning in from the back seat. "Looks like that neon green number Cliff Acton wears so Avery can keep track of him."

"I have to admit Avery's at the top of my list of people who might want to make me look bad," Ellie said. "Just the other day she was arguing with me about allowing the sophomores to read *Clockwork Orange*. She said, and I quote, 'it's all weird sex and dead bodies.'"

Viv cocked her head. "And you're thinking Avery put a dead body in your car in protest?"

"Maybe not a protest"—Ellie sounded less sure—"but it certainly wouldn't be a good look for a potential school board member. If anyone found out, I'd have to drop out of the race."

"Avery would love that, but she wouldn't touch a dead body," Viv insisted. "She's too prissy. Although she might've asked someone she trusted to do it—Cliff maybe."

"Would be interesting to know where Cliff was on the night the body showed up," Julia said.

Viv leaned forward again. "My mom told me she saw Avery at the Baptist church meeting that Thursday. She was trying to rally support."

"What about Cliff?"

"No Cliff, just Avery."

"If Cliff's the man on the Ring video, why didn't he leave the body in the trunk?" Julia asked. "We have an anonymous tip line now. He could've called the police and caused a real scene."

Ellie rubbed her temples. "If this was a campaign stunt, it was poorly done."

"Maybe Cliff was worried they'd trace his cell phone?" Viv mused.

Julia tapped her fingers on the steering wheel. "The crucial questions is, where would they get a body in the first place? I mean it's not exactly something the average person has lying around the house."

"I'm not sure I want to know where you get a body on short notice," Ellie buried her head in her hands. "Maybe this is the start. Maybe Avery and Cliff are planning another prank."

Julia started the engine. "If they try again, we'll be ready for them."

"Will we?" Ellie said.

Viv gave Ellie's shoulder a squeeze from behind. "Of course we will."

FAUST

Once again, Ellie arrived late to book club and was stuck parking on the street. She looked around nervously as she entered the side door at Viv's but saw no one. Tonight's book was *Faust*. No one had read it as far as Ellie could tell, and Viv had laid out margaritas and nachos for no reason other than she liked them. As the weeks passed, book club was getting to be less about culture and more about catering.

Ellie poured herself a second margarita, or was it the third? Under the not-so-subtle influence of the tequila, the memory of the body was receding. Four weeks to the day and there'd been no reports of a dead body in the papers, no missing persons. Ellie believed they'd been mistaken. There was no dead man. After all, they hadn't actually touched the body. Maybe it'd been a lifelike dummy. Avery and Cliff's idea of a practical joke. The thought made her feel better.

* * * *

When the last stragglers had departed, Ellie and Julia helped wash and dry the plates and cups. Viv put the plastic margarita glasses Ellie had loaned her into an old Amazon box and the three women walked out to the curb.

"I'll be glad when next week's over," Ellie said. "I have to admit I'm not feeling confident about the election. Avery's supporters are so vocal."

"But not numerous," Viv assured her.

"I hope not." Ellie popped the trunk to allow Julia to load the box in the rear but stopped short at Julia's shriek.

Shaking her head, she hurriedly stepped back from the car. "I thought you two were imagining things before. I was worried about you—really, I was."

Ellie steeled herself to look in the trunk. There was another white sheet and another body. A young man this time. The same gray-white pallor, and the same sense of panic and revulsion firing her anxiety response.

"Oh God, oh God." Viv walked in circles flapping her hands as if trying to exorcise the vision from her mind.

Ellie crouched to the ground, her head in her hands as she rocked back and forth. "Not again. I'd convinced myself this was all a bad joke. But he's real, isn't he? And so was the other one. Where are they coming from?"

"Okay. Everybody breathe." Julia gingerly approached the open trunk and peered closely at the young man. She sniffed and then turned to Viv. "Do you have any old Covid gear in the house. Gloves maybe?"

"I'll go see." Viv couldn't get away from the scene fast enough, but she returned quickly with a half-empty box of surgical gloves and tossed them to Julia. Julia pulled out a pair and slipped them on before approaching the body in the car—scientific curiosity besting her revulsion.

She lifted the covering and examined the body. "This man's been dead for some time. He's cold, almost frozen, and you can smell the formaldehyde. To be honest, I caught the same smell in your trunk last time, but it didn't really register then. Also, there's a metal loop on his right big toe. I'd guess he's been tagged and in the morgue."

Ellie looked up. "You think someone's borrowing bodies from the morgue? Then what? They return them like a late library book?"

"Maybe. It would explain why we saw nothing in the papers."

"You can't just walk in and check out a body," Viv insisted. "You'd have to have access."

"Avery's husband, Cliff, is a pediatrician," Ellie said, rising stiffly.

"That means he works at the hospital," Viv said, "but would it give him free run of the morgue?"

Julia stepped back from the body. "Morgue's not exactly a secure location. I mean, no one's worried about the occupants getting up and leaving."

Viv stood to the side, pressing a hand to her stomach. "Still, you couldn't wander in."

"Theoretically, you could," Julia admitted. "Hank took me in one time. Before things blew up with you two," she clarified for Ellie's sake. "I'd run out of formaldehyde for a project we were doing in AP Bio, and he got me some. The backdoor key's kept behind a loose brick in the wall. I know that—Cliff might as well."

"But surely they'd notice a missing body?" Ellie said.

Julia pulled off the gloves and walked to the end of the drive to drop them in the trash. Raising the lid, she frowned before reaching down and pulling out a crumpled piece of manila paper. "This could be our answer. John Doe. 23 years old. Unidentified male," she read aloud. "The intake date was two months ago. They must've been keeping him in a deep cold storage."

"You mean no one's claimed the body?" Ellie asked.

"I'd guess so. Maybe there is no one."

"Poor thing," Viv said, her eyes filling with tears. "He's a kid. What will happen to him?"

"I don't know," Julia said.

Ellie looked into the trunk once more and registered the curly blond hair, the young face, and the small lightning bolt tattoo on his right shoulder. A Harry Potter fan. Barely older than the young wizard himself. Someone's child. A wave of intense sadness swept over her. What had this poor soul done to wind up here?

Viv pulled out her phone and searched. "It says under state law unidentified bodies are cremated and placed in a communal grave after sixty days."

"That means he's about hit his sell-by date," Julia said.

Viv looked up from her phone. "Julia. What an awful thing to say."

"I don't suspect he minds at this point," she replied, covering his face with the sheet.

"What do we do with him?" Ellie said.

"Call the police?" Viv said without conviction.

"Maybe we could return the body to the morgue and leave it outside the backdoor," Julia said. "He'll be found then and dealt with."

Ellie shook her head vehemently. "What if we're seen? The only thing worse than being found with a corpse in my trunk would be being caught returning a stolen corpse to the morgue."

"Maybe if we go in the house like we did before and think for a bit, whoever left the corpse will take it away again," Viv said hopefully.

"That would mean they're watching us now." Ellie looked up and down the street, but there was no sound, no movement.

"Viv's right," Julia said. "Let's go in, make a plan, then come back out and see if our friend's still here."

* * * *

A large pot of herbal tea and two Xanax later, the debate continued.

"It's Cliff and Avery. It has to be," Ellie insisted again. She was feeling a bit woozy from the combined effects of the tequila and the borrowed sedative, but also strangely more decisive. "No one else has any reason to do this to me."

"What about Hank?" Viv said.

Ellie waved a hand dismissively. "Why would Hank put a body in my trunk? Our divorce was nasty, but it's been over for more than a year now."

"He spent your entire married life gaslighting you," Viv insisted. "Trying to make you feel ignorant at best, and crazy at worst. He's despicable."

"And that's why I divorced him. We've closed that chapter of our lives."

"You sure he's not trying to write a new story—a horror story?" Viv asked.

"He hated you having anything of your own," Julia observed. "The idea of you on the school board must be driving him insane."

"And Hank works at the hospital," Viv added.

Ellie pursed her lips. "Nope. It's Avery and Cliff. He'd do anything she demands, and she'll do anything to win this election."

"It's a ballsy move," Julia pointed out. "And Cliff's usually quite sweet. It's Avery that's not."

Ellie leaned forward. "Even so, it's them. I feel it in my bones. Wish I knew where they were tonight."

"That's easy," Julia said. "Avery's having a campaign event at the country club—pulling out all the stops."

"Going overboard I think," Viv said. "I heard her arguing with Cliff Saturday night at the Dairy Queen about how much she'd spent on giveaways."

Ellie frowned. "Giveaways?"

"Pickle ball paddles with *Score One for the Clean Team* across the face."

Ellie snorted. "She's buying votes."

Julia looked dubious. "With pickle ball paddles?"

"I should confront them," Ellie said, attempting to stand.

"Absolutely not," Julia said. "What if you're wrong?"

"And even if you're right, she'll only deny it," Viv observed.

Ellie finally made it to her feet and paced in circles before stopping and facing Viv and Julia. "Then I won't confront them verbally, I'll just give them a taste of their own medicine."

"I don't like the sound of that," Viv said.

"Then you're going to hate the reality."

* * * *

The parking lot at the country club was full when they arrived. Avery's brand-new BMW convertible was parked well away from the other cars on the outer edge of the lot. Given Ellie's condition, Julia was driving, and she parked the Taurus in the narrow side street adjacent to the club.

"Poor Harry deserves better than this," Viv lamented. She'd insisted that they couldn't keep referring to him as John. She was certain he was an orphan, alone in this cruel world, and now, as far as she was concerned, he was Harry.

"He certainly deserves better than lying unclaimed in a small-town morgue," Ellie said. "Now at least, he's performing a community service."

Viv stepped away from the car. "I don't think I can do this."

"Then wait here," Julia said, extending a pair of plastic gloves to Ellie. "You sure about this?" she asked once more.

"Absolutely," Ellie replied. "Avery's behind this. It's only fair. We'll see what a naked, dead man does to that new car smell of hers."

"He's heavier than he looks," Julia muttered as they struggled to leverage Harry's torso into the BMW.

Ellie swung his legs onto the narrow backseat. Harry flopped in—half on the bench and half on the floor. Julia reached across the front seat and positioned him with an arm draped along the back of the seat to raise him up. It gave him a sort of creepy insouciance.

"At least wrap him up a bit more in the sheet," Viv directed from a distance. "It's chilly out here."

"Don't think he minds," Julia said through clenched teeth. "Let's get out of here."

Viv and Julia started toward the street, but Ellie veered off across the parking lot and lurched into the bushes next to the club. "Where are you going?" Viv hissed.

"I want to see what's happening."

Viv and Julia slipped into the bushes next to Ellie, flattening themselves against the wall as she stood on tiptoe to peer through the window.

"I see Avery, but not Cliff. Do you think he's out looking for Harry?"

"Ugh. I'm standing in an ant bed," Viv said, scrambling out of the bushes and onto the sidewalk in front of the club while swiping at her ankles.

"Viv?"

Vivian turned and saw the man himself approaching. "Cliff, uh, how's it going?"

Julia and Ellie stood frozen in the bushes behind her.

"Okay, I guess. What brings you out this way? I know you're not here for Avery's event."

"No way," Viv said, scratching her ankle with her toe. "I was just taking a walk."

Cliff stepped closer and lowered his voice. "Did you know Hank's here?"

"Hank?"

Cliff nodded. "I overheard him telling Avery about the stash of porn Ellie keeps under her bed."

Viv's eyes grew wide. "You can't believe that?"

"No, I don't, but you know Hank. Always tells people exactly what they want to hear."

"Bastard."

"Can't say I disagree there." Cliff pulled out a cigarette and lit it.

"I never knew you smoked?"

"It's been a rough few weeks."

"What's going on?" Viv asked.

"Mom had a heart attack. I've been in Cleveland most of the last month dealing with her. Dash home on the weekend for a mess of kid's soccer games; then dash back. I'm exhausted."

"I'm sure." Viv moved closer. "Nice of you to come back for this."

"Avery insisted. Almost didn't make it," Cliff admitted. "My flight was delayed, and I was really late. She's fuming. You'd think I did it on purpose."

"But you're here now," Viv said, speaking loudly in the direction of the bushes behind her. Cliff was out of town for the last two book club meetings and this one as well. He couldn't be responsible for the bodies. Viv could hear a shuffling in the background and fervently hoped the other two were on their way to move poor Harry before he was discovered.

Cliff took a long drag on the cigarette. "Suppose I'd better go get Avery's car. She sent me to move it round front. She has so many of those damn pickle ball paddles leftover—not sure they'll all fit in the trunk."

"No rush," Viv said, placing a hand on Cliff's arm. "You know Avery, she'll still be yapping away. Tell me more about your Mom."

Cliff hesitated, then launched into a detailed description of his mother's struggles with her heart. Viv hoped it was giving the others the time they needed.

As the tale of medical woe wound down, several couples emerged onto the front steps of the club.

Cliff looked over his shoulder. "I'd better get moving, but thanks for listening, Viv."

Viv walked away, heading rapidly toward the main road. On the far side of the club the Taurus pulled up. She jumped in and hunched down in the back seat.

"Where's Harry?"

"In the trunk," Julia said, turning on the street adjacent to the park and pulling up by the playground.

Ellie was leaning against the headrest breathing heavily.

"You heard what Cliff said about Hank?" Viv asked.

"We heard," Ellie said.

"Hank's absolutely despicable," Julia said. "He must be the one behind this game of musical corpse we've been playing. He has access to the morgue, and as an administrator, he's probably the one filing out the paperwork to authorize the removal and cremation of bodies."

"I can't believe Hank would do this to me," Ellie said, "but then again, I can. I'm totally screwed. If I go to the police, they'll ask questions I can't answer, and I'll look guilty. I can't prove a thing." Ellie seethed internally. Her impulsive reaction had nearly made things infinitely worse, and what was more, Hank believed he'd won.

"What do we do now?" Viv said.

Ellie took a shaky breath in and exhaled slowly. "We give poor Harry a respectful burial. We owe him that much."

"What if Hank tries again?" Julia asked.

"After the election we can call the police, but be realistic," Ellie said. "How many unclaimed bodies can there possibly be in Longwood? Even two is stretching it."

"I like the idea of burying Harry," Viv said. "But I'm not sure I can manage to dig a grave. My back's already killing me."

"And we might be seen," Julia pointed out.

"I have an idea," Ellie said. "I had a compost pit on the edge of the woods by our house. Hank's house now. I know it's been unused since I left. A nice deep hole with lovely soft soil. We can lay Harry to rest there without digging. Just cover him up and say a few kind words. No one will ever know."

"Except us," Julia said.

"Somehow, I think Harry would like that," Viv said softly.

* * * *

All had been quiet since the service for Harry. No tricks, no bodies. When election night rolled around, things turned out far better than Ellie could've imagined. The race was close, but when the last votes came in, she'd snagged a narrow victory. She smiled across the room at Viv and Julia who stood together drinking champagne. They raised their glasses.

Ellie stepped back to allow Avery to make her concession speech. As Avery droned on, Ellie retreated into the hallway of the school, phone in hand. Avery's phone. She'd picked it up from the table when her rival made her way to the stage to speak. Ellie had a call she wanted to make.

Alone in the hallway, she dialed the police tip line.

"Can I help you?"

"Yes. I'd like to report the location of a body."

WAX ON, WAX OFF

NINA MANSFIELD

It all began with the Body Hair Acceptance Movement.

Singer/Songwriter and sometime bikini model Audra Kling had been paparazzied on a Belize beach with stubbled legs and a bit of bush poking indiscreetly from her nether-regions.

There was an outcry on social media. The trolls called her a grizzly bear. Her supporters lauded her bravery. Some said it was all planned because less than two weeks later Kling launched her single, "No More Wax," which included the ear-worm inducing refrain: "No more waxing, It's too taxing, Toss those razors, Let it grow."

And suddenly, American beaches felt a little more European.

My elderly mother was disgusted. My teen daughter embraced the movement. I was torn. Not that I enjoyed having Tammy—my slightly too gabby bikini wax maven—rip hair from my loins on alternating months. But I was pushing fifty. Too old to be re-socialized into the new normal.

Body hair was a choice. For a while. Until a militant branch of the Body Hair Acceptance Movement, the Hair Radicals, picketed the waxing parlors. A laser hair removal boutique was bombed. Mass razor meltings were organized.

Even clean-shaven men were publicly shamed.

The Olympic committee was persuaded to ban waxed swimmers.

And eventually, legislation was passed in twenty-eight states prohibiting unnatural hair removal for profit. "Unnatural" included everything beyond a haircut and a men's shave.

For a while it looked like hair dyeing, perming, and straightening might be under attack along with hair removal. The moral dilemma seemed to be: if we can't remove body hair, should we be drastically altering our head hair?

Classes of hair were established. This led to the passing of the Head Hair Protection Act, which meant I could stay blond, and all those partially bald men could continue to shave their heads. But the man with a rug of back hair that made him look like Sasquatch—he was stuck in the same boat with all us women unless he was going to DIY his waxing treatment.

Which is how I found myself in an alley three blocks from the courthouse waiting for a signal to descend the steps to Tammy's Downstairs Boutique. "Downstairs Boutique" had become a euphemism for an illegal hair removal facility.

The Tammys of the world had gone underground.

The alley smelled vaguely of hair straightening chemicals and chlorine, most likely from the hair salon around the corner. Salons had to up their prices as services were cut. A door crept open, and a woman in full-on incognito garb—trench coat, sunglasses, Chanel scarf—swept by me. There was something vaguely familiar about her gait, and I recognized her perfume. *Eau du Resistance.* As her tasteful flats pattered past, I regretted not disguising my appearance in any way. The penalties for noncompliance with hair removal laws were steep. The fine itself I could handle. But the public shaming, not so much. A not-for-profit body hair acceptance organization, funded by the Hair Radicals, had taken it upon themselves to out transgressors via social media. Violators were known to lose jobs and feel unwanted glares in the grocery store. Recently, a local celebrity health-food chef had lost her streaming contract. Della Cookies—yes, her last name was really Cookies— had a "healthy" molten lava cake that was to die for. She also had these perfectly arched eyebrows. Someone produced a photo from high school where she sported a unibrow and fuzz on her upper lip. Where was it now, the trolls wanted to know. Was Della really tweezing her own brows at home?

But who had outed Della Cookies? One possibility was the Cookie Cutters, a group of online haters who argued that Della Cookies's claims on healthy cooking were fraudulent. They insisted her signature sugar-free organic sweetener, Cookie Sweet, was misrepresenting its ingredients and causing a diabetes epidemic. The Cookie Cutters were known for stalking Della at public events and posting unflattering pictures of her and her food on their blog. One of them had most likely snapped the photo of Della on the waxing table and just like that *Della Cookies Cooks* was off the air.

Okay, so I was never in the same league as Della Cookies. But I was Andrea Kalinski, PTA treasurer, locally known mommy-blogger, and founder of The Ageless Change, a recently launched skin-care line that targeted peri-menopausal women. Our motto was: "A woman of a certain age can do anything." I was premiering a new product in two days at BeautyConn 2040 in Rio de Janeiro, where incidentally Della Cookies was scheduled to speak. Brazil's body hair laws were non-existent. Hence my need to professionally de-fuzz.

The trench coat wearer rounded the corner, and silence filled the alley for three long breaths.

Then a creak. A shadow at the door.

"What's the word?" I heard a voice say.

"Follicle," I replied.

The door opened and I descended the staircase.

The shadow belonged to Jacob, Tammy's wayward ex-husband, whom she'd convinced to work security for her once she'd taken her business underground. He'd been perpetually out of work when they were married, so it seemed like a win-win.

"Room three, dude." Jacob said dude a lot, often out of context, and seemed to have a never-ending supply of Hawaiian shirts.

The hallway was dimly lit by a flickering fluorescent light. Greenish linoleum tiled the floors. The walls were bare. I got the sense that Tammy's new digs had been one of those massage parlors—the kind that provided a little more than massages—once upon a time.

Jacob strutted down the hall, his faux leather sandals squeaking, and opened the door to room three. Jenny, Tammy's former assistant, now business partner, stood stirring the wax. Her sleek black hair was pulled tightly into a bun. Cat-rimmed eyeglasses balanced on the tip of her nose. "I'll be ready for you in a moment, Andrea."

"Where's Tammy?" I asked.

Jenny blinked at Jacob. I followed her gaze. He nodded.

"She's not in today," said Jenny.

"I scheduled with Tammy." I tried to keep the annoyance out of my voice. Getting hair ripped off one's nether-regions was bad enough. But Tammy could always distract me with lurid gossip and somehow make it seem less painful. "You'd be surprised what people will share with me," she told me once. And if she wasn't spilling dirt on some minor celebrity, she was filling me in on her latest sugar detox or micro-greening adventure. Tammy, a child of diabetics, was a proud health nut. She had a way of making me think about the sugar content of my daily iced latte, rather than the wax strips she was yanking off.

Jenny, on the other hand, made the experience feel like I was being interrogated by terrorists.

"We don't know where she is, dude," Jacob said. "We're actually pretty worried—but what can we do? We can't call the police. We're not exactly a legal establishment."

I was leaving for Brazil in two days, and I had a PTA breakfast I couldn't get out of the next morning. Sure, I could've gotten a bikini wax in Brazil, but for a procedure so personal, I didn't want to go to some random stranger. I could feel my face tightening up into Karen-mode. "Do you think Tammy will be back tomorrow?" I asked, trying to modulate the tone of my voice.

Neither Jenny nor Jacob had time to answer.

The lights flickered. An obnoxious rock ballad blared through the sound system. "Someone tripped the alarm," Jacob whisper-screamed. "It's a raid!"

"In here." Jenny grabbed my arm.

Next thing I knew, I was shoved into a supply cabinet. Jenny and Jacob followed me. They shut the door. Our bodies smushed together. I was overcome with the aroma of hot wax mixed with sweat. I could feel someone's heart beating against my cheek.

"Stay quiet, and they won't find us." Jacob said. "And if they do…" He held up something that looked suspiciously like a revolver.

"Careful with that thing," I whispered.

"Don't worry. Jacob doesn't believe in ammo," Jenny said.

I closed my eyes, and at that moment, I wished I was having my pubes painfully ripped from my loins.

And then the cabinet door flung open. My Brazilian bikini wax would have to wait.

* * * *

To be clear, I've never been arrested. But I knew we still had some semblance of civil rights in our country, even though they were mostly for show. Ordinary citizens weren't generally blindfolded, gagged, and shoved into car trunks.

Nor were police station interrogation rooms painted garish shades of pink. I could spot the walls through the edge of my blindfold. When I peered down, I could make out the edge of my captor's tasteful flats. And the smell… I recognized it. Like lavender with a hint of ginger. *Eau du Resistance*.

When my blindfold was removed, I realized I'd been in this pink room. I'd eaten cucumber sandwiches in this room. I'd planned a Greenville High School PTA budget in this room.

"Diana?" I asked. A figure stepped out from the shadows. Sure enough, my captor was none other than Diana Jimenez, super-mom, PTA President and pole-dancing entrepreneur.

"What the hell, Diana? Are you some kind of Hair Radical?" I demanded. I struggled. My hands were tied behind my back.

"Absolutely not! I could ask you the same thing. What were you doing in Tammy's Underground Boutique?"

"Um…you know I'm heading to Brazil in two days. What do you think I was doing?" I looked around. I thought that maybe Jenny and Jacob had been "arrested" along with me, but it turned out I was the only one who'd had the pleasure.

Diana contemplated her manicured hands. She'd chipped a nail—probably kidnapping me.

A note about Diana Jimenez. One does not become PTA president in the town of Greenville without knowing where the bodies are buried. Diana was the type of woman who could organize a carnival, balance a budget, and get the school administration to fully support her son's emotional support peacock, without the accompanying doctor's note. All of this while raising five kids and running The North Pole, her family friendly pole dancing classes out of the basement of the Westside Congregational Church.

Diana released my wrist restraints and brought me a box of water.

"I apologize for our tactics, Andrea, but it was a necessary precaution," Diana said. "The truth is, we think someone at Tammy's has been compromised by the Hair Radicals. And I couldn't risk losing you to some ridiculous hair removal scandal. You know we have our PTA breakfast tomorrow, and I'm counting on your quiches."

"Well, yeah. I've been busy making them all morning." That was a lie. I was planning to pick some up at the Healthy Way Market later that day. But I was confused. "So, you kidnapped me to make sure you had quiches for tomorrow's breakfast?" I knew Diana took her job as PTA president seriously and the next day's breakfast was one of our biggest suck-up-to-the-school-board events, but this was too much, even for her.

And that's when Diana told me, that in addition to everything else, she was also the leader of WAX.

* * * *

Until that moment I thought WAX (Women Against eXtremism), an underground organization battling against the Hair Radicals, was a myth. They provided protection to underground boutiques. They smuggled wax in from out of state. They funded out-of-state laser hair removal. I'd heard they held virtual masterclasses in DIY depilatory creams. WAX was supposed to keep an eye on places like Tammy's, not raid them.

"But you...why did you...?"

"I recognized you on my way out of Tammy's this morning. The fact that you were going in there undisguised was...well...stupid. And suspicious. Plus, I'd learned that Tammy was missing, so my senses were on high alert. If you weren't afraid of having your identity discovered that meant you were either hopelessly naive, or you were a Hair Radical spy. Or maybe you didn't realize that Tammy's was a compromised location—in which case, I needed to get you out of there. Either way, I decided to act fast."

"Um...thank you?"

"Plus, have you ever gotten a bikini wax from Jenny? Let's say, I did you a big favor," Diana added.

I couldn't argue with that.

I took a swig of my boxed water. "So...WAX is real," I said. I was still processing the information.

"It is. And the truth is, we could use your help."

* * * *

Diana went on to explain that WAX had recently been on the hunt for whoever was snapping photos of celebrities and outing their illegal hair removal activities on social media. According to Diana, the now infamous photo of Della Cookies mid-eyebrow wax had been taken at Tammy's.

"If you look really close at the picture, you can spot one of Tammy's long, bedazzled fingernails at the edge of the frame."

"But surely you don't think Tammy was involved in outing Della?"

"That seems unlikely, but maybe someone who works for her."

I thought about Jenny and Jacob and the look they exchanged that morning.

"The truth is, Andrea, I'm practically flying solo these days. My number two gal went into labor last night, and our third member is keeping a low profile after she almost got busted in a real raid."

I wasn't sure what to say. Sure, I was honored she'd chosen to confide in me about WAX, but I wasn't really sure I was the woman for the job.

"Look, Andrea. You know I can't run for PTA president next year because of our term limits. You help me—us out—and I can guarantee the position is yours."

I could have declined. I could have told her no matter how much I agreed with WAX's mission, I wasn't about to engage in anything illegal. But over the past few years, the line between legal and illegal had blurred. And even though I already had a full plate—blogging, single parenting, and launching a new skincare line—it wasn't in me to say no when someone asked for help.

Plus, I really wanted to be PTA president.

"What do you need me to do?" I asked.

"We need you to find Tammy."

* * * *

Finding a missing person was definitely outside my skill set, but I was going to practice what I preached in my social media posts: "A Woman of a Certain Age Can Do Anything." I decided to start at the source. After dropping my daughter off at her jiu jitsu class and letting her know I'd probably be late picking her up, I rushed home to don my disguise. Diana had lent me a wig and a nose prosthetic. I knew from experience that the last appointment of the day at Tammy's Underground Boutique was scheduled at five p.m. I arrived there at 5:10 and waited in the alley. As the last customer exited, I caught the door before it closed and slipped inside.

As I entered, I heard strange noises emanating from one of the rooms. I thought the last customer had left, but maybe I was wrong. I paused, listened. Grunting. Panting. Like someone was in pain or enjoying their waxing session a little too much. Stealth was hard in stilettos, which is why I was glad that I had worn Crocs and yoga pants. I tiptoed down the hall and peered through the partially open door of room three.

There, I spotted Jacob and Jenny *in flagrante delicto*. What shocked me more than their coital embrace was the amount of body hair they sported. Jenny had bushy pits and carpet legs that made it clear she never partook of her own services. And Jacob had disturbing tufts on his shoulders and the middle of his back.

They were truly the beast with two backs, and way too hairy for people who literally had melted wax at their fingertips.

I would need to question them. But now certainly wasn't the time.

While Jacob and Jenny continued their live-action Kama Sutra, I decided to go snooping. I strode by another waxing room and found something that looked like an office. Desk. Filing cabinets. Bingo! Large old-fashioned appointment planner, open wide. I was relieved that they weren't using a computer for appointments. Computers could be hacked.

I flipped through the appointment planner. Everyone was identified by initials. DC, AK, QRX. Of course. An underground salon needed to be discreet. There was always the possibility of a raid—a real raid, not like the one Diana had staged. An appointment planner could fall into the wrong hands.

I checked my phone for the time. I had thirty minutes before my daughter's jiu jitsu class would end. A text popped up. It was from Diana.

"If you are at Tammy's, get out now," it read.

Another ping, and a link to an article appeared. I clicked.

The headline read: "Body of Illegal Hair Removal Maven Found Near Popular Coffee Establishment."

Tammy was no longer missing. She was dead.

* * * *

I hadn't signed up to investigate a murder. I wanted to battle an unjust law and wear a thong at Ipanema Beach. I was about to take Diana's advice and leave the premises when I was interrupted by the metallic clang of a door being swung open.

Jenny materialized in front of me wielding a tweezer. Jacob stood behind her, holding the revolver I'd spotted in the storage closet.

"Don't move," Jenny squeaked. "What do you want here?"

Luckily, I remembered what Jenny had said about Jacob's lack of ammo while we were huddled in the supply cabinet.

"Why don't you tell me which one of you killed Tammy?" I said.

Jenny's mouth dropped open. Jacob lowered the gun. "What?" he said. His lower lip quivered.

"She's not dead," Jenny blurted. "She can't be."

I held up my phone so she could read the article. Their distress seemed genuine.

"And while you're at it, why don't you tell me why both of you are in serious need of hair removal? You're Hair Radicals, aren't you?"

"What? No? This business is my life! Why would you say that?" Jenny said.

"Because you are both so…hairy!"

"Dude, we have made a choice. The way you have made the choice to have your hair removed, we have made the choice to have our hair grow *au naturel*. Shouldn't everyone be able to make the choice that's right for them?"

Who knew Jacob could be so profound?

"But if you didn't kill Tammy, then who did?"

Tears formed in Jacob's eyes. "You've literally given us heartbreaking news, and now you are like, asking all these questions we can't answer. You, a trespasser. A total stranger who for some reason seems oddly familiar."

At that moment, Jenny reached over and plucked the prosthetic off my nose and the wig off my head. "Did you really not recognize her?"

"Whoa. That's pretty wild. But why the disguise?" Jacob asked.

"We thought you were arrested," Jenny added. "We felt really bad that you got taken up in the raid."

"Yeah, no. It's kind of a long story. But let's say, I'm on your side. I wanted to help find Tammy. But since she's…" I didn't want to be insensitive, but I also still needed to get waxed. "Do you think you could squeeze me in for an appointment between noon and three tomorrow?"

"I'm all booked up at that time. How about now?"

"Uh…sure," I said, a little surprised Jenny would offer to work after receiving such bad news. Then again, I had recently been abducted from her supply closet. "But could we not use room three?"

* * * *

While Jenny ripped the hair off my body I tried to meditate—let my mind drift off to somewhere where I couldn't feel excruciating pain. If Jenny and Jacob weren't involved in Tammy's death, then who was? And if they hadn't leaked the photo of Della Cookies, then who had? I wasn't sure if the two events were related, but their proximity told me they might be. I looked around the waxing room. The photo of Della needed to have been taken from inside the room. There were no windows, and the vent was too small.

Sure, Jenny and Jacob might have been lying, but as the mom of a teenage girl, I had a pretty good sense of when someone was hiding the truth from me. But that meant only Tammy could have taken the notorious photo. But why do that? Tammy wasn't a Hair Radical. She was putting herself on the line every day to provide much-needed hair removal services to the women of Greenville. Why would she risk losing one, or even all of her clients? None of it seemed to make sense. Unless… As Jenny ripped another wax strip off my body, I figured something out.

* * * *

Two days later, I was lounging on Ipanema Beach. The PTA breakfast had been a success, my mom was playing chauffeur for my daughter for the next few days, and I had successfully launched my new moisturizer at BeautyConn 2040. I was fuzz-free and feeling fabulous.

My phone buzzed. It was a text from Diana. "You were right."

Sure enough, Della Cookies had been arrested for Tammy's murder. The authorities had been helped out by an anonymous tip. Full disclosure: I was the anonymous tipster.

I realized, while suffering through my Brazilian bikini wax, that Tammy must have been a Cookie Cutter. She was always railing against the evils of sugary foods, always giving me her latest health tips. Della's outing on social media had nothing to do with the Body Hair Acceptance Movement, and everything to do with the sugar content of her supposedly low-calorie sweetener.

Della must have realized right away that Tammy had been the one to out her, the one to ruin her life and career. There was plenty of motive for murder. Plus, who knew what other secrets Della might have spilled on Tammy's waxing table?

It only took a few clicks on social media and a visit to the Cookie Cutters's latest blog post for me to ascertain that Della was sipping a latte in a downtown coffee shop at 9:27 the morning of Tammy's murder. That was three blocks from the crime scene. I also knew that she was headed to BeautyConn 2040 the same time I was—to Brazil, a country with which we no longer had an extradition treaty.

I didn't support what Tammy had done to Della, but murder was murder. Della Cookies belonged behind bars, even if her "healthy" molten lava cake was the best I'd ever tasted. But I retract my earlier comment. It wasn't to die for. No one should die for cake.

Me, I was going to enjoy the rest of my conference. I stretched out on the beach. Somewhere, someone blasted the latest Audra Kling hit, titled, "Injustice." The lyrics were catchy, as usual. "I didn't know my words would serve, to spread injustice, undeserved…" I let my eyes unabashedly ogle all those gorgeous, hairless bodies, and I wondered what it would be like to live in a country where we had a choice. Certainly smoother, and maybe a little more beautiful.

POLLY WANTS A FREAKING CRACKER

SYLVIA MAULTASH WARSH

I woke up from the sleep of death. My mouth was dry, my eyelids heavy, my whole body felt wrong. And when I opened my eyes, I was behind bars. That couldn't be—I was a lawyer. In my family law practice I helped put other people behind bars, usually men who'd beaten their wives.

But these bars were different. They were gold.

I wasn't in jail. I was in a cage. A small cage. But how did I fit into it? I'm six feet tall.

Beyond the bars was a kitchen, but not my own, though it looked vaguely familiar. Suzy had recently renovated ours into something spectacular, spent a fortune on backsplashes and Subzero appliances. I loved my darling so much I didn't tell her I had to take out a line of credit to pay for it. Legal aid only paid a quarter of my hourly rate, but those were the clients who needed me.

A movement startled me; I wasn't alone. There was a bird in the cage. A large bright green parrot sat on a perch staring at me with huge beady eyes, its black pupils circled with amber. The red patch on its forehead spooked me. Were parrots dangerous? Was it going to attack?

I lifted my hand in greeting. "Hi!" My hoarse voice surprised me. The parrot raised its claw at the same time and croaked. I was starting to get a bad feeling about this. I blinked. The parrot blinked back. I tilted my head. The parrot did the same.

Only then did I notice the mirror. I was watching myself in it. The bird was *me*. *I* was the bird.

Oh gawd! This couldn't be. I peered around the cage and saw a newspaper lining the bottom. I turned my head to read the headline:

LAWYER KILLED IN HIT & RUN

I caught my breath.

Police are investigating the death of lawyer Paul Spano whose body was found on the street near his home—

My tiny heart raced as if it would burst from my chest. I tried hard to remember, closing my eyes, struggling to find my way back to the human Paul. Running. Yes, I was running. Leg muscles straining in rhythm, sneakers pounding the asphalt. The sudden rev of an engine behind me. I turned just as a monstrous beast with horns crashed into me. In the minute it took before I stopped breathing, I remembered confusion. My track suit was supposed to make me visible at night, with its fluorescent stripes down the legs and shiny square across my butt.

I'd been murdered! And now I'd come back as a—parrot? What kind of Karma was that? I'd always been kind to animals.

I stared at myself in the mirror. Murdered! Who the hell wanted me dead? I could think of three men right off the top of my head, clients' husbands who were either wife beaters or deadbeats, angry at being forced to pay alimony and child support. But angry enough to kill me?

"*Meow.*"

An orange tabby slunk into the kitchen and peered up at me. Oh, great. The cat sat in front of the cage, lifted its front paw and methodically licked it, sandpaper tongue flicking in and out. A pretense, I realized, as it studied me. No doubt deciding which part of me to eat first.

A boy with a familiar stiff gait entered the kitchen, and pieces of the puzzle fell into place. Benny, the ten-year-old son of Ella Frayne, a client whose husband slapped her around until I convinced her to go to the police. Kirk had spent a short time in jail and his pay as a car mechanic was now being garnisheed. The man hated me, blamed me for all his troubles. He had a restraining order, so he didn't get to see his kid either. Also my fault. Had Kirk killed me? That would be a terrible irony, landing in the home of my killer. Was that how Karma worked?

"Cool it, kitty," Benny said, approaching the cage. "He's our new pet parrot. He's replacing Polly."

What? When he came to the office with his mother, I'd never been able to understand the boy's grunts. He was autistic and didn't have words. Even Ella could only guess at what her son was trying to say.

"Benny," I croaked, just to hear my voice.

The boy jumped. His brown eyes, magnified behind his glasses, watched me. "You know my name."

He had words! "I'm Paul," I croaked, embarrassed by the awful sound of my own voice. "The lawyer."

Benny's eyes widened. Had he understood? "*Mom!*" he called out.

Ella ran into the kitchen, her wavy brown hair uncombed. "What's wrong, Benny? I'll make you breakfast."

Benny pointed at the cage. "It's Paul, the lawyer."

She looked at me and nodded. "You like the bird? It's a pretty green color. Just like Polly. You see? One flies away and another one comes."

She hadn't understood her son, as usual. She opened a cupboard and took out a box. "Polly want a cracker?" She offered it to me through the bars of the cage.

"It's Paul," I croaked. "*Paul!*"

"Polly want a cracker?" She wiggled the cracker in front of me until I took it in my beak.

Once I tasted the salty crunchiness, I gobbled it up. I hated myself for taking the next two crackers she gave me. *Focus!*

She turned back to the counter.

"Benny!" I croaked.

The boy was all attention.

"I need to read the other side of the newspaper in my cage." Gawd, it was hard to talk in this raspy voice. "Can you turn it over for me?"

He looked down. "But there's poop on it."

I was terribly embarrassed. Green-brown pellets laced with white lay scattered on the paper.

"The edge is clean. Just lift it up so I can read the back."

He opened the cage door and very carefully raised the paper.

According to Spano's wife, Suzanne, he went out after dinner every evening for his daily run. The neighborhood was quiet with few cars. She said her husband wore track pants with fluorescent stripes to stand out at night. When he didn't come back at his usual time, she stepped outside and found his body lying on the street. Police are asking for any witnesses of the hit and run to come forward.

They thought it was an accident!

"Okay," I croaked miserably. Benny released the paper and closed the cage.

I paced along the rope bridge, trying to organize my thoughts. Paced is the wrong word. Edged sideways like some circus acrobat, my weird toes grabbing the rope with each step.

"Benny, open the door. Let me out."

Benny looked around at his mother. She paid us no attention. "Promise you won't poop?"

"Promise," I croaked. My lawyerly instincts hadn't abandoned me like my body had. Of course, I'd poop. I was a bird.

Benny quietly opened the gate. I flew out and landed on top of a cupboard. Ella glanced at me, clicking her tongue.

Benny sat at the kitchen table and I watched him cut out pictures and headlines from the newspaper his mother had brought home from the school where she worked. This was the one thing he was good at, she'd told me. He meticulously snipped around the photos and letters and put them in a box.

"Benny," I croaked. "Open the back door."

"You'll fly away."

Ella turned and smiled at her son but otherwise ignored our conversation. It must be terrible to be so unaware.

"I'll come back," I croaked. "I promise." I hated to lie to Benny, but I had no idea if I would make it back.

Benny crept to the kitchen door that opened onto the backyard. He peeked to make sure his mother still had her back to him, then he creaked open the door. Just as Ella turned, I squawked and flew out.

"Benny! Why did you let him out?"

"He promised to come back." It was a good thing she couldn't understand him.

Their words faded. I spread my emerald wings and soared into the wind. *Yippee!*

Exhilarated, I glided on an air current, ascended higher, then floated down again. I had never felt so free. My tiny heart filled with—joy?

That was ridiculous, my cynical lawyerly self kicked in. I could get the same thrill on a rollercoaster.

No, no, *look at the view from up here!* my parrot brain cried. Rooftops and treetops and toy cars. All the stupid little stuff everyone worried about was nothing up here. But the euphoria didn't last long when I remembered where I was going. I swooped down to land on a bush in front of a four-story building.

Kirk had moved to a crappy apartment only a few blocks from Ella's small tidy bungalow, close enough to keep her afraid. She was a teaching assistant at Benny's school with a salary low enough to qualify for legal aid. I had accompanied her to Kirk's one weekend when he hadn't returned Benny on time, and she didn't know who else to call. Suzy said I should've been a social worker.

In the back parking lot, Kirk's shitbox was easy to spot, a 15-year-old Chevy van, all rust and scratches. I landed on the bumper, scouring it for evidence. There were dents on both sides but nothing that looked new.

Back in front of the building, I perched on a bush, watching and waiting. Finally, the front door opened, and a couple walked out. I sailed past them, making it inside just before the door closed.

I pecked in Kirk's code in the rundown lobby.

"Who is it?" Kirk answered on the intercom.

I squawked my name.

"Get lost!" Click.

A young girl approached the glass door. When she opened it, I flew in above her head.

"Whoa!" she said. "You're welcome."

I didn't touch the filthy staircases as I flew up to the third floor. At his door, reality sunk in. What was I doing there? What could I, a bird, possibly do to Kirk, a man? Yet he was the main suspect in my murder.

I tapped on the door with my beak. Kirk opened it but didn't look down at the floor where I stood. He stuck out his bald head, peering around. I took the opportunity to fly inside.

"Hey! What the—" Kirk watched me swoop around until I landed on the back of a kitchen chair.

I didn't remember what a big fellow he was, since I was just as tall. In my other life. His T-shirt stretched across a beefy chest, a black K tattooed on his neck.

"Get outa here!" He tried to swat me away.

I squawked and flew out of his reach. "Killer!" I croaked.

I hoped my muscular little parrot tongue would help me enunciate words better.

Kirk squinted at me, then stepped to the door and stuck his head out. "Ella? This your idea of a joke?"

"You killed me!" I croaked.

Kirk fixed fierce eyes on me, then disappeared into another room.

I flew to the kitchen table and spotted a letter addressed to Kirk from the Family Responsibility Office.

"Your application to discontinue ongoing child support for the minor Benjamin Frayne has been denied. You may appeal this decision by applying to…"

It looked like Kirk had tried to stop them garnisheeing his wages, without success.

I picked up the sheet with my bill just as Kirk returned, wielding a baseball bat. It smacked the table a second after I flew off and landed on top of the fridge.

Ugh, didn't the guy ever dust?

When Kirk waved the bat at me, I flew to the top of a cupboard, out of reach. Kirk snarled, pulled over a step stool. I flew to the opposite cupboard. Kirk moved the stool. I could do this for hours, but it was boring.

I flew into the bedroom, still clutching the sheet in my beak. *That's* what I was looking for. An open window!

Kirk lunged at me, swinging the bat. I flapped my wings and shot out the window. I soared up. *Ha!* A human couldn't have done *that*.

I climbed into the sky. Pointing westward, I found a current going my way. The stream carried me like a magic carpet, my wings spread out. Far below, the leaden waters of Lake Ontario stretched far into the distance, like an ocean.

The houses grew tiny, turned into Monopoly pieces, with trees like pom-poms. Farther west, the gray high-rises of downtown Toronto could have been LEGO, only without the fun. The wind tunnels created by the business district monoliths buffeted me. I fought to keep the paper in my beak. Finally, police headquarters loomed below, glass cubes and pink granite squatting on College Street. The Pink Palace. People were going in and out the huge blue double doors, so it was a breeze to fly inside above their heads.

I sneaked in behind someone stepping out of an elevator and pushed the floor number with my beak before anyone else could enter.

I'd been lucky to get this far. When the elevator opened, I swooped along the hall looking for Morrie. My luck held out. He was sitting in his usual spot in a room full of desks. I landed with a thud on his desk, exhausted from my trip. The sheet slipped from my beak.

"Hey! Who belongs to the bird?" Morrie gave me his detective onceover, his cool gray eyes stymied for a change.

I hadn't seen him for a while and looked him over, too. He'd filled out in the wrong places and lost some hair. Morrie and I went way back to when we shared a room as undergrads at the University of Toronto. After he graduated from the police academy, he was my go-to cop when I needed an opinion or advice. Maybe I should've listened to him years ago when he said I was too soft to be a lawyer.

"Don't you shit on my desk!"

Why did everyone think I was going to drop a load on them? I pecked my bill at the sheet of paper.

He looked down. "What's this?" He picked it up. "Kirk Frayne. Rings a bell."

I hoped so. Morrie was the cop I'd told Ella to call the last time Kirk beat her up.

He leaned back in his chair observing me, his pot belly round beneath the blazer. "What is a parrot doing here, bringing me—" He looked down at the sheet.

"He killed Paul!" I croaked. "He killed Paul!"

"Bless you."

I guess my enunciation still needed work. Even to my ears, it sounded like *Hikipaw*.

He tapped the sheet against the desk, distracted.

"Paul Spano!" I squawked. "Paul Spano!" That was better; I was getting the hang of it.

He sat up. "What did it say? It sounded like—" He shook his head. "Need some more coffee."

Suddenly everything blacked out. I could see shadows through the sweater someone had thrown over me.

"I got 'im! What d'you want me to do with 'im?" An unfamiliar voice.

"Geez. Just take him downstairs and throw him out."

Good old Morrie.

****

By now I was tired. I flew between the buildings, heading north, away from downtown, shuttling around hydro towers that straddled great swaths of green. I was getting close when the ribbon of the Don River glinted below. My eyes were soothed by the leafy banks and the weeping willows leaning into the water. Swooping down, I hung a right into my street and finally arrived at my house. I longed to see my wife.

Though it looked a lot bigger now that I had shrunk, the familiar two-story plucked at my heartstrings. I flew 'round the back to land on one of the patio chairs outside the kitchen. And there she was, my darling Suzy, sitting at our kitchen table, her sister Didi's arm around her shoulder. The glass patio door was open; their voices carried through the screen door.

"I miss him terribly," Suzy said, her pale face tear stained. She stared out at nothing.

I remembered the first time we met. Late for a meeting, I'd rushed into Hudson's Bay to buy some new underwear—I was behind on my laundry and wearing my last clean pair. She was straightening out a cardboard palm tree in a tropical display for March break. Out of breath, I mumbled for directions to the men's socks. I figured they'd be in the same section, and I wasn't going to ask a pretty woman for men's skivvies. She looked up at me.

"Oh, I'm not—"

I was about to apologize when she gave me a smile that hooked me. Without another word she led me to the right aisle. After she turned to go, I picked out a pack of tighty-whities. To my horror, she pivoted, then coyly tilted her beautiful blond head toward a mannequin wearing champagne-colored boxers festooned with pineapples. I still have that pair.

Didi's voice brought me back. "I'll always be grateful to Paul. I don't know where I'd be if he hadn't gone after Lenny like a pit bull. I would never have found those offshore accounts without him."

Didi had discovered her husband, Lenny, in the arms of a young assistant in his condo development office and filed for divorce. Her admin job wasn't going to keep her in the style to which she had become accustomed, and Lenny was crying broke. So I went after his invisible assets, found more than I expected, and made him cough up. Hated me for it.

Hey! I thought. How much did he hate me? Enough to roll over me in his Porsche Cayenne?

Before I knew it, Suzy had gotten up and stuck her head out the screen door. "Hey, little cutie, where'd you come from? Are you lost?"

She was talking to *me!* I took my opportunity and flew into the house.

"Geez, Suzy! You let it in!" Didi covered her head with her arms as if I was going to attack her.

Suzy's face brightened as I landed on top of a white lacquered cupboard. The kitchen reno had cost a bucket but it sure looked grand. She had hit it off with Xavier, the hunky contractor, who went all out to please her.

Didi lowered her arms. "Well, at least it made you smile." She picked up a magazine and stood, about to shoo me away like a mosquito.

"No, let him stay." Suzy studied me with those sky-blue eyes. "He's a beautiful green."

"Suzy!" I croaked. A horrible sound.

"He talks," she said. "Sort of."

"I love you!" I tried again, but even I didn't recognize the words.

She went to the cupboard and took out a box. "Is it true they like crackers?" She placed a Ritz on the counter, then stepped away.

I couldn't help it—my body ruled—I flew down to snatch the cracker, then high-tailed it back to the cupboard. The cracker was gone in a flash. Yum!

Her smile widened. She took out a handful of crackers and left them on the counter.

"You're crazy!" Didi announced. "It'll crap all over the kitchen."

Again with the poop.

While I was chowing down on the cracker feast, the doorbell rang. Suzy left to answer it.

I could hear her talking to Xavier, the contractor, in the hall. "I hope you don't mind, Suzy. Thanks to your design the kitchen turned out gorgeous. I just want to take some pictures for our website."

"I'm flattered," she said. "Go ahead."

He strolled in like he owned the place. And he still might if Suzy couldn't pay off the line of credit I had taken out to foot the bill. He was too good-looking for my liking, with a man bun and muscles bulging under his brown T-shirt.

He nodded at Didi, but she might as well have been part of the marble island. Then he saw me and scowled. I was just polishing off the last of the crackers. "You got a new pet?"

Suzy smiled at me. "Just visiting. Unless he decides to stay."

His scowl turned into a glower. "Birds are filthy. Just say the word and I'll get rid of it." He took a cracker from the box and said in a melodic voice, "Polly want a freaking cracker?"

He looked about to pounce, sending me back to the top of the cupboard.

"No, really. I like him."

Tough guy! I felt like showing him just how filthy I could be, but I didn't want to prove him right.

He knelt and stooped as he took shots of the kitchen on his phone, flaunting his perfect physique. When he finished, he stood too close to Suzy, showing her the pictures.

Didi picked up her purse. "I'll be going."

After she left, Xavier's hungry eyes roved over Suzy, as if she was going to be his next meal. "How about going out for coffee? Or dinner?"

"That's very sweet, Xavier, but I'm not up to it."

"You got to move on. You're still young and beautiful. Paul was a great guy, but…"

He had never liked me. I wondered now if it was because he had the hots for Suzy.

"…you can do better. He had no style sense. I mean, who wears sweatpants that make their ass glow in the dark?"

She stuck out her chin. "It was supposed to keep him safe. He had a great sense of humor."

Something pinged in my puny brain. How did he know about my fluorescent butt? The newspaper article only mentioned the stripes down my pants. He could only know that if he was the one who ran me down. The fluorescent square would have been an easy target.

Livid, I swooped down and pecked at his head, unravelling his man bun.

"Hey! Get the hell off me, you freaking—"

Suzy opened the patio door. "Shoo!" she cried. "Shoo!"

Demoralized, I flew out.

Maybe I was wrong. Maybe somebody at the cop shop had blabbed about my shiny butt and there were posts all over social media. How would I know? Parrots don't have smartphones.

I flew to the driveway to inspect his pickup, "Uno Renovations" Lettered on the sides. Aha! There was a crack in the bumper, hard to spot since it was black. Looking up, I suddenly quivered with terror. Embedded in the grill, a skull-like ram's head ogled me, its silver horns looming ferociously. Xavier drove a Dodge Ram! The moment flooded back, running on the sidewalk, an engine revving, turning around to see the silver monster just as it…

He'd killed me and now he was after my girl. I always sensed he wanted her, but I never would have guessed he was a psycho who would murder the competition. Was she in danger? Hell, yes! How could I protect her? To my relief, Xavier stepped out the door and headed to his truck. I sailed up and landed a good one on his door. His curses mollified my rage a little as I made my escape.

All I could think about was that he'd get away with murder because I couldn't tell anyone. Unlike my fellow parrots, I was unintelligible. Maybe reincarnation was mucking about with my tongue. Nobody could understand me. Nobody but Benny.

I struggled back to Ella's house, tuckered out from all the flying. Benny wasn't back from school yet and the cat lay on the lawn, so I dozed off in a maple tree across the street. In my dream, Suzy was lying in my manly arms, when I was rudely awakened by a squirrel jumping on my head. Half asleep, I looked down and panicked before I remembered I could fly.

Ella and Benny were just coming up the walkway. When I sailed down to the porch, Benny laughed and stroked my feathers.

"You came back!"

I was chuffed and if a parrot could grin, I would have.

Ella clucked her tongue but smiled at her boy.

Inside, while Ella turned on a soap opera in the living room, I had a heart-to-heart with the kid. "I need you to do something for me, Benny. It's important."

He beamed, his eyes widening behind the glasses.

I asked him to bring out his box of newspaper cut-outs and spread the headlines on the kitchen table. "I want you to cut out these letters." I pointed out each one, 32 altogether.

He hunkered down with his scissors, relishing the task. I picked up each one he cut and placed them in order on a sheet of paper.

They spelled out, "Xavier Uno killed Paul Spano. Save Suzy."

Benny's eyebrows shot up. I'd been wrong to blame Kirk and was relieved he hadn't done it, for Benny's sake, though I was sure he was guilty of something.

Benny pasted the letters onto the paper with his glue stick, and I was good to go.

Energized now, I flew with new purpose down to the cop shop, the sheet held tight in my beak. I found good old Morrie at his desk and dropped the paper in front of him. He looked at me, about to utter an expletive, but then he saw the black letters.

"You back again? Where'd you get this?"

I was thrilled he was talking to me. "I'm Paul!" I croaked. "I'm Paul!"

"I thought parrots were supposed to talk," he said, and I knew I'd failed again.

"Who's Xavier Uno?" He looked up the name on his computer and found some outstanding traffic violations.

"Go to Paul's house!" I rasped. "Go to Paul's house!" I flew to the door then back to his desk twice, three times, the way Lassie used to do to get people to follow her.

He couldn't possibly have understood me, but maybe he remembered Lassie because he got up and followed me outside. He headed for his car while I took off as the crow—or parrot—flies. I prayed Morrie was heading in the same direction.

When I arrived at my old house, Xavier's truck was in the drive. Raised voices sounded inside. Desperate, I pecked at the doorbell. Suzy opened the door and ran outside, her hair disheveled, her blouse askew. Dashing out behind her, Xavier grabbed her and pulled her back into the house. I flew in before he closed the door.

"I don't want to hurt you." He held onto her arm while she wriggled, trying to get away. "I love you."

"Let me go!"

I flew around his head to distract him. He tried to swat me with his ham fists, but first had to release Suzy.

"What the hell!"

Suzy ran to the kitchen where she stood against the island. Looking for a weapon, I spied a long barbecue fork hanging decoratively on the wall. When he appeared, I grabbed the handle of the fork with my beak and divebombed at him, aiming the sharp spikes at his juicy bicep. Bull's eye! Blood poured from two holes in his arm. He only had time to gasp before Suzy whacked the back of his head with a cast iron pan. Down he went.

I squawked with excitement and landed on her shoulder.

The doorbell rang. Better late than never.

Suzy ran to the door. "Morrie! Thank heavens you're here," Suzy said, leading him into the kitchen.

He stood over Xavier where he lay unconscious on the floor, handing her the sheet with Benny's letters: "Xavier Uno killed Paul Spano. Save Suzy."

"He killed Paul?" She burst into tears, Morrie patting her back awkwardly.

When she was all cried out, she took the paper. "Where'd you get this?"

He nodded at me. "The parrot dropped it off."

They looked at me, puzzled. I wished I could explain. I wished I could make myself understood, but something weird was happening. I hoped it was indigestion.

Suzy was safe, that was all that mattered. A great wave of relief rolled over me, flattening me, reshaping me, forging something new, till I didn't recognize myself. Till I *wasn't* myself.

* * * *

Where was I? How'd I get here? I was *so* hungry.

"Polly want a cracker."

Two people I didn't know stared at me with their mouths open. The woman spoke first.

"That's the first time I understood what he said."

"Me, too."

Who were these people? I liked the blonde better than the fat guy. Her pretty face looked familiar. Hey, look, she's taking out some crackers. I like her hair. I like the crackers. Maybe I'll stay.

While the fat guy took out a shiny thing and talked into it, the blonde said, "I think I'll call him Paulie."

A PANDEMONIUM OF PARROTS

SUZANNE FLAIG

"9-1-1, what is your emergency?"

"Murder! Murder!"

The 9-1-1 operator heard a high, squeaky voice. Possibly a child or a frightened woman. "Can you tell me your address?"

"Murder! Murder!"

The operator spoke into the headset. "It's going to be okay. The police will soon be there." Luckily, they had ways to determine the location, as long as the caller stayed on the line.

"George is dead. George is dead."

"Is the perpetrator still in the house?"

The only answer was a repeated, "George is dead."

The operator heard a flurry of noises in the background and other voices repeating, "Murder! Murder!"

"Is someone else with you?" she asked. "Who's in the house with you?" If the caller was a child, there might be other children in the house. Had these children watched someone kill their father? "The police are on their way," she said. "Stay on the phone with me until they get there, okay?"

"Stay on the phone, stay on the phone," the voice repeated.

* * * *

Officers Sanchez and Anderson responded to the call at the upscale home in the historic downtown district. Gun drawn, Officer Anderson knocked and yelled, "Police! Open the door!"

From within, several voices echoed, "Police! Police!" accompanied by a rustle of movement.

Anderson tried the doorknob, and the door opened a crack. He looked over at Sanchez, who nodded. You never knew what might be behind a closed door. Sanchez raised his fingers to signal: one… two…. On the sign of three, Anderson flung open the door and entered a room filled with parrots, swooping and squawking. He ducked, nearly shooting himself in the foot. The birds repeated, "Police! Police!" as they flew one by one into cages lined up along one side of the room.

Sanchez slammed the door shut. "What the hell?"

One parrot remained, perched on an ornate mahogany table in the center of the room, guarding a landline telephone. The receiver had been knocked off its cradle.

A man's body lay in a pool of blood on an oriental carpet.

The parrot squawked, "Murder."

A voice on the other end of the line asked, "Have the police arrived?"

The parrot repeated, "Police, police."

Sanchez walked over to the phone, pulled a handkerchief out of his back pocket and picked up the receiver. "This is Officer Sanchez with the police department. Is this the 9-1-1 operator?"

"Yes, sir," she replied. "Are the children who called okay? It sounded like they were in a real panic. Now that you're there, I'll get off the line."

"Don't worry," he said, "no children are in jeopardy. But make sure you save the recording of this call. You're not going to believe the situation we've got here."

Sanchez and Anderson secured the scene, then called in the coroner, crime scene techs, and the homicide detective.

When Detective Ramos of Metro Homicide Division arrived, he asked, "What's the situation, Officer?"

"The coroner's inside with the body," Anderson said, as he led the detective into the spacious living room. "It's quiet now, but when Sanchez and I arrived at the scene it was pandemonium."

Ramos surveyed the row of cages along the wall. "*A* pandemonium, Anderson. That's what they're called."

"What?"

"The parrots," Ramos explained. "A group of parrots is called a pandemonium. Like a group of cattle is a herd, or a group of lions is a pride."

Anderson shuddered. "Well, that sure as hell was a pandemonium we walked into. Those damn birds were screaming and repeating everything we said. They're lucky I didn't shoot every last one of 'em."

Ramos laughed. "Then I'd have to arrest you for shooting the witnesses."

Anderson scowled. "They attacked me first. I almost shot myself."

Sanchez, standing next to the coroner, snickered. "It was kinda funny. But after we came in, they shut up and flew into their cages. All except that one." Sanchez pointed to a light gray parrot with a black beak perched on the table. White feathers surrounded intelligent black eyes. "He won't budge."

Anderson rolled his eyes. "We're assuming he placed the 9-1-1 call."

Ramos stopped at the table, bent over, placed both hands on his knees, and peered into the bird's eyes. "So, you placed the 9-1-1 call, did you?" The bird cocked his head to the side, staring back. Ramos nodded, then turned his attention to the coroner, who was kneeling over the body sprawled in the middle of the floor. "What've you got, Jimmy?"

"Adult male, approximately seventy years old. Cause of death multiple stab wounds to the abdomen. He bled out."

"Did you find the murder weapon?" Ramos asked.

Jimmy shook his head. "The murderer must have pulled it out after stabbing the victim. Unless your people find it here somewhere, he must have taken it with him."

"Can you tell what kind of knife caused these wounds?"

"Not until I get him back to the morgue for a more thorough examination."

"Okay, then, I'll let the techs do their job." Ramos straightened and looked around the room at the birdcages, then at the lone parrot perched on the table. He took a notebook from his breast pocket. "I guess I'd better question the eyewitnesses."

Anderson shook his head. "You've got to be kidding."

Ramos watched the coroner and his assistant zip the dead man into a body bag and lift him onto a gurney. As they wheeled it toward the door, the parrot who had been on the table took flight and landed in a cage that had a placard labeled "Oskar." Ramos considered his next move. Maybe he was crazy, trying to interrogate a bird. On the other hand, the parrot had been smart enough to peck the numbers 9-1-1. And the damn thing kept repeating "Murder," so he must have some information. The detective approached the parrot's cage.

"Hello. My name is Detective Ramos. What's your name?"

"Oskar."

"Did you see what happened here?"

The parrot replied, "Murder!"

At the sound of that word, the other birds, who had been quiet since the detective arrived, began squawking, "Murder, murder," and flapping their wings.

Startled, Ramos raised his arm and said, "Stop!" The room got quiet. Even the crime scene techs paused and turned toward the detective. "I understand, Oskar, you witnessed a murder." He held his breath, hoping the word didn't cause another outbreak. The parrots remained quiet, and the techs returned to their duties.

Ramos continued. "Can you tell me the name of the dead man?"

Oskar replied, "George. George is dead."

"Is George the owner of this house?"

Oskar seemed to be nodding. "George is dead."

"Did you see who murdered George?"

The bird repeated, "George is dead."

Ramos rubbed the back of his neck. This was going nowhere. Did Oskar see someone stab George? Did he see who did it? Would he be able to identify the person who did it? He knew these questions were doubtful at best, and even so… would a bird's testimony be admissible in a court of law? The whole idea was nuts, but it was all he had.

Ramos turned to the crime scene techs. "I want all twelve of these parrots locked in their cages and taken back to headquarters. They're to be treated as witnesses and possible persons of interest in a murder investigation."

* * * *

Lieutenant Granger called the detective into his office. "What the hell do you expect us to do with these damn parrots, Ramos?"

"I thought we could put them in one of the interrogation rooms, sir." Detective Ramos raised his head with a look of assurance he didn't really feel. "They are my only eyewitnesses, and one of them called it in."

The lieutenant blinked twice. "You expect me to believe a parrot made a phone call?"

"Yes, sir. I've got the 9-1-1 tape as evidence."

Lieutenant Granger sat down and rubbed his hand over his bald head. "What do you plan to get out of these… birds?"

"They can speak," Ramos said. "I know a little about parrots. Although most simply mimic what others say, I've heard of trained parrots who learned to understand their owners and were able to make associations with the words they've heard over the years."

"You think these birds are that smart?" Granger asked.

"Some are highly intelligent, sir. The one who made the 9-1-1 call—Oskar—is an African Grey, one of the most intelligent species."

"So, you really think they can help you solve this case?"

"I believe they can. At least Oskar can. So far, all he told me is the victim's name—George—and that he was murdered. But I think I can get more out of these parrots, given time."

"You *think*," Granger said. He sighed. "I'll give you forty-eight hours, Ramos. Put them in Interrogation Room Two."

"Thank you, sir. I'll get results, sir." Ramos trudged out of the office wondering where to begin. He followed the parade of parrots into the interrogation room where the cages with the squawking birds had been lined up against the wall. Onlookers in the adjoining room could watch the proceedings through the one-way mirror.

Starting with the first cage on the left, Ramos asked the same question of each parrot: "Did you see who murdered George?"

Every time the detective mentioned the word 'murder,' the birds flapped their wings and repeated the word. He tried another yes or no question. "Did you see who came to George's house this morning?" He got no response. Maybe this wasn't going to work, after all.

But when Ramos got to Oskar, whose cage was positioned on the far right, he stared into the bird's eyes. The parrot turned his head, one bright eye gazing intently back at the detective. Ramos asked Oskar the same question: "Did you see who murdered George?"

The bird's feathers shook, and his head bobbed back and forth. Clearly agitated, he replied, "Don't know."

"Did you see who came to George's house this morning?"

The bird hung his head and said, "Too many came, too many went."

"You called the police, Oskar. What did you see?"

Oskar replied, "Can't tell."

"What does that mean? You can't tell me the murderer's name, or you can't tell me what happened?"

Oskar flapped his wings and repeated the word, "Murder!"

This parrot is an intelligent bird, Ramos thought. He wants to tell me who killed his owner. He doesn't know how to give me the information I need, and I don't know how to get it from him. But I'll figure it out.

"I'll be back, Oskar," Ramos said.

The detective returned to the squad room. The only witness he needed was the African Grey, so he called the local bird sanctuary. They were happy to take the rest of the parrots, saying George McPherson had donated money to their charity over the years.

* * * *

The victim, seventy-two-year-old George McPherson, a retired art dealer, collected rare paintings, sculptures, and antique furniture. He never married and had no children of his own. George's sister had passed away three years ago. His two nephews, Roger and Thomas, lived nearby, and were in line to inherit George's fortune, putting them at the top of the suspect list. Money is always the most likely motive for murder. And family members the most likely suspects.

The detective stopped at the morgue. He asked the coroner, "Do you have a time of death, Jimmy?"

"Sometime between six and nine a.m."

The detective nodded. "Makes sense. The call came in right after nine. If the parrot saw it go down and he made the call, that fits the timeline."

"Ramos, you're a real piece of work."

"What do you mean by that?"

"You really think a bird will help you solve this case?"

"He saw it go down, Jimmy."

"Yeah, and so did my dead Aunt Ophelia. But she's not talkin' either. You better stick to facts and forensics, my man."

"Okay, okay. I'm not ignoring the facts. Oskar is just another piece of the puzzle. Now what about the weapon?"

Jimmy said, "A run-of-the-mill kitchen knife. Nothing special. The crime scene techs didn't find one at the scene, and none seem to be missing from the man's kitchen, so we're assuming the killer brought it and took it away afterwards."

"Thanks, Jimmy. Maybe he dumped the knife nearby. I'll have my guys search the area. We'll get search warrants for the nephews' places, too. We might get lucky and find something."

"Hold on, Ramos. Don't rush off yet. The techs found a strand of blond hair in the carpet fiber near the body, and more on the victim's shirt. They sent them to the crime lab for analysis. I asked for a rush on the results, but good luck with that."

* * * *

The following day, Detective Ramos contacted George McPherson's nephews and asked them to come down to the station for questioning. He put them in separate interrogation rooms.

George's nephew Roger wiped sweat from his forehead. "Is it warm in here?"

"Not really," Ramos replied. "Are you nervous?"

"No, no… well, maybe…. Why am I here? Am I a suspect?"

"I just have a few questions." The detective leaned forward. "To rule you out. You understand. Standard procedure."

"Oh. Okay."

"Where were you yesterday between six and nine a.m.?"

"Yesterday morning?" Roger asked. "Probably asleep, until seven-thirty when my alarm went off. Then I got ready for work and arrived at the office a little before nine."

"Can anyone corroborate that?"

"Well, yeah, my wife can tell you when I left the house—it was about eight-thirty—and everyone at my office can vouch for the time I got to work."

"Where do you work?"

"Parker and Jones, on Third Street. I'm an accountant."

"All right. We'll check that out. Thanks." Ramos stood up. "And we'll verify the time with your wife, as well."

Roger pulled at his collar. "Uh…sure."

The detective said, "Just one more thing, Roger. Will you follow me?" He led the man into the room where Oskar sat in his cage with the door open.

Roger blinked. "What? Hello, Oskar."

Oskar flew out, landing on Roger's shoulder and began pecking at his blond hair. "Roger has a rug, Roger has a rug."

Roger's face turned beet-red as he tried to swat the bird away. "Stop it, Oskar!"

Ramos asked, "Did you take one of your uncle's oriental rugs?"

Just then, Oskar plucked the toupee from Roger's bald head and flew back to his cage, dropping the "rug" with a childish laugh.

Roger stomped over to the cage, retrieved his hairpiece, and turned to Ramos. "Oskar's really intelligent but he's always looking for attention. Even at the expense of others."

The detective stifled a smile. "I'm sorry about that. Thank you, Roger. I'll be in touch."

Next, the detective went in to speak with Thomas. When asked about the parrots, Thomas spat out, "Uncle George treated them like his children. He spoke to all of them and they answered just like another person in the room. Especially the oldest one, an African Grey named Oskar."

"You sound jealous of your uncle's parrots."

Thomas leaned back. "Well, maybe a bit. Even when Roger and I were kids, Uncle George played with his birds and ignored us."

Ramos asked Thomas, "Where were you between six and nine yesterday morning?"

Thomas folded his hands on the table and smiled. "I was in New York on business. Didn't get back in town until two p.m. You can check my flight schedule."

Ramos had checked Thomas's schedule and already knew about the business trip but had wanted to see the man's reaction. He sighed. Both nephews seemed to have solid alibis.

"Follow me, please," the detective said. He took Thomas into the room with the parrots. Oskar immediately perked up and said, "Hello, Thomas."

Thomas mumbled, "Hello, Oskar."

"How's business?" the bird asked.

Thomas took a step back. "Why ask about my business?"

"Maybe he heard your uncle ask you about your work," Ramos said.

"I suppose," Thomas said.

Ramos shook his head. Thomas had seemed shaken when the subject of his business came up. Something to look into.

After they left the room, Ramos said, "Thomas, I'm curious. You told me that your uncle spoke to his parrots like people, and they answered him. Could Oskar answer questions in full sentences, or did he just repeat the words George said?"

"I've seen that parrot do some amazing things over the years," Thomas replied. "Sure, I saw him actually hold a conversation. At least with Uncle George." Thomas sneered. "Never with me. But then, Oskar considered my uncle his family. Maybe they shared a special language."

The detective thought he'd better learn that language, or his only witness would soon fly the coop.

Ramos sent Thomas home, contemplating his next move.

The parrot hadn't reacted violently to either nephew. That seemed to rule them out as the murderer, at least according to Oskar.

But what if one of them had an accomplice? The detective would look more closely into the private lives of the two men and their finances. Who knew what kinds of people they associated with? Possible criminal elements? Birds of a feather, and all that.

Ramos returned to the parrot. "Oskar, talk to me. I know we want the same thing. I want to find out who stabbed George. You can help me find his killer."

Oskar turned his head from side to side. "George is dead, George is dead."

"I know. Who killed him, Oskar? Can you give me a name?"

"No name, no name." The bird shook his feathers. "Don't know."

Ramos asked, "Why don't you know the name of the person who killed George?"

If parrots could cry, Detective Ramos believed Oskar was about to shed tears.

The detective buried his face in his hands. Another dead end. The killer must be a stranger. Was this simply a random break-in? Yet none of George's money, expensive art, antiques, or anything of value had been stolen from his home.

* * * *

Still questioning whether George's murder had been orchestrated by one or both of the nephews, Ramos executed a search warrant for the homes of both men. "What are we looking for?" one of the officers asked.

"I'm not sure," Ramos replied, "but I'll know it when I see it."

Ramos interviewed Roger's wife, who could not corroborate the exact time her husband left for work the morning of George's death. She said she thought he left about eight-thirty, as he claimed, because that was his usual departure time. Yet she admitted she had slept late and didn't awake until after nine. None of Roger's neighbors saw or heard anything. But one middle-aged woman, who seemed to have her ears on the neighborhood gossip, reported that "Roger's wife often had a gentleman caller in the afternoon while her husband was at work."

When Ramos rang Thomas's doorbell, he complained about the search warrant. "What's the meaning of this? Am I a suspect? I cooperated with you. You know I was out of town at the time of Uncle George's murder!"

Ramos placated the man, saying, "It's standard procedure. Just to cover our bases and to rule you out. We did the same at Roger's home."

The detective questioned Thomas's next-door neighbor, who told the detective about Sharon, Thomas's girlfriend who often spent the night. Thomas had made a point of telling his neighbor Sharon would be in the apartment while he went out of town on a business trip.

"Did you see Sharon the morning of George McPherson's death?" Ramos asked.

"She left the apartment early that morning. At least I assumed it was her. A blond woman drove away about six-thirty in his car."

"And the next time you saw either of them?"

"I guess it was later that afternoon when she and Thomas returned from the airport," he said. "Probably around four."

"Thanks for your help." The police had notified Thomas of his uncle's death after four o'clock. Since Ramos hadn't been the one to deliver the news of George's murder, the detective wondered what Thomas's initial reaction had been.

* * * *

The next day, Lieutenant Granger called Detective Ramos into his office. Granger's bald head shone like a polished bowling ball. "Your forty-eight hours are up, detective. What have you found out from your *witness*, if I can call him that?"

"I've had a slight setback with the parrot, sir. My main suspects were the two nephews, Roger and Thomas. They are George's only living relatives and seem to have the only viable motive. I thought the bird would react violently when he saw the old man's murderer and hoped that Oskar would incriminate one or both nephews. But the parrot acted friendly with both men." Ramos chuckled. "Although the bird did pull a prank on Roger."

The lieutenant raised an eyebrow. "It makes sense the parrots would know George's nephews if either of them visited the old man frequently. And be on friendly terms."

"True. Problem is, when I questioned Oskar, he said he didn't know the name of the person who murdered George."

"So, you're back to square one," Granger said, "and if the bird can't help you, it's time to get rid of him."

Ramos sighed. "Yes, sir. I already sent the other parrots to the bird sanctuary. I'll call them back and have someone pick up Oskar." Then the detective perked up. "I do have another thread—or actually a hair—that might lead to the killer. The crime techs found strands of blond hair on the victim's body and in the rug nearby. George's nephew, Roger, is a blond, so I'm hoping the lab results will come back soon."

Granger snorted, "And I hope this isn't another one of your 'harebrained' ideas, Ramos."

Before contacting the sanctuary, Ramos received a phone call. He had left a message with George's lawyer to find out the details of the old man's will, assuming the nephews would inherit McPherson's substantial fortune. If he was forced to rule them out as suspects, who was left? The detective had hit another dead end, and his forty-eight hours with the avian witness was over.

When the lawyer called, Detective Ramos learned that George's family members weren't the only ones who might benefit from his death. McPherson's passion was his parrots—no surprise there—and George had donated annually to the local bird sanctuary. These eccentric rich types often left their money to charity when they died. George McPherson was no exception. Apparently, several years ago, he had written his nephews out of the will and left everything to the Pandemonium of Parrots Sanctuary.

Maybe money was the motive for George's murder after all.

Detective Ramos made another call to the bird sanctuary. The owner, Millie Malone, answered. She agreed to come to the station that evening to pick up Oskar. Ramos had to admit he'd be sad to see Oskar leave. Over the past two days, he had become attached to the intelligent bird. He considered adopting Oskar once this case was solved.

While he waited for Ms. Malone to arrive, Ramos received another file by courier from George's law firm. They had discovered a new will, signed just two days before the old man's death. Ramos made another call to the estate lawyer. The lawyer confirmed what the detective suspected.

Later that evening, an officer escorted a middle-aged blond woman to the detective's desk. The officer said, "This is Ms. Malone, from the Pandemonium of Parrots Sanctuary. She asked to see you."

"Yes, I've been waiting for her," Ramos said. "She's here to collect the parrot. Would you ask Lieutenant Granger to join us in Interrogation Room Two?" He thought, *I want to make sure he knows I kept my side of the bargain to get rid of Oskar*.

When the detective opened the door and ushered Ms. Malone inside, Oskar immediately flapped his wings and began squawking, "Murder! Murder!"

The woman backed up and tried to get out. She flattened herself against the wall, screaming, "What's going on? Stop him!"

Oskar screeched, "No money for you!"

Ramos blocked the doorway. Lieutenant Granger came up from behind. "What in the world set that bird off? I thought the woman from the bird sanctuary was here to take him away."

"She is, Lieutenant," Ramos said, "and apparently my *witness* just identified the murderer."

Granger watched the pandemonium and saw the woman cowering in the corner.

Detective Ramos said, "Is that a good enough identification for you, Lieutenant?"

The lieutenant's red face said it all. "Enough to hold her for questioning, detective. Cuff her and put her in Interrogation Room One. Then tell Jenkins to call someone else from the bird sanctuary to come and take that damn parrot away."

As Ramos took Ms. Malone into custody, she screamed, "I had to do it! He was going to change his will. Those parrots deserved that money!"

The detective sat her down. "You were too late, Millie. George changed his will two days ago, after he found out you embezzled the funds he'd been donating over the years."

Detective Ramos left to have a final conversation with Oskar. "It seems you solved the case for me after all, old buddy. The case is closed."

Oskar flapped his wings. "Case closed! Case closed!"

DIE ALREADY, WILL YOU?

DONNA CLANCY

"I never realized you'd be more of a pain in the ass dead than alive," Cannon Times said. "Why don't you move on already?"

"But, partner, I'm here to help you."

"Help me right into the funny farm," he yelled. "And right out of a job!" He turned and she was gone.

"I need a drink. People will never believe me. They'll say I've lost it because of feelings of guilt," he said, pouring himself a full glass of whiskey. "Hell, I don't believe it myself."

Two months ago, Cannon's partner, Anita Jean Myles, was killed in a shootout with a drunk husband turned wife-killer. AJ, as she was called, was ambushed as she entered the house and never knew what hit her. She was dead before her body hit the floor. The guy, realizing he had just killed a cop, turned the gun on himself before Cannon could stop him.

The funeral service was well-attended, as AJ was extremely popular. Cannon spoke at the church and as tough as he was, he had a difficult time getting through his eulogy. As he choked up, he heard someone behind him say, "Keep going." Turning around, he saw no one there. At the end of his speech, he could have sworn he felt a hand on his shoulder. Again, no one was near him.

Cannon took some time off after the funeral. He knew he was going to be assigned a new partner and wanted to be mentally ready to give his all to the job again. He was still having flashbacks of that day and was well aware of the fact if he had gone in first he would be dead, not AJ.

While he was home, strange things began to happen. Things moved around in the apartment, and when he would pour a drink and come back to it, the glass would be empty. He didn't remember drinking it, but it was gone just the same.

It all became clear to him the night before he returned to work. He sat in his recliner, staring blankly at the television set when it shut itself off. He sat straight up, looking around the darkened room. It started as a shimmer in the corner and grew larger and larger until AJ was standing next to him.

"Hello, handsome," she said, smiling. "Did you like my entrance?"

She always called him handsome when out of the earshot of others. He sat back, staring. He looked at his glass of whiskey and it was still full.

"No, I'm not drunk," he muttered.

"I bet you never thought you'd see me again, did you?"

"But you're dead," he stated.

"Am I? I don't feel dead."

"I watched you get shot. You're…" he said.

"Free is the word you're looking for. I'm not tied down to a body anymore like you are. I can travel anywhere, walk through anything, listen in on any conversation, and the best part is, I will always be here to help you."

"Like I was for you…" he muttered.

"Stop beating yourself up. You couldn't have done anything to change the outcome. It was my time, plain and simple. You need to stop drinking, pull yourself together, and be the great cop I know you can be."

"This is ridiculous. I'm having a conversation with a dead person. I need some sleep."

That was the start of it. He woke up the next morning thinking he dreamed the whole episode, but he soon found out it wasn't a dream.

Cannon met his new partner, Stanley Putz. It was hard for Cannon not to laugh when they were first introduced, because he couldn't envision himself yelling out Putz every time he needed his partner's help. Stanley looked at him, knowing what was running through his mind, and told him to get all the jokes out as there would be nothing he hadn't heard before. They sat down at the same table at rollcall.

"Putz, that's a hell of a name," AJ's ghost whispered in Cannon's ear.

"Get away from me," he mumbled.

"If you want me to sit somewhere else, just say so," Stanley replied, standing up to move to another table.

"No, you're fine where you are," Cannon insisted. "I wasn't talking to you."

"Okay," he said, sitting back down.

"Pay attention. We had another murder last night in the downtown district," the Captain said, entering the room. "Everything points to it being the same guy who has hit six times before, in that same area."

"Who was it this time?" Cannon asked.

"Marilyn Gotts."

"Daughter of the newspaper magnate?" Cannon asked in disbelief.

"Yes, which makes this a very high-profile case, and the media will be watching our every move," the captain replied. "That's why I want Times and Putz on the case. Go to the penthouse and see what you can find out."

"Solve this one and it could be a major career boost. You always wanted to make detective," AJ said, poised on the end of the table with her dress blue skirt that she was buried in hiked high on her thigh.

"Get lost," Cannon mumbled under his breath.

"You have a problem with my request?" the captain asked, staring at Cannon.

"No, sir, just talking to myself."

"Solving this case and catching this killer is our number one priority. Keep your eyes and ears open and talk to your sources to see if they've heard anything on the streets. Someone knows who this guy is. That's all."

"That's our captain. Pleasant as always," AJ stated as Cannon stood up.

"Yeah, he probably misses your smiling face," he replied, sarcastically.

"Did you say something to me?" Stanley asked.

"No."

"I get it. Talking to yourself again? Do you do that a lot?"

"I just started lately, and frankly, it's none of your business," Cannon replied, heading for the door.

"I knew a guy who talked to himself all the time. He did some of his best thinking out loud. He made detective in less than two years," Stanley said as they walked to the parking lot.

"You see, he doesn't even care you're talking to me. I kind of like this guy," AJ said, floating through the closed door and waiting for them on the other side.

"I drive," Cannon said. "I always drive."

"Even though you suck at it," AJ said from the backseat.

"Fine," Stanley replied, crawling into the passenger seat of the cruiser.

When they pulled up in front of the hotel, Cannon glanced in the rearview mirror and breathed a sigh of relief when he saw AJ was gone. From the outside, you couldn't even tell a murder had occurred on the premises. Once inside, there was a heavy police presence in the lobby.

Near the elevator, Robert Gotts, the victim's father, was arguing with the cop who was blocking his way. He was threatening to sue the police department and anyone else who got in his way. Many years ago, Cannon dated Marilyn Gotts, and he knew Robert and his temper.

"Cannon, tell this officer to let me by," Robert insisted as Cannon walked up to join them.

"You know I can't do that, Robert. The penthouse is a crime scene, and it has to be processed before anyone but the police can enter."

"But I need to see my daughter."

"Tell him he needs to remember her the way she was and not what he would see now," AJ said. "It's pretty gruesome up there. It looks like she put up quite a fight."

"Robert, let the police do their job," he said, ignoring AJ's advice and being straightforward in dealing with the distraught father. "You want us to catch who did this to Marilyn, don't you?"

"Of course I do. She was my only child and poised to take over my newspaper empire."

"Go sit on the couch and I'll have the bartender bring you a drink. Now, I have to go upstairs. Promise me you'll sit there and not cause the officers anymore problems," Cannon said.

"I will, and Cannon, you do know only you can get away with speaking to me the way you have," Robert stated. "Find out who killed my daughter."

The Crime Scene Unit arrived and was loading their equipment into the elevator. Cannon and Stanley caught a ride up to the penthouse with them. The front door to the residence was open. Cannon stopped in the doorway. Blood trailed from the entrance, down the hallway, and into the living room. It looked like she had made a run for it but was dragged back into the interior.

"Are you okay?" AJ asked him. "I know you dated Marilyn a long time ago."

"I'm fine," Cannon muttered, swatting at the air like he was pushing someone away.

"Are you okay?" Stanley asked.

"I'm fine. I wish everyone would stop asking me that," Cannon snapped.

Stanley stared at Cannon, knowing he was the only one who had asked him that since they got there. He was really beginning to wonder if his new partner was stable enough to return to the job after the shooting.

"Please put white boots on before you enter," one of the CSIs requested. "And avoid stepping on any blood as you walk around. There's a lot of it in there and we haven't taken any pictures yet."

Donning booties and gloves and slowly entering the suite, they stood at the end of the hallway that opened into the living room. Marilyn's body was lying in the middle of the room, in a large puddle of blood that had soaked into the Persian carpet underneath her. The CSI agent was right; there was blood everywhere.

"Man, it looks like she put up a hell of a fight," Stanley said, shaking his head.

Cannon returned to the door to look at the door jamb. It had not been jimmied or tampered with in any way, which usually meant the victim knew the person and let them in willingly. As he returned, he scanned the bloody footprints that ran both ways, up and down the hall. It appeared to him that there were three separate sets of prints. He deduced there had to be two intruders and not just one as originally thought.

"The bedroom is a total wreck. It looks like the intruder ransacked everything," the CSI stated.

"Intruders," Cannon corrected. "There's three distinctive sets of prints in the hallway. One had to be Marilyn's as she tried to run. They must have whacked her right inside the door, where the blood splatter begins, and chased her inside. And from the size, they look like men's sneaker prints."

"It looks like she tried to escape to her bedroom, probably to lock herself inside. There are bloody handprints on the inside of the door and a pool of blood that doesn't extend any more than a foot away from the door," Stanley said, returning from the bedroom. "They must have dragged her back out to the living room before she could get the door locked."

Cannon entered the bedroom and looked around. The jewelry boxes had been emptied and left on the floor. The bureaus drawers, the same. The walk-in closet was in disarray, and the intruders had found the hidden safe located in closet. It was still closed and locked.

"Make sure you print the safe. They might have left prints behind trying to open it," Cannon told the CSI agent.

"We know how to do our job," the CSI stated, insulted by Cannon's attitude.

"I'm sorry, man, this one is kind of personal," he replied.

"Wow! Check this out," AJ said from the back of the closet. "It looks like Marilyn was into S&M. Check out the leather corset."

"Marilyn wasn't like that," Cannon stated.

The CSI looked at him and walked away.

"I would have looked good in this one," AJ said, pointing to a bright red leather dress with a matching whip. "Wouldn't you have liked to see me in this?"

"Really? That's all you can think of when there's a dead woman lying in the living room? How good you would have looked in leather?" Cannon asked, leaning into the closet.

"I hope you're not talking to me about looking good in leather," Stanley said from behind him.

"Ah, no. I was thinking out loud again," Cannon said, trying to cover up his anger with AJ. "I wonder if it could have been someone Marilyn was seeing. Look at all this stuff."

"Whips and chains. People are into this stuff, and it can get pretty intense, pretty fast. A lot of people hook up online. Her computer and phone should tell us who she's been seeing lately."

"It's possible this has nothing to do with the other six murders in the area," Cannon stated. "They just wanted it to look that way."

"I'll talk to hotel security and get any surveillance video they have," Stanley offered.

"So, you didn't answer me," AJ said after Stanley left the bedroom.

"What? I'm in the middle of an investigation. You want to play games, go somewhere else to do it," Cannon replied angrily.

"Would you have liked to see me in leather or not?" she asked, posing seductively.

"Go away, woman. I'm busy here," he replied, searching the area around the bedroom door.

"Stick in the mud," AJ mumbled.

"Go away!"

"Okay, but I won't tell you what I overheard listening to the bellboys. They agreed not to tell the cops because they didn't want to get in trouble or lose their jobs," AJ said, starting to shimmer out.

"Get back here. If you know something that will help solve this case, tell me."

"Okay, but first admit you liked the leather."

"Fine, I liked it. Are you happy now? What did you hear?"

"Your Miss Marilyn was sleeping with all the bellboys who worked here. She also had many men coming in and out of her penthouse at all hours of the night. She was quite the swinger. They saw the two guys who were here last night but are afraid to say anything."

"I need to talk to them. Are they still here?" Cannon asked.

"They are."

"Stay here and see if the CSI agents discuss anything I should know about," Cannon requested.

"You still didn't tell me if I would have looked phenomenal in red leather," she yelled as Cannon left the suite.

Four bellboys were sitting in the far corner of the lobby. Cannon headed straight for the group and sat. Two of them started to walk away.

"Sit down, if you want to hold onto your jobs," Cannon instructed.

They hesitated but eventually sat back down.

"I know you don't want to talk to the cops because you're all sleeping with Marilyn Gotts," he started. "I could care less about your sex lives, and I won't tell management if you cooperate with me."

"The two on the far left were with her last night. They passed the killers in the penthouse elevator when they were returning to work," AJ said.

"I told you to stay upstairs," he mumbled.

The bellboys exchanged bewildered glances.

"You, Joey and Nick. You were up with Marilyn last night and passed two guys getting off the penthouse elevator when you were leaving."

"How do you know that?" Joey asked, eyeing Cannon.

"It doesn't matter how I know; I just do. Now, did you recognize the two guys? Have you seen them here before?"

The bellboys remained silent.

"Look, we can do this here or we can take it downtown. Make it easy on yourselves and tell me what I need to know," Cannon stated.

"A lot of men go in and out of Marilyn's place. We don't know most of them," Joey said. "Those two guys last night didn't look like Marilyn's type."

"She had a type?"

"Yea, skinny guys, mostly nerds, that she could boss around," Nick replied.

"These guys all fit that description," AJ said, laughing.

"Shut up, will you?" Cannon said to AJ, ignoring the weird stares he was receiving. "And these two guys were different?"

"Yeah, they were both built like brick shithouses. They were looking right at us as the elevator doors opened, but as soon as they saw us standing there, they looked down and tried to hide their faces."

"It looked like they knew where the security cameras were in the hall because they avoided looking in their direction," Joey added. "They stood at Marilyn's door and didn't knock until we entered the elevator and the door started to close. And then we heard them knock."

"I'd like you to go with one of the officers to the station and work with a sketch artist," Cannon requested.

"Do you think those two guys killed Marilyn? Are we in some kind of danger because we saw them?" Joey asked.

"Ask them about the videos?" AJ said, blowing in Joey's ear and laughing while he batted at the air around his head.

"Grow up," Cannon said to AJ, glaring at her.

"Don't be such a grouch. I'm just having a little fun," AJ replied. "Ask them about the videos."

"Did Marilyn video tape your sessions?"

"Again, how did you know that?"

"I used to date her many years ago and I know what she liked," Cannon said, not wanting to admit he was getting his information from a dead cop.

"She recorded everything."

"I'll be right back," AJ said, disappearing through the ceiling.

"You mean everything in the bedroom?" Cannon asked.

"No, I mean everything in the penthouse. Marilyn catered to some big-time politicians and important people. She wanted to protect herself from retaliation. Somewhere in her suite is a vast library of recorded hook-ups."

"Sounds like she turned high society call girl," Cannon muttered.

"She always said something would happen to her because of who she serviced. We never paid her, we were just her playthings," Joey admitted. "And we were the ones who were paid, not the other way around. We didn't mind visiting her as the money was good. It definitely helped with our college bills."

"But if our manager finds out, we'll lose our jobs," Nick added.

"As far as I'm concerned you saw the suspects in the lobby. You two need to go to the station and sit with the sketch artist. I won't tell your boss about any of your meetings with Marilyn, just stay away from the penthouse for a while," Cannon said.

"Wait until you see what I found," AJ stated, coming out of the wall. "Go back up to the suite so I can show you."

Cannon headed for the elevator. He turned just in time to see AJ grab one of the bellboys on the butt. Nick turned, but no one was there.

"AJ! Upstairs, now!" Cannon ordered, realizing too late that he had said her name out loud and the other cops around the lobby heard it. "Oh, crap."

He fumed in the elevator and then entered the suite, mad at the position he was now in because of his dead partner. Word would get back to the station and then to the captain, who would order him to psychological testing.

Why didn't I just tell her to go away the first time she showed up? Now, my job is on the line.

"Psst, Cannon, over here," AJ said.

"Why are you whispering? No one else can hear you," he muttered under his breath.

"You never know," AJ countered. "I'm going to hand you your detective shield."

"What the hell are you talking about?"

"I told you. I can go through walls. I found Marilyn's secret stash of videos and there is a camera still recording the hallway facing the front door."

"Don't screw around. Where is it?" Cannon demanded.

The others were watching him talk to himself. Across the room, Stanley was suddenly having serious doubts about his new partner's stability. He walked over to join Cannon and ask him what was going on.

"Pretend to be looking around. Don't go straight to the spot where the camera is or you'll have trouble explaining how you knew exactly where it was located," AJ stated.

"How can I go to it if you won't tell me where it is?" Cannon asked angrily, totally ignoring the fact that all eyes were on him.

"Hey, Cannon, do you need a break? I know you dated Marilyn and maybe this is getting to you after just losing your partner," Stanley asked.

"I'm fine. You wouldn't understand," he replied, looking back at everyone who was staring at him. "None of you would understand."

Cannon perused the wall opposite the front door. Stanley walked toward the same wall. He suddenly fell, as if someone had tripped him.

"What the hell?" Stanley asked, eyes wide.

"He was heading directly for the spot where the camera is hidden," AJ said. "I didn't want him to find it. I want you to find it."

"So, you tripped the poor guy? Really?"

"A girl's got to do what a girl's got to do to help her man."

"I'm not your man," Cannon mumbled, going to help his partner.

"I don't know what happened. It felt like someone tripped me but— Just clumsy I guess."

"The bellboy told me Marilyn recorded everything. This wall would be a great spot to place a camera to catch anyone who entered the suite. Let's check it out," Cannon suggested, feeling bad for what his dead partner had done to his new, living partner.

"What are you doing? I handed you this case on a silver platter and you are going to share the credit with someone named Putz? Really? It will be the last time I try to help you make detective."

"He's my new partner whether you like it or not," Cannon said.

Angry, AJ rushed into the wall. All the pictures flew off and fell to the floor with a crash, along with a large porcelain vase that was sitting on a table. Six people witnessed what happened and stood there with their mouths open. No one spoke a word.

"I'll explain it to you later," Cannon told Stanley, under his breath.

"No, you won't," AJ said, sticking her head out of the wall.

"Oh, yes, I will," he countered.

"Whatever…" Stanley replied.

"I think Cannon Times has totally lost it," one of the CSI's whispered to another.

"Are you going to put this in the report?" the other CSI asked.

"We have to. I feel bad for Putz. He got stuck with a real lulu."

"Let's look for cameras," Cannon said, trying to ignore what was being whispered behind his back.

Stanley was the first to find a camera. It was hidden behind a statue of a nude male, poised on the top of a bookcase, and pointing into the living room. Seconds later, Cannon found a small hole in the wall next to the same bookcase, facing the front door.

"There's another camera hole here," Cannon said. "We need to see if the bookcase moves. There's got to be a way to get to the camera hidden behind the wall."

"Of course it moves," AJ said, appearing out of nowhere.

"Of course it moves? Awfully sure of yourself, aren't you?" Stanley asked, still searching for cameras.

"The Putz man heard me?" AJ asked. "I'll be damned."

"Look for a lever or something to open the bookcase," Cannon said, running his fingers along the edge of the wood.

"Hey, Cannon, how'd you know about the cameras?" Stanley asked. "She told you, didn't she?"

Cannon stopped what he was doing.

"She who?"

"AJ, I've seen pictures of her. I saw her right before she rushed into the wall and disappeared. And I just heard her a few seconds ago."

"AJ?"

"Yeah. Don't play stupid. Your dead partner. I wasn't sure she was haunting you, but I am now," Stanley answered. "I opened up my abilities and there she was."

"Keep it down, will you? I don't need everybody and their brother knowing I'm getting help from a ghost," Cannon replied.

"You want to open that bookcase? Grab the statue's penis," AJ announced. "It's the lever you're looking for. Push it down."

"I'm not grabbing any penis," Cannon said.

"Oh, for cripes sake, Cannon, just grab the penis. Do you want to solve this case or not?" AJ demanded.

Putz stood there, laughing.

"Come on, Cannon. Grab the penis," Stanley teased his partner.

"Damn, he can hear me," AJ stated. "Putz, you do it."

"This is Cannon's case, not mine," Stanley said, "I'm the newbie, remember?"

"You two are such losers," AJ said, trying to grip the statue's appendage but her hand passed right through it.

Putz stepped in front of Cannon and pushed down on the penis.

The bookcase silently swung open to reveal a small room lined with shelves that held labeled recordings of Marilyn's clients. The camera in question had stopped running. On the far wall were eight monitors, one for each camera concealed around the suite.

"Wow!" one of the CSIs said. "This is amazing. Look at some of the names on those tapes. Politicians, CEOs, and even some cops."

"It seems Marilyn had a very high class of clientele," Putz stated.

"I can't believe I dated her and never even had an inkling of this wild side she had," Cannon replied. "Her father is not going to want this to go public."

"In order to solve the murder, it will have to be made public," AJ replied. "Why don't you view the tape in the camera facing the front door? It should tell you all you need to know."

Cannon took the cassette out of the camera, inserted it into the VCR on the table next to the monitor, and hit rewind. Five minutes in, they saw two men enter the suite and Marilyn trying to run from them. She screamed, but nobody heard her. They hit the back of her head with a bat as she ran for the bedroom, but she kept going, trying to get the door closed behind her.

The two men were too strong, forced the door open, and dragged her back into the living room where they finished the job. They checked the body several times to make sure she was dead.

"It's a little messier than the Senator wanted, but she's dead and won't be blackmailing him anymore," one of them said, standing over the body.

"Now he'll have the election in the bag," the other one replied. "And I don't know about you, but I can sure use the money he paid us."

"Let's get out of here before those bellboys return. We'll call the Senator from the car to tell him the job is done."

"I recognize those two," a CSI said from behind them. "They're bodyguards for Senator Biggins."

"You process the room. We're going to take the tape to the station to get arrest warrants issued for these two and the Senator," Cannon stated.

They took the elevator down to the lobby. Marilyn's father was still there. Cannon took him aside and told them what they found. He wasn't happy but he wanted to get the people responsible for his daughter's death regardless of what came out in the news. Cannon promised to stay in touch.

Later that afternoon, the Senator and his two bodyguards were arrested at a rally for his reelection. He threatened lawsuits against the police and everyone involved in his arrest in front of the media, claiming they had no evidence he was involved with the murder.

Later that night, Cannon was home, sitting in his usual spot, drinking his nightly glass of whiskey.

"You don't need that stuff, you know," AJ lectured, walking through the TV.

"You still here?" he mumbled.

"Yea, but not for long."

"I thought you were never leaving?"

"I wasn't, but Putz is a good man, in spite of his stupid name. You'll be okay with him as your partner, if you lay off the booze. And I was listening at the station. They were talking about putting you up for detective for solving the Gotts case."

"I'm sorry, AJ. I wasn't there for you," Cannon said, taking a slug of whiskey.

"In more ways than one," she replied.

"What are you talking about?"

"I loved you, but you never saw it."

"I saw it, but I was selfish, and my stupid career came first."

"I figured as much. You have your career now. Stop drinking and make the most of your life."

"I'm drinking because I lost you," he mumbled.

"You haven't lost me."

"I don't deserve you watching over me. Move on like you're supposed to."

"Move on? Never! I'm going to be side stage at the Adele concert when I leave here. I'll have the best seat in the house and then I'm going to the after party. I can go anywhere now, remember? It's time to live it up, even if I'm dead."

"AJ, I did love you."

"Better late than never, handsome," she said, vanishing into the wall.

THREE COUSINS
WALKED INTO A BAR

SUSAN LOVE BROWN

Blitzen Christmas, Epiphany Christmas, and I (Holly Noelle Christmas) walked into the Old Philly Tavern off Rittenhouse Square on the evening of the winter solstice to celebrate Blitzen's birthday, but it was not an auspicious occasion. The evening began under a cloud—not the ones hanging over the city of Philadelphia threatening snow, but the one clouding Blitzen's mind.

The jewelry store where she worked as both a designer and a salesperson had been robbed that afternoon. The sun had started to abandon the day, anticipating the longest night of the year, and in the course of its cessation, two people walked in, masks over their faces, dressed all in black, hoisting mean-looking guns in front of them. One held the two salespeople—Blitzen and her colleague Joe—and three customers at bay, while the other one grabbed all the jewelry in sight and put it into a rather stylish hobo bag, moving from necklaces and bracelets to rings, and then to brooches, mostly one-of-a-kind holiday pieces designed by Blitzen. Among them was one she had designed especially for our grandmother, Merry Christmas, our beloved family matriarch.

Blitzen was so distraught she yelled out, "Don't take that. It's for my grandmother!"

"Shut up!" the man yelled back, tossing the pin into his bag. Then, as he raised his gun threateningly at Blitzen, the customer standing nearby grabbed his arm, and he turned and shot him almost reflexively.

Blitzen screamed, as did the other two customers. Joe ran to the downed customer, and the two thieves ran out the door as sirens blared and lights flashed. Joe had hit the silent alarm.

After being interrogated by police on the scene, Blitzen made her way to my condo at 20th and Walnut, where Epiphany and I were waiting.

Blitzen arrived at my door shaken, her black wool coat covered in melting snowflakes, which didn't bode well for our planned night on the town.

"You're late!" Epiphany said, never one to mince words.

"We were robbed!" Blitzen cried, collapsing on my couch without even taking off her coat. She blurted out what had happened in detail, as if telling the whole story would purge the shock from her system. "They shot the man who tried to keep him from shooting me. I have a headache. Do you have any aspirin? I can't believe this happened on my birthday."

I got her the aspirin. "Maybe we can just stay here and celebrate," I said.

"Oh, no," Epiphany said. "I didn't drive all the way in from Ardmore to sit around this homage to Christmas commercialism."

Epiphany was taking a dig at my decorations: my six-foot tree, thick with extravagant ornaments and flashing LED lights with a teddy bear on top, my collection of Santa Clauses scattered throughout, and the multi-colored lights strung over mirrors and doorways. The place positively glowed. It was not like Epiphany's restrained use of white lights to outline the contours of her house—the old Christmas family house in Ardmore off County Line Road taken over by her father, and now by her. Normally, those would be fighting words, since Epiphany and I had had a longstanding combativeness since we were children. But I chose to ignore Epiphany in deference to Blitzen and her birthday.

"I know a nice, quiet tavern just on the other side of Rittenhouse Square where we can go," I said.

"In this impending snowstorm?" Epi said, looking down at her four-inch heels sitting under my coffee table. This evening it was the Jimmy Choos instead of the Louboutins. A sensible person would have worn boots.

"I'll call an Uber."

And so, we all bundled into a car driven by a guy named Tony, who took us to Saul's Old Philly Tavern, tucked away on a street that still had cobblestones. Its neon window sign belied the atmosphere that Saul had created inside, which sought to replicate a colonial vibe, more something Hollywood would have created than a revolutionary barkeep. Nevertheless, it was a neighborhood place where we could unload our troubles, and it wasn't too far from Mom-Mom's house near Rittenhouse Square.

Saul had cleverly provided an area for coats and other weather-related paraphernalia, so when the three of us walked into the tavern proper, heads turned.

My cousin Blitzen had an explosion of corkscrew curls in brown and golden hues that emphasized the beautiful features of her smooth-as-silk and slightly round, brown face with naturally long lashes. Unlike my retro, very short Afro and Epi's braids, she was the essence of a young woman making her way in the world in which variety was the current trend.

Mom-Mom had told us stories about straightening combs on the stove, hot grease and her tender-headedness, the first Afros (called Naturals) that emerged in the Sixties at the same time that white kids rebelled with long straight hair for girls and very long hair for boys. This so-called age of hair led to Geri curls, and more until multi-colored, artificial hair even made the scene. But Blitzen was adorable, and beneath her mop of curls, she dressed in a black jersey sheath with pearls and stylish boots, projecting an air of sophistication beyond her now 21 years but totally appropriate for the upscale jewelry store on Walnut Street.

My cousin Epi had braids growing out of her scalp, and she sculpted them into interesting designs, depending on what she was wearing. Tonight, she had swept them up in a beehive, and she wore earmuffs and a Burberry scarf around her neck to avoid disrupting the hairdo. She wore red leather pants, her only homage to the holiday, a matching cashmere sweater, and a camel coat tied at the waist with a belt. And the Jimmy Choos, which signified her winter impracticality and obsession with shoes.

As for me, Holly Noelle Christmas, I wore my hair natural and as short as I could get it without being bald, plus leggings covered with tiny Christmas trees, a bright red turtleneck with a string of Christmas lights around my neck, and a big, fat bubble coat that Epiphany looked askance at, plus thick, furry boots.

Yes, all heads turned when we walked into the Old City Tavern. Then they turned away again and went back to their food and drinks.

Saul, the owner and nascent history buff of all things colonial Philadelphia, was tending bar, while Maggie Merchant collected trays of drinks, swishing her barmaid skirt as she moved toward the customers seated at the wooden tables and booths. Bows of artificial greenery festooned with white lights in the shape of candles hung around the perimeter, and there was a colorful tree at one end of the bar.

A couple of young brothers, presumably old enough to drink, had settled at the bar and paid attention as Saul greeted us cousins.

"Well, if it isn't the Holly Christmas," Saul said.

"Saul, this my cousin Blitzen. It's her twenty-first birthday today."

One of the brothers spun around on his bar stool to face them. "And who are you two, Dasher and Dancer?" he snorted, laughing at his own cleverness.

"No," Epi said. "Prancer and Vixen. She doesn't dash, and I don't dance."

The other brother guffawed and slapped his thigh. "Good come back."

"I bet yo mama wears combat boots," the first brother said in retaliation. I hadn't heard that one since elementary school.

Epi rolled her eyes. As sophisticated and above it all as she purported to be, and how beneath her it was, she considered playing the dozens with this guy. She reverted true to form with a rejoinder, "And your daddy licks them."

"Your mama's so dumb, she tried to make an appointment for a checkup with Dr. Dre," the brother said.

"You mama's so dumb, she kept it," Epi retorted.

The second brother guffawed again, and people at the tables had started paying attention to us again.

"Cool it!" I said to Epi. "Let's get a table."

Blitzen just stood there. "Really lame ranking," she commented.

Epi shape-shifted back into her old, sophisticated self, and we settled at a table for four in the middle of the room.

The Old Philly Tavern menu attempted to fuse contemporary Philly food like cheesesteaks, hoagies, soft pretzels and other favorites with imagined colonial fare and a few oddities. The result was what the food critic at my paper, *The Broad Street Broadsheet*, called Con-Fusion.

I ordered a Philly cheese steak. "Tell me you don't put Cheez-Wiz on it," I said to Maggie, the ersatz barmaid.

"No, indeed. Benjamin Franklin over there wouldn't hear of it," she said, pointing to Saul, who effected the esteemed scientist and publisher with a broad brimmed hat and wire spectacles, but looked more like the guy on a box of Quaker Oats.

"What do you recommend," Epiphany asked, back to her snooty ways.

"Anything that doesn't crawl," Maggie replied. She had Epi's number.

"All right. Cheese grits and shrimp." That was one of the oddities.

Blitzen's bad experience hadn't curbed her appetite. "I'll have the Franklin apple-a-day salad, a side of scrapple, and a black-and-white milkshake."

Both Epi and I failed to hold back our grimaces. Nevertheless, it looked like Blitzen was rebounding from her earlier mood.

"How about drinks?" Maggie asked.

"Champagne all around," Epi piped in. "It's our cousin's birthday, and we want to toast. Do you have Perrier Jouet?"

"No, I'm afraid not. But I'll see what I can find with bubbles."

"Well, in the meantime, I'll have a glass of your house white," Epi said.

"Bring us a whole bottle," I said. "Does white wine go with scrapple?"

Maggie didn't bother to answer. She scrawled the order down and left.

"So, how does it feel to be twenty-one?" Epiphany asked.

"Like I was robbed," Blitzen said, dashing all hopes of celebration and revelry. "That pin I made for Mom-Mom was one of a kind, her name in silver and gold and tiny diamonds."

"How could you afford that?" Epi asked.

"I made it with leftover materials and stuff I found from searching pawn shops and other places," Blitzen said. Blitzen was the one who always showed up at the Christmas Christmas dinner with cute trinkets for the little cousins like bracelets of jingle bells or cute miniature tree ornaments.

"Do you have any clues about who they were?" I asked. "Do you think they cased the joint?"

"Oh my god," Epi said. "You sound like a bad cop show. Must be all that hanging around those detectives."

"What detectives?" Blitzen asked.

"Holly has become enamored of a homicide detective named Ross whom she met when she and Mom-Mom helped solve that murder at The Fifth Season a couple of years ago."

"You solved a murder?" Blitzen said, suddenly rising out of her slouch.

"Mom-Mom and I *helped* solve a murder," I said. "But you know all about that, Blitzen. Don't you remember?"

"I guess," Blitzen said.

"Anyway, these homicide detectives appeared again on another case Holly and Mom-Mom got involved in, and now they seem to show up at a drop of the hat. Anyway, ever since then Holly fancies herself a crime reporter for *The Broad Street Broadsheet* in addition to being a cultural critic."

"I do not!" I snapped at Epi. "I just happen to be around when those things happen."

"Be careful, Blitzen, not to follow in her footsteps," Epi warned. "There aren't enough cute homicide detectives to go around."

Before Blitzen could reply, a strong, cold breeze blew through the room, and Epi shrank down into her seat.

"What's wrong?" I asked.

"One of my students just walked in," she said in a whisper. Epi was an assistant professor at a liberal arts college out in Radnor, which she never let me forget, always dissing my MFA in theatre as less than her doctorate in literature.

I spied a young man enter the tavern with an attractive young woman on his arm. He had on one of those black hats that reminded me of the Cossack dancers in The Nutcracker Suite and very red cheeks. She had black hair halfway down her back, wore a long-sleeved royal blue dress, had a bag slung over her shoulder, and glittered with a panoply of jewelry. He acknowledged Saul with a salute, and the second brother at the bar looked the woman up and down and then turned back to the drink he was nursing. The first brother said, "Boy, you'll let anybody in here, Saul."

"Don't worry," the second brother said. "You'll bounce."

"Why, Dr. Christmas," the young man said, approaching our table. "I'm surprised to see you here."

Epi recovered her composure. "Good evening, *Mr*. Cranston."

"This is my date, Evvie," *Mr*. Cranston said.

Epi nodded politely, but I could see she was assessing the young woman's appearance. We'd hear all about it later, I assumed. Blitzen feigned a smile and then lowered her gaze to the table.

"Evvie, this is my English teacher, who seems to think I'll never amount to anything because I never diagrammed a sentence."

"She says the same thing about me," I interjected, just to annoy Epiphany.

Just then, Blitzen jumped up and left the table. After consulting with Maggie, she bounded down the stairs toward the ladies' room.

"Hello, I'm Epi's cousin, Holly Christmas. Would you like to join us?"

"Actually, I would have asked," Epiphany said, glaring daggers at me, "but this is a private celebration for my cousin."

"We wouldn't want to intrude, Dr. Christmas," *Mr.* Cranston said. "We'll just grab a table over there. Nice to meet you."

"Have fun," I said, waving my fingers as he ushered away his date, Evvie-no-last-name.

Epi glared at me. "Thanks a lot, Cuz."

"Any time," I said.

Maggie arrived with two bottles, one in a bucket of ice and one that she twisted and uncorked with expert precision and poured into three champagne flutes, which she sat before us.

"Your orders will be up soon." She put the ice bucket on the table, and off she went to make her rounds.

Epi leaned in. "You really piss me off sometimes, Holly, and I know you do it on purpose."

I smiled in saintly fashion. "Really? I never mean to."

"Where is Blitzen? She's been down there quite a while."

"Do you want me to go down and fetch her?" I asked.

"No!" she snapped.

Eventually, as the bubbles evanesced from our champagne, Blitzen reappeared.

"We should go," she said. "We should go *now*."

"Not a chance. Sit down," Epi said. "Pick up your champagne. We're toasting your twenty-first birthday."

"You don't understand," Blitzen said.

"What?" I asked.

Just then, the already dim lights receded still more, and Maggie and Saul appeared with a small cake festooned with twenty-one candles, Saul singing out in his loud voice the Happy Birthday song. Everyone joined in—the two brothers at the bar, Epi's student and his date, and a few customers.

Everyone applauded at the end of the chorus, and we waited expectantly for Blitzen to blow out the candles. Just as she did, searing blue and white lights began flashing outside the window.

"They're here," Blitzen said, her eyes wide.

A stream of uniformed police officers flowed in until the room was surrounded in dark blue, badges shining in the fake candle lights.

"Just keep calm, Everyone," one of them said. "And please stay right where you are."

But *Mr.* Cranston stood straight up with a scowl, while Evvie no-last-name gawked. The two brothers twisted around to face the room, and loud murmurs rose. Maggie and Saul were trapped in the middle of the tavern. Maggie rested her weight on one hip. Saul looked confused and removed his Franklinesque spectacles.

Everyone paused as two men walked in, one in a camel wool and cashmere overcoat and scarf that matched his handsome face, and the other man in a worn dark overcoat and faded red knit hat that matched his puffy cheeks, both with badges affixed to their outer garments.

"Well, if it isn't Detective Ross and Detective Clemente," Epi exclaimed, looking directly at me. "What did I tell you?" She directed this at Blitzen.

They walked over to our table.

"Good evening, ladies," Detective Clemente said, pulling off his knit hat and showering us with melting snowflakes.

"What are you two doing here?" I asked.

"The jewelry heist on Walnut this afternoon. The bystander died an hour ago. We got a 9-1-1 call about the perpetrator being here." Detective Ross explained. "Which one of you called?"

None of us owned up. Then Blitzen spoke. "It's that couple in the corner. Woman in the blue dress with the Merry Christmas pin."

Detective Clemente scanned the room until he found the couple. *Mr.* Cranston was still standing, calling attention to himself.

"You two come with us please," Detective Clemente said, indicating *Mr.* Cranston and Evvie no-last-name.

"Why? What's this all about?" *Mr.* Cranston asked, a uniformed officer taking him by the arm, which he shook off.

"Cuff them," Clemente ordered.

The uniformed officer did so, starting with Evvie's date and then her. A second uniformed officer joined him.

"I'm just his date," Evvie-no-last-name said as the officer walked her toward the door. "I haven't done anything."

"They're just taking you downtown for questioning," brother two shouted out as they passed by, followed by the stream of uniformed officers.

"Hey, man, we're already downtown," brother one said.

"They're bringing them in," brother two said.

"They're *taking* them in. You bring from far to near. You take from near to far." brother one explained.

"It's not that far," Saul piped in.

"Gentlemen, we have an English professor here who can settle this if you wish," I said.

"Do *not* drag me into this inanity, Holly," Epi snarled.

"Do you know how to diagram sentences?" I asked brother one.

Epi rolled her eyes again, as she was wont to do around me.

Once again a cold breeze blew through the tavern and in walked someone else we didn't expect.

"Happy Solstice, all," she said. It was our grandmother, Merry Christmas.

"Mom-Mom!" Blitzen shrieked and found her way over to Mom-Mom's arms, hanging on for dear life and starting to cry.

"Will someone please explain what's going on?" Saul asked. "Nice to see you, Mrs. Christmas."

"First, champagne all around," Mom-Mom said. "My treat to the entire room. It's my granddaughter's twenty-first birthday," Mom-Mom said, kissing Blitzen on the cheek and then handing Saul her credit card.

A cheer went up in the Old Philly Tavern, and people started shouting out thank-yous and hoisting their drinks in Mom-Mom's direction.

Mom-Mom was a spry seventy-six, decked out in her red furry coat, leggings, and boots, her Christmas scarf wrapped around her white hair and tied beneath her chin. She coaxed Blitzen to sit and then took the fourth chair at our table. Maggie gave us another glass, and Mom-Mom poured her own champagne and topped off ours.

As Maggie made the rounds, bottles and flutes in hand, Saul reluctantly opened a bottle for the two brothers at the bar.

Then Mom-Mom noticed the homicide detectives.

"Won't you join us, detectives?" Mom-Mom said. "Pull up a couple of chairs."

"Sorry, Mrs. Christmas, we're on duty," Detective Ross said. "Let's go, Clemente."

And off they went into the night, Laurel and Hardy in black and white.

Mom-Mom then stood, raising her glass. "To my granddaughter, Blitzen Christmas, on her twenty-first birthday, for her bravery and creativity with love."

Shouts of "here-here" rang out.

"It's the solstice, you know," brother one said, raising his glass and downing the liquid in one gulp and turning to the bar for more.

"You were born on a pagan holiday," brother two said to Blitzen.

"Can it. Let her enjoy her celebration," Saul warned. "You guys are too sloshed to drive home."

"That's why we walked," they said in unison. Then they both broke into laughter.

Mom-Mom then told us that Blitzen had called her and told her that a stolen piece of jewelry—namely, the piece she had designed for Mom-Mom—was worn by a woman who came in with Epiphany's student.

"It wasn't just that," Blitzen said. "That bag she was carrying—"

"The designer hobo bag?" Epi asked. Of course, she had noticed.

"Yes!" Blitzen exclaimed. "That was the bag that they put the stolen jewelry in. I didn't make the connection that the second thief—the one holding the gun on us while the other one collected the stuff—was a woman."

"Oh my god, Blitzen!" I shrieked. "You solved the case!"

"I did?"

"Yes, you did," I said.

"For her own safety I told her to wait in the rest room until the police arrived," Mom-Mom said.

"I tried, but I felt bad about abandoning you two. You didn't know what was going on. I was afraid you might say something or do something that would get you into trouble," Blitzen said. "When I came back and tried to get you to leave you wouldn't listen. Luckily, the police came in shortly thereafter.

"I called 9-1-1, explained the situation, and they referred me to some sergeant. After that, I thought I'd better get over here to make sure you three were all right," Mom-Mom said.

"Why didn't you ask us what to do, Blitzen?" I said.

"Yes, we were right here," Epi said with a frown.

"You two never agree on anything," Blitzen said. "I was afraid to say anything, in case you two started arguing, set one of them off, and we all got slaughtered."

"Honestly, Blitzen, you have a vivid imagination," I said. "I don't think they were armed."

"She could have had anything in that hobo bag," Blitzen said.

"Mr. Cranston is no crazed killer," Epi said. "You should have said something."

Mom-Mom just smiled. Blitzen was absolutely correct. Epi and I would have raised such a ruckus that the guilty parties would have probably just upped and fled.

"So, you didn't call Ross and Clemente, Mom-Mom?" I asked.

"No, I didn't. I don't know why they ended up here."

"I suspect that wherever Holly goes, Ross isn't far behind," Epiphany said with a smug smile.

"Whatever do you mean by that?" I asked.

"See, they're at it again. Who are Ross and Clemente again?" Blitzen wanted to know.

"Two homicide detectives that Holly and I ran into a couple of years ago in unfortunate circumstances," Mom-Mom said. "We'll explain it all later. In the meantime, let's kill this bottle of champagne, eat, and then we can go over to my house."

I tore into my Philly cheese steak, Epi scarfed down her cheese grits and shrimp, and Blitzen killed her salad, gobbled down her scrapple, and practically inhaled her black-and-white milkshake.

After we had trudged through the accumulated snow, including Epiphany in her four-inch heels, and we were all warm and cozy in front of a crackling fire in Mom-Mom's living room, we joined Mom-Mom in a round of Amaretto sours. Mom-Mom spilled the beans about Detective Ross and his undercover attentions to me, and how we kept running into him and Clemente when murder occurred at the cultural events I covered for *The Broad Street Broadsheet*.

Blitzen took it all in and then fell asleep, her head on Mom-Mom's lap like she used to do when she was a little girl.

The phone rang and Mom-Mom answered.

"Hello, Detective Clemente." She paused, listening. "Wonderful. Why don't you both come over for a nightcap?"

After she hung up, she said. "Detective Clemente wanted us to know that they've made arrests in the jewelry heist case."

"And of course you invited them over." Epi rolled her eyes, obviously thinking that Mom-Mom always seemed to facilitate the occasions upon which Detective Ross and I were in the same room. She didn't dare say it, but *I* knew that *she* knew that *I* knew exactly the same thing.

"Was the murderer *Mr*. Cranston or Evvie?" I asked Mom-Mom.

She shrugged. "I'll let the detectives explain." She woke Blitzen and helped her sit up. Blitzen shook her head full of curls as if clearing her brain, already marinating in scrapple and alcohol.

"We're expecting company," Mom-Mom told her.

"I've got to pee."

"Then do it," Epiphany said. "You don't have to announce it like it's some great event."

"Leave her alone," I said. "You're such a bully sometimes."

"This is not exactly how I expected the evening to go," Epi said. "Luckily, I don't have any classes. The semester is over. I was ready for some fun."

"Instead, you got intrigue," Mom-Mom said.

Mom-Mom went to the kitchen to make coffee and tea, being ecumenical where caffeine and even decaf were concerned. It wasn't even midnight yet.

A few minutes later, Mom-Mom returned and set a coffee and tea service on the large table in the middle of the seating area.

Then the doorbell rang.

"Stay put," Mom-Mom said, eyeing me especially. "I'll get it."

And so, she did. After divesting themselves of hats and coats and scarves in the vestibule, in walked the two detectives, looking cold and weary.

Clemente plopped down in the chair next to the fireplace and began rubbing his hands together, as if to fight off frostbite. Ross took the chair between me and Epiphany. No man's territory.

Without asking, Mom-Mom poured them each a mug of black coffee. Clemente wrapped his hands around it. Ross nodded his thanks and did the same.

"Are you going to tell us what happened?" Blitzen blurted. "Who did it, Cranston or Evvie?"

Ross deferred to Clemente.

Clemente said. "Turns out that the young woman, Evvie, has a boyfriend, with whom she decided to rob the store. I'm afraid Cranston dropped her and went home dejected."

"On, no!" Epi cried. "If he's in my class next semester, I'm going to have to deal with broken heart syndrome."

"What's that?" Detective Ross asked.

"When students want deadlines extended because of some emotional trauma brought on by a breakup."

"Well, maybe it will become an incentive to learn how to diagram sentences," I said.

"No one teaches that anymore, not even the composition and rhetoric teachers. I must have blurted it out in frustration over a paper or something," Epi pouted.

"I'm devastated that the bystander didn't make it," Blitzen uttered, on the verge of tears again. "He was trying to protect me and Joe." She hung her head, and tears started flowing.

Mom-Mom gathered Blitzen in her arms again.

"Turns out that the bystander was part of the gang. He was carrying out surveillance and gave the go-ahead to the others," Ross said. "Also, he instructed the two who robbed your store to maintain surveillance of Ms. Christmas here, because she could identify him. He was not counting on dying by the wobbly hand of one of his own gang."

"What surveillance?" Epi asked. "Not my student, Mr. Cranston."

"No," Ross said. "Those two guys who were at the bar."

"Those buffoons?" I said, incredulously.

"The same. We noticed they were following you when you and your grandmother walked home."

"You were keeping us under surveillance?"

"Yes," Clemente said. "We were sitting in our car after we left the building, just waiting for you four to emerge. They followed you out but kept their distance. They weren't as drunk as they pretended. Anyway, we notified the precinct, but they'll probably walk, since they didn't really break any laws.

"So, they were part of the gang that planned the heist," Epi said.

"No," said Ross. "They were hired separately by Evvie's accomplice. Her date with Cranston was a way to keep an eye on them. She just made the mistake of carrying that bag and wearing that pin."

"Why didn't you tell us?" Epi wanted to know.

"Because we needed you to act normally," Ross said. "And by the way...."

He handed Blitzen the pin she had designed for Mom-Mom.

"Didn't you need this for evidence?" she asked, pinning it onto Mom-Mom's turtleneck.

"We found some of the stolen jewelry in the hobo bag that Evvie was carrying, so there's plenty of evidence," Detective Ross said.

"You Christmases are a weird lot," Clemente said, raising his cup. "Crime seems to follow you around at this time of year."

We laughed and took it as a compliment.

"Yes," Ross concurred. "There's no telling what can happen when three Christmases walk into a bar."

ROMEO, ROMEO, WHEREFORE ART THOU, ROMEO?

ED RIDGLEY

"Where are you heading?" Frederick said.

"Virginia Beach," Romeo replied.

"I'm heading to Richmond."

"I can find a ride from there."

"Maybe I'll go to the beach, too. Hop in."

"I appreciate it."

"What brings you to the beach?"

"The Virginia Sports Hall of Fame. I want to visit as many Halls of Fame as I can before I die."

"How many have you visited so far?"

"This will be my first."

"A good start then."

"Hold on, I'm getting a call," Romeo said.

"Sure," Frederick said.

"What did the cops say? The detectives? Jeez, how many? No, I didn't do it. Okay, I'll call you back when I get a burner phone. It wasn't me. Bye."

"Trouble afoot?"

"It was me."

"What did you do?"

"I forgot to say my name. I'm Romeo."

"Really? Romeo?"

"Yes, really."

"Sounds made up."

"It's my street name."

"Why did you pick Romeo?"

"I love to steal."

"Don't hold back now."

"I'm not. I have no shame about it. It's an addiction, really. I don't like the actual having gotten the thing, it's more about the getting."

"Enoy the journey, not the destination?"

"Yes, something like that. What's your name, by the way?"

"Frederick. My dad was from Frederick County. Said it was the best place on Earth."

"He still around?"

"No, he left us a few years back. Died in his sleep. Went to sleep thinking of Frederick as Heaven on Earth and woke up in the next best place. He was fond of saying that."

"Sounds like a great guy," Romeo said.

"He was," Frederick said.

"My dad taught me how to be a pick pocket."

"I suppose that's a worthwhile skill."

"It'll do in a pinch, for sure, but it's too risky for me. I prefer the stealer's way of life. If I ever write a book, I'm going to call it *The Stealer's Way*."

"Good title."

"Subtitle will be *How I Found Peace Through Thievery*, or something like that."

"You've thought about this a lot, I see."

"I've started on the first chapter."

"I'd love to read it when you finish it."

"It's still a work in progress. What did your dad do?"

"A bar owner. The man never met a stranger."

"My dad might have been one of his patrons."

"Your dad fond of the drink?"

"Called it liquid courage."

"Yep, I heard my dad say that many times when fights broke out at the bar."

"There's another thing I think about a lot."

"What's that?"

"There should be a Criminals Hall of Fame."

"There used to be one at Niagara Falls but it's closed now. It was a wax museum."

"What do you do with wax figures after that?" Romeo asked.

"That's a good question. Probably would make a good topic of conversation at someone's house," Frederick said.

"Can we stop at the next exit so I can get a burner phone?"

"Sure, but it just occurred to me that I'm harboring a fugitive. What did you steal?"

"I stole it for another guy. He was too close to the situation and would have been nabbed right away. I really should have turned it down. My heart was never really in it. Seems his wasn't either cause after I did my thing, he had an attack of conscience and—get this—his fiancé said he should come clean. It's why I don't get attached."

"That can be a lonely life."

"Oh, I'm hardly ever alone."

"A ladies' man, huh?"

"I do all right."

"But are you lonely?"

"Never."

"That's good."

"What about you, got someone to come home to?"

"No, newly unattached here."

"Sorry about that."

"It's okay. I don't miss her."

"But your aim is getting better?"

"Ha, no nothing like that. Same old story, we just grew apart."

"It happens."

"So you never said, what did you steal?" Frederick asked.

"It was a rare coin. Thing was supposed to be worth over a million," Romeo said.

"Nice."

"Turns out it wasn't nearly that much. I checked."

"Had a guy check it out?"

"Yeah. Told me he didn't know why the guy said that but that he'd be lucky to get a buck oh five out of it."

"That's quite less than a million."

"He was exaggerating, of course, but tried to tell me through his laughing frenzy. I wanted to get rid of the thing right then and there."

"Why didn't you?"

"I wanted to shove it down the guy's nostril first."

"The appraiser?"

"No, the other guy."

"Did you?"

"Yeah. It was after that that he told his fiancé about the whole thing."

"Here's a good exit so you can get that phone."

"Thanks."

* * * *

"Did you make your call?" Frederick asked.

"Yeah. It was my sister. She lives with our Mom, takes care of her," Romeo said.

"Is everything okay?"

"She's not sure. Told me to lay low for a while."

"We're about 30 minutes out of Richmond. Do you think you'll be okay?"

"Yeah, it's going to be fine. They got the coin back and the guy confessed he was part of it. He's even taking the blame, so I don't think there'll be much of a dust-up about me."

"Hopefully," Frederick said.

"I don't think I ever asked you, but what are you going to see in Richmond?" Romeo asked.

"The Poe Museum."

"Really? Like Edgar Allan Poe?"

"Yep."

"I had no idea there was such a place."

"I got up this morning and decided today was the day I was going to see it."

"Are you a fan of Poe?"

"Yeah, one of my favorites. Do you have a favorite?"

"I don't really read. I mean, I read newspapers and magazines, but not really books."

"But you're writing a book."

"What can I say? I'm an enigma."

"Well, if you ever decide to read a book, read Poe. I recommend his short stories."

"I'm more of a music guy."

"Who's your favorite band?"

"Dave Matthews Band."

"Why them?"

"Not long after my dad died, "Lying in the Hands of God" was playing on a radio at an outdoor arts festival near a river, and I looked out at the water thinking how God's hands could reach in and scoop all the water up and how I wouldn't mind being swooped up too."

"That's a really cool story."

"I didn't know who sung that song, but I walked over to the person near the radio and asked them and they told me. The rest is history. I've seen them over 20 times."

"Over 20 times? Are you serious?"

"Yep. Just can't get enough. Never known what enough means, really. Same goes for stealing and picking pockets, I guess."

"Do you practice your craft at the concerts?"

"I can't help myself. It's a two-birds-with-one-stone kind of thing."

"I can see that. What have you stolen?"

"Like I said, it's more about the thrill of the chase. I always give the thing back."

"Every time?" Frederick asked.

"Every time," Romeo said.

"Give me an example."

"Well, one time I stole this guy's first edition books."

"Why did you do that? You don't read books."

"Guy was going on and on about them at a party. One of those Monopoly Guy types, like what was on that movie *Ace Ventura*."

"I loved that movie."

"Me too. Anyway, he was bragging about an Ernest Hemingway this and an Ezra Pound that. Regurgitating. I just wanted him to feel what I feel."

"Which is what?"

"I wanted him to feel vulnerable, to feel loss, to feel dread, to feel regret. I bet he hadn't felt those things in a long time, if ever."

"You assume a lot."

"Maybe, maybe not. But if I was wrong, what's the harm?"

"Good point," Frederick said. "Tell me more."

"Those books were objects to him, his reason for being. I wanted to give him something else to care about," Romeo said.

"What exactly?"

"Anything."

"Some would say that's projection."

"I care plenty, maybe too much."

"What do you care about?"

"My bucket list."

"But what after that?"

"There's not anything after that. I won't be finishing it."

"Not enough money?"

"Not enough time. Let's just say my doctor is going to outlive me."

"I'm sorry."

"Don't be. The way I see it, I've already lived two lives."

"What do you mean?"

"A long time ago, when I was about 20 or so, I picked a pocket from an undercover cop. He felt it and turned around and grabbed me and yanked me up to his face by my collar. And then I recognized him. I didn't know he was undercover or I wouldn't have said anything but I said, 'Hey, Leroy, how's it going, man,' ya know, hoping he would let me go and all. Well, he glared at me and then one of the other guys said, 'Hey, why did he call you Leroy?' I said, ''Cause I know this guy. We go way back. Leroy Phillips.' The other guy says, 'I thought you said your name was Sal Doyle.' 'Sal Doyle,' I says. 'Who is Sal Doyle?' Leroy whispers to me, 'I'm undercover, moron.'"

"Holy crap," Frederick said.

"Yeah, holy shit is more like it," Romeo said. "So I said, 'Oh, wait, you're not Leroy. My bad, man.' By then it was too late though. I blew his cover. And the bullets started flying faster than a NASCAR race. I ran one way, Leroy/Sal ran the other. I made it—barely—he didn't. Spent a month in the hospital rebuilding parts of me."

"That's a hell of a story."

"So I've lived a second life since then."

"What did you do after that?"

"I decided right then and there I would be more selective on whose pocket I picked."

"Most people would find religion or something like that."

"I guess I'm not most people. Can we pull over a second? I think I'm going to be sick."

"Sure."

* * * *

"Feel better now?" Frederick asked.

"Yeah, much better. Thanks," Romeo said.

"How much longer did the doctor give you?"

"Said I had about six months."

"Man, that's rough. Tell you what, let's skip the Poe Museum and go straight to the beach."

"Are you sure?"

"Yeah. I can see it anytime."

"I don't know what to say," Romeo said.

"You don't have to say anything," Frederick said. "Do you need to call your sister and tell her where you are?"

"Yeah, I guess so. Hold on."

"Okay."

Romeo dialed the number. "Hey, sis. Yeah, this is my new number, at least for a while. Have you heard anything? What? Well, that's not what I wanted to hear. Okay, I'll be careful. Yeah, yeah, I'll stay in touch. Bye."

"Not going good, huh?"

"Could be better, for sure. She said the police visited her house asking about me and said they needed to question me, that the guy now says I planned the whole thing."

"That's not good."

"Tell me about it."

"What are you going to do now?"

"Go to the beach. What else?"

"Will they be trying to find you somehow?"

"Who knows. Oh, look, a stray dog. We have to get it."

"I don't know."

"Oh, come on. Don't you like dogs?"

"Yeah, I love dogs, but it's a stray. What if it's mean or has fleas or something?"

"We can't leave it to get hit."

"Okay, I'll pull over."

* * * *

"See, he's a good boy," Romeo said. "Look how happy he is."

"Here, give him water out of this bottle," Frederick said.

"Thanks."

"Did you ever have a dog growing up?"

"Yeah. His name was Tippy. Best dog in the world. A good squirrel dog. I tell ya, that dog could find a squirrel quicker than I could pick a pocket. And the sweetest thing ever."

"What kind of dog was he?"

"A German Shepard/Collie mix. Smart as a whip. What about you? Did you have a dog?"

"Yep. His name was Huckie. Named him after Huckleberry Finn, my favorite book."

"Is that right?"

"Your dog was the best? Mine was the best, too."

"What kind was he?"

"A dachshund."

"A wiener dog."

"Yep, a wiener dog. I would lay on the floor to read or watch TV, and he would lay on my back and go to sleep. Just curl right up there. God, I miss that dog."

"So what do we name this little fella? Huckie or Tippy?"

"Let's name him Tippy. You saw him first."

"Tippy, you hear that? Are you okay with Tippy?"

"I think he likes the name."

"I think you're right. Hey, are you seeing what I'm seeing?"

"What are you seeing?" Frederick asked.

"Flashing lights," Romeo said.

"Oh, yeah, I see them now. Let me ease over into the slow lane."

"Oh, man, this is it. I'm done for."

"Now hold on. They just might be needing to get somewhere in a hurry, or maybe there's an accident up ahead or something."

"It looks like they're slowing down."

"It does, doesn't it?"

"I told you. I'm done for."

"Well, they're going to think I'm helping a fugitive so we're in this together, I suppose."

"I'll tell them you don't know nothing."

"Don't know anything."

"What?"

"Never mind."

"They're getting closer. Slow down and see if they slow down, too."

"Good idea."

"Oh, God, they're slowing down, too," Romeo said.

"Are you sure? I'm not so sure," Frederick said.

"They are. I can tell it."

"How?"

"I can. I just can."

"It looks like they're going to go on by," Frederick said.

"I don't know," Romeo said.

"See, I told you. They have other things on their mind."

"I should probably tell you something."

"What's that?"

"That coin I told you about?"

"Yeah."

"It was worth over a million dollars."

"But you said—"

"I switched it. I have it right here."

"What? You're on the run *and* you have the coin?"

"Look at it. I mean, it's just perfect. It was made in 1849 and it's gold."

"Let me see it."

"Don't take your eyes off the road."

"I won't."

"Here."

"Wow, this thing is heavy. What's the name of it?"

"It's the Liberty Gold Coin, 90 percent gold."

"What's the other 10 percent?"

"Copper."

"Wow. And it's worth a million?"

"No."

"How much?"

"Fifteen million dollars."

"Fiftyf?"

"No, fifteen. One five," Romeo said.

"Still. I mean, wow," Frederick said.

"I know."

"What was all of that before about thrill of the chase?"

"I lied. I'm a bit of a liar, too. Can't help it."

"Is your name really Romeo?"

"That part is true."

"If you lie all the time, how do I know that's true?"

"I said I'm a bit of a liar. I don't lie all the time. Nobody lies all the time. Or at least I don't think they do. Who knows?"

"Still. Fifteen million. I can see now why you got so paranoid about the flashing lights."

"That, and, well, I stole another coin too that the guy didn't know about."

"What?"

"Yeah, I know."

"What else did you steal?"

"It was just laying there, almost like it was talking to me. There was this gold coin and then this silver one. It's like they were a couple. I couldn't break up a family."

"That's a creative way of thinking."

"I swear the Liberty Coin lady looked at me with tears in her eyes when I picked her up and didn't get the other one."

"You may need help."

"I'm lying, of course, but that's the way I felt."

"So how much is the silver coin worth?"

"Over six million dollars."

"Wow. So you have two coins worth over 21 million dollars," Frederick said.

"I'm not good at math," Romeo said.

"What are you going to do with them?"

"Keep them."

"But you'll be hunted for the rest of the time you have left."

"What a way to spend six months, right?"

"Do you really want to spend it in fear like that, though?"

"I'm not fearful."

"You sure looked like it when those cop cars went by."

"Well, yeah, that, but not always."

"You'll have to constantly look over your shoulder."

"Well, there's that, too."

"Do you even have a plan?"

"For what?" Romeo asked.

"For the coins, for the end, for anything," Frederick said.

"I don't want to involve my sister, so I'll send her a letter. We've talked about everything anyway, and, besides, she has enough on her plate already."

"But you'll need some pain medicine or something."

"I guess so. I haven't thought that far ahead."

"I'll tell you, I did not see today going like this when I got up this morning," Frederick said.

"I didn't either, to tell you the truth," Romeo said.

"So now you're telling the truth?"

"As good a time as any, I suppose."

"What did your sister say exactly when you called her earlier?"

"She said the police had an all points something out on me."

"An all-points bulletin."

"Yeah, that's it."

"An APB."

"Yep."

"They are serious then."

"I'm their number one priority apparently. I've never felt so special."

"I guess that's one way of putting it."

"You said you didn't see how this day was gonna be like this before. Well, me too. I mean, I got me a ride to the beach, a friend to be with along the way, and this little buddy, my new Tippy. The way I see it, this is the best day of my life."

"The best day of your life includes every law enforcement officer alerted to finding you? Hell, you may even make it on the FBI's most wanted list."

"Wouldn't that be something? Now *that's* how to go out on a high note."

"Something just occurred to me."

"What's that?"

"When you said you had six months left, how long ago was six months?"

"Five months ago," Romeo said.

"Let's get to the beach," Frederick said.

"Sounds good to me. You know what my sister said to me? By the way, she loves Shakespeare. That's why I chose the name Romeo for my street name. She always called me that growing up on account of my fondness for the opposite sex. I hit on every friend she ever had. Anyway, after all this that's going down, she was joking with me."

"You two are close."

"She's my best friend."

"What did she say to you?"

"'Romeo, Romeo, wherefore art thou, Romeo?'"

SIX-ARMED ROBBERY

ASHLEY-RUTH M. BERNIER

Who don't hear will feel.
　　　　　　　　　　—Caribbean grannies everywhere

If you stop to think about it, this whole mess was Sister Alice's idea to begin with. Well. Not the robberies themselves. That idea came straight from Nessa and D and me. Our part in this wasn't exactly small, and I've never denied that. It's just that, when you hear Sister Alice talking about *distress* and *anguish* and all those other phrases she's been throwing around, it might not be such a terrible thing to remember it was something she said that inspired it. Like that poster she has in her office… you know, the one that says you have to take full responsibility for the seeds you plant?

That's not what it says? Seriously?

Okay, scratch that, then. The point is, I never would've even thought about the robberies… and I really hesitate to call them *armed*… if it hadn't been for Sister Alice's words. I know that's a big accusation. But once you hear the whole story, I bet you'll agree.

The robberies never would've happened if it hadn't been for Sister Alice's *actions*, either. When my mom sent me down here to spend the summer with her Auntie Jeanette, I knew exactly what I was getting into. I haven't lived here since I was three, but there's plenty I remember… like Auntie Jeannette's little red house with her big backyard full of fruit trees. Like chasing iguanas and catching crabs at the beach. Like all the time she spends at church. I knew this wasn't going to be the glamorous summer all my Raleigh friends imagined when I told them I was spending six weeks in St. Thomas… but I knew I'd get lots of beach time, and the plan I had to make a little money before the start of eighth grade was the kind of thing I could do anywhere as long as I had my computer with me. I know Sister Alice might have a different opinion, but there's really nothing *wrong* about being hired to write essays about the parts of a cell or Revolutionary War heroes for kids in the class below me. People get paid for things they write for other people all the time. I looked it up online—it's called ghostwriting, and it's perfectly legal.

...It's called *cheating* in middle school? Is that written down somewhere?

Um, let's debate that another time. Thing is, because word of my essay-writing service had gotten lots of attention around school, I had a ton of jobs lined up for next year—and my aunt's choir practices and dinners at the church were the perfect time to work on them. They were getting ready for the Joyful Noise Caribbean Choir Competition in August, and even though Auntie Jeanette said never to repeat this, Sister Alice was really hellbent on winning. Since Sister Alice is the choir director, she wanted them to have an early dinner before practice every weekday evening. Like I said, it wasn't glamorous, and between us, the singing was a lot less *joyful* and a lot more *noise*, if you know what I mean. But three full hours with my computer in the back of the church, with a belly full of stew chicken and potato stuffing and all the other good meals Auntie Jeanette and her choir friends brought? It felt... cozy and calm, and that golden hour light fading into evening blues helped me to focus and write.

I'd taken a tiny break from an essay about the Boston Tea Party one Tuesday, and I didn't even notice the choir was on their own break until Sister Alice swooped down and snatched the computer right off my lap.

"You back here playin' games, young lady?" she'd snapped, and then her beady eyes nearly bulged right out of her head when she saw exactly *what* I was playing. "Jeanette! Are you *aware* of deh nonsense your niece is engaged in back here?"

The *nonsense* was, um, an online game. Maybe you've heard of it—"A Mercenary Habit?" Yeah, it's the one all over the news about the nun catching car thieves in the streets of Chicago with an assault rifle. I don't know why everyone's so upset about it... doesn't it just, like, teach kids that stealing is wrong and that nuns can kick butt when they need to? Both are important lessons, if you ask me. Sister Alice didn't think so. She held up her computer for my aunt and all the other choir members to see.

"I had no idea," Auntie Jeanette gasped, which was enough to make me feel terrible. Auntie J's the best, and what she doesn't understand about technology she makes up for with what she *does* understand about throwing down in the kitchen.

"This is what idle time creates," Sister Alice said. Most of those other mean old ladies in the choir nodded and clucked their disappointment. "Dangerous distractions and inappropriate interests. Iss a good thing I noticed."

I began to explain this was just a teensy little lapse in judgment, but she wasn't even listening. She just plowed on ahead about the evils of video games and unregulated free time in that *voice* of hers.

...yes, it kinda *does* sound like a parrot with a head cold. Exactly. But, um, those are your words, not mine.

In any case, the evening ended with Sister Alice convincing Auntie Jeanette to let her keep my computer locked away in the church office for the rest of the summer. It was bad enough that I wasn't going to get to play the nun game, but what it *really* meant was that I couldn't write those essays I was charging $20 bucks apiece for. Even worse? She'd found me another "job" to do during those choir practices, although I'm using that word really loosely. You get paid for a job. This was more like... involuntary servitude, and yeah, I already learned in social studies class what those words *really* mean. Turns out Sister Alice had a few thousand books in the school library next to the church that needed new plastic covers, stickers on the spine, and a stamp on the front cover. She could've paid some of the teachers, like Auntie Jeanette, to do this, like she was paying a whole lot of the other ones to teach summer school all day for high-schoolers on academic probation. But she had a different idea in mind... one that wouldn't cost her any money at all. I think you can see where I'm going with this. Instead of spending my summer writing sentences, I'd be spending my summer *serving* one.

Sister Alice convinced Auntie J that working in the library all day would help me grow in character, and that clearing the dishes and straightening up after their choir practice dinners would help me grow in virtue. I tried to explain to my aunt that I'd done enough growing—I'm one of the tallest kids in my whole grade—but I wasn't the one she wound up listening to. I started my work at the library the very next day.

There was *one* good thing that came out of this, though. Two, really, because if I hadn't been assigned to books and busgirl duty, I would never have met Nessa and D. I noticed them first when I walked into the library on my first day, not the piles of books behind the table where they sat. Nessa's the same honey brown as I am and almost as tall, and we learned pretty quickly that we both liked car thief video games and heist movies. D was—different. A lot shorter than me, and Nessa, too. Deep brown complexion and eyes that reminded me of the ocean, not because they were anywhere even close to blue, but because they were gentle and warm. Everything about him was gentle and warm. Well. Mostly. Because D could be pretty hardcore, too, if the moment called for it.

I mean, yeah, maybe I thought he was cute. Or... maybe I *will*, in a couple of years. This summer, it wasn't like that for us. We were just friends. Special friends, the three of us. Because once we'd known each other for a few days, we became a trio.

Turns out Nessa's situation wasn't all that different from mine. She'd gotten roped into the library chore after her grandmother spilled to Sister Alice that Nessa's stepmother was letting her work a few hours—with pay—at her beauty supply store. "Sister Alice told Granny that a girl my age should be surrounded by Whitman and Walker instead of wigs and weaves," Nessa grumbled to me the day after we'd met. And D? He was one of Sister Alice's victims, too. She'd snatched something of his at a choir rehearsal also—a handheld gaming system—and one of the game chips fell down into an air conditioning vent behind a pew. It was her fault, but Sister Alice convinced D's grandmother he didn't need to replace it—that D didn't need gaming as much as he needed godliness. Yeah, she liked her alliteration, for sure.

Having a common enemy helped us bond. Like I said, it made us a trio. But once we heard Sister Alice and her friends at dinner one night… once we had that *idea*… we became something more. We became a crew.

The idea came to us about four days after I'd started working in the library—meaning four long days of stamping, stickering, and plastic-wrapping hundreds of books—but it didn't actually come to us *in* the library. We were on meal clean-up duty, scraping plates and bringing dishes and pans back to the church social hall kitchen to clean. Nessa and I were wiping down folding tables while the choir members talked.

"—that's why she isn't here tonight," old Mrs. Braithwaite was saying to the crowd of ladies gathered around the fruit punch table. "Six iguanas on deh terrace! Said she chased dem with a broom an' all, but she was so shaken afterwards, she didn't think she could sing tonight."

"Lord sen' help," Mrs. Warner sighed. "Glad it was Glenda and not me. Those *disgustin'* creatures… I can't even get mehself near them."

"I don't mind iguanas," Auntie Jeanette spoke up, "but don't let me see a gecko. Or—good Lord, those big grasshoppers? The way they jump? May as well call deh priest for my Las' Rites."

"That's how I am about frogs. And they jump even higher," Ms. Flores shuddered. "I can't stand to even *look* at any amphibian. Jus' causes all deh bile to rise in my throat."

"It had four cockroaches got into meh car one evening after a rain," Mrs. Chesterfield announced. "I pulled off the road and walked two miles home along Mafolie Road. I decided the car was theirs for the night."

"That's absolute nonsense," Sister Alice declared, snapping her fingers at me for a refill of her tea. "You'd think someone would be able to rob you blind just by waving some kind of insect in your direction."

"Oh, you could certainly rob me with a roach," Mrs. Chesterfield chuckled. "I'd fight a robber with a gun or a knife. I'd throw meh whole purse at a robber with a cockroach."

"Or a frog," Ms. Flores added, and all the other ladies chimed in with their agreement.

"Ridiculous," Sister Alice said. "I could understand, perhaps, a *gungolo*. Those things deserve their space. But all those other creatures you mentioned? They jus' need a simple reminder about the natural order of things. That there's a hierarchy. That they're at the bottom. They need to realize their place in the world and who's actually in charge." I handed back her cup of tea, and she raised her eyebrows at me. "Kind of like children."

She left a pile of dirty dishes for us to clean that evening, but that's not what I was thinking about when I went back to the church hall kitchen with Nessa and D. And it wasn't until I was certain that we were alone that I actually let the idea out.

"Did you hear what they just said?" I asked D as we scrubbed a lasagna pan.

"When they were talking about all the kids in summer school this year?" D asked.

"No, not that. About the bugs and the lizards."

"Yeah, they're scared," Nessa snickered. "Like a roach or a li'l lizard could do anything to them."

"That's what I mean," I said. "They're all terrified of these little creatures that *look* scary but can't actually hurt them. So scared that they'd leave their car on the side of the road and walk home. Or even…"

D paused in the middle of washing a pan and looked at me, but Nessa's the one who spoke first. "What are you thinking?"

"She's thinking about that other thing Sister Alice said," D said before I could answer. There was a slow nod. He understood. "About being robbed with a roach."

"Think about it," I told them, dropping the plate I was holding and climbing onto the counter next to the sink for a seat. "Sister Alice has my computer, and now I can't make money the way I planned to this summer. Nessa—you were supposed to work in your stepmother's beauty supply store, but Sister Alice butted in and you're not getting paid, either. And D, it's not like she's ever going to pay to replace your game."

"Now we doin' all *this* for free," Nessa grumbled. "And it's not like any of the others spoke up for us."

"Exactly," I said. I felt something rising in my chest and my cheeks, something warm and crackling like electricity or—soda bubbles, you know, when you drink it too fast. Whatever it was, I felt it behind every word I spoke. There was no way I could hold them back at that point. "I'm not scared of any of those animals. You?"

Two head shakes, both no. "I didn't think so," I continued. "Remember what Sister Alice said about the 'natural order of things'? Knowing who's actually in charge? My science teacher told us that there are something like 2 *billion* bugs on this planet for every human. They could crush us all if they wanted to. If they knew how to organize." I paused and fixed them both with a stare. "If they had a plan."

"You got a plan?" Nessa asked. Her eyes got wide and bright, like they did whenever she started talking about a good car heist game, and her smile matched.

"She's got a plan." D's voice was quiet, as usual, and it was hard to read his face at first. He said nothing for a few moments, and then, finally— "No one touches our own grandmothers—or your Auntie Jeanette. That's my only rule." He nodded. "But I'm in."

I guess you can figure out what happened next. Nessa and D and I got our plan straight—planned everything down to the last second, which we'd need to do in order to pull it off. After that, we started our preparations. Over the next week, we spent our free time sneaking around and collecting as much wriggly wildlife as we could. Roaches, lizards, grasshoppers… D even found an iguana he was able to smuggle into an old dog crate he had at home. His parents have tons of hibiscus bushes and a huge mango tree, so the iguana was happy to lounge around in the crate as long as D had some ripe fruits and flowers for him. Nessa talked her little brother into walking up from the house to help us, and just like the iguana, he was happy to help as long as he got paid in mangoes. The two of them raided their older brothers' closets. Nessa searched the discard bin at her stepmother's store for supplies. It was all coming together. I just had… one lingering little question, and I asked D about it one afternoon while we were catching tiny lizards hiding in the cracks throughout the old blue-stone wall behind the church.

"What's a gunlo?" I asked.

He'd just pulled a newt out from its little hole and put it gently in the bin I was holding. "A what?"

"Maybe I'm not saying it right," I muttered. "Sister Alice didn't seem to be scared of frogs or roaches or lizards, but there's one creature she talked about, and she… sounded different when she did. She called it a gunlo."

"Gungolo," D corrected me. He wasn't laughing when he did. D never laughed at me—at least, not for things like that. "They're like slimy black millipedes. Not too big, maybe deh size of your finger. You've seen them around your house, I bet."

"I have," I said slowly, thinking I'd seen several since I'd landed on-island a few weeks earlier. "I never thought about picking one up or anything, but—"

"Don't." D stopped his search and turned to me. His brown eyes were deep and… *intense*, like a sandstorm. "Look, everything we've caught? They ain' fun to look at, but they're not dangerous. A gungolo is."

"Seriously?" I shook my head at him. "If it's what I'm thinking about, they look like slimy licorice cheese puffs. And if *that's* the one thing Sister Alice is scared of…"

"I know what you're thinking," he said quietly, "but you have to leave those alone. You have to promise, all right?"

So I did. I promised. Not because I actually was scared of something that looked like a dark chocolate gummy worm, but because D asked me to. And for a crew to really work together well, there has to be trust.

The next night, we put our plan into action. Nessa, D, and I robbed the sopranos of Sister Alice's choir of all the money they had in their purses. And no, we didn't rob them with weapons. We robbed them with roaches.

And toads. And lizards. And D's big ol' iguana.

I got Mrs. Flores first, right when she was squeezing out of her car at the far end of the parking lot. With a fat frog in each of my hands and faking a voice that made it sound like I had a third one in my throat, I told her to throw all her money in my direction or I'd let the amphibians jump. I swear she called on six generations of New Testament ancestry before she flung three twenties at me and ran away.

Nessa got Mrs. Chesterfield out on the front road at the same time—told her she'd let all the cockroaches out of their jar if she didn't see the green. Mrs. Chesterfield had a fifty and a twenty on her that day.

D didn't get quite so lucky with Mrs. Warner and the iguana. She only had thirty dollars tucked away inside a compartment in her car. But I heard her scream all the way from the back parking lot. A scream like that, the whole island probably heard it.

By the time everyone had collected themselves and reported what had happened and gave the three of us in the library a second thought, Nessa, D and I were settled back down at our tables, working on those books just like we were supposed to be.

…How did we do it? Good question. Normally I'd keep something like this to myself, but I guess I don't really have a choice, and I don't mind sharing. It was a pretty good idea, if I say so myself.

Like I told you earlier—timing was everything. The robberies needed to happen right after the big kids in summer school got dismissed for the evening. It was easy to slip out of the library and disappear into the crowded hallways, especially since Nessa and I are so tall… and with the old school uniforms and backpacks the two of them found in their older brothers' closets, we blended right in. We kept wigs from Nessa's stepmother's store and some masks we made with old t-shirts in our backpacks. We pulled them on once the high-schoolers were gone. Our marks only saw tall kids in long pants and polo shirts, with wild wigs and a mask hiding everything except the eyes.

Of course, Sister Alice held a meeting with all the summer school kids the next day, but without any evidence, what could she do? She did stop and glare at the three of us in the library after the meeting. D asked in his sweetest voice whether there was anything he could help her with… and even though she looked as murderous as the nun in my game for a couple of seconds, she said nothing at all before she stormed off.

Even so, we waited another week before we struck the altos. Everyone had been rattled for a day or two after our first hit, but that had slowly faded away into… geez, what's the word? Yes—*complacency*. They forgot to be on guard, and that's exactly when we got them again. Mrs. Bryan with big grasshoppers. Old Ms. Baptiste with an extra-large coqui frog Nessa caught on the side of her cistern. Mrs. Aquino with three hairy-legged flying roaches that even gave *me* a bit of a chill. But by the end of that run, we'd earned an additional $96.

We also earned ourselves a visit from Sister Alice. By the time she'd made it to the library after the second hit, Nessa, D and I were back in our regular clothes doing our regular job. She growled something and raged through the room, looking under tables and behind bookshelves. The evidence had already been chucked back into our bags and sent home with Nessa's little brother, and the best part about using natural weapons was that we could release them right back into the wild after the job was done. There wasn't anything left for her to find.

"I know allyou did this," she hissed after searching the entire room. "Don't know how, but I know it was you."

"Did what?" Nessa asked innocently as D shrugged.

"We don't know what you're talking about, Sister Alice," I followed up.

"You know exactly what I'm talking about." She placed her hands on her wide hips and fixed me with a horrible stare. "*You* know. Pride goeth before a fall, and I expect you're about to take a mighty big tumble."

I probably should've kept quiet. Probably should've just listened and nodded, like D and Nessa did. But I felt that thing inside my chest and my cheeks again—that crackle of energy like a light switch with bad wires, and what *actually* took a tumble were those words, falling out of my mouth. "Oh, I don't know, Sister Alice. I'm pretty sure-footed," I answered. "Like I learned from my Sunday School teacher—'whoever walks in confidence walks securely.'"

"That's not the way that proverb goes," Sister Alice snipped, "and while we're talking about ol' time sayings, maybe you've lived away long enough to forget this cornerstone of West Indian wisdom." She took a step closer to me and twisted her face into a frown angrier than a trapped wasp. "'Who don't hear will feel.' Those who don't heed advice will face unpleasant consequences. Don't ignore that, young lady. I've taught generations of students. I know this is one piece of prudence that never… *ever*… fails."

D and Nessa tried to make me feel better after she was gone. Nessa called me a badass for speaking back like that, and D said I was braver that moment than he ever would be. It was another moment I should've just been happy to live in—something I should've moved on from. But I didn't. I just couldn't let it go.

So much so that, after a long night with almost no sleep, I decided to break my promise to D.

The next day was Saturday, a day with no library duty *and* no choir practice. My auntie always used that free afternoon to go grocery shopping, and I'd learned from her a few weeks earlier that Sister Alice used that time to do paperwork in her office. As soon as Auntie J left, I grabbed my wig and my mask—along with a few little *friends* from the yard outside—and took the back roads to the church. The school gates were closed but not locked, and nobody was around to see me pull on my disguise and hide my face. Then I pushed open Sister Alice's office door, ready to hear her scream.

Only she didn't. She didn't even seem surprised. She turned to see me standing in her doorway, and all she did was sigh. There was kind of an annoyed little shrug as she tossed the papers she was holding on top of her desk. "I was expecting you a li'l earlier," she said. "You almos' missed me. I usually go home for a cup of bush tea before evening mass."

I have to admit her calmness, her... *nonchalance*, if that's the right word... threw me off a bit. I didn't know how to answer that, and I saw a mean smile crack on her lips. "I should call Jeanette right now for you," she said, folding her arms over her chest.

I'll also admit I was surprised here, too—that she knew exactly who I was. Maybe that's why I didn't even bother to argue the point. "You won't, though," I said instead.

"No? Perhaps iss because I should be calling the *police*. You and your friends stole 250 dollars."

"256, actually." I tried my best to make my voice sound as strong as hers. "But I'm willing to give it back."

She raised her eyebrows. "Oh?"

"Yup," I said. This is when I pulled my mask and wig off. "I'll give back everything I took if you do, too. Give me my computer, buy D his game, and give Nessa a chance to do something she *really* wants to do this summer."

Sister Alice stepped around her massive desk. "*Spare deh rod an' spoil deh child*," she muttered under her breath. "Listen, young lady, I have friends in *very* high places. But I'm willing to go easy on you, maybe march you home right now with a notebook to copy the entire book of Proverbs... *twice*. Clearly you have a lot to learn about pride. What makes you think I would cater to any of your demands?"

I cracked my own smile. "These do," I answered, and reached into my pockets for the gungolos I'd gathered from Auntie Jeanette's bougainvillea plants. Two in one hand, three in the other. They were sticky and wriggly, but the shock on Sister Alice's face was worth it.

"Put those down." Her voice wasn't shaky or thin—it was every bit the opposite. "I'm very serious, child. Step outside and put them on the ground."

I felt tingly and bubbly all over again. "These little millipedes? Do they scare you?"

"They should scare you," she answered. "Didn't Jeanette or Vanessa or Deuteronomy explain to you what those can do?"

Curiosity about the answer to her question won out over the shock of hearing D's real name, but it was a close race. "All they said was to leave them alone."

"As they should've. Every child growing up on this island knows they can spit in your eye. Some children insist that it's... urination, but that's—"

"—ridiculous," I finished for her. "All of it. We studied millipedes in science class this year." I brought my left hand up to my face for a closer look at the wormlike creatures. "One thing I know for sure, Sister Alice, is that they definitely can't spit in anyone's eye."

Well. I'm sure you know exactly what happened next. I guess you heard it from Sister Alice, though, because it was kind of a blur for me. Literally. I brought my hand up to my face and the next thing I knew, everything above my neck felt like it was melting, and I couldn't see *anything*. There was a lot of screaming and a trip to the hospital, and a few days full of medicines and bandages on my eyes. It was on one of those days when D came to visit, and he quietly explained that the species of millipedes in the Virgin Islands... unlike the ones I see sometimes in Raleigh... can spray toxins up to eight feet away. And yeah, the doctor explained that the acid in those toxins is strong enough to blind, so I'm lucky the ER staff acted quickly. Lucky the choir ladies accepted my apology. Lucky Auntie Jeanette only spent a day or two being shocked and disappointed before she finally believed how sorry I was and forgave me with a long hug and some fresh johnnycakes. Auntie J really is the best ever.

I'll be honest, though. When Sister Alice told me she had friends in high places, I didn't think she meant a former student who's a whole *police captain* now. I thought she meant... um, a more heavenly connection. I know she wanted you to talk to me about laws and rules... and maybe pride, too, but I've learned my lesson, and I've got burn scabs to prove it. Feel free to tell me anyway, since you probably already planned to—

I'm sorry? You *weren't* planning to talk to me about any of those things?

Well—yeah, I'll be back next year. D might be taller by then, and Nessa and I are both excited about "A Mercenary Habit 2" coming out. And yes, I'm interested in the Junior Police Corps you mentioned. I can see myself as a detective or lieutenant too, one day. Oh, I agree—it's definitely better to have this mind of mine working on your side than on the other.

Not sure you meant that as a compliment, but I'll take it.

In the meantime, I hope you'll excuse me. I've got this notebook, and a whole lot of proverbs to copy.

MANDATORY RETIREMENT

SARAH BEWLEY

When we stepped into the garage, Bobby Lou literally fell over the body. I was behind her, so I only stumbled into Bobby Lou, but cracked my chin on the back of her head because she's so damn short. It hurt like hell, and I chipped a front tooth. That would cost me, and I was not happy about it at all.

"Oh, good Lord! It's Madeline!" she said.

I looked down, as I was the only one still standing, and saw Madeline's wide dead eyes staring up at me. Creepy as all hell.

"What is she doing in our garage?" I asked.

Bobby Lou looked up at me and said, "Waiting to be found?"

I squatted down and looked her over. She had on the usual sweater set, pearls, and neat black slacks. Her shoes matched the blue of the sweater set. Her hair looked a little mussed, but her make-up was perfect, as always.

Bobby Lou rolled over so she could get a better look. "I'm not seeing any blood," she said.

"If she was dead when she got here, she wouldn't be bleeding," I said. I moved from the second step to the garage floor and took a closer look. "Her hair's messed up."

Bobby Lou got up to her knees and leaned down to check what I was seeing. "Yeah, let's take a look." She gingerly picked up Madeline's head. Her hair parted a little right at the crown of her head with a neat hole about the size of a Sacagawea dollar coin. The hair on the back of her head was stiff with blood.

"How the hell did that happen?" I asked.

"No idea, but looks like she bled quite a bit."

"Put her head down and I'll call the Sheriff."

Bobby Lou braced her hand on the floor and slowly got to her feet. She brushed off the knees of her jeans. "Damn, these are my good jeans," she said.

I pulled my cell phone out of my purse and dialed 9-1-1. Elise Carlyle from dispatch answered. "Elise, this is Evelina. Madeline Howard is lying dead in my garage. Bobby Lou just fell over the body as we were going to the car. I don't know who's on today, but someone needs to get forensics and someone from the Medical Examiner's office out here."

Elise snorted. "She must be dead, because that's the only way she'd end up in your garage."

"Yeah, that's true," I said. Bobby Lou snorted. Madeline had not approved of our kind even existing. If she'd been alive to see where she'd ended up, she'd be mortified.

"I'll get someone out there right now," said Elise. "Does her death look natural?"

"Not unless you'd call trepanning natural. She's got a hole in the crown of her head that's about the size of a dollar coin."

"That does not sound natural," said Elise. "Let me get someone out there."

I disconnected and said to Bobby Lou, "I'm moving the car. I don't want someone telling us we can't have it until they've cleared the scene."

"You do that. I'm going to go get myself some sweet tea."

Personally, I was getting a beer as soon as I moved the car out to the street. Finding a dead Southern Baptist in my garage had frayed my damn nerves. Once I parked the car in front of the house, I went in through the front door and headed straight into the kitchen.

Bobby Lou stood at the kitchen counter eating a huge piece of red velvet cake with a scoop of ice cream and holding a tall glass of iced tea in her left hand. I went to the refrigerator and pulled out a beer.

"Are you going to drink that before the sheriff gets here?"

"I certainly am," I said. "I need something to calm me down."

"Do you really think it's smart to be drinking alcohol before we're questioned about Madeline Howard's body in our garage?"

"I think it's absolutely necessary."

Bobby Lou turned back to her cake and ice cream. "Some people just have no damn sense of decorum at all," she muttered.

"Some people don't decide to eat their weight in cake and ice cream after tripping over a dead body in their garage."

"Sugar is soothing."

"So is beer."

"Fine."

"Fine."

I popped the top on the can and took a big gulp. I swallowed and then opened my mouth and let out a loud burp.

Bobby Lou snickered. "You are awful."

I grinned at her. "You like me."

Bobby Lou looked at me and grinned. "I have bad taste in women," she said.

We both sniggered at that.

Someone knocked at the garage door, and I went to open it. Carl Jenkins stood on the other side next to the steps.

"Hey, Evelina," he said. "You got a dead body in your garage."

"No shit," I said. "You are a master of detection, Carl."

"Yeah, that's why they pay me the big bucks," he said. "I'm going to tape off your garage as a crime scene. You got anything in here you need?"

"Nope," I said, "Tape away."

He nodded and walked back to his patrol car. I closed the door and went back to drinking my beer. I'd had a sandwich just before we started to head out to run our errands. I felt it sufficient to keep me from getting drunk on a single can.

Bobby Lou finished her cake and ice cream and poured herself some more sweet tea. "I don't know what it is about sugar, but it always makes me thirsty as hell after I eat it."

In the next thirty minutes our garage filled up with people and equipment. A van from the Medical Examiner's office was in the driveway, a car from forensics had parked behind our car in front of the house, and Carl's patrol car parked in front of our car. Bobby Lou and I sat on the front porch and watched as the neighbors suddenly decided two o'clock in the afternoon was late enough for their dog's evening walk, or to check the mail that never came before four. The attempted nonchalance of the rubber-necking failed them all miserably.

Sheriff Rupert pulled up and parked behind the Medical Examiner's van in the driveway. He waved at us and then got out of the car. "How are you ladies holding up?"

Bobby Lou spoke before I could, "We're just fine, Sheriff Rupert. How are you today?" I elbowed her, but she ignored me.

"Evelina," said the sheriff. "How's retirement treating you?"

"Well, it was going fine until Bobby Lou tripped over Madeline Howard in our garage. Messed up her good jeans, so I suppose we're going to have to replace them. And then I have all my old co-workers showing up here and taking up the parking space. 'Bout the only difference in my life right at this moment, over before I retired, is that I'm not wearing a uniform."

"You get a good look at the body?" he asked.

"No, I closed my eyes and turned around and went right back into the house."

The sheriff took off his hat and smoothed his hair. It was a nervous tic I well remembered from my former time serving under the man. "Any idea what killed her?"

"Might be that big hole in her head," I said.

"Gunshot?" he asked.

"Definitely not. Looks like someone drilled a hole in her skull about 5mm wide. Blood in her hair, but nothing on the floor under her, so she must have been dead when she was dropped off."

Bobby Lou elbowed me.

The sheriff watched us both closely. "Any idea why she was dropped off in your garage?"

I shrugged. "Other than the fact that we didn't like each other, nope. I'm sure whoever did this figured you'd look at us first as the killers. Give them a chance to get rid of evidence and such."

The sheriff sighed audibly.

"You can check our garbage, and in the car, and we don't own a drill."

"Evelina, I don't for a minute think you killed Madeline Howard."

"Huh," I said. "That's awful white of you, Sheriff."

The sheriff put his hat back on. "Do you always have to be a pain in my ass?"

I nodded. "Yeah, I'm pretty sure it's mandatory upon retirement."

He shook his head. "Bobby Lou, did you get hurt when you tripped over Madeline?"

Bobby Lou laughed. "I'm probably bruised, but I managed to get back up without aid, so I think I'm fine."

"I'm glad to hear that. Excuse me, ladies, I'm going to go see what Dr. Hamilton has to tell me."

We watched Sheriff Rupert walk into the garage and then Bobby Lou turned on me. "Can you just this one time try to be a little bit nice to the sheriff? It is not his fault mandatory retirement is 55."

"Unless you're the sheriff. Then you can work as long as you get elected. He's 60. I have to retire at 55, and he's still in uniform. I could kick his ass any day of the week, but I'm not fit to work."

Bobby Lou shushed me. I flipped her off. She swatted my arm, and I licked the side of her face. She began to spit and sputter and wiped her face with her sleeve.

A Toyota pulled up and double parked next to our car.

"Oh, no. Let's head inside."

"Why?"

"That's Elmond. He's going to want to know what's going on."

Bobby Lou and I both got up and went into the house. I locked the front door because I knew Elmond well enough to know if it was unlocked, he'd just open the door and walk right in. He still had dreams of being either Woodward or Bernstein. The newspaper was barely staying alive, and he wanted to break one last big story before he faded into the ignominy of being a never-was.

He banged on the door and called for me or Bobby Lou. I held her back from answering. She hated not answering the door because she thought it rude, but I didn't care. I'd spent my entire career keeping him away from crime scenes.

"You answer that door, and I will invite your mother to have dinner with us."

"You wouldn't!"

"Don't test me, Bobby Lou."

She stomped into the kitchen where I joined her. I grabbed her glass and refreshed her sweet tea. She took the glass back and shook her head. "Elmond isn't that bad."

"You never had to say 'no comment' a hundred times in a row to get him to leave."

"Fine."

"Fine."

The door into the garage opened and the sheriff walked in. "Doc's moving the body. We're going to need you to lock this door and stay out of your garage for a couple of days."

"Certainly, Sheriff," said Bobby Lou.

I gritted my teeth. I loved the woman, but she was way too polite to people who annoyed the hell out of me. "Can you run Elmond off before you leave?" I asked.

The sheriff nodded. "Least I can do."

"That's true," I said, and Bobby Lou stepped on my foot. I glared at her, but she ignored me.

The sheriff walked through the living room and opened the front door. We could hear him telling Elmond to meet him at the station. Elmond protested, but the sheriff made it clear that he had to leave us alone.

We heard someone close the garage door and pretty soon all the official vehicles left. I rinsed my beer can and tossed it into the recycling bin. "Let's take a walk. I feel like a saunter," I said.

"Saunter my fanny. You know the sheriff's got someone over at Madeline's right now, checking her house."

I grinned, "No, they've already been there."

"What do you think you'll find they didn't?"

"No way of knowing until I get there. You want to come with me?"

"I'd better. No telling what kind of trouble you'll get into if I'm not there."

Madeline Howard's house was on the other side of the highway from our neighborhood. The houses were larger and the lawns landscaped, but other than that it didn't look all that different from our neighborhood. The main difference was there were three colors the houses were allowed to be painted there. One was an off-white, one was a pale blue, and the third was a light gray. Madeline's place was pale blue. Only native plants were allowed, so her home was surrounded by white azaleas. The azaleas were in full bloom.

The front door was sealed with yellow and black crime scene tape. It clashed horribly with the pale blue of the house and the blue door with sand blasted glass. An undeveloped lot bordered hers on the right-hand side. I walked into it and turned left into the stand of oak trees that lined the back of the vacant lot. When we stepped out of them, we stood in the backyard of Madeline's house. The back door to the house had been taped, but the screen door had not.

I walked up and opened it, using the hem of my t-shirt to grab the latch. "Madeline never was good about locking the screen," I said.

"How did you know that?"

"Remember that possum that got into her house four years ago?" I asked.

"You didn't!" said Bobby Lou.

"I thought it was her cat."

"Evelina, she nearly had a stroke when she found that thing in her kitchen eating crackers!"

I shrugged. "Madeline was always kind of excitable."

I walked up to the sliding glass doors and opened them, again using my t-shirt to cover my hand. Bobby Lou made a surprised noise, but she followed me right into the house. It still being light outside made it easy to find our way through the house. Sheer curtains covered all the windows.

The living room showed no sign of human habitation, but then it had been Madeline's, so that didn't surprise me. We went into the kitchen and the white tile floor was spotless. We headed back toward the baths and bedrooms. The guest room looked like a model room in an unoccupied house. Also not surprising. Madeline didn't have friends. She had cohorts, and they all lived in her neighborhood. The en suite bathroom was the same, right down to the flower shaped soaps at the sink and in the shower.

The master bedroom had yellow tape across the open door. I ducked under the tape. Bobby Lou chose to drop to all fours and crawl under it. Nothing seemed out of place. I started to walk toward the bathroom and noticed something shiny just under the foot of the bed. I reached down and saw that it was an opal earring. I pulled a tissue from the box on the vanity and picked it up.

"What's that?" asked Bobby Lou.

"An opal earring. Pierced earring." I set the earring back where I found it. If it was evidence of someone else being here, I certainly didn't want to have it in my possession. But it would be something to think about.

"I don't ever remember seeing Madeline wearing opals," said Bobby Lou.

We walked into the bathroom and saw that the sink had blood stains in it. All the towels were missing, as was the bathmat.

"Looks like someone cleaned up after themselves," said Bobby Lou.

"Why would they leave blood in the sink?" I asked aloud. "Of course, if it's all Madeline's blood, I guess the killer thought it wouldn't be traced back to them. I want to take a look in the garage."

We retraced our steps and opened the garage door. Madeline's Mercedes sat in the middle of the space. We walked around and found nothing. "Well, the murder weapon must have been brought by the killer," I said. "This place doesn't have anything other than the blood in the sink."

Bobby Lou got down on all fours and looked under the car. "There's something under here," she said.

I got down and looked. I could see something, but I had no idea what it was. I pulled the tissue out of my pocket and stretched my arm until my tissue-covered fingers could just reach the thing. I pulled it out. "I have no idea what this is," I said.

Bobby Lou came around and looked at it. "Let's take a picture. Maybe we can identify it on the computer."

I set it on the floor, pulled out my phone, and took several photos. Then I used the tissue to put it back under the car.

"All right, let's get out of here," I said. We retraced our steps, went back through the oaks and wandered along the street, pointing to flowers and flags until we felt we could make our way back home without looking suspicious.

Once we got home, we each got something to drink, and I emailed the photos to my computer. I couldn't believe how quickly I got a match to the image. It was a diamond drill bit used for creating holes in stone and ceramic.

"How did someone get her to lie still for that?" asked Bobby Lou.

"I don't imagine she was conscious," I said. "Maybe she was drugged and then someone drilled into her head."

"Why go to all that trouble? I mean you could just shoot her or something."

"Guns are more traceable than a diamond bit, I'd think," I said.

"Oh," said Bobby Lou. "I guess so."

"Also, according to the internet, the thing only costs about $25."

"That's a lot cheaper than a gun," said Bobby Lou.

I closed my browser and turned the computer off. So we found what made the hole in her head. That was something, and I wanted to call the sheriff and tell him whoever searched her place did a crappy job. But then he'd want to know how I knew, and that wouldn't go anywhere good.

Bobby Lou and I decided to have dinner and make an early night of it. Her knee was sore, and I was having a moral dilemma, which wasn't something I was used to at all. We both figured that a good night's sleep would make things better in the morning.

It might have made Bobby Lou's knee better, but it didn't do spit to ease my mind.

The sheriff showed up about mid-morning. He said he needed to talk to me, so Bobby Lou decided she'd run the errands we hadn't done yesterday.

The sheriff and I faced off over the kitchen table.

"Do you have any idea who might want to kill Madeline and screw with your life as well?"

"I'm a former deputy and a lesbian in a small town in North Florida. I think the pool of suspects would be pretty large."

"You had to have at least one enemy in common," said the sheriff.

I thought about it and sipped at my coffee. "I've been trying to think who might want to kill Madeline, and I think she's probably pissed off as many people as I have just by existing. She was not a nice person."

"Yeah, that's pretty much what I'm getting. I haven't found anyone who seems sorry that she's dead."

I laughed. "Got any ideas about how that hole in her head got cut?"

"Doc Hamilton thinks it had to be a cranial drill, but he doesn't know how anyone would get one."

Oh, I wanted to just reach across the table and slap him. Cranial drill. No one in this town could afford one. We didn't even have a hospital. We had to drive an hour to get to one. "I don't suppose it's occurred to either of you to think of something that someone in town could actually afford?"

The sheriff frowned. "Do you know something you're not telling me?"

"You ever heard of a diamond drill bit?" I asked.

"No," he said.

"Cuts stone and ceramic," I said.

"Since when do you know anything about cutting stone and ceramic?"

"Since I went on the damn internet. I figured you'd need something strong to cut through bone, and the hole in Madeline's head wasn't big, so I did a Google search and found out that you can get a drill bit that cuts stone that's called a diamond bit."

The sheriff stared at me. "Why did you look that up?"

"Because the hole is neat. It wasn't punched like with a claw hammer or something. I got a pretty good look at it when Madeline was lying on my garage floor."

"Huh," he said. Then he messed with his coffee mug. Finally, he looked at me and said, "You always were one to puzzle about things."

"Yeah, I like using my head for something besides a hat rack."

"Diamond bit, huh?"

"Yes. Anybody who just tiled a place might have one."

The sheriff looked at me and smiled. "She just had tile laid in her kitchen. One of her neighbors said she and the tile guy got into a big argument, and that she threatened to make sure everyone knew his work was unsatisfactory."

"That sounds like Madeline," I said.

"Maybe I'll go talk to him," he said. "You think you might want to come along? Just to observe?"

"You want me to come observe you questioning a potential suspect?"

"Just thought you might have some insight on things," he said.

I was sure he knew that I knew more than I was telling him. But it would sure as hell be more interesting than running errands or sitting in the house all day. "Sure," I said.

The two of us went out and got into his patrol car. I'd stuck my wallet in my back pocket and brought my phone, just in case. Soon we were pulling up in front of Kirkland Tile and Flooring. I followed the sheriff inside where a woman stood behind the counter. The sheriff asked to speak to the owner, and the woman said her husband was out on a job.

I stepped a little closer. She was wearing a large opal on a chain around her neck. "That's a nice necklace," I said.

The woman touched it. "Thank you. It's my birthstone."

"Really pretty. You wear opals a lot?"

"All the time. My husband buys me opals every birthday."

"Nice," I said. "I think your husband did the work on our bathroom when we first moved into our house."

"I don't recognize you," she said.

"Oh, he probably worked with Bobby Lou. My hours were always unpredictable. Bobby Lou Daniels?"

The woman smiled, "Oh! I do remember that job. She's really sweet. Paid right on time and never complained about anything. Mike even did a back splash in your kitchen for her at a reduced rate because she was so sweet to work with!"

The sheriff looked at me. Then he looked back at the woman. "Could you have him call me when he's available to talk? I need to ask him some questions about Madeline Howard."

The woman frowned. "I can have him call you. Probably won't be until tonight."

"Do you know anything about the argument he had with Miss Howard about her kitchen tile?"

"Not really. I just know he said she wasn't satisfied, and she wanted him to redo some of the work."

"That's aggravating, I imagine," said the sheriff.

"That woman is more than aggravating. My husband does good work. It's going to eat up our profit having to go back and redo work."

"I'm sorry to hear that," said the sheriff. He pulled out his business card and left it on the counter. "If you could have him call me."

"Certainly," she said.

We walked back out to his car. I looked at him and said, "Have you had Madeline's house searched, yet?"

He looked at me over the top of the car. "You think there's something to find?" he asked.

"Maybe. You never know what could be important."

"Any place you think we might have overlooked something?"

"I know that Carl sometimes doesn't look closely at floors. I did more than a few searches with him over the years and found things after he claimed to have searched a place. I think he's so tall he doesn't really see stuff that's down low."

"I'll have a couple of deputies go through the house again."

"Don't forget to search the garage. It's real easy to miss things under a vehicle or back behind a waste container."

"Thanks, Evelina. I'll be sure to have them take a closer look."

Two days later the front doorbell rang, and Bobby Lou went to answer it. I heard the sheriff's voice. Bobby Lou called out for me to come to the living room. I sighed. The man probably wanted to remind me that as a retired deputy I should keep myself out of his business. But damn, the woman had been left in my garage. It was my business, too.

I walked into the living room and Sheriff Rupert stood with Bobby Lou. She smiled like she'd just won the lottery.

"Sheriff," I said.

He held out a badge to me. "You know I'm allowed to appoint deputies," he said. "I checked into it, and appointed deputies don't fall under the mandatory retirement rules."

Bobby Lou punched me in the arm. "Well, take it, Evelina. The man is hiring you back as a deputy!"

I reached out and took the badge. The damn thing was pretty. I'd always liked our badges. "Is this a joke?"

The sheriff shook his head. "Evelina, we arrested Donna Kirkland today. We found the towels and the diamond drill in a garbage bag at their house. We also found the sedative she'd doped Madeline with in the bathroom cabinet. Mike Kirkland has a prescription for chronic insomnia."

"Did he know?"

The sheriff shook his head. "He's pretty torn up. He had no idea. She knew about you from him having done the tiling here. She'd heard Madeline trash talk you at church."

"Damn," I said.

"You up for coming back?" asked the sheriff.

"Hell, yeah," I said. "You up for dealing with me again?"

He nodded. "You're a pain in the ass, but you're a good deputy."

"Yeah, I am," I said. "Both."

"Good. Start next Monday?"

"Yes, sir. Next Monday sounds great."

Bobby Lou threw her arms around my neck and kissed me. I looked over at the sheriff and he was blushing. Man, I was going to give him no end of shit for that. I kissed Bobby Lou back.

THE MANCHURIAN CANINE

HUGH LESSIG

Old Mr. Halderman says my dog wants to kill him. To be fair, he also says mole people live in Prohibition-era tunnels under the town, and the Amazon delivery guy is a doppelganger whose fellow look-alikes have invaded the neighborhood. My dog is Max, a hairless Chinese crested with a purple mohawk. He needs occasional suppositories for constipation, but sure, he's an assassin.

This morning, I'm weeding the flower bed when Old Mr. Halderman ambles over from next door. One hand fiddles with a twisted paper clip that cinches his pants six inches above the waistline. Mom always called him High Pockets. Her memory almost makes me laugh for the first time in weeks.

"That dog of yours."

"Max, yes."

"He's a-something, that one."

"Quiet voice, please. I haven't had caffeine."

"Last night, he snuck into my kitchen and tried to enter the basement. He's cavorting with the mole people who've come up from the tunnels." Arms crossed, chin jutted, he stamps his foot with an air of finality.

"Mole people. Not the doppelgangers?"

"Good God, is everyone crazy but me? The doppelgangers are a separate population. They're walking the neighborhood. The mole people are in the tunnels, and now they're in my basement. I've locked the door so they can't get out, but they call me—by name."

Somewhere in Penn's Landing, a kindly soul would ask the difference between mole people in tunnels and doppelgangers walking the neighborhood. That soul is not me. "Mr. Halderman, what's gotten in to you? I've only been back home a few days, but I don't remember you having these... problems. You were just the weird old man who lived down the lane. Every neighborhood needs one."

The insult rolls off him. "I've got a bad heart because of all this. Your mom didn't believe me, either."

"Mom liked you."

"She was a real clown."

He walks away before I can thank him for the complement. Mom was indeed a clown. She worked birthday parties and carnivals around Penn's Landing, making balloon animals and finding coins behind the crusty ears of children. Three weeks ago, I lost my marketing job in Philly to the boss's son, fresh out of college with a bachelor's degree in beer pong. Mom told me to come home and sort things out, but first, she insisted I trash the boss in a company-wide email. She could always make me laugh.

Two days after that conversation, mom died in a car cash. Her Volvo was T-boned on Interstate 80 near the New Jersey line. Through tears and fury—*I thought it was a prank call! I almost hung up on the police! Volvos are the safest cars around!*—I fulfilled her last wish, scorching my company's inbox with all-caps screamer, including that time I spotted our vice president at a local comic convention, where he cosplayed a kitten and flirted with a chain-saw-wielding French maid before discovering she was a he, then switched to stalking anime girls in plaid skirts and knee socks who shouldered meat cleavers on their crisp, white blouses. Writing that email was fun. I imagined mom applauding it, and I smiled. But I'm not back to normal, not by a long shot.

Now I'm alone in the family homestead, where mom and I shared everything. She was only eighteen years older than me. Dad left when I was born, and talking about him was forbidden. Mom was very big on moving on, and I should listen to her. Penn's Landing is no longer the town I remember. Downtown is overrun with convenience stores and payday lending outlets. Harrison's Drug Store, which featured an old-fashioned soda fountain, is a blood plasma donation center. Stately homes have been chopped into rentals with overgrown front yards. Even Old Mr. Halderman has somehow devolved.

What's worse, I don't know what to call him. Growing up, he was always Old Mr. Halderman. Is he now *Older* Mr. Halderman?

The question answers itself that night, when he becomes Dead Mr. Halderman.

* * * *

A frantic pounding at the door interrupts my nightly dose of Anderson Cooper. Keeping the chain in place, I open the door a few inches to labored wheezing and cigar-scented hot breath. A withered hand shoots through the opening and grabs my fingers. In the glow of my porchlight, Mr. Halderman stares daggers at me.

"That dog." He takes a gulp of air. "That dog of yours. I swear."

"Enough with the dog, Mr. Halderman. I'm in fuzzy pants here."

Speaking of pants, the old man has none. He wears rubber goulashes and a wristwatch and good God but that's it. With his free hand, Mr. Halderman clutches the gray hairs of his chest. "He has spectral powers. I swear. I ran here to tell you."

I can't think or form words. The universe is out of balance. At some point, it occurs to me that an old man running with a bad heart isn't a good idea, with or without clothes. That's when he releases my fingers and slides to his knees. He hiccups twice, then stops breathing. He stares at nothing. Anderson Cooper welcomes his expert panel on the situation in Gaza. Max materializes out of the darkness and jumps on the front porch, wagging his tail.

"Max. Did you chase him here?"

He barks once.

"Could you have brought pants?"

A phone call brings two paramedics who extricate the old man from my door and confirm the obvious. After a few minutes, they go to their truck and leave me alone with the victim, covered to his chin with a blanket. Even in life, Mr. Halderman's face was made for an open casket viewing. The grim mouth. Those crinkled eyes. His future is finally looking up. Neighbors will toddle from the funeral home, whispering to each other: *Didn't he look good? I thought he looked good.*

I pat his head. "Why was my dog so interested in you? No one else is."

After the paramedics leave, a police officer pulls up in a white SUV. He looks ten years younger than me, with a weaker chin and skinnier forearms. A Batman-style utility belt barely rests on his hips. He wears a proper police-man's cap, and his name badge says Hanson.

"We got a call for a 10-27. That's an unresponsive male."

"He also fit that description while alive."

Officer Hanson cocks an eyebrow. "Did you see what happened?"

"I can't un-see it."

"Name of the deceased?"

"Mr. Halderman from next door. First name Harry."

He stares into the front yard, as if clues will sprout like dandelions in the dark. Max comes up from behind and sniffs his pant leg. Hanson flinches. "What's with the hairless cat?"

"That is a dog."

"It looks like one of those hairless cats a villain would have."

Max growls. Hanson smooths his shirt and tightens his belt another notch, checking various pouches and pockets. He reaches down and tentatively pats Max on the head. "Did Halderman say anything before he collapsed?"

"Nope."

"He wasn't screaming about doppelgängers?"

"Not even mole people. You've heard his conspiracy theories, too."

The officer points down the dark road. "Worse than that. A while back, he started this cockamamie newsletter full of his theories. He tacks it on telephone poles all over the neighborhood. At least he doesn't get on the internet." Hanson checks his phone. "I must go. Have a good night, ma'am."

The next morning, I gaze out the kitchen window at the Halderman bungalow, which hasn't changed since I was a child. It has the same sagging porch, the leaning foundation, the odd arrangement of backyard junk. The front door appears ajar. A woman at the police department answers the non-emergency number and says today is a great day in Penn's Landing. I immediately detest her.

"Not to be a Karen, but I'm calling about the Halderman house. He died yesterday, and his property is an eyesore. I don't think he had any survivors. I'm wondering what will happen to it."

"What's your last name, Karen?"

"It's Georgette Winston."

"So, Karen is your middle name."

"Just—okay. Can you find Officer Hanson and put him on? Last night, he came to my house after I called 9-1-1."

"Officer Manson? Like in the stabby family?"

"Hanson. H-A-N-S-O-N."

"No one named Hanson works for this department."

"That's ridiculous. He wore a blue uniform and drove a car with the police logo."

"Our officers wear khaki, not blue. The chief says it's ass-slimming. His words. For the record, it is not."

"This Hanson had a badge and everything."

"Really, a badge and everything? Did he have a belt with stuff hanging from it?"

"Um, yeah."

"He must have been legit. No way could a regular citizen obtain such things. If only we had a system of computers connected worldwide, in a sort of web, and we could buy anything by using handheld devices that double as telephones, but gosh, ma'am, until that far-off day arrives…"

"The vehicle," I say. "The logo."

She asks for my phone number. A beep signals an incoming text. It is a photo of the Penn's Landing Police Department logo. "Did it look like that?"

"Uh, no."

"The next time your friend comes trick or treating, let us know. We'd like to have a conversation with him. I'm hanging up now, Karen. Have a blessed day in Penn's Landing, gateway to the Poconos."

I stray into the kitchen, feeling like a stupid twelve-year-old seeking Mom's comfort. Except now I'm looking for cabernet sauvignon instead of licking cake batter off a wooden spoon.

* * * *

The next morning, Max and I walk down the road and find Mr. Halderman's most recent newsletter stuck to a telephone pole. It is a single sheet of paper printed on both sides and looks like something made on a Smith-Corona typewriter, spit out by a hand-cranked mimeograph machine. The name was conjured up in a hot fever of creativity.

THE HALDERMAN NEWSLETTER

The top headline is a bit more sparkling.

DOPPELGÄNGERS STALK PENN'S LANDING!

The story says several people who have been sighted in the area appear to be copies of each other. One dresses in a shirt and tie and carries a clipboard. Another wears bib overalls and delivers vegetables. A third masquerades as a police officer. The photo accompanying the story has been distorted through the printing process. It shows a man in a police uniform that could be the fake Officer Hanson, walking between my house and Halderman's.

Great. The twitchy fake cop has body doubles, and he knows where I live.

I return home and lock the doors and windows. Theories run through my head, but none explain why an imposter cop would stalk me and have look-alikes around the neighborhood. Mom never mentioned keeping a gun in the house, but I search her bedroom anyway. All I find is her clown makeup case, a three-tiered box of vials and gels and pencils. In a way, it was also her medicine chest. She never got over dad leaving us, but she self-medicated her grief by putting on a different face and making others laugh. She told me that being a clown worked better than Prozac.

"Always have fun, Georgie," she would tell me.

It gives me an idea.

That afternoon, I drive downtown and find an office supply store. I buy new cartridges for my printer and a stack of paper. During the drive, I try not to see the closed storefronts and homes with For Sale signs in the yard. Back home, I fire up my laptop, find a newsletter template and match the font and purple type of The Halderman Newsletter. It takes less than an hour to publish a two-sided sheet. The back page has two stories: a ghost locomotive that runs along an old railroad bed that is now a hiking trail, and glowing orbs rising from abandoned coal mines to impregnate farm animals.

Hey, I'm in marketing.

On the front page, the lead story is the jewel in the crown.

"MANCHURIAN CANINE" STALKS DOPPELGÄNGERS

Recent reports of a body stalking Penn's Landing have caught the attention of Max, an assassin dog. A hairless Chinese crested, Max's fur balls are tipped with a slow-acting toxin. Styled after the infamous Manchurian Candidate, Max is controlled by an unseen enemy. Anyone who pets Max will soon fall ill, and death comes in a matter of days unless the victim receives an antidote.

One hour later, the latest issue of the Halderman Newsletter hits the telephone poles. Let's see if that brings any fake police officers out of the woodwork.

* * * *

The rescue organization where I adopted Max is one hour south of Penn's Landing. The director's name is Pete, and he picks up on the first ring. Of course, he asks about my marketing job. Then he wonders how mom is doing. I tell him the bad news and the worse news.

"I'll stop asking questions now."

"On the bright side, Max may have helped kill my neighbor. I was hoping to board him with you until things blow over."

"I… wait."

"Try to keep up, Pete."

I summarize the last twenty-four hours: Max's odd obsession with Halderman and his house, the old man turning up dead on my doorstep, the fake cop, the newsletter, and my attempt to draw the imposter into the open with a story about Max's fur.

"You have a future in marketing, Georgette. But we're booked up here. What happens if this guy shows up at your door?"

"I'll get a photo and give it to the police. I wanted Max out of the picture. This fake cop has seen my dog, and I have a bad feeling. All of Penn's Landing gives me a bad feeling. I've lived elsewhere for ten years. I don't know what's happened since I've been away."

"Finally, a question I can answer," Pete says. "You're in coal country, right? Look up the Hudson Investment Company. They buy houses and convert them into crappy apartments. Businesses get divided into smaller storefronts that change every year. Maintenance never gets done. The newspapers have run stories. They're land vultures, snapping up properties where the economy is depressed."

He starts to say something else, then stops.

"What else about this investment company?" I ask.

"It's not that. It's about Max. He has a… a certain skill. Max was part of a pilot program down here. The idea was to run non-traditional dogs through a drug detection program. Let's say the police did an assembly in a high school or set up a booth at a job fair. You bring a dog like Max, who seems more like a pet. People let down their guard and approach him. If they've got drugs, bingo."

"That sounds… weird."

"It was privately funded and never got off the ground. But Max went through most of the training. He was given up for adoption after the money ran out. To be clear, your dog is not a certified drug detector. But he completed much of the training. It's interesting that your neighbor attracted Max's attention."

Last night, he snuck into my kitchen and tried to enter the basement. He's cavorting with the mole people who've come up from the tunnels.

"Thanks Pete. You gave me an idea."

* * * *

That night, Max and I walk to Mr. Halderman's bungalow and push open the unlocked door. The stench of musty old men—a mix of stale sweat, pine cologne, and frying grease—nearly knocks me sideways. Max sneezes while walking into the kitchen. A leaning tower of crusty dishes rises from the sink. My shoes stick to the tiled floor. A fridge wheezes and shudders in its final death throes. Max stops at an old wooden door and pushes it open. Steps descend into darkness.

Do I deal with mole people or open the fridge?

I'll take mole people for five hundred, Alex.

Downstairs, the milky glow from a laptop screen allows me to find a switch that activates overhead lights. I'm standing in a basement twice the size of the bungalow. It extends beyond the original foundation in all directions. Next to the laptop are two large speakers and an old map marked with colored pens.

Storage crates line the far wall. The concrete floor is immaculate. A shiny metal hatch marks the center of the room. Max ambles over to the crates, barks twice and lifts his leg. Then he goes to the hatch and circles excitedly. I walk toward him and take in the sweet stench of weed.

The crates are full of marijuana, wrapped in neat bales.

College memories return in a fog. Marketing memories are clearer. Pennsylvania doesn't allow recreational weed, unlike New Jersey and other neighboring states. It certainly doesn't allow *bales* of it. My marketing company worked for an organization that was trying to change that, lobbying state lawmakers in Harrisburg. It didn't work. Only medical marijuana is authorized in the Keystone State.

The floor hatch opens to a ladder. Down in the darkness, men grunt and swear in the distance. One sounds like fake officer Hanson, who says, "We need to keep moving product. Aunt Alma expects better from us, and I'm not feeling well. I petted that dog. Did you read the latest newsletter?"

The other man laughs nervously. "If it makes you feel better, we'll kill the neighbor's dog, cut off its head, and take it to be examined."

"That's for rabies, idiot."

I shut the hatch and pick up Max, who nuzzles my neck. "I won't let anything happen to you, boy. Those morons sound too afraid to put one foot in front of the other. Let's look around some more."

The old map draws my attention. Colored pens mark different areas of a tunnel complex. I jiggle the touchpad on the computer and see a spreadsheet with a title. Dots connect.

"I get it now, Max. We need to do some work and make a phone call."

* * * *

Thirty minutes later, we're back in the basement. I open the hatch and climb down. Max rests in my backpack. The tunnel is silent and pitch black. I turn on my neck light, great for reading in bed, navigating through a power outage, or moving through creepy tunnels with your fake assassin dog, currently looking over my shoulder like a pirate's parrot.

Five minutes later, we come across stacked cases of beer. Harsh voices split the silence up ahead. I switch off my light. Flashlights wave back and forth, getting closer.

"I need a doctor," Hanson says. "It's the fur. The slow-acting poison. I think it's getting dark."

"It *is* dark."

"Darker then."

"Fine. Let's go tell a doctor you petted the toxic fur of an assassin dog who is controlled by unseen forces," his companion says. "We need to finish this move, then go get the dog. Maybe knock that woman around a bit. These tunnels give me the creeps."

The flashlights stop at an intersection of tunnels. A single bulb hangs by an orange extension cord, the two men backlit against it. I retreat to the beer cases and pick up a full can. Staying in the dark, bending my knees for balance, I toss the can at the bulb.

And hit it.

Sort of.

The plan was to break the bulb and throw everything into darkness. Instead, I hit the cord and the bulb sways wildly, throwing light at crazy angles.

Maybe that will work just as well. I rush into the clearing and scream at the top of my lungs. The men turn toward me. Fake officer Hanson still wears his policeman's uniform. The other man could pass for his younger brother. Same weak chin. Same clueless stare.

They see me and run the other way.

Because I'm not me.

My skin is deathly white. Dark circles ring my eyes. A crazed smile extends halfway to my ears, and my hair is a rat's nest of gray stalks that sprout from my head.

I've heard that mole people live in tunnels under Penn's Landing. And I have mom's makeup case to thank for it.

Max jumps from my backpack and chases the men. They must smell like weed, as did Mr. Halderman when he finally worked up the courage to enter his basement and find a drug distribution network under his living room, complete with a map of the Prohibition-era tunnels.

On the night he died, was he running to tell me what he found?

I run after Max and do my best to scream like a mole lady, whatever that's supposed to sound like. Ahead of me, light stabs through the darkness. The men have climbed another ladder and opened a new hatch, but they're not escaping. Harsh voices order them to show their hands. They ascend into the light. As Max reaches the bottom of the ladder, a supernatural growl comes from his throat. A flashlight shines on him.

"Chief, what the heck is that?"

I grab Max and pull him away. For a split second, I look up and lock gazes with a police officer wearing a ball cap and protective vest. I wonder if he's the guy who answered the phone less than an hour ago, when I called in a tip on Mr. Halderman's landline phone, telling police to look out for drug dealers in the Penn's Landing tunnel complex. Thanks to the old map marked with exits, I could tell them where to stake out.

The police officer gasps in horror.

"Never mind the chupacabra. Who is *that*?"

* * * *

The next morning, the same officer who looked down the manhole at me shows up at my door. He wants to know about the night Mr. Halderman died. His name is Josh Ripley and he doesn't seem to recognize me—yet.

"There was an incident at Halderman's house last night. Two brothers were using his basement as a hub for their marijuana distribution ring. The house was built by a bootlegger in the 1920s and sits near an intersection of tunnels. They could move weed in different directions, imported from other states. Mr. Halderman's name was etched on the inside of the crates. We found a laptop with a fake profile in Halderman's name. The guy never got on the internet, so he didn't know about it. Had it been exposed, it would have looked like Halderman's operation."

"I'm glad you caught the brothers red-handed then."

"We received a tip last night, phoned in from the Halderman house." Officer Ripley eyes me up and down. "It was a woman's voice."

"Maybe it was the mole people. Mr. Halderman insisted he heard voices in his basement."

"He was telling the truth. The brothers played ghostly voices on that laptop. It must have spooked the old man, and he wouldn't go down there. But he wasn't crazy. We think he overcame that fear and found the basement operation before ending up dead in your yard."

Because Max led him down there. Mr. Halderman couldn't tell the police, because his name was on the crates and the computer records.

Ripley flips open a notebook. "Those brothers delivered weed around town in the light of day. They'd dress up as different people: vendors, a farmer delivering produce or cops."

"Doppelgangers. Mr. Halderman saw them."

"Exactly. Fred Gorman listened to a police scanner and must have heard paramedics rush to your address when the old man died. He got curious because you're Halderman's neighbor. He even drove an SUV with a bad version the department's seal."

"So I hear."

Ripley looks over my shoulder. "This is Mary Winston's old house. She was quite the clown."

"I get that a lot."

"Are back here to settle up the estate?"

"I'm not sure. I thought Penn's Landing had nothing for me, but I need to give it more thought. I haven't been back here in a long time."

"That's strange. You seem oddly familiar, Miss Winston."

TWO MONTHS LATER

At six in the morning, a persistent knock rouses me from sleep. I open the front door to find a lemon-sucking woman with a helmet of blue hair. It even has Nazi-like flares instead of split ends. Although a foot shorter, she somehow backs me into the house.

"You're the woman behind these Penn's Landing Conspiracy Tours," she says.

"That's my new project, yes."

"The lady with the dog."

"Also me."

"Whose mother was a clown."

"You've hit the trifecta, ma'am. How can I help you? The tours are self-guided. Just download the app and pay online."

Her mouth twists into a full grimace, and it was already halfway there. "I have no intention of supporting your ill-conceived tour. Some people will do anything for money."

"I'm in marketing. Conspiracy theories run rampant in Penn's Landing, and I'm just trying to monetize them."

"Monetize? Exploiting people's fears is more like it."

"Oh please. It's harmless fun, and a portion of the proceeds go into an economic development fund. It'll provide seed money to residents who want to start businesses. Maybe one day we can clean up these decrepit apartments."

"Those are *my* apartments, young lady." She rises to her full height, which is still munchkin level. "I am Alma Gorman, managing partner for the Hudson Investment Company. We own many buildings in the area. I resent your insinuation that they are run down. This conspiracy tour is the last thing I need. I've been dealing with bad publicity since the arrest of my nephews."

That night in the tunnels, one of the Gorman brothers referred to "Aunt Alma." She must have managed the weed distribution network. This diminutive woman doesn't fit the profile of a menacing drug dealer. Maybe that's her secret.

"So, you're Alma Gorman, drug kingpin."

Did I just say that? I just said that.

"How dare you? I'll sue you for slander."

Max comes to the door, yawning and leaning against my leg. At the sight of Alma Gorman, he perks up. He circles the old woman, then paws at her oversized purse, a saddlebag that would make John Wayne proud.

"Max seems to like you. Or something you're carrying."

The old woman stalks away, muttering to herself. Halfway to her car, she drops her purse and Max races for it. He burrows inside and begins to run. The purse sprouts four hairless legs with tufts of fur at the ankles. The old lady screams. A blue shard of hair disengages itself from that steel perm and stands up straight. She waddles down the sidewalk, chasing her purse, screeching like fingernails on a blackboard.

I can hear mom laughing.

I join in.

THE SWEET FERN AND THE JUNIPER

P.J. NELSON

My Aunt Rose left me a bookshop in her will. She'd been a Broadway actor for thirty years, more understudy and chorus than leading roles, but still a life in the theatre. Her baffling retirement plan was to return to Enigma, Georgia, where we were both raised, and make her ancestral manse, a dilapidated three-story Victorian on the edge of a tiny town, into The Old Juniper Bookshop. More baffling than that: it worked, largely owing to the nearby Barnsley College, an oasis of education in a landscape of gnats.

It was the end of the summer, but temperatures were still over a hundred degrees every day. No rain in sight and not a whisper of a breeze anywhere in town. That kind of heat will make you do crazy things.

So there I was, fanning myself with a comic book version of *The Moonstone*, dressed in rust-colored linen shorts and a white seersucker shirt I'd found in a thrift store. I was swatting at bugs and sipping gin and lemonade, when up roared the town police car—the only one—and out flew Billy Sanders, the law in our little slice of heaven.

"Maddy," he said breathlessly, flying up the porch steps. "Look!"

He held out his hand. In it there was a receipt from my shop, wrinkled and a little soggy, for "Once More On The Lake" by E.B. White.

I looked at it. Then I looked at Billy.

"Do you want a refund?" I asked him. "You'll have to give me the book back."

He shook his head, trying to catch his breath. His face was contorted, and his eyes were a little wild.

"What is it, Billy?"

"They found a dead body at Dillard's Lake. She had this in the pocket of her cutoffs." He swallowed. "I thought you might be able to tell me who she was."

That was unusual. Billy knew everyone. He grew up in Enigma. He was also one of the calmest people in the state and I'd never seen him so disconcerted.

"I didn't recognize her," he confessed, police hat off, shaking his sweaty head. "I guess she's a student at the college."

I set down my drink and reading material, took the receipt, and stared.

"I remember this little book," I began. "It was something that Philomena special ordered for her Perspectives class. It's an essay."

Dr. Philomena Waldrop, head of the Psychology Department at the college, was Rose's closest companion and my surrogate aunt. It was thanks largely to her that the bookshop did such sterling business.

"Would she know this kid?" Billy asked.

I stood. "Of course she would. Come on."

I headed inside. Billy followed.

The inside of the bookshop was lit by the last light of the day, dust motes floating golden in the air and the irrepressible scent of books, old and new, all around. The place was empty except for Cannonball, the world's largest black cat, who had commandeered the old desk in the parlor that we used as a cash register.

I sat at the desk. Billy stood beside me impatiently. Cannonball opened one eye.

"Mind if I use the phone," I asked the cat.

Cannonball did not immediately object, so I placed the call and Phil answered almost immediately.

"Hey," I said quickly. "It's Madeline. Got a question for you."

She was silent for a moment. Then: "No small talk? No 'Hot enough for you'? No—,"

"Billy's here," I interrupted. "He found a dead girl at Dillard's Lake."

"Drowned," Billy volunteered. "Looks like."

"Oh." Phil's voice changed instantly. "Who was it?"

"That's why I'm calling," I said. "The kid had a receipt in her pocket for that E.B. White essay book you had your students get, so I thought maybe you'd know something."

"Oh," she said again, more distressed. "One of my students?"

"Don't you think?" I asked.

"Well."

Philomena was a riddle. She seemed so fragile on the outside, but I knew she had a core of granite. She and Rose had raised me more than my parents had, and I knew her better than I knew most people. Still, I was shocked to hear her suggestion.

"I guess I'd better have a look at the body, then," she said.

I glanced at Billy. "You want to look at the body? I thought maybe we could just go through the receipt book here and figure something out."

"Everyone in the Perspectives class bought the essay," she said dismissively. "The semester is only two weeks old, so I don't know everyone in the class yet. You stay right where you are. I'm coming over."

And she hung up.

I held the phone a second longer, then gave up. There's no arguing with a dial tone.

"She's on her way," I told Billy.

"What?" He took a sideways step and shot a look out the window, as if she might already be outside. "Dr. Waldrop is coming here?"

I stood. "You know what she's like."

He did. He'd taken courses from her. He was working on his degree in Criminology. He had aspirations. You had to have aspirations in a town like ours. Billy and I went into the kitchen for coffee.

Phil arrived twenty minutes later. She was as flustered as she was concerned. Dressed in her college professor uniform: navy shin-length dress, hair up in a tight bun, glasses on a pearl chain around her neck.

"Tell me what happened," she demanded even before she was in the kitchen.

Billy stood; it's the way he was raised.

"Baxter Jennings, over at the Dillard's Organic Farm, he found her just after dawn this morning," Billy began. "But he was scared, and he didn't know what to do, so he didn't call me until around two this afternoon."

Phil slid into a seat at the kitchen table. The kitchen was huge, the ceiling was high, and the wooden floor was battered and scarred from over a hundred years of wear and tear. It also felt like the safest place in America. I couldn't have told you why, exactly, except that it was also a room filled with memories of thousands of loving southern meals and a hundred thousand caring embraces and a million tears—happy and sad. A room absorbs that kind of thing, keeps it in the walls and the ceiling and the air.

"That poor child," Phil said, barely above a whisper.

"I didn't recognize her," Billy went on. "But I found the receipt from this place in her pocket."

"Anything else?" I asked. "No wallet, obviously, but—"

"She was holding a kind of odd mug in her hand," he said.

"And the receipt was for the essay book?" Phil confirmed.

Billy showed it to her. She looked down at it and sighed.

"'Summertime, oh, summertime,'" she quoted softly. "'Pattern of life indelible, the fade-proof lake, the woods unshatterable, the pasture with the sweet fern and the juniper forever and ever.' The essay is White's musing on the patterns of Time, with a capital T—what it changes, and what it doesn't. I use it in the course—"

"So where is the body now?" I interrupted, setting down a cup of coffee in front of Philomena.

"Still out in the field by the lake," Billy said, obviously miserable about it.

"You just left her there?" Phil raged.

"The coroner from Tifton couldn't get away. He won't be here 'til seven, and he told me—I mean, I knew already not to move the body. I left old man Dillard there with her."

"Let's go!" Phil stood so suddenly that it toppled her chair.

Ignoring the flying furniture, she headed toward the front door like a bulldozer. Billy and I looked at each other. Billy got up and put the chair aright. I followed Phil through the shop.

"Can you answer the phone while I'm gone?" I asked Cannonball.

Cannonball looked at me, head upside down, but otherwise remained noncommittal on the subject.

* * * *

Dillard Lake strained the definition of the word; I would have called it a pond. But Dillard Organic Farm was a genuinely great enterprise. Best vegetables and peaches I'd ever tasted.

The lake was on the outside edge of the twenty-acre peach orchard. The peak of the peach season had passed, but there was still fruit to be had, pink and gold in the last light of day.

There were two people sitting in the grass at the edge of the lake. One was Pierce Dillard, the scion of the family, about sixty and dressed in overalls. The other person was his granddaughter Ellie, cut-off jeans, baseball cap, and a T-shirt that advertised Juicy Girl tomatoes. She was a student at the college and a frequent patron of the bookshop. She looked like she'd been crying.

As we approached them, they stood up silently.

Philomena brushed past Billy and me as she rushed forward to see the body that the Dillards had been guarding.

When she stopped and gasped, I assumed that she recognized the deceased. I went to her and looked down. I also recognized the girl lying there on her side but couldn't have said who she was. Like drowned Ophelia, she was decorated with a few pond weeds. In her left hand she held some kind of arcane mug with a grotesque, three-dimensional face on it, glistening in the late light.

"It's Laney Bascombe," Phil whispered. "From down in Willacoochee. Worst student I've ever had."

At that Ellie Dillard burst into tears again and said to Philomena, "This is all my fault!"

Billy stared. I glanced between Phil and Ellie. Philomena rushed without hesitation and took Ellie in her arms.

"Why would this be your fault, sweetheart," she whispered to the distraught girl.

"Because!" Ellie was inconsolable. "The club was my idea."

The lake, the orchard, the setting sun all took a moment of silence before Billy stammered, "What club?"

Ellie explained, sniffing and sobbing.

The Enigma Swim Association began as a drunken dare. Who in her dorm would be willing to go to her family's farm, drunk as they were, and swim across Dillard Lake at midnight under a full moon? There had apparently been many such outings.

"Last night it was just three of us," Ellie concluded. "We got here at about eleven, drank a whole lot, and then me and Jill Haydon jumped in."

She glanced at the dead body, and then went on, but her voice had changed dramatically.

"Only Laney...she was already passed out. Me and Jill swam across the lake. I don't quite remember what happened after that. I woke up this morning in my dorm room, still in my wet clothes. I come over to Grandpa's to have supper about an hour ago. That's when I heard the news."

"Uh huh," Phil said with just the right tone of condemnation. "But Maddy told me that this child bought a copy of the E. B. White essay at the Old Juniper."

"She did," I volunteered. "I remember her."

Phil flashed a look my way. "She's not in that class. My Perspectives class. She failed my Intro to Psych class. It's a prerequisite for Perspectives."

"Anyway," Billy grunted impatiently.

But before Billy could go on, the sound of a four by four broke through the orchard behind us. It was driven by Grandma Dillard, and her passenger was the coroner from Tifton. I couldn't remember his name, but we'd met before.

"All right," Billy said with a hint of authority, "let's clear out, let the coroner do his job."

The coroner got out of the four by four; Ellie and her grandpa got in and drove away.

"Why would Laney buy that essay?" Phil asked, mostly to herself.

"Hey," the coroner said suddenly. "I thought you said this was a drowning."

Billy walked toward the coroner. "It's not?"

"She may have been in the lake, but there's not any water in her lungs, I can you tell that already. But mostly, look here."

The coroner rolled the body slightly and pointed. There, sideways in her chest, was a small, red-handled knife.

* * * *

Billy delivered Phil and me back to the bookshop and left. Phil was going to her office for Laney Bascombe's address and phone number so that Billy could contact her family.

"Is Ellie Dillard in your Perspectives class?" I asked Phil as she was getting into her car.

"Uh huh," Phil answered distractedly. "She and Jill Haydon, the other girl Ellie mentioned."

And with that, she was gone. The sun had set but twilight lingered. The crickets and cicadas set loose their low music. As I climbed the stairs up the front porch, my brain would not slow down. Because somebody killed a girl who bought a book from me. For some reason, that made it personal.

So, I turned over some of the possibilities. One of the other two girls in the so-called swim association had killed Laney. Unthinkable. Or the farm worker that found the body, Baxter Jennings, did it. Unlikely. Baxter had lived and worked on the Dillard farm forever. What motive could he possibly have had? After that, my mind went wild. College boys, aware of the swim club, tantalized by the possibility of drunken young women under the moonlight, followed the club to the lake, found Laney passed out, tried to take advantage of her, and stabbed her when she woke up and objected. But that was too much like a bad television plot and Enigma wasn't that kind of town. Of course, the question closest to home for me was why would she buy a book for a class that she wasn't taking?

Once inside, I caught sight of Cannonball. He was still lolling on the desktop where I'd left him.

"Did anybody call while I was gone?" I asked him.

His sat up and licked his chest.

I thought about eating. I thought about drinking some more. I thought about just going to bed. But in the end, I found my car keys, jumped in my car, and headed for Barnsley College.

* * * *

It wasn't difficult to find Jill Haydon's dorm room. Wisely or unwisely, there was a register posted at the bottom of the stairs right inside the front door. So up the stairs I went, two steps at a time, hoping Jill was in.

Room 207 was at the end of the hall. The door was open, and to my surprise, Otis Redding's "Sad Song" was emanating from the room. When I got to the door, I tapped on the frame and peered in. A young woman in a pale blue T-shirt dress was sitting on the bed, singing along with Mr. Redding. She hadn't heard my tapping.

"Hi," I said a little louder than I needed to.

She jumped, stood, and stared.

"Sorry," I said instantly. "Sorry. I...my name is Madeline Brimley and—"

"I know who you are, ma'am." She sighed heavily.

"Yeah, I was hoping to speak with you," I told her, trying to ignore being called ma'am, "about your little swim last night."

She instantly burst into tears and collapsed back onto her bed.

I stepped into the room. It was meticulously cared for, nothing out of place, which seemed to me an anomaly in the empire of dorm rooms. On the wall by the bed there was a poster of Einstein on a park bench. He was talking with Marilyn Monroe.

"I didn't mean to upset you," I began.

"Laney's dead and it's my fault," she sobbed.

"That's just what Ellie said." I took a few more steps into the room. "Now it's *your* fault?"

"It's this *heat*; I believe it's made me lose my mind." Jill did her best to compose herself. "You got no idea how hard college is."

Didn't seem like an answer to my question.

Otis concluded his Sad Song and started singing about the Dock of the Bay.

I waited.

"I'm on a HOPE scholarship," she finally told me. "My parents could never afford to send me here. Or. Anywhere, tell the truth. And if I don't keep up my grades, then I lose the scholarship, I go back home to Ty Ty, I work on my family chicken farm, I get pregnant by some stupid redneck boy, I get emphysema from the air in them big old coops, and I'm dead before I'm thirty."

And she began to cry again.

"Well," I said as calmly as I could, "that's quite a vision of the future. And I've been in some of those industrial chicken coops. The air is terrible. But what does that have to do with Laney?"

Jill reached over and switched off the music just as Otis was explaining that he'd left his home in Georgia.

"You can't tell nobody this," Jill whispered. "Promise."

"Tell them what?" I asked, reticent to promise something that I wouldn't do.

"Laney was the smartest person I ever met," Jill said.

That didn't seem to agree with Philomena's assessment of Laney's poor academic standing. But I kept quiet. Sometimes keeping quiet is the best thing for a conversation.

"I guess I was jealous of her. Sometimes she made me feel so stupid. She could do math in her head, she could remember long quotes from books, and she could read faster than—than the wind."

I was unaware of the wind's ability to read at all, but I kept quiet.

"It was some people, some teachers here, even, that thought she wasn't so smart," Jill said. "But if Laney was in a class and she got bored, she just quit going to that class and, I mean, she failed. Like a bunch of times."

"Okay, but I'm still wondering," I said, "what this has to do with Laney's death."

She nodded and sat up straight, preparing for her confession.

"I wasn't doing so well in Dr. Waldrop's Perspectives class. I only passed the Intro to Psych class because of Laney. So I asked Laney to help me again. She went and bought that stupid little book about the lake. She wouldn't take mine; I don't know why. She tried to explain it all to me. But, I mean, what even is the metaphysics of time?"

She had a difficult time pronouncing the word metaphysics.

"That's a tough one," I agreed, trying not to get pulled into a philosophical discussion. "So Laney was helping you with the class."

"Uh huh," Jill said, not looking at me. "And then…we went swimming last night in Ellie's lake."

* * * *

It was ten minutes before midnight by the time the three young women decided to swim across the lake. They'd been drinking a concoction called Bee's Knees: lemon, honey, and gin. They'd already finished one batch and were well into a second by the time Jill lit into Laney.

"You think you're so smart," Jill said, involuntarily spitting as she spoke. "You think you're so much smarter than me!"

Laney just smiled. "I don't think I'm smarter than you. I just am."

Ellie tried to stop things before they got started. "Jill, this girl has helped you before and she's helping you again. What are you doing?"

Jill turned her ire on Ellie. "What am I doing? I'm telling off a know-it-all. What's she doing here anyway? If she's so smart, why ain't she in some better college in some better town?"

Laney answered. "I picked Barnsley College because it was in a town called Enigma. The *town* is called *Enigma*. Plus, it's pretty, the campus. What do you call all those shrubs that have flowers on them?"

"Azaleas," Ellie answered absently. "Jill, you've had too much to drink."

"I ain't had enough to drink," Jill answered. And then she took two or three healthy swigs from her red Solo cup. "You're nothing, Laney! You don't never sleep. You always drink out of that stupid face mug you love so much. You're shaky all the time. You got no boyfriend, you got no friends at all, truth to tell. Nobody likes you. Why don't you go back where you come from?"

And at that Jill reached into the pocket of her gym shorts and produced a red-handled Girl Scout knife, opened it, and stood up.

Jill got to her feet too, but Laney stayed where she was.

"This is exactly what I would expect from a drunken bumpkin," Laney drawled. And then, "Drunken bumpkin. That's hard to say when you've had a lot to drink."

Ellie grabbed Jill's arm then and pulled her toward the water. "Come on, Jill. It's midnight. Let's get into the water now. Cool off."

Ellie pulled again, hard, and Jill dropped the knife on the ground at the water's edge. One more tug and both girls fell into the shallows and began to swim across the lake.

* * * *

"I don't exactly remember what happened then," Jill concluded. "But I know me and Ellie swum across the lake, and it sobered me up a little. At least enough to swim back to apologize to Laney because I didn't mean it. I didn't mean what I said. But when we got there, Laney was dead."

"What do you mean?" I wanted a clear picture.

Jill's voice was barely above a whisper. "I mean she took my knife and killed herself. It was there, sticking out of her chest. She done it because of what I said. Because of how mean I was to her. Because of me."

After that, Jill couldn't put together any more coherent sentences. I gathered that she and Ellie just left Laney at the water's edge and ran.

I took out my phone and called Billy.

"I know how Laney Bascombe died," I said, very proud of my investigative skills. "I've solved your case for you."

"Uh huh," he said, and then he chuckled. "Maybe hold off on that for a minute."

"Why would I do that?" I asked, a little incensed at his attitude.

"Well, mainly because Laney ain't dead."

I don't know how long I was silent—seemed like an hour—before I said, "What?"

"Come over to the Urgent Care on 82," he said, and I could actually hear him smiling. "I'll explain everything. And Maddy, you ain't about to believe it."

* * * *

I arrived at the Urgent Care Center on the highway about a half an hour later. Billy was waiting for me.

"What the hell is going on?" I asked him before he had a chance to get in a word.

He just laughed, then, and waved me down the hall, so I followed.

There, sitting up in the hospital bed in Room Two, with a woman in scrubs standing next to her holding a chart, was Laney Bascombe, pale and confused, but alive as she could be.

I turned to Billy then. "You have got to explain this to me."

He nodded. "Lemme let the doctor do that."

The woman in scrubs turned our way. Her name tag read Dr. Harris, and she just shook her head.

"I've never seen anything like this," she began, walking toward Billy and me. "I've only heard anecdotal stories. Let's step out of the room, let Laney rest."

We moved. The hallway smelled like rubbing alcohol. The florescent lights were a little too bright. The linoleum floor was far too clean.

"After we left the Dillard's," Billy told me, "the coroner went to work and got quite a shock. He found a pulse. He called this place and told them to get ready, and then he called me. Long and short: I got Laney here. Dr. Harris revived her."

Billy was doing his best to sound official, but there was a kind of unsteady awe in his voice.

"When they told me the circumstances," Dr. Harris said softly, "I didn't know what to think."

"There wasn't much blood where the knife was," I realized.

"That's just it," Billy began.

"We think she just rolled over onto the knife when she fainted," the doctor concluded. "The wound was only superficial."

"Then…what did happen?" I asked.

"I was at a loss and I asked a lot of questions," Dr. Harris said. "And then Officer Sanders told me about the face mug he'd found in Laney's hand, and something clicked."

"I had the mug in the squad car," Billy added. "I went out and got it."

"It's an antique, probably quite valuable." Dr. Harris smiled. "And it has a thick lead glaze."

I looked at her, then at Billy, then back at her before I came to my own conclusion.

"Lead poisoning?" I asked.

They both nodded.

"Laney was able to fill in some of the blanks," the doctor said. "She told me that her favorite drink—"

"Bee's Knees," I interrupted. "The lemon leached the lead, and it got into her system. But that had to happen slowly, over a long time."

"They call it the bucket theory," Billy supplied. "It means that you can take so much without any reaction before your bucket overflows, and then you got a problem."

"Which is what happened to Laney," the doctor concluded. "One sip and she was okay; the next sip and she was unconscious."

"I reckon she went down," Billy explained, "tried to get back up, got to the water's edge, rolled over the knife, and then passed out."

"Isn't it kind of a miracle that she's alive?" I asked the doctor. "She was lying out there for almost twenty-four hours."

"Well, essentially, she was just asleep for a long time," Dr. Harris responded. "She's young and healthy, but mostly I think she was incredibly lucky. And once I gave her an injection of EDTA, she came right around."

"What's that?" I asked.

"EDTA?" the doctor said. "It's calcium disodium ethylenediaminetetraacetic acid."

I rolled my eyes. "That's easy for you to say."

"And by the way, the face mug was a prize that Laney won in high school," Billy concluded. "For outstanding academic achievement."

* * * *

It was a couple of weeks before Laney Bascombe was back in her dorm room. And a couple of weeks after that, as summer was finally giving way to autumn, she and Ellie Dillard came by the bookshop just as we were about to close.

"I wanted to thank you for your part in my resurrection," Laney said to me.

Her face was considerably brighter than the last time I'd seen her. Her black cotton dress and combat boots belied the lilt in her voice.

"I didn't do anything," I protested.

"Well, you sort of got Jill to confess to my sort-of murder or suicide or whatever," Laney said. "If you'd written it all in a story, that would have been the end of it and you'd be the detective hero."

That made me laugh, probably more than it should have. I invited them both into the kitchen for coffee and we talked for a couple of hours. Jill Haydon, they told me, had transferred to Valdosta State, a little farther south of Enigma. Laney had helped her to get a scholarship.

"And Dr. Waldrop tells me," I said to Laney, "that you're doing a lot better in your classes. In fact, she admitted to a rare lapse in judgement where your academic abilities were concerned."

"She allowed me to re-take the final exam for the Intro to Psych," she said. "This time I passed."

"She did more than that," Jill announced. "She got a perfect score!"

"Well," Laney said shyly, "I guess I have a lot less lead in my head now."

"Or maybe cheating death gave you a new attitude?" I suggested.

Laney was admitted into the Perspectives class, and, by Ellie's assessment, was the star student. That position was apparently cemented by a paper that Laney read in class about E. B. White's use of the dragonfly as a symbol in his "Once More to the Lake" essay.

"It symbolizes change," Laney told me after a little encouragement. "And new beginnings. Like you said. I have a new attitude. An idea which I embrace primarily by deciding never again to drink Bee's Knees out of my face mug."

And just at that moment, a dragonfly landed on the backdoor screen in the kitchen.

"Look," I said. "It's your new academic advisor."

"Or my new therapist." She stood up from the kitchen table. "I'd better go see what she wants."

With that, all three of us went outside and watched the dragonfly as it flew from one Black-eyed Susan to another. We watched, in fact, until the night turned into fireflies, and the first cool breeze of autumn filled the air.

POACHED

MELISSA WESTEMEIER

Holly Christiansen blew into her hands to warm them while she stared hard at the back entrance of the Three Bear Lodge in West Yellowstone. She'd parked behind a green metal garbage dumpster and was currently huddled low in the front seat, no way Kyle would notice her. Not that observation skills were his strong suit, or he'd have clued in about how wild she was when he left town two days ago. But just in case that self-centered, no-good, dirty lowdown liar bothered to look past his nose, she'd smeared her Minnesota license plates with mud and tucked her curly blonde hair beneath a knit cap before taking off after him.

A figure appeared at the glass door and Holly leaned forward. A young woman wearing jeans and a polo shirt braced the door open with her hip while heaving a black trash bag over her shoulder and carrying over it to the dumpster. The hotel employee didn't give Holly's car a second glance and Holly settled back in her seat to focus on the pulsing blue dot on her phone screen. Kyle's location on the app and his truck parked in the lodge's back lot convinced her she'd tracked him down. She'd had two days alone in her car to contemplate what she'd do after catching him in the act. It comforted her to know Minnesota was an equitable distribution state when it came to divorce settlements.

At first, she hadn't paid attention to Kyle's casual announcement about this "business trip" since he took one every month or so. But then he started scrambling to hide his phone screen from her whenever she walked in a room. A little sleuthing turned up the credit card transaction involving this hotel reservation. He'd told her his destination was Denver. She still didn't know who he planned to meet since stalking his social media accounts turned up nothing but cold trails. Didn't matter. Holly was determined to catch him and tear his heart out. Or something. She applied a fresh coat of cruelty-free banana-berry lip balm, tossed the tube into her purse, and resumed tapping her black-painted fingernails against her phone case.

Suddenly the door swung open, and this time Kyle walked outside, wearing jeans and a heavy fleece with his winter jacket. He still looked hot, but she reminded herself to overlook that fact. Holly frowned as her husband slung a duffel bag over his shoulder and strolled across the parking lot to his truck, alone, looking like he didn't have a goddamn care in the whole world. She waited for him to drive out of the parking lot before starting her car and following him. *What the hell was he doing? And where was his lover? Was he on his way to meet her somewhere else?*

She lost her cell phone signal a few miles after the entrance to the national park. Switching off her phone, she concentrated on the insanely narrow two-lane highway cutting through endless acres of lodgepole pines. Holly kept Kyle's taillights in view, driving far enough behind so she wouldn't attract his attention. Her fuel gauge crept closer to Empty, making her jittery. She had no clue how far he'd drive before stopping. Lots of shops and restaurants around the park had already closed for the season by mid-October and Holly suspected her options were limited. But that meant Kyle's were, too. Pressure built against her bladder, and she regretted not sneaking in to use the restroom at the Lodge. By the time her fuel gauge hovered in the red, Kyle finally pulled over. Holly noted the sign for the Mount Washburn trailhead before driving past and winding up at the Canyon Gas and Service Station.

Gas tank refilled, her bladder relieved, and an assortment of snacks ready to fortify the next hours of her stakeout, Holly returned to Kyle's parked truck. No other vehicle. *Weird. Was he alone?* She cautiously turned off her engine and watched from her window while counting to a hundred. Then to two hundred. She studied the landscape for any sign of activity before getting out to check his backseat. That truck hadn't been a-rockin', though, so it came as no surprise to find it empty. Footprints marked Kyle's path from the driver's seat to the bed, back to the side of the truck, then down a damp dirt trail toward the woods. One set of tracks. *And an empty gun case.* Holly narrowed her eyes. She knew why he was alone. Her fury burned deep in her chest.

Scum-sucking liar. She listened hard and tried to see through the towering stand of fir trees until her toes cramped with cold. Time to move.

* * * *

A bitter wind yanked the door loose from Chief Ranger Tanner Jessup's grasp and slammed it against the wall of the ranger station. The building shuddered and Leah Hill glared at him while smacking her palms on top of the papers on her desk so the gust wouldn't send them flying. Tanner muttered an apology while shoving the door closed with the sole of his boot; getting the latch to click always made a racket. The building was old, and like most of the facilities in Yellowstone National Park, needed repairs and upgrades.

The papers quit fluttering and Leah continued her conversation into the receiver wedged between her ear and her shoulder. "...sorry, Mrs. Christiansen. I can take down your information and share it, but this is really a matter for local law enforcement. Uh-huh. Uh-huh. I see. Okay…" Leah rolled her eyes at Tanner as he passed her desk on his way to his office. She regularly fielded calls from people demanding more than they were equipped for or, in this case, qualified to handle.

Tanner shed his Carhartt jacket and draped it over the spare chair in his office before sitting at his desk. When he'd joined the Park Service thirty years ago, his work kept him physically fit, but as he rose through the ranks, he spent more time exercising his jaw and finger muscles than his arms and legs. He'd spent the morning driving the Upper Loop of the park to meet Lou Miller, the West District Ranger, to sign off on staffing and fire safety paperwork as part of his annual audit. Driving, talking, filling out paperwork. All the sitting in his truck and sitting in meetings made his legs feel restless. Tanner turned on his computer and stood while he tried to think of an excuse to get outside, even with the sky growing dark with an incoming storm. Dress for it, and you can be outside in any weather.

Leah rapped her knuckles on the door frame before crossing her arms and leaning against it. "You look like someone who wants to go somewhere," she observed. They'd worked together for twenty years. Leah could read him better than his wife.

"What you got?" he asked hopefully.

"Possible missing person." Leah waggled her eyebrows at him. "Kyle Christiansen, age forty-eight. His wife says he failed to check in. Says he's here in Yellowstone."

"Who's he with? Where's he staying?" Tanner reached for his jacket.

"Says he's alone, staying at Three Bear Lodge."

Tanner considered this information. Unusual to visit the park alone, especially off-season. In his experience, solo travelers were up to one of two things: they were escaping off the grid in search of their soul/purpose/solo adventure, or they were keeping their activities private because they were up to no good. A guy alone in the park this late in the season? Tanner bet on the latter. "He got a habit of disappearing?"

Leah gestured to her desk. "What's it say on my nameplate out there? Nancy Drew? No, I don't know if he's got a habit of disappearing." She slapped a yellow Post-it on his office door. "You want to play detective, go nuts. I've got two months' worth of meeting minutes to type up." She turned on the worn-down heels of her Hoka sneakers and left him to decipher the chicken-scratch on the note. Tanner shook a toothpick free from the slim metal holder he kept in his shirt pocket and stuck it between his teeth. He thoughtfully glided his thumb over the smooth edge of the case before replacing it in his pocket. Then he dialed the phone number.

"Holly speaking." Holly sounded young and breathless, like she'd sprinted up a flight of stairs to answer his call.

"This is Chief Ranger Tanner Jessup at Yellowstone National Park. You called to report your husband's missing?"

"Thank you for returning my call." Her voice shook a little, like she was holding back tears. "Kyle's supposed to call me every evening. He didn't call last night, but I assumed he'd gone out and lost track of time. Wouldn't be the first time that happened. But then I didn't hear from him this morning and he's not picking up when I've tried to call him. We use one of those phone locater apps, you know? Anyway, the signal shows him in the north part of Yellowstone. Near Canyon Village I think?"

"Hold up," Tanner interrupted. "You can see his phone signal?"

"You know, the Find My Phone feature? Yeah, I think it shows him kinda near someplace called Canyon Village?"

"You sure about that?" Tanner worked the toothpick to the other side of his mouth.

"What do you mean?"

"I mean cell phone service isn't exactly great inside the park."

"Oh." She fell silent for a moment. "Well, I'm looking at my phone right now and that's what it shows."

"Huh. And you're sure he's alone?"

"Uh-huh."

Tanner tried to keep his skepticism out of his voice. "What's he doing in the park?"

"Ummm, what do you mean, exactly? By doing. What do people usually do in Yellowstone?"

"Like, is he hunting? Hiking? Taking photographs?" A guy alone better not be hunting out of season. He sensed she was stalling. Either she knew and didn't want to tell him, or she didn't know.

"Uh, I don't really know."

Okay, Kyle was up to no good. Tanner sighed and reached for his coffee mug. He tipped it back and discovered it empty. "Ma'am, if you want to find your husband, if you really believe he's missing, you're gonna have to do better than that."

Another silence filled the line and when Tanner was about to hang up, she sighed. "You can't just find him if I share his location?"

"Nope. Gonna need to know what he's up to, otherwise we don't know what we're up against."

Another long silence.

"Okay then," Tanner said, indicating the call was over.

"Wait!"

He knew what she'd say before the words left her mouth.

"Kyle's hunting."

After Holly texted over a recent picture of her husband, Tanner gave it a cursory look before forwarding it to Billie Spirling, the desk clerk at Three Bear Lodge. A quick phone conversation with Billie confirmed that yes, Kyle Christiansen was a guest at the lodge. He'd paid using a credit card in his name, left early yesterday morning, and had the room for three more nights. "Can't remember seeing him come through last night. Need me to knock on his door?"

"No. But keep an eye out for him, all right?" Tanner said before removing his toothpick from his clenched teeth and cracking it in half between his fingers. He bet Kyle would turn up for dinner and drinks tonight at the lodge. When Billie called to report this, Tanner would send a warden over to check the guy's vehicle. Depending on what they found, they'd make an arrest or issue a warning about poaching and keep a close eye on him until he left Yellowstone.

* * * *

"I still haven't heard from him!" Holly's voice sounded frantic when she called the following morning and Tanner suppressed a heavy sigh. He'd suspected trouble when he never heard from Billie last night. Holly's husband was probably lost in the back country, tracking whatever he'd shot.

After giving assurances they were doing their best, Tanner radioed Hayden, the Canyon Village ranger. "Can you put eyes out for a missing person?" He provided the details—truck make and model, license plate, description of Kyle Christiansen before adding, "I think he's hunting out of season, so be careful."

Tanner got off the call and gnawed on a fresh toothpick while he gazed at the dripping eaves outside his office window. Then he pulled on his jacket and told Leah he was going over Canyon Village way.

"Thought you sent Hayden out to look for this guy." She poked her index finger against the spreadsheet on her desk so she wouldn't lose her spot.

"I did. I just have a feeling." They stood a chance of catching this guy in the act. If they caught Kyle tracking a bear, a wolf, whatever the hell he'd shot, they could showcase him as an example. Tanner wasn't stupid, he knew illegal hunting happened all the time. Sometimes people pleaded ignorance, not knowing the restrictions set in place to manage populations and protect endangered species. Most people knew exactly what they were doing though and didn't care because they wanted to get their trophy. Yellowstone was too big to effectively patrol, but they could capture one poacher and send a message.

At the trailhead for Mount Washburn, Tanner pulled up behind Hayden's vehicle and surveyed the other truck, a silver Ford F-150 with Minnesota plates. Presumably Kyle's truck. He pulled on heavy winter gloves and snugged his cap over his ears before leaving the warmth of his own truck. The air was calm this morning and he could hear the chatter of mountain chickadees. Hayden's footprints left a clear path through the fresh snow from last night's storm, and Tanner found him over a mile up the trail on a steep north-facing slope deep in a thicket of trees.

"Well?" Tanner asked. While he caught his breath, he studied the scene while Hayden pointed out a snow-dusted lump beneath a tree. The spot was ideal for elk. He hunted a similar hillside himself on land his brother owned.

"That's your guy."

Tanner followed Hayden toward the lump and as they drew closer, he noted the tree stand strapped around a trunk about fifteen feet up.

"I found the truck and figured the guy took the trail back here, even though I didn't see any tracks. I remembered there's this great timber stand, spot's teeming with elk, and sure enough, I find this." Hayden reached into his jacket pocket and held up a scrap of fabric pinched between his index finger and thumb. "It was snagged on a branch. Last I checked nothing out here wears this shade of blue. Especially not in a synthetic blend."

Tanner cracked a grin. Hayden was a funny guy.

"Plus this clown left a path of broken branches. Practically led me straight to his stand!" Hayden gestured to a spot southwest of the tree stand where Kyle must've sat for a spell while deciding where to set up. The soft earth looked trampled behind a blind of young spruce and fir trees. He could see divots beneath the coating of snow.

"You sure he's dead?" Tanner suddenly asked.

Hayden's lips curled up and he snorted. "See for yourself."

Tanner stepped inside Hayden's footprints on his way over to Kyle's body. The heavy, wet snow had already begun to melt and water dripped off the tree limbs, slapping the ground around them. Tanner regarded the still form on the ground, the snow around the man disturbed by Hayden's activity. Kyle Christiansen bore little resemblance to the picture his wife had sent. His skin was pale, and lips stretched into a grimace had turned blue. Tiny ice crystals glazed Kyle's camouflage overalls, coat, and cap.

"Yep, he's dead," Tanner agreed.

Hayden had already sent the call over the radio and they waited for the medical team to arrive, partly to guide the team to the correct location. After helping him spread a tarp across Kyle's body to protect it from weather or critters, Tanner craned his neck to study the stand. He recognized the brand, an expensive accessory, ultralight, with padded seat and armrests. After a moment Tanner frowned. The top rung of the ladder had cracked free on one side.

"Yeah, I'm guessing that's what killed him, too," Hayden said.

"Where's his gun?" He pulled back the tarp.

Hayden pointed the toe of his boot at the muzzle of a rifle half-buried in snow beneath Kyle's shoulder. Guy must've been carrying it in a sling. Tanner unzipped his jacket and reached for his stash of toothpicks. "All right. We're figuring he fell from—" Tanner paused and chewed on the soft wood stick in his mouth as he estimated the distance. "We think about fifteen feet?"

"Yep."

He knelt to inspect the ground around Kyle's body. The ground was still soft beneath the snow, but he didn't observe any sign of a struggle, that Kyle had flailed around, tried to roll over or crawl away. "Think he died on impact?" He hoped so.

"'Spect so. Broken back or neck maybe." Hayden wiped his nose with the back of his gloved hand.

Tanner nodded. The coroner would let them know for certain. As much as he loathed poachers, the guy hadn't suffered. *We should all be so lucky— dying doing what we love.* It occurred to Tanner that it was no different for most birds and mammals. One minute you're grazing or flying or moving to your den, then BAM! You're dead. *Unless your hunter's a bad shot*, he reminded himself. *Then you're wounded and suffering and struggling.*

"How long do you think they'll be?" Tanner asked.

Hayden checked his watch. "Maybe another forty minutes?"

The sun was higher and moved the shadows away. Tanner wandered around the perimeter of Kyle's hunting spot. *His poaching spot*, he corrected himself. Vapor from his breath drifted across Tanner's line of vision while he looked for other signs of the man's activities. "Suppose we can't charge a dead man for poaching, eh?" he called over his shoulder.

Hayden laughed. "Nope. But there's a good lesson about the dangers of hunting alone, out of season."

Suddenly Tanner thought about Holly Christiansen, the worried wife who'd called to report her missing husband. *Maybe it's true what people say about a sixth sense. She might've felt he was in danger.* His mother swore to her grave that she knew the instant his older brother, Clayte, died in a plane crash. She claimed she froze while gardening and a vision of Clayte's face flashed through her mind. He worked the toothpick to the left side of his mouth. Then he remembered something.

"Hey, you find this guy's phone?"

Hayden shook his head. "No."

"Check again." Tanner drew closer to watch Hayden kneel and search through Kyle's pockets.

"He might have a pack on his back. When medical gets here, they can look." Hayden held out a tin of tobacco. "Want some?"

Tanner shook his head. That's why he chewed on the damn toothpicks, to keep from smoking or chewing. While Hayden helped himself, Tanner noticed the area around Kyle's armpits. Straps for a gun sling, but no pack. "Show me that fabric you found again."

Hayden produced it and frowned at Kyle's body. "No match."

"Unless he came out earlier wearing it." Kyle was dressed in camouflage hunting gear with a black neck gaiter, no blue clothing. Tanner took another loop around the area and found himself in the spot he'd noticed earlier, where the ground was trampled. Almost like an animal had bedded down behind the low-growing trees, but instead of tufts of fur, Tanner noticed footprints faintly marking bare patches of earth. He bent closer. The prints were deep, whoever'd made them had stood in one spot for a while. The toes left clear marks of ovals and squiggly lines. Tanner compared the width of the footprint to his own boots. *Were Kyle's feet this small?* He hadn't noticed.

He returned to examine Kyle's boots. They looked normal sized to him. "What size you think his boots are?" he asked Hayden.

"Why? You thinking of taking them? I think your feet are bigger."

"You're an idiot. No, I'm not taking a dead guy's boots. This isn't World War I. Jesus." Tanner rolled his eyes. "Those footprints further over aren't the same size."

"Weird."

"Yeah."

* * * *

After dispatching Kyle's body with the medical team and hiking back down the trail, Tanner watched Hayden turn out of the trailhead and head back toward Canyon Village. He drove back to his office where he smelled a fresh pot of coffee. "I love you sometimes," he told Leah while he poured a cup.

"Only when the coffee's hot," Leah replied. "The rest of the time you tolerate me. So, you found the missing husband."

"Yeah." He felt Leah's eyes on him while he carried his coffee mug back to his desk. Tanner wasn't much for social media, but he found Holly Christiansen on Facebook and scrolled through her photos, trying to get some sense of her. There were pictures of her and Kyle on a beach somewhere tropical, at a concert, at a party, and on a boat. He clicked on one image to enlarge it. A blonde woman with sharp brown eyes and high cheekbones held her arms tightly around Kyle's shoulders. She looked down at him with a happy smile. Kyle grinned directly at the camera, showing even white teeth. His large hand covered hers, like he was proud they were together. He wore a wedding band.

Tanner scrolled through the comments.

Beautiful couple!

You've caught a trophy husband, Holly!

You 2 are perfect together!

Can't believe u finally landed Mr. Right!

Tanner's eyes widened when he clicked on Holly's posts.

* * * *

Tanner heard plenty of hunting stories, and he knew certain elements got embellished—the chase, the wait, the danger. Tanner signaled to the bartender for another round before getting to the good part in his hunting story. His wife and their friends waited with expectant expressions on their faces.

"I followed her trail from West Yellowstone to Canyon Village where she'd stopped to buy gas two days ago. She returned that same day to buy a small tool kit." He shook his head at Holly's stupidity. "She might've gone unnoticed in summer when the park was crowded with visitors, but not at this time of year. Holly was so focused on her target that she hadn't bothered to conceal her tracks. Then she drove far enough to get a signal so she could call and report him missing." Tanner chuckled at how he'd thought she was breathless with panic. She was breathless from setting a trap for her unsuspecting husband.

"We reckon after her husband packed it in for the day, she snuck back to tamper with his hunting stand. She unscrewed the top rail on one side, which made it dangerous enough, but the snow probably made it slippery, too, so he never stood a chance once he started falling." Tanner could imagine the guy's panic. Falling fifteen feet, all alone in the woods like that. He knew he was a goner before he hit the ground. "Footprints along the trail matched her boots, and Hayden found a scrap of fabric torn from her jacket, that's what led him to the body. When Holly called again the next day, he was already dead, and she was halfway back to Minnesota."

"But what made you suspect the wife?" Mike asked. He stood behind his wife, Bella, one foot hooked on her barstool, his arm slung around her shoulder.

Tanner grinned at his best friend. "Because of what she'd said on the phone. She told me she'd traced his cell phone signal to just outside Canyon Village."

Heads nodded with understanding. Char gazed at him with admiration and Tanner stood up straighter. Impressing his wife didn't happen very often after twenty-seven years together.

"Exactly. There's no cell phone service *anywhere* near there. The only way she could've known his location was if she'd been there herself. The guy's phone was in his truck, incidentally. Turns out she'd had a bead on him from the minute he'd left their house and she tracked him into the park.

She called to provide herself with an alibi." Tanner took a long swallow of his beer. "I guess she thought he was having an affair, but it turned out to be something worse."

"What do you mean? He wasn't cheating on her, he'd just gone hunting!" Bella held up a hand to stop the others from correcting her. "He was *poaching*. And yes, I realize poaching is against the law, cheating on your wife isn't—don't even think about it, Mike," Bella shot a warning glance at her husband who laughed harder. "But I don't get it, how did you figure she killed him from all of this?"

"How do the kids say it again, honey?" Tanner gave Char's thigh an affectionate squeeze. "I *stalked* her online and learned she's big into animal rights. She posted all these quotes and links to articles about not eating meat and not wearing fur and how hunting is bad and farming is evil. Not sure where she thinks the food she eats comes from." Tanner shook his head in wonder. "When she figured her husband was on a *hunting* trip, she must've lost her mind!"

"That's diabolical!" Bella exclaimed.

"That's genius!" Char cried.

"I don't think I like you calling a killer 'genius,' honey," Tanner told her.

"Better not piss her off, then," Mike said.

"Anyway, that Find My Phone app she mentioned? Well, police used it to trace *her* location and prove she'd taken a little side trip to Montana."

"So, you hunted down the woman hunting down her husband, who was hunting elk," Bella giggled.

"*Poaching*!" Char and Mike corrected her.

"Yes, poaching," Tanner grinned. "I mean, I had a little help from the police in Minnesota, but yeah. I got her."

"To Tanner!" Mike raised his glass. "For chasing down his prey!"

Tanner touched his bottle to Mike's glass before adding, "And last I checked, there's no bag limit for murderers!"

THAT DARN DOG

PATRICIA GOUTHRO

I set the metal dog water dish on the pavement in front of the I Scream Terrific Treat Shoppe and watched as a small Labrador puppy with a red and white checked kerchief knotted around his neck darted over and began to slurp noisily.

"Hot enough for you, Angel?" asked Sam, who owned the barbershop next to my store. I preferred Angela but was resigned that my grandfather's peers weren't going to change the practice of using the diminutive version of my name, since they'd been calling me that for the last twenty-two years of my life.

"Goin' to be a scorcher," I agreed, already feeling the heat from the Tidewater sun, still low in sky before we opened at 10:00 a.m. Sam had been at work for a full two hours already, but he'd be closed and home for supper well before I shut down at 9:00 p.m. Summer hours were long but necessary in the seasonal ice cream business.

"What's that darn dog doing here?" he asked with an irritable nod at the puppy who was slopping water over the sides of the bowl. "Looks like he escaped from Lucy's yard again. Going to get hit by one of the cars driven by all these tourists one of these days."

"I hope not," I said, looking around the already busy streets. The odd local darted through the bumper-to-bumper traffic and throngs of visitors flooding the sidewalks. Sam was right. It wasn't safe for the little puppy to be out without his human, as my best friend, Kyla, would say. "Do you know who his owner is then?"

But just then a barrel shaped man greeted Sam warmly and my next-door business neighbor disappeared into the barbershop with his latest customer.

I picked up the puppy, looking around the crowded streets with dismay. He wriggled in my arms, a golden bundle of furry enthusiasm, torn between excitement at being held and a desire to race around and investigate his surroundings. I couldn't just leave him on the sidewalk without someone to claim him. He was so little—what if he darted into traffic? But at the same time, as a food establishment, I couldn't risk bringing him into the kitchen of my business. It would be just my luck that the food inspector would show up that morning. And it was only five minutes to opening time.

Just then I saw Margo, the owner of a gift shop two doors down, carrying a cappuccino. It was rumored that she spent half of the proceeds of her annual sales supporting her caffeine addiction at Cuppu Joanne's, the local café where she had a standing account. Margo was a well-known animal lover, who campaigned continuously for the nearby animal shelter. I stopped her to explain my predicament, and she kindly agreed to take the puppy into the back room of her shop until more of my staff arrived and I could slip out to see if I could return him to his owner.

The morning passed in a blur as I served a steady stream of customers. The crowd has just thinned enough that I could consider leaving to check on the puppy when a police officer stepped into my shop, the short sleeves of his dark FBI uniform revealing a pair of powerful tanned upper arms.

"Hello." I mentally gulped as I looked up at Officer Biceps. He gave me a disarming smile in return, grey eyes creasing slightly above a set of chiseled cheekbones.

"Good afternoon," he greeted me, as I stepped aside and motioned for one of my staff to take my spot in front of the tubs of ice cream lined up under a half dome of glass. It was a relief to straighten up and pull my head out of the cooler. I was conscious that messy wisps of blonde curls had probably escaped from my ponytail holder. Hygiene took precedence over style in my line of work.

"I was wondering if you'd noticed any unusual customers lately?" he asked. His voice was gently courteous, his dark brows lifted in a slightly quizzical manner, but the intensity of those grey eyes was a little disquieting.

"Unusual how?" I crinkled my nose as I frowned to recall the parade of customers that I'd already served that day. "Their orders?"

There'd been one mother who'd handed out pouches of pureed vegetables to her twin toddlers, ignoring their pleas for ice cream while she waited patiently for her triple scoop of Death by Chocolate. It was a bit unusual, but not the first time I'd observed parents who had double standards in healthy food expectations for their offspring.

"Possibly," said Officer Biceps, "or unusual looking".

"Well, there were those two chocolate chips in a waffle cone..." My voice trailed off. The biker couple had had matching improbably colored bright copper hair with silver zebra stripes, collar neck tattoos and tattered fringes on their faded leather jackets. Their appearance suggested more 'in desperate need of fashion advice' rather than criminal intent, however.

"We're canvassing the neighborhood to see if anyone observed anyone or anything unusual because a local woman has been murdered."

"Murdered!" I exclaimed. "Here in Chincoteague?" Our little tourist town, crowded each summer by visitors who came to enjoy the beaches and see the wild ponies in the nearby state park of Assateague, was generally a safe and quiet community. Our local police force, which had less than a dozen officers, rarely had to contend with more than the odd drunk-and-disorderly or texting while driving offenders.

"We found the victim this morning after we received a phone call from her niece, who reported a kidnapping and that the family had received a ransom demand," explained Officer Biceps. "The victim was visiting her sister, and when we checked the house, we found that the sister had been murdered. There was no sign of the kidnapped woman, although her belongings were still at the house."

"That's terrible!"

The officer nodded, looking grim. "The missing woman is Helen Maitland. She's an older woman, slim and tall, stylishly dressed." He held up his phone so I could see a picture of a woman with expertly cut grey hair and vivid blue eyes.

"Oh—I've seen her, but it was a few days ago." I grimaced as I recalled the less than enthusiastic visitor. Most adults who visited my store looked at the walls lined with glass jars of gummies, stacks of brightly wrapped chocolate bars and colorful packets of candies with delight as they pointed out different types of treats recalled from childhood, but this woman had worn a disdainful expression the entire time.

"What do you remember about her?"

I shrugged. "She opted for a child's scoop of mango sorbet in a paper cup. We don't like to do that for adults because it's usually because they're being cheap. In her case though, I think she really wanted the smaller scoop. She was with another woman who was shorter and heavier, and she made a snide comment to her because she ordered a double Rocky Road."

"Would this be her?" The office held up his phone with another photograph. I looked at the picture of a woman with flyaway grey hair, and a round face with laughter lines spanning out from her eyes and the corners of her smiling mouth.

"Yes—she's not—dead?" I asked hesitantly.

He nodded, looking grim. "She was the victim."

I felt slightly nauseated at the thought, even though my encounter with the two women had been very brief. Wow. It just confirmed my belief that life is too short. You never know what's going to happen next.

"That's horrible," I said out loud, "but I'm glad she ordered two scoops."

Officer Biceps looked momentarily taken aback and then amused at my comment as a small pair of dimples appeared at the corners of his mouth. He really did have distracting looks for someone who had chosen to make his career in law enforcement. But then he got back to business.

"The victim's name was Lucy Witteger. She retired last fall from her career as a university librarian and moved here to a house that had been bequeathed to her by an elderly aunt. Had you met her before?"

I shrugged—we had so many customers in the summer, I couldn't be sure if she'd ever been in my shop before. But then the name Lucy rang a bell.

"Did she have a dog? A Labrador puppy?"

Officer Biceps looked thoughtful. "I don't know, but now that you mention it, there was some dog paraphernalia in the house—a half empty food dish, and a leash hanging from the wall hooks, but no dog."

I explained to him about the puppy drinking from the water dish that morning and how I'd brought him over to Margo's to look after until I could get a chance to return him to the owner. "Sam, the barber at the shop next door, said the dog must have gotten loose from his owner who was named Lucy."

As I was talking another influx of tourists entered the shop, so many that some were standing in the open doorway with the air conditioning gushing out.

"I'll talk to him." Officer Biceps ducked into the crowd who parted without protest to let him navigate his way out to the sidewalk.

I'd just finished with three single strawberries and a double banana when he returned. The crowd once again parting magically, although I noticed two shifty looking teens who'd been prowling around the candy selection slip out without purchasing anything. I couldn't tell if having an officer of the law in the shop was helping to rid us of potential shoplifters or if it was driving away possible customers.

"Can you come with me?" he asked, and I nodded, pausing to inform Liezel, the oldest high school student I had assisting me in the shop, that she would be temporarily in charge. Liezel's eyes lit up with enthusiasm at the prospect of this heightened level of authority being bestowed upon her. I hoped she wouldn't be too assertive with her sister, Reyna, who was only seven minutes her junior, but who was constantly being reminded by her twin that she was the younger sibling. However, it wouldn't take long to run over to Margo's to check on the dog.

But when we got there, Margo was looking distressed.

"I was going to call you," she said. "Your puppy escaped. I had a delivery arrive while I was busy out front with some customers, and the driver heard him whining. He thought perhaps he'd gotten accidentally trapped in my office, so he opened the door and the dog shot out and ran through the delivery door that he'd propped open. I'm so sorry!"

There wasn't much that could be done then to retrieve the puppy, which Sam had confirmed was indeed Lucy's pet.

"I'll give you my card." Officer Biceps handed it to me as we walked back towards my shop. "Give me a ring if the dog shows up again or if you remember anything else." One heart-melting smile and he disappeared into the tourist crowds.

I sighed and looked at his card, smiling as I read his name.

Jake Byers. My nickname for the FBI officer was not too far off after all.

* * * *

I was on my own closing up the shop when a skinny man wearing a navy ball cap and a dingy white t-shirt stepped inside. He grabbed a plastic bottle of lemonade and a couple of chocolate bars without taking the time to carefully peruse the selection, as most of my customers did.

"We have this same lemonade in the cooler if you'd like a cold one," I said, as I rang in his purchases. Even though the sun was lowering in the sky he'd kept his dark sunglasses on, a scruff of beard obscuring his features.

"Good enough for her," he replied dismissively, grabbing his items off the counter. The door jangled noisily as it closed behind him.

Odd.

My Spidey senses tingled. That was a strange response. 'Good enough for her'. Who was 'her'?

I stepped outside onto the sidewalk and looked down the street. The man ducked into the cab of a black pick-up truck and pulled out into the thinning traffic to drive by. I could see a big dent in the driver's door. A car following too closely behind the truck obscured my view of the rear licence plate.

An odd order, a strange response. Was that enough to call Officer Biceps—correction, Officer Byers?

Just then I heard a little yip, and I looked down. It was the Labrador puppy who'd made his escape earlier that morning. He was at the water bowl, which had been drained by a previous canine visitor.

"There you are!" I exclaimed, reaching down to pick up the wriggly puppy as well as the empty water dish. I wasn't about to let him out of my sight this time. My store was now officially closed, so I figured I could bring him inside to the back storage and office area while I rang the FBI field officer.

After I filled the water dish for the thirsty pup I punched in the number that the officer had given me into my phone.

"Hello. Jake Byers."

"Hi Jake. This is Angela McKenzie, from the Treat Shoppe." I briefly summarized my story and told him that I had the puppy with me in the back of my store. A few minutes later I heard a loud tapping at the window—that was quick! But when I looked out, I saw that it was my friend, Kyla, waving at me. I opened the door, making sure to hold the wriggly puppy tight so that he couldn't escape again.

"Who's this handsome fellow?" she cooed, just as Officer Byers stepped into view behind her. Although her words echoed my thoughts, I realized she was referring to the golden fur bundle in my arms.

"Hi Angela."

Kyla glanced around with interest as Officer Byers stepped inside behind her, closing the door to ensure that the dog wouldn't escape again.

"Jake Byers, FBI," he said, introducing himself to Kyla.

My friend blinked. "FBI?"

He nodded, and briefly summarized the situation.

"So a woman was murdered and her sister was kidnapped? Here in Chincoteague?" Kyla's voice mirrored my own sense of disbelief. That was the kind of thing that happened in DC—not in our small little community.

"That appears to be the case," Jake concurred, running a hand through his short dark hair.

He looked over at me, and behind his back Kyla rolled her eyes towards him and mouthed the syllable 'Wow!' Ever since she'd gotten engaged to her high school sweetheart it seemed like she'd made it her mission in life to become my personal matchmaker.

I struggled to keep my face expressionless as Jake continued to talk, obviously focused on the case. "Angela, you said that you also had a strange encounter with a customer?"

I nodded and repeated my story of the odd man who'd purchased a bottle of hot lemonade.

"Sometimes people buy drinks off the shelf instead of from the cooler because they will put them in the fridge at home to drink at another time. But it was odd, the way he said, 'good enough for her.'" I shook my head, still slightly troubled by the encounter.

I set the puppy down on the ground while I recounted my story. He snuffled and nuzzled around Kyla's feet. She reached down to pat him absently, watching the two of us with interest. Then, as she glanced down at the dog, Kyla suddenly did a doubletake.

"Angie, what's this dog wearing around his neck?"

I looked down and realized that the red and white gingham kerchief had been replaced by a scarf with vibrant colors.

Kyla unknotted the large square of fabric and shook it out. The material had a bright jeweled pattern of dragonflies and flowers in tangerine, scarlet, and jade colors set against a cream silk background. "Is this a Hermes scarf?"

"He wasn't wearing that this morning," I said.

The three of us looked at one another.

"You said that the daughter had received a ransom note for her mother who is missing—Helen Maitland. Is she wealthy?" I asked.

"Very," confirmed Jake. "Her husband started Maitland Construction." I recognized the name of a large and well-known Maryland firm.

"That means she could afford to have a Hermes scarf for everyday wear," said Kyla, who ran a clothing boutique and was much more knowledgeable about fashion than I am. "Their scarves run between $700 and $1500."

I blinked. That amount was more than I'd spend on my entire summer wardrobe.

"Could she have knotted this around the dog's neck?" I asked, voicing what we were all thinking. "As a clue for anyone who found him? If so, maybe he can lead us back to her."

"It's a long shot," said Jake, a little dubiously, "but we could try a tracking device."

Jake pulled out his phone as my mind raced.

"Wait—I have one here." I held up my key fob. "It's one of those luggage trackers. I keep it on my key ring because I kept losing them. We could put the scarf back around the dog's neck, loop the leather fob holder around it and use my phone to follow him."

"Let me call this in and talk with my supervisor first," said Jake.

He wandered over to the far end of my storeroom to have his conversation while

Kyla expertly tied the scarf around the dog's neck again, this time with my leather fob that had the silver disk tracker knotted into it under a clever fold so that it wasn't immediately visible.

"Alright—my boss thinks it's unlikely, but rather than wait to get a proper tracking device brought over, which will take a while, he suggests we try the key tag on him and let him go," said Jake.

I felt a bit anxious as we stepped out into the back alleyway and then let the puppy loose. He yipped a few times and then darted off down a narrow road behind a dumpster.

"Can you stay here in case he comes back?" Jake asked Kyla. "Angie and I will take my car and see if we can follow him using her phone."

We ended up behind Hiram's Steakhouse, where I saw a cook serve the puppy a dish with some leftover scraps. Jake and I chatted as we sat in the darkened car. As the son of a naval officer Jake had lived across the country, from Boston to Hawaii and then settling in Norfolk. I told him about how I'd continued the family business after I inherited my grandparents' store here in Chincoteague after they'd retired.

"He's on the move," said Jake, as the puppy finished his scraps and trotted off down a narrow pedestrian alleyway. "I think we'll have to follow him on foot."

We took off out of the car, Jake in the lead.

"He's going right!" I exclaimed, watching the telltale dot move across my phone screen.

Jake darted behind the building and then I heard a loud metallic crash, followed by some muttered curses and the loud demands of woman as to who was out there. I turned around the corner just as Jake picked himself up and calmed down a large irate woman illuminated in the back doorway of one of the shops.

I held back, sharing his frustration, as I watched the dot on my screen move further away. The woman finally slammed the door behind her after Jake finished straightening up the trash can after reinserting its contents. Something smelled fishy, and I realized that unfortunately, it was likely to be my partner in crime solving.

"This is not going to work." Jake stomped past me towards the car. Once back in the vehicle we looked at my phone screen again, which showed a dot behind Peppito's pizzeria.

"It looks like your dog is working his way through a three-course meal," muttered Jake. Just then his phone rang, and he spoke briefly to the person on the other end before signing off.

"We have a new lead that I should follow up on, but it's out in the country. If I drop you on main street, can you make your way back to your shop?"

"Sure." I was a little disappointed, but I could see that following a dog with the hope that it would take one to a kidnapper was hardly a common FBI investigation strategy. "I'm sorry this didn't work out."

"Worth a try." Jake shrugged and gave me a fleeting smile before stopping at the corner of the main street. "See you later."

"You too," I said, as he drove off. I pulled out my phone to ring Kyla.

"You may as well head home." I hoisted my backpack onto my shoulder. It was a little heavy because I'd filled it with treats earlier that afternoon, planning to stock up at home in anticipation of the arrival of my brother, his wife, and my two nieces, who were coming to visit for the weekend. "Tracking the dog was a bust. It seems like he's a puppy with street smarts who has lots of people who like to feed him. Jake's gone to pursue another lead and I'm going to head back to the house. I still have to get beds made for Mark and Priya and the kids."

"Okay—did you make any plans to see Jake again?" asked Kyla. "I thought those tv shows with hot FBI agents were not very realistic, but I'm beginning to rethink my career options."

"Right—like you'd even notice another man if Trent was in the room."

"Well, I did notice this one—but with you in mind," said Kyla. "What did you think?"

"I don't know—I can't see it working out," was all I said. After the embarrassing end to our foiled dog chase, I doubted Jake would be ringing me any time soon.

After we said goodbye, I took one more look at the tracker on my phone. My steps quickened as I realized that the dog was a couple of streets back in a residential area, not far from where I was walking. I followed the map to walk in that direction. Then I saw it—the truck with the dented driver's door parked in a driveway.

The neighborhood was quiet. No one else was out walking, so they wouldn't see me if I scuttled up to the side of the bungalow. Light spilled out of a side window, and I crept beside the hedge that divided the property from its neighbour.

Inside was a kitchen that was brightly illuminated. At the table sat the man who'd purchased the lemonade and chocolate bars earlier that evening. Across from him was a woman that I recognized as the missing sister—Helen Maitland. While he was slouched forward reading his phone, she sat up stiffly—and then I realized that was because her hands were bound behind the back of the chair.

I gasped as I heard the yip of the dog, scratching at the back screen door. The skinny man stood up and opened the door.

"Hey fellow," he said, scratching the dog's ears. "What are you wasting your time coming to see this old girl for? She doesn't care about you."

Helen's eyes flashed, but she didn't say anything. Then the expression on the man's face changed as he fumbled around the dog's neck at the scarf.

"What's this? Who put this on here?"

Fear flashed across my brain as I realized that the man had spotted the leather holder with the tracking device that had been attached to it.

"Did you do this?"

He turned fiercely to face the woman. No longer haughty, she looked alarmed as he whipped out a gun and aimed it at her.

I scurried back to the front door, terrified that the man would shoot her before I could call for help. I rang the front doorbell and then scrambled out of sight behind a tall bush set against the side of the garage.

Flattened against the wall, I hauled my phone out and dialled 911.

"Hurry—a man with a gun on Doherty Lane," I said breathlessly, and then shut it off before the operator could respond.

I unzipped my knapsack, wondering if there was anything in there that I could possibly use as a distraction. The skinny man swung open the front door, and the puppy raced out into the yard, barking loudly. He sniffed, and unfortunately headed right in my direction, whining with delight at having located a friend.

"Who's there?" The man demanded, storming down the couple of concrete steps to the path leading directly by the shrubbery where I was hiding. Before he could get any closer to where I was, my hands closed around a plastic bag inside of my knapsack as I remembered its contents.

"Someone there?" He reached into his back pocket and pulled out his revolver again. The puppy barked. Before the man could get any closer, I took the bag out and hurled the contents over the path. Dozens of round hard balls of candy skittered across the path and around his feet, startling him. The puppy raced back and jumped at his knees, tripping him up, as I dove and knocked him forward onto the pavement. The gun went off with a loud blast, and I heard a woman scream. For a moment all was chaos as the man tried to shove me off his back and fought to get to his feet.

"Hands where I can see them!" hollered a familiar voice. I rolled out of the way as Jake suddenly appeared, a gun of his own tightly aimed in front of him. Sirens blared and then cut off as he was joined by a contingent of law enforcement officers.

"Angela, are you okay?" As soon as other officers took over the arrest, Jake steadied me, his hands lightly brushing down my arms as he looked me up and down. "I thought you were up to something when I saw you going off looking at your phone. I knew you'd keep following that darn dog, and sure enough, I saw you sneaking over to the side of the house. You should have called the police. What were you thinking?"

"I did call—but there was no time. When I went around the side of the house I could see into the kitchen, and I saw that Helen was tied up to a chair. Then the man let the dog in, and he saw the tracking device. He started yelling at her and then he pulled a gun. The only thing I could think to do was to distract him by running to the front door to ring the doorbell. I called 911, but then I didn't have time to get away."

"Well, I'm glad you're alright," said Jake. He dropped an arm over my shoulders as we stood to one side while the emergency responders assisted Helen out of the house. One of them kicked a couple of balls of candy out of the way. "What are those?"

"Jawbreakers," I said. "I was bringing a bag of them home because my brother is coming to visit this weekend, and he loves them."

We looked over to where an emergency responder had passed a large compress to the skinny man who was now under arrest. He used one fist to jam it up against his chin as an officer placed a hand on top of his head to guide him into the back seat of the patrol car.

"Appropriate," said Jake, grinning.

* * * *

The next day I was back at work, feeling a little sore after having tackled a murderous kidnapper the evening before. It was late by the time I gave my statement to the police and contacted my family to assure them I was all right in case they heard about what had happened in the news.

There was a momentary lull in the stream of customers when I heard the front door jingle. My neighbor, Sam the barber, shepherded an older woman into the store, who I recognized as Helen Maitland.

"There's your angel," he said, giving me a thumbs up.

I smiled as Jake stepped past him and our eyes met. The goodnight kiss Jake had given me after he drove me and the puppy home last night hadn't been exactly professional, but it had certainly helped to end what had been a rough evening on high note.

"I hear that I have you to thank for rescuing me," said Helen, "and for catching that terrible man who murdered my sister.

"I'm so sorry for your loss." I moved around the counter to face the older woman, "but I'm glad that you're alright."

Helen's eyes teared up for a moment as she looked around the shop appraisingly.

"I came here with Lucy, and she was so excited to show me this place. 'Do you remember coming here when we were children?', she asked me. She thought it was so wonderful, and at the time all that I could think was that there wasn't a single healthy thing to eat in here."

"I guess not," I agreed. But it was a treat shop, after all, not a health food store.

"My sister always lived life with gusto, right until the end." The corners of Helen's mouth lifted in a soft smile. "Could I get a Toffee Almond Fudge, please? And can you make it a double?"

CATCHING THE EARLY FLIGHT

JEAN MACALUSO

"Damned rain," I grumbled to my sister. "Drapes in a hot sheet motel are more transparent than this windshield!" Lee didn't rise to the bait.

"We get plenty of rain at home," I persevered, "but at least Georgia doesn't have the audacity to call itself 'The Sunshine State.'" Silence prevailed.

Florida's subtropical April Showers weren't just obscuring the road, they were threatening to throw us off schedule. Maybe *that's* what was distracting Lee.

We'd checked out of the Leesburg bed-and-breakfast at 2:00 a.m. on the dot. The trip from there to Orlando International Airport normally takes little more than an hour. In the middle of the night, dodging cloudbursts (and allowing for Florida drivers who've yet to master those *goldarned complicated* turn signals), it's a crap shoot if you haven't allowed extra time. That's why I was piloting a gutless Ford Escort rental—in the dark, on just a couple hours' sleep.

Out of nowhere a big white Yukon careened past on my left, throwing blinding sheets of water across my line of vision. I shoved the wiper into high, then back to intermittent. Good thing this stretch of US 441 East runs straight as Uncle Joe making a beeline for the bar; otherwise, we'd have landed in a ditch.

When I could see again, the nearly empty countryside didn't afford much to look at besides gloomy trees—fog-shrouded oaks, stubby cabbage palms, stunted orange tree groves—and the occasional shuttered fruit stand. Under a leaden sky, sodium lamps stationed at ridiculously long intervals were the only light source for miles on monotonous end.

Still, it was a restful change from the omnipresent swarms of motorcycles we'd put up with these last few days. A jawbreaker of a yawn overcame me, so loud it penetrated Lee's mental cocoon.

"Shall I take over, Jess?" she offered half-heartedly from the passenger seat. "It's a shame we had to get up so early, but you know we can't afford to miss our, um, connection this morn...." And she trailed off again. For the past several miles, she'd been so mesmerized by her side mirror that she didn't even comment when the Yukon whooshed by. It's a wonder she heard me yawn.

"Nah, it's okay." I squared my shoulders and wriggled my butt. "Really, Lee. I'm fine," I lied. "See? Bright-eyed and bushy tailed." At least my antics elicited a raised eyebrow.

One of us had to stay sharp, and *I* was the designated driver, so I didn't push her. Besides, I'm older by five minutes. We're twins sired by two different men—a fact that embarrasses our mom to this day. Nor do we *look* related. Lee's the show-stopper sister to my Marian-the-Librarian looks. She's blonde to my brunette, tall to my short, stacked to my barely B cup...and strategist to my improvisationist.

* * * *

We'd had a busy week in central Florida, shuttling between Leesburg, Lake County's oldest city, and Mount Dora, where arts and crafts flourished.

Our stay in Leesburg coincided with that city's annual *Bikefest*, an event that commandeered the entire downtown. Concert stages were set up in the streets to showcase bands from across the musical spectrum—country to heavy metal—going amp-to-amp over a million loudspeakers. At pedestrian level, vendors hawked food and beer and bike gear. Sidewalk tattooists plied their trade alongside elaborate displays of motorcycle art. 'Death's heads to right of us; Death's heads to the left....' Also depictions of skeletal eye sockets, bleeding purple roses, and snakes—lots of coiled snakes. Hard to miss the theme.

Impromptu bike demonstrations sustained the vibe. Let me tell you, when you've seen one Harley V-Twin lit up with multicolored LEDs synchronized to engine RPMs, you've seen 'em all. [Did you know the very first V-twin was mounted to a frame in 1909? Bikefests aren't just about the bikes, the booze, and the noise; they're educational, too!] Trust me, after more than one biker's exhaust pipes *accidentally* wither an innocent bougainvillea *(or a bystander)*, the novelty palls.

Lee and I weren't really *into* macho bikes, or overwrought stainless steel jewelry, or the weird nostalgia of stock traders who want to revel (weekends only) in the counterculture of *Easy Rider*. Nor did we relate to those who seek to inhabit (however briefly) Brando's outlaw persona from *The Wild One*. However, Leesburg offered more reasonably priced accommodations than Mount Dora, whose Art Festival was scheduled for the same week as Leesburg's *Bikefest*.

This year, Lee was the Mount Dora Art Festival's primary honoree. As such, an exhibition of her work was featured at the Arts Center for the entire week. Lee had already made a name for herself at home in Brunswick. Her Low Country scenes (Georgia has scads of palm trees, too, and Lee's painted most of 'em) tastefully arrayed on the walls of art galleries and upscale retailers in Old Town, go over big with the well-heeled visitors passing through on their way to and from resorts on the Golden Isles barrier islands.

Evidently Lee's fame has spread to Florida. She was chosen as the first recipient of Mount Dora's new "Artist of the Palms" Award. *That* and an E-Pass will get you a ride on a Florida toll road! Big whoop! Aw, I shouldn't make fun. Lee may not be Monet incarnate, but she's a damned good artist—light and shadow to my stick figures, for sure.

Bunking in Leesburg rather than Mount Dora also made sense for us because Auntie Ruth, Ma's younger sister, lived there. In Florida, where almost every resident was born in some other state, that virtually makes us natives. Ruth lost her husband some months back, and Ma wanted us to express our condolences in person. During our obligatory visit, her phone didn't stop ringing, and she continually sneaked peeks at her computer as we chit-chatted about family. When asked if we were *interrupting* her, she claimed that staying busy kept her from missing the dearly departed. Lee later remarked that Auntie didn't seem overly distressed at being a widow. I had to agree. Uncle Joe had been in and out of jail for most of their married life. Knowing there'd be no more call to fork over bail money and legal fees probably tempered her grief.

Lee and I didn't put up at Ruth's house. Not that she offered. Good thing we didn't count on it, even though she owns an apartment complex on the edge of town. Impressed? Don't be. It's a converted two-story motel that wouldn't have qualified for even a *quarter*-carat AAA Diamond rating. Auntie and Uncle Joe fumigated the godforsaken derelict, painted the exterior, then transformed it into low-income rental units—one room at a time over ten years—in between his visits to the 'pen.' Nevertheless, should anyone ask, we could pass for locals…thanks to Auntie.

We were moderately satisfied with the quaint B&B in the heart of downtown. It was packed to the gills with mostly female bikers who preferred to bathe daily within the confines of walls and a roof. They didn't bother us, and we mostly ignored them. From this base, we maintained a sedate profile while exploring Mount Dora to the east and The Villages to the north. We also stayed out of the local bars and businesses. Even the pervasive street noise failed to ruin our slumber, not to mention permanently damage our eardrums. We had come prepared—our padded headsets over industrial-strength earplugs did a bang up job *(pun intended)*. We slept like babies, with the glaring exception of last night/this morning.

During the day yesterday, we ate a late breakfast, did some banking, then napped until early evening. The Artists' Champagne Reception in Mount Dora was compulsory. As honored guest plus moocher, we mingled, listened to thinly disguised fund-raising speeches, and waded through enough finger food and booze to enable us to skip supper. Eventually they presented Lee with an inscribed bronze palm leaf and a five-hundred-dollar check. We took the money (and plaque) and ran…straight back to the B&B.

We'd had a trying day, and needed to be at the airport extremely early. Our plan to go straight to sleep was shot to hell the minute we sailed through the door. A cluster of biker babes waylaid us near the reception desk. They were abuzz with news of a bank holdup *right here in River City*. And, get this, the robbers were bikers!

No! Really?

The babes had the details down pat because as soon as the TV news crews vacated the scene, they'd swept the teller into the nearest saloon and 'ministered' to her shock. Here's what happened, as Lee and I pieced it together.

According to Biker Babe #1, "A bank around the corner was robbed in broad daylight." She couldn't remember which one, but "it had a 'funny' name." Obviously an out-of-town babe.

Florida does seem to have more than its share of banking institutions with monikers touting virtues that tourists supposedly look for—sun, sea, and sand—rather than emphasizing safety and liquidity! Think Suncoast Credit Union and Ocean Bank. Sometimes the PR effort goes awry. Climate First Bank, for example, readily evokes sunstroke and catastrophic flooding in some minds. Personally, I'd hesitate to put my money in "Flying Flamingo Trust," let alone "Sinkhole Savings & Loan." But…I digress.

Biker Babe #1 resumed her tale: The *bandidos* entered the lobby just before three o'clock closing, as a lone teller counted out twenties to her sole biker customer. [The manager had made the questionable decision to open on a Sunday to accommodate *fest* attendees who might want to cash some traveler's checks before returning to their mahogany desks on Monday. *Does anyone use traveler's checks anymore?* He's boxing groceries at the local Winn Dixie now.]

Biker Babe #2 picked up the narrative: One of the bad boys was tall and powerfully built; the other was short and stocky. Both wore full-face bike helmets. [Note: Florida law doesn't require helmets of riders twenty-one and older *if they have medical coverage*, thus ensuring a ready supply of organs for folks on transplant lists.] The miscreants sported heavy black leather jackets wrapped in chunky chains, gauntlet gloves with giant studs on wide cuffs, and unisex, metal-toed, knee-high biker boots.

Wide-eyed, I told the bevy it was a wonder the robbers could walk upright with all the weight they carried. I got a puzzled group stare in return. [Gee, I hate to waste snark.]

Biker Babe #s 3 & 4 took over the chronicle: When the robbers walked in, the short one locked the door, flipped the sign to "Closed," and drew the blind. The tall one lifted an arm to reveal a gun barrel protruding from his right sleeve into his palm, a gloved finger resting on the trigger. He gestured to the terrified "captives" to dump their phones in the waste basket. It was a silent stickup; not a word was uttered. Meanwhile, "stubby" handed the quivering teller a black nylon bag and pointed to the cash drawers, and then to the safe (which she finally opened after considerable fumbling). When the bag was full, the shorter thief snatched it back and shoved it into his jacket, snugging it against his prominent beer belly. Teller and customer were then herded into the bathroom.

The felonious duo proceeded to unlock the front door, stroll into the crowded street…and disappear. Who needs a mask in a sea of visored helmets?

It didn't occur to the rattled hostages to try the knob immediately, and valuable time was lost in sounding the alarm. It seems the bathroom door was latched, but not *locked!* Biker Babe #5 shook her head in disbelief as she shared this last tidbit.

The babes twittered on about how *close* the bank was to our B&B. They'd all been in the vicinity, wandering from exhibit to exhibit. Why, the robbers could've brushed right past them! They lamented that this incident would "give bikers a bad name."

That last point exhausted our stores of commiseration. We escaped to our room, where we laid out nondescript travel outfits, packed in record time, and crawled into bed. Sadly, we were so wired that decent sleep was a lost cause.

* * * *

On the move in the wee hours of Monday, we steadily narrowed the gap between us and the airport. On the far side of Apopka, we abandoned US 441 (it wanted to slew south and call itself Orange Blossom Trail) for SR 436, aiming due east before skirting Casselberry and turning south to the airport. The rain had stopped and visibility improved, but it was still dark out there. I flicked off the wipers. An occasional car whizzed past, but we stayed within the speed limit, and out of the fast lane.

Lee remained absorbed by whatever she saw in her wing. Then….

"Don't pull over, Jess." Lee's urgent tone put me on high alert. "If you feel a bump or jolt, DON'T stop the car!"

"Okay, Lee. Fine." She was scaring me, but I complied. "If something happens, even if a tire blows, I'll just drive until…. Isn't there a big, well-lit Wawa ahead?"

"Just. Don't. Stop. No matter what!"

Right! Okaay!!

With Apopka behind us, we'd expected the lighting to improve. It was busy (and safe) enough by day, with neon signs identifying strip malls and fast food joints. In the predawn, this area was an urban dead spot. We passed unlit churches, dense parcels of undeveloped green space, and at least one cemetery.

We were still west of the Altamonte Springs interchange for the I-4, which snakes through the state from Tampa on the Gulf, across-and-up to Daytona, Jacksonville, and points north. Cars rushing through would not be inclined to stop and shop. Nary a headlight pierced the atmosphere, in either direction. So, what had rattled Lee?

Before I could ask, I was distracted by a wavering set of headlights traveling toward us at breakneck speed on the opposite *westbound* side of the median. The driver, either drunk or high, abruptly swerved through a gap in the divider, and hung a U-ie into our eastbound traffic. Miscalculating, he barreled across the middle lane, cutting in front of us and missing our near fender by inches on his trajectory to the slow lane. Ricocheting off the curb, he cut across our path a *second* time. Fortunately, I'd instinctively decelerated. But he was oblivious to the near misses. Finding himself in the inside lane *where he should have been all along*, he shot away from us, his tail lights diminishing in the distance. At no point did his foot touch his brake.

"That bozo almost T-boned us!" I swore like a trucker and felt better for it. "There's never a cop around to...."

"Don't stop the car," Lee ordered.

Again?

A black spectral shape, without headlights or internal lighting, glided past us in the right lane. "Don't slow down, Jess. Don't change lanes."

Suddenly the interior of our car was flooded with light.

"What the...?"

A police car materialized on the passenger side, its cherry light spinning. It was eerie because they weren't using their siren. We held our breath as the cruiser slid abreast of us...and kept going. We exhaled.

A mile or so later, rotating beacons illuminated the shoulder. The patrol car that passed us had been joined on the verge by another. The cruiser must have radioed ahead. While two officers searched the 'ghost' car—a dark, nondescript sedan—two others stood with their guns trained on the driver splayed on its hood. The police had been chasing *him*. Not us.

"Whoa! I thought for sure the cops were going to wave us down," I said in a shaky voice. Not that we'd done anything wrong. "The guilty flee where none pursue...," I probably misquoted. Then I turned to face my sister. "What just happened here?"

Calmly, Lee 'splained it to me.

That bastard had been trailing us since Tangerine!

"His lights were off," Lee said, "He paced us from within your blind spot, Jess. You couldn't see him, but he could see us. Two women alone on a dark road. He'd 'clip' us and claim it was an accident. We'd stop, because 'that's what good citizens do....'" Then he'd steal our money...or worse!"

"Jeez, Lee, how did you know...?" I was appalled. "And why the hell didn't you say something sooner!?"

"Once I spotted him, I kept my eyes glued to the side mirror." she said. "But I lost him after the Yukon splashed us. I suspect he left the highway, skirted around Apopka, parked under a tree, and waited for his prey...." Sensing my agitation meter spiking, she reassured me. "I had my taser, Jess! We weren't in any *real* danger."

Silly me, to be so worried! Then it hit me.

"That whacko has run this con before." I snapped my fingers. "That's why the cops were around.... It was a stakeout!"

"Yep. Uncle Joe told me one of his cellmates used the same gimmick... once too often, apparently." In a heartbeat, Lee can make *me* feel naïve. How does she do that?

* * * *

We made it to Orlando International with time to spare. The airport proper doesn't open 'til four, so it was still pretty dark (as planned) when we drove into long-term parking and transferred all our belongings to our beloved '93 Mercedes S-Class. I drove the Ford over to the rental car lot, paid the machine, and walked back to long-term. We changed into more stylish (and flattering) getups, fluffed our hair, and touched up our makeup. We like to travel in style. Lee settled into the driver's seat and I rode shotgun.

There's no law that says you can't use an airport's parking garages unless you're catching a flight. It's assumed you're going by air, but who's checking? Lee took I-4 North, reaching I-95 North just as orange and red streaks stained the horizon. We stopped at a Dunkin' Donuts at the Ormond Beach exit, but hopped right back on 95, munching contentedly through the breaking dawn.

* * * *

Beautiful downtown Jacksonville filled our rearview mirror as we bounced over the bridge spanning the St. John's River. Soon we'd cross the state line into Georgia; an hour later we'd be home.

"What should we do with all the biker regalia, Lee?" Those leathers had cost a bundle.

"Hmm! Let me think." She tapped her dimple with a pearly pink fingernail. "I know! Cousin Rodney in Savannah has a birthday coming up next month. He's tall, has big feet, and is mad about 'cycles. He'll love my outfit."

"Good plan," I told her. "I think I'll give mine to our mechanic's kid. He told me he's saving up for a dragster. He'll easily unload my biker paraphernalia (minus the padding) to a buddy for a decent price."

"It would have been a different story, Lee, if that clown who crossed the divider had crashed into us," I said, broaching the subject we'd both avoided while we were still on Florida soil. "That would have been a heavy-duty hit-and-run. We could have lost a limb…or our life!"

"Maybe so. But what if the *other* creep, the one in the 'ghost' car, had ambushed us and hijacked my beautiful palm leaf plaque along with our recent bank withdrawal? That would have been a tragedy!"

"True that. Everybody knows there's nothing worse than being victimized by an art-loving highwayman!" I snorted, then sobered. "Come to think of it, either one of those close calls could have exposed us to a lot of unwelcome scrutiny.

"Absolutely! The trunk might have popped open. Imagine the cops pulling us over because a black bag was snagged on the undercarriage and greenbacks were flying across the Interstate," said Lee, refusing to be serious. "Oh, look! That turkey vulture has a twenty-dollar bill in its beak!" She's always been good at keeping things in perspective.

We were confident that no one would associate us with the heist around the corner from the B&B—which conveniently possessed a seldom used secondary entrance overlooked by a *nonworking* security cam. We'd shown zero interest in the motorcycle culture, instead spending our days at art galleries or flea markets in *other* towns. Moreover, the bank perps were manifestly guys—*burly, scary guys*. There was even less reason to link the rickety Escort to our ritzy S-Class. Tourist-driven Florida bans rental cars from displaying telltale agency signs that would make it easier for thieves to target visitors. Cruising around in our rented 'beater' with Florida plates (instead of an upscale foreign car with a Georgia peach on its license plate) rendered us practically invisible.

"By the way, we have to return little Billy's rifle," Lee reminded me. "He screamed like a banshee when he 'lost' it. Let's toss it over the fence into their vegetable garden. His mom will find it when she picks her tomatoes."

"You know, Jess," she mused, reverting to a favorite tangent, "I still believe a taser is safer for everybody, but…. Damn! Toy guns are so realistic these days. Isn't it great?"

I fiddled with the visor; my side of the car was in the sun. *Don't encourage her!*

"Not to change the subject, but have you given any thought to where our next job will take us?" I said, hoping to divert her by changing the subject.

"Oh, I meant to tell you. There's an Art Invitational at The Armory in New York City the last week in October and…," Lee said modestly, "I've been asked to enter some canvases." I must have looked surprised. "Hey, I'm not just good with palm fronds." She grinned. "My autumn leaves are *dynamite*."

"What about it, Jess? Halloween in The Big Apple!—Broadway, Bergdorf Goodman, the Met. Throngs of people in costumes! It'll be a cinch to melt into the crowds. What do you say?"

"I'm in! I'm in!" She had me at New York, New York—richest city in the world. "Chase Manhattan, Citibank, the Federal Reserve!"

As Willie Sutton put it so poetically, "*...that's where the money is!*

OH, HOLY NIGHT

VICTORIA DOWD

"This is utter murder!" Olivia Marchmont threw down the donkey's head. Her face was as puce and sweated as the old, boiled ham set out on the church hall's trestle table. The Delights of Christmas buffet had a leftovers look about it right from the first day the cling film was pulled back to reveal the weary offerings provided for the actors. The biscuits began life soggy, the cake was dry the moment it emerged from the tin. The tea urn had been maintained at a constant tepid temperature over the entire course of those so-called dress rehearsals.

"Absolute bloody murder," she repeated and kicked the sad donkey's head that lay on the floor.

"You want to count yourself lucky." A thickset man stood up straight behind Olivia. Placing his hands into the small of his back, he arched over and winced. "At least you're not the back end of the donkey."

"Ben, let me tell you, it's like a furnace in that head. I'm sweating cobs."

"You don't need to tell me that. I've spent hours wedged up your—"

"Ben Lucas, your mother would be ashamed!" a sharp voice of authority cut in.

The young man might well have been Upper Brimstock's fastest fly half and darling of the touchline, but in the face of Philomena Goodbody's wrath, he wilted just like everyone else in the village.

"Sorry, Miss." Ben Lucas flushed all the way through his dark, highly groomed stubble, his fingers fiddling with the tufted fur on his donkey suit trousers.

Like most people under the age of thirty in Upper Brimstock and the surrounding areas, he'd been one of her pupils at St Mary's. Philomena Goodbody never really stopped being their headmistress.

"At least you've got a bleedin' costume." A slender young man with a long platinum ponytail and a callous face threw down his tinsel star and ripped off the children's sparkly pink fairy wings.

Philomena shook her head. "Really, Ezra, that is hardly fitting behaviour for the Angel Gabriel."

"You can stuff yer halo where the sun don't shine. I'm off for a pint."

"Not in my pub, you ain't. You're barred." Raymond Mayhew, the landlord of the *Hope and Hoop* folded his arms over his beer-barrel stomach.

"What, for havin' a fumble with yer wife? That'd be half your customers gone."

The landlord's eyes flared. "Why you—" He began to lunge.

"Stop!" Philomena commanded.

And he did. Even the middle-aged publican had once been a pupil.

She cast a disparaging eye over the object of so many affections—his wife. Serena Mayhew, the Virgin Mary, was attractive in a rather obvious way for the mother of Jesus.

A frivolous little laugh broke from one of the three people holding a stuffed toy sheep.

Philomena's expression narrowed into impatience and came to rest on the giggling teen. Alice Fairchild, the Second Shepherd with the naturally woolly hair, immediately faded into embarrassment.

But however much authority Philomena Goodbody might command, she could not argue with the truth of her angel's statement. There were still no proper costumes for the village production of the musical nativity, and it was the night before Christmas Eve.

Casting adults had seemed like such a good idea that would invigorate this year's Upper Brimstock Christmas Nativity. No more forgotten lines, nose picking wise men, dropped baby Jesus or weeping angels. This would be a slick production with individuals cast based on auditions, rather than those whose mothers had the loudest voices on the PTA. For one sacred moment in Upper Brimstock's history, the audience would see these select residents in a very different light. The three wise people were not merely the local reporter, a thief, and a grocer. They were a holy trinity of baritone, tenor and descant. Ezra Freeman was no longer the surly odd job man but the Angel Gabriel with a surprisingly angelic voice. Sylas Logan wasn't just the village lothario but a handsome Joseph who stood by his wife. His Mary wasn't just the flirtatious, adulterous wife of the pub landlord. Serena Mayhew was the very image of radiant virtue. Raymond Mayhew, her husband, was not just a cuckolded publican but a ruddy faced innkeeper willing to lend a space next to his lowing cattle to this pregnant virgin. For one holy moment, the villagers of Upper Brimstock were to be transformed as seamlessly as contestants on *Stars in their Eyes*.

Only they weren't.

The costumes emerged from the old wicker hamper and the realisation hit that this festive tale of a pregnant virgin had only ever been performed by the village children. None of the costumes were adult sized, except that of the donkey that doubled as the yearly pantomime's horse.

The Christmas miracle of transformation was looking very unlikely.

Philomena found it increasingly difficult to inspire her new disciples as the opening day drew nearer and they still had no costumes, except for the ungrateful donkey.

"I ordered them all from Amazon ages ago," Philomena protested. "I even paid extra for Prime!" she added with a note of appeal.

"Snow on the roads in *Lower* Brimstock." Jack Avery (First Shepherd) spoke as if it was some distant land from Upper Brimstock. "An' a tree down." He pushed the stuffed sheep under his chair and took out a sandwich from his pocket. There was no wrapper on it and his fingers had crescents of dirt beneath every nail, but dirt never harmed him or the generations of farmers before him.

The cast stared out at the wet slate sky and watched the small flurries of snow drift in and out of the light cast by the church hall.

The three wise people took off their paper crowns in a co-ordinated act of abdication.

"We look proper fools." Leo Masterman shook his head, the light skating over his beetle black hair. He'd spent years perfecting a cockney accent to make him sound more streetwise. The whole effect ended up sounding more St Trinians' spiv than East End hardman. The biggest heist he'd pulled off was stealing a lorry load of frozen kebabs from the pub last summer, all of which defrosted in his mother's bathtub. The smell of rotting meat hung over the whole of Upper Brimstock for weeks. The victim of this crime, the pub landlord, Raymond Mayhew, wanted to beat the incompetent thief with his own pork knuckles, but his wife Serena had interceded.

"Leave it to me," she'd purred.

Her punishment had been far longer and more brutal than any her husband could have imagined. Leo Masterman (First Wise Person), the most unsuccessful criminal in Upper Brimstock, spent a year cleaning those pub toilets and everyone bore witness to it. By the end, he didn't know which was worse, the public humiliation or the constant stench from that very well-used public convenience.

"Well, I'm not about to be made a fool of," Serena announced.

The other two wise people, Gabbie Finnegan, the local reporter, and Augusta Heft, the grocer, nudged one another and raised their eyebrows. They would have been better cast in a Roald Dahl production and neither would have required a costume.

"Hark at Miss Job Centre," Gabbie stage-whispered.

They both laughed on cue.

Serena glared and pursed her full, glossy mouth.

Alice Fairchild (Second Shepherd) clutched her sheep tight and looked confused. "Job Centre?"

"Do be quiet, Alice." Philomena scrolled through the endless emails from Amazon on her phone.

"Aye," Gabbie sneered. "She's been through more professions than the job centre has pinned up. First there was the milkman, then the gardener, delivery drivers, postmen, window cleaners—"

"How dare you!" The colour was burning up Serena's face.

"That's enough!" Her husband, slammed down the old fashioned, green teacup, sloshing its muddied liquid into the saucer. His eyes remained fixed on his wife like a man who was worried she might disappear if he looked away.

There was only one thing that could distract his attention—the self-satisfied leer of Upper Brimstock's very own Romeo: Sylas Logan, Joseph to his wife and a lot of other things as well.

The wrath in Raymond Mayhew's old eyes was truly Biblical. "You sleazy b—" he flew at Sylas, who artfully dodged to the side in a way that suggested he was no stranger to a husband's fists.

The laughter did nothing to quell Raymond's indignation as he fell to the floor. "You'll pay for that."

"It's here!" Philomena hurried across the room, past the sprawled-out body on the floor and the laughing wise people, past the coquettish Virgin Mary and the disgruntled donkey—front end and back. She flung open the doors of the church hall with the kind of ceremony and drama that might have been more suited to Westminster Abbey. The snow was spiralling through the air but had not settled yet. Standing there in the shaft of light was the bedraggled driver holding out a large box marked with the Amazon arrow.

"Thank God!" she proclaimed as if there might well have been some Divine intervention. She held the box in reverence. They would no longer be a defeated landlord, the sneery wise people, or grumbling donkey. Even the sight of her Mary and Joseph standing over in the corner and locked in a very inappropriate embrace could not derail this show now. They were *all* about to be transformed. "Tonight, Matthew, they will be the Nativity!"

Philomena turned back to the door. "Thank you. We are saved!"

It all seemed so convincing then, even to the most cynical eyes in the room. Perhaps they were *all* going to be truly saved.

But no, not *all*.

Every tale of redemption requires a sacrifice.

* * * *

There was a childlike Christmas excitement, almost merriment, amongst them as they ripped open the box and began taking out the costumes. Some might have described it as a convivial scene of festive joy.

Philomena took a moment to admire the scene gathered round the baby doll swaddled in the nursery school cradle.

The Nativity was brought to life during that next precious hour in the dim glow of a village church hall with a snowstorm building outside. Just how the birth of Jesus should be, Philomena thought. It was truly a miracle.

It was not one that would last very long.

"Right. Much as it pains me to love you and leave you," Sylas crooned. "I've got someone…somewhere I need to be."

"Oh?" Serena frowned.

He gave no further explanation, just a shrug. It was that shrug of apology Serena had been dreading. Just a downturn of his mouth and slight tilt of his head was enough. "*I am what I am*" kind of gesture—a helpless sorry from a man at the whim of his own desires. "I can't help it" was an expression that came very naturally to his face. It was swiftly followed by a final smile that said, "you knew that."

Serena stood up, knocking over the cradle. "You can't just go."

"Serena…" her real husband cautioned.

When she looked at him, she saw all those days spreading out at the pub, and there was another all-too-brief encounter leaving.

Sylas sighed as if it pained him just as much. But it didn't. "I'm just not an exclusive kind of guy," he said unironically. "We've still got the Nativity, Babes." The last remark felt like a twist of the knife.

Tears pricked her eyes.

The cast waited.

Philomena waited.

Serena exited stage left—pursued by no one.

Sylas pulled open the heavy safety door of the church hall and the wind instantly slammed it into the wall. Cold rushed in as if a vacuum had been pierced. The light from the hall lit the angry air outside and shimmered on the twirling flakes. The night was thick with snow, the ground glistening and piled high.

"You can't go out there!" (Second Shepherd) Alice's mouth hung open.

Leo Masterman set down his crown and kingly sword. "Well, I ain't stayin' 'ere either, that's for sure."

Sylas laughed and pulled up his collar. "It's only a short stroll." He headed out into the storm and was immediately swallowed by it.

"I've got a pub to run," Raymond announced, fastening his coat over the inn keeper's outfit. He followed Sylas out into the darkness.

The troupe watched the empty doorway.

"I need a slash," Ezra the Angel Gabriel announced, pulling off his halo. He left by a side door.

"Well, I'll be sayin' evenin', as well then," Masterman called before heading out into the night.

They scattered like a disappointed audience on first night, through various doors and as fast as they could. Those who remained caught in a vacant silence.

The next sound they heard was an engine starting up and driving away.

They looked to Philomena.

"Right." She sighed. "Well, perhaps you should get changed. I don't want my... the brand new costumes to be ruined. They were very naughty to run off so quickly in them. They'll have to pay for any damage." She bustled towards the door next to the stage leading into the kitchenette and offices that served as a green room. She held open the door like an expectant headmistress.

Slowly, her flock of shepherds, wise people and the donkey (front and back) filed through.

It was the front of the donkey, Olivia Marchmont who was the first to find the body. Her scream lit up the sombre corridor of the church hall.

* * * *

"Touch nothing!" Philomena ordered.

They gathered at the door to the small office, their faces cut with horror and disbelief.

Slumped in the chair, facing them, was Serena still dressed in her Virgin's costume, her blind eyes wide, her mouth cracked slightly open. There was almost an ecstasy to the last expression life had left behind on her beautiful face.

Philomena stepped towards Serena and felt her neck. She shook her head and peered closer. "Strangled." Her voice was church quiet. "With this, I think." She pointed to a long length of bubblewrap that had burst in places. It was twisted and stretched to the point of thin plastic string.

There was a small almost indistinguishable tinkling noise as Ben Lucas lifted the murder weapon.

"Don't touch that!" Philomena shot. "It's evidence. Put it down."

He dropped it immediately but noticed something on the floor and picked that up instead. "Looks like a child's badge. It's a minion."

"For goodness sake, Ben. Stop contaminating everything. We need to preserve the scene. Everybody out."

In the black window behind her, a face suddenly appeared with zinc-white eyes. Hands began beating on the window.

Olivia screamed out again.

"Be quiet, girl," Philomena ordered. She walked to where the newly widowed Raymond Mayhew was hammering on the glass. He opened the window and climbed through.

"What's happened? What have you done to my Serena?" A line of spit travelled down from his mouth to the floor. He stared at the fallen figure in bemusement as if the picture made no sense.

Philomena closed the window and folded her arms as she locked eyes with the landlord. "*We* have done nothing. *We* were all together."

He fell at his dead wife's feet, gripping her knees. She was unmoved. Then he paused and looked around the group. "What do you mean? You can't be suggesting—"

"What's happened?" It was Ezra, no longer an angel, at the door. He was wrapping a scarf around his neck but paused, one arm holding it around his neck. "What's going on?"

The group parted for him to see.

Philomena began, "Serena has been strangled, we think with this." She glanced down at the floor.

Ezra's arm didn't move. "I… I just went to the loo."

"Is that right, lad," sneered the dirty fingered Shepherd, Jack Avery.

"You can't think I had anything to do with this?"

"Why not, Ezra?" Philomena raised an eyebrow. "Were you not barred from the pub by her husband who caught you *in flagrante*?"

"In what? It was just a snog and a bit of a fumble. Nothing else. I was never in—"

"Mr. Ezra Freeman! I put it to you that you were the only member of the party to be out here with the victim at the time of her death."

They all looked on in astonishment.

"This isn't for us to investigate." Gabby (Second Shepherd) said, pulling out her reporter's notebook. "We should call the police."

"No chance." Jack spat on the floor as if to confirm it. "Phones is out." He held up a mobile in his dirty fingers.

This injected fresh panic into the room. More than one voice started shouting until the whistle cut through everything.

Philomena took her fingers from her mouth and waited in the new silence. "That's better. Now, let the suspect speak!"

All eyes transferred to Ezra.

"Suspect? What the hell? I came past this room and heard voices. The door was slightly open but I could only see Serena."

"Voices?" Philomena questioned. "Whose? What were they saying?"

The group were in awe of her ruthless efficiency.

"I… I don't know. A man—"

Ezra was interrupted by another round of hammering on the window. They all turned in concert to look, except for Serena whose lifeless gaze remained focused on some fixed point ahead of her.

It was a man.

Two men.

Sylas Logan, the victim's stage husband, and Leo Masterman (First Wise Person). They stood in awful wonder at the dimly lit scene within before Sylas opened the window. An icy wind circled the room.

"What the hell is going on?" Sylas searched first Philomena's face and then looked at the body dressed as Mary. "Jesus Christ," he whispered and climbed through ahead of Masterman.

"Why are you here, Mr. Logan, Mr. Masterman?" Philomena spoke with absolute patience. She closed the window, and the storm was muffled once more. The only sound the tiny fingertip tapping of the snowflakes on the glass.

The room was crowded now. Twelve good, and not so good, men and women staring at the empty face of the murdered victim. Her real husband still wept at her feet.

"We heard a scream." Sylas spoke as if he was coming too from a dream and unsure where he'd woken up, not an unfamiliar sensation to him. "We came running through the snow."

"You were together."

He glanced at Philomena. "Yes. Leo caught up with me and we decided to walk back together. It's bad out there."

"Yet you didn't return sooner?"

He straightened up. "Listen, I had no reason to kill Serena. Far from it. I suggest you look closer to home." He stared down at Raymond, who slowly rose to his feet.

"You shut your mouth, Sylas. Don't even look at her." Raymond's face tightened into an angry ball. So did his fists.

Philomena stood between them. "Boys! This will not help. We must leave our lady in peace." She widened her eyes. "We must all go back to the hall, now."

There was something unquestionable about Philomena but when she started taking photographs of the dead woman on her phone, it seemed like a good moment to leave. She took more of the weapon, the floor, and the window.

Raymond was the last to leave, tears blistering his eyes. "Why?" he whispered.

She studied him for a moment. "You ask why? One thing we are not short of, Mr. Mayhew, is *reasons* someone might want to kill your wife. Particularly you."

He started to huff in astonishment, but Philomena had already turned her back on him and was leaving.

In the cold hall, there was no longer a warming scene of a blissful nativity. It was a stark setting with plastic chairs gathered in a circle. The cast were seated as though they were attending a support group meeting and about to make a confession. A chair had been set aside for Philomena and when she entered, they all fell into a hush. She seated herself and straightened her skirt.

"Ladies and gentlemen, we are all aware Serena, our Virgin Mary, has been murdered."

Her husband, the real one, made a strangled noise as he settled into a chair.

The lights flickered and another member of the cast shrieked.

"We have no telephones so cannot phone the police."

"Someone could go for them," Ben Lucas (donkey's rear end) offered.

Philomena shook her head. "The weather is too bad. It's over a mile walk to the first house. Also, we may be letting the killer go scot free before the police have been contacted or had time to get here."

She paused for them to consider this before adding, "Or we may be sending someone into danger."

"What?" Gabby (Second Shepherd) looked confused and terrified. "Are you saying they're out there? Now? How could they have got in? We were all here. In the hall."

"Well, that, at least, is simple. The window to the room Serena was in was not locked. Mr. Mayhew opened it from the outside to come in. The killer could very easily have been outside, entered, killed Serena then gone back out." She looked around the circle with ominous eyes. "It could have been any one of Mr. Mayhew, Sylas Logan or Mr. Masterman. Each had a motive."

"Me? Why would I kill her?" Sylas scoffed.

"Mr. Logan, we all witnessed you breaking up with Serena. Did you slip round the corner of the hall, see her through the window, quarrel and kill her with the packing material in the office?"

He looked stunned.

Philomena didn't waste any time on his reaction. "Or perhaps it was Mr. Mayhew, the husband she betrayed on multiple occasions, who came in and argued with her before murdering her and leaving."

He only sobbed in response.

"Or the third unwise man who was outside at the time of death—Mr. Leo Masterman."

"That's just ridiculous," he laughed.

"Is it? A whole summer of humiliation at her hands being made to clean the very public toilets at the *Hope and Hoop*? Revenge would have been sweet, Mr. Masterman."

He turned away.

"Or perhaps our killer was inside all along and still is now. Ezra was on his own out there where the offices are and, as we know, had a motive in that he too shared relations with her that were cut short."

Ezra snorted.

"He tells us he heard voices. Serena was talking to someone. Either Ezra's lying or it was someone she knew or expected perhaps."

"Is the murderer here? Now?" Olivia cried.

"No," was all Philomena said.

"So, someone is out there—the killer—waiting?" Augusta sounded even more frightened.

"No," Philomena repeated.

Sylas leaned back on his chair. "Well, it has to be one or the other."

"Don't rock back on your chair."

His mouth dropped and he put the front two legs of the chair back on the ground.

Philomena straightened. "There is a third option."

They all stared like rabbits pulled from a hat.

"The killer only wanted to kill Serena."

"But how can you know that?" Ben Lucas had not been keeping up.

Philomena pulled out her phone. "Three wise clues. The murder weapon." She held up the photograph before scrolling to the next one. "The snow." Again, she showed them a picture.

"Snow outside the window to the office?" Leo voiced his thoughts.

"Precisely. Look at the snow. What do you see?"

"Snow," Ezra said.

"And…"

She waited. He stared at her blankly.

"Let me help you. I didn't ask you what you expected to see but what you see—*exactly* what you see. I see two parallel lines. A set of tyre tracks. We heard an engine after Sylas and Leo left. After Serena had left. Yet the three men who left here didn't travel so far because they were on foot."

"So, someone drove here, killed her, then drove off."

"Yet there is only one set of tyre tracks in the snow and it's highly unlikely they drove away exactly over the other tracks."

"They were already here!" Olivia announced.

"No…"

"They're still here?" Augusta queried.

"No. They were here before the snow came but left after it started. After they killed her."

"This makes no sense to me," Sylas sighed. "Are they invisible or something?"

"Oh yes, often. These people are often here but seldom taken notice of. They walk amongst our everyday lives and very few of us could describe them." She scrolled through her photos again.

"Let's look at the final clue. A minion." She held it up.

Leo Masterman squinted at the screen. "That's not a minion." They all looked at him, then back at the photo of the small, child's badge with the character on it. "Minions are yellow not orange. That's a Peccy."

"A what?" Raymond asked, wiping his tears.

"A Peccy. It's their mascot. He's orange. Look, he even has the arrow for his mouth. I should know, I worked in their warehouse for long enough." He looked round them. "The Amazon warehouse."

They all stared at him as the meaning of the words began to rearrange.

Philomena finished their thoughts. "Someone did drive here before the snow settled. They stood at the door and witnessed the woman they loved canoodling with someone else. The woman who slept with all manner of visitors to the pub, postmen, milkmen and… delivery drivers. People who walk through our lives and we pay very little attention to. He saw her and what she was doing with Sylas. He waited. We never heard an engine at that point. He didn't drive away. Then he saw her through the window and climbed in. They spoke and presumably she made it very clear she wasn't interested. That's when he killed her with the packing material so readily available to him. The bubblewrap. Unfortunately, the mascot badge of Amazon, the Peccy, dropped to the ground in the scuffle. He left through the window and that is when we heard the engine drive away and create the track in the snow."

They sat in astonished silence.

Until the ping of a phone.

"We've got signal!" Olivia cried.

"It's mine." Philomena looked at her phone. "A message. From Amazon. My package was delivered."

THE BOOK

STEVE SHROTT

The man removed my blindfold as he spoke in a guttural voice. "Glad you could make it, Miss Holden."

My eyes snapped open as I realized the man was Tony Marcino, a local mobster. My legs shook all the way down to my four inch heels, and I prayed I would leave with the same number of legs I came in with. "I, uh, really didn't have a choice when the man with the scar came to my door holding a gun. I didn't want holes through my Gloria Vanderbilt underwear."

Marcino rubbed his receding salt and pepper hair and stood up from behind his large desk. I figure guys get large desks to compensate for their lack of self-esteem, but this dude looked like he could tear apart a dump truck with his pinky.

"So sorry about that, Miss Holden, but I desperately need your assistance."

I stared at him a moment wondering why a mobster would need my help. I was a writer. The only crime I'd committed was too many sentences with dangling participles.

Marcino picked up the book I'd written from his desk and patted it as if it were a badly behaved Chihuahua. "You see, our situation is somewhat similar to The Leicester Affair you recount in chapter three where you investigate the robbery of your client's art collection. How you deduced that the perpetrator was five feet three inches tall, forty-seven years old, bore a scar on his left cheek, and smoked a Fuente cigar but only during the day, astounds me—especially considering you untangled all this from a tiny scuff mark on the parquet flooring."

Oh my God! He apparently thought the book I had written about my PI adventures was all true.

Well in fairness to him, it did say 'All True' in big red letters on the cover. I had written the book because my agent told me true stories about crime sell in a big way. So, I made up stories about the PI career that I never had.

But now the book seemed like not such a great idea.

Marcino paced for a few moments, then spoke in a somber voice. "Miss Holden, I need you to go to the National Bank with Fredrico, one of my lieutenants."

I was hoping Fredrico just needed help figuring out why his bank statement had an overcharge of thirteen dollars and seventy-three cents, but I had a hunch there might be more to it than that.

"You see when Fredrico returned from last week's robbery, a hundred grand was missing from his briefcase. He claimed he was hijacked by another of my lieutenants—Hendricks—who I dismissed instantly. I didn't take any stronger action at the time as I had suspicions that Fredrico might be behind this thievery. Miss Holden, I need you to use your superb deduction skills and figure out if he is indeed responsible. If it turns out that he is, I'd ask you to take him out." He gave me a big toothy smile.

"Take him out?"

"Yes."

"You mean like take him out to a deli—and have a chat with him?"

He laughed, his belly shaking up and down as if it were about to explode like some lava-filled volcano. "There is that great sense of humor you share with us in the book. No, no, Miss Holden, you must dispose of him."

"Dispose, as in get rid of, eliminate…ex-ex-terminate?"

"Yes, exactly."

At this point, I probably should have come clean and said I made everything up. But considering there were rumors Marcino was involved in shootings, drownings, and stranglings, I thought maybe I should put a pin in that idea. So what I said was, "The thing is I'm a, uh, PI, and we don't take people out."

"Yes, the normal PI. But you are not that, are you?"

"What?"

He flipped through a few pages of the book. "In chapter one, you talk about being head of the Tomaso Crime Family before you turned your life around to become a private investigator."

Damn I'd forgotten about that. Damn me again for being so damn creative. Damn.

"As I recall, Diego, one of your lieutenants, surprised you with nunchucks hoping to usurp your position. Little did he know you were an expert in nunchuckery, and moments later, he lay on the ground, his heart no longer inside his chest."

"Yes, well, uh, the thing is, I'm not really a nunchuckery exp…"

"Then you discovered Fernando had bumped off Salvador, your consigliore, and you used your vast knowledge of Akito, Kyokushin Karate, and Krav Maga to take him down."

I blew out air, cursing myself for ever having written that stupid book (except for the fact that I still get royalties.)

"So let's get started. I've already informed Fredrico that you will be assisting him with the bank job."

* * * *

That night snow fell, a ballet of perfect whiteness choreographed by the gentle winter breeze. See I told you I'm a writer. I was in the front seat of a black sedan with Fredrico at the wheel. He wore a black toque, a black scarf, and a long black coat. Black must be in this year for the well-dressed mobster. In his coat pocket I saw a bulge that I assumed was a firearm. If that wasn't ominous enough, in the backseat, a briefcase lay on top of a brightly colored quilt with the picture of a man holding a knife to another man's throat.

"Interesting, uh, quilt."

"Took me weeks to get the tints and tones just right."

"You made this?"

"Crime is a high stress career path, lady. When you're not robbin' or murderin' you need an avocation."

Up close Fredrico looked mean with his stony face and dead eyes. But, you know, first impressions can be wrong, and someone like him can be the nicest guy in the world.

He stopped at a light and turned to me. "I gotta tell you somethin'."

"Uh huh."

"No disrespect, but I would like to push the engine to eighty, tie you to a heavy rock, and toss you out the window into an alligator-filled swamp."

Okay sometimes you gotta go with first impressions.

"The only reason you're here is we've been getting pushback from the other crime families about not being gender balanced."

"I don't under…"

"Apparently we don't have enough ladies for some people. But as I've always said, chicks shouldn't be in crime. They just don't have the goods."

This was unbelievable. Not only was I going to be involved in a robbery, and told I might have to take someone out, but worse yet, I was going to be subjected to these anti-feminist vibes.

When we arrived at the bank, Fredrico parked on the street, grabbed the case from the backseat, then handcuffed me to the steering wheel.

"Hey what's…"

He slammed the door shut and left.

I know this is hard to believe, but so far, this has not been my best day.

It seemed like hours later when the bank alarm rang, and Fredrico raced toward the car gasping for air as his face turned the color of an over-ripe tomato. I admired the commitment but the man really needed a full cardio-vascular work up. He held the case in front of him, but it was open, exposing the bills. Luckily, as he reached the car, he was able to snap it shut and load the case into the backseat. He obviously hadn't removed any of the money, which was good news, as it meant Marcino would be happy, and I wouldn't end up at the bottom of some swamp somewhere wearing cement shoes. Not my favorite location or footwear.

As we drove back to Marcino's office, I felt like Fredrico and I had bonded as he hadn't mentioned anything about tying me to a rock, tossing me out a window, or alligators—always a good thing in a new acquaintance. Although I doubted we would ever be on a rollercoaster together eating from one another's candy floss.

After a few moments, he stopped the car and parked in front of a forested area so he could take a leak. As he walked toward the tall trees crowding together, I was surprised I had missed how chunky he was. But I didn't think it was my place to suggest that a gangster who could probably shoot the hairs out of a fly's nose from twenty feet away to check out Jenny Craig.

* * * *

When we arrived at Marcino's office, Fredrico finally undid the handcuffs, and we walked inside. Marcino immediately jumped up from his chair like a child receiving a new toy, and snatched the case from Fredrico. I was astounded at how spry he was. I guess whacking people keeps a guy in pretty good shape.

He placed the case on his desk and opened it. I peered inside with a smile on my face which gradually morphed into disbelief and then terror at what I saw—nada, naught, zilch, zip, diddly-squat, zot.

To translate, zero cash.

Fredrico spread his hands. "I told you on the phone, boss, she buried the money when she took a leak."

What the hell was going on? "I never went for any damn leak in the woods. I'm not going to the bathroom, the same place a moose goes. Do you know what their hygiene is like? Fredrico is the one who went for a leak."

I thought I'd cleared that up, but I realized I may not have been as successful as I hoped when Marcino brought out a gun and made me go outside to his car. He pushed me into the backseat alongside Fredrico. I couldn't even look at him after how he'd lied about me. I thought we had something together.

Once we started driving, Fredrico began rubbing his feet. I couldn't believe it—a mobster with athlete's foot is not a good look for the organization. I think they're really gonna have trouble at their next membership drive.

We finally arrived back at the forest where I had supposedly taken a leak. Fredrico pointed to numerous footprints that led toward a Willow Tree. "That's where Holden buried it."

Although I hadn't buried anything, I figured, with my luck, when they dug up the snow and earth they'd find the money.

Bingo.

Marcino tapped Fredrico on the back and told him to gather up the cash and take it to the car.

After he left, a scowl appeared on Marcino's face as he told me to stand against the tree. "Tried to bilk me, eh, Holden."

"I didn't take the money."

"Uh huh."

"There's got to be another explanation." I had a hunch he didn't think there was another explanation by the rage etched on his face and the fact that he was reloading his gun with what seemed like way too many bullets. I was astounded. I'm like six inches away from the dude, and he can't get me with one shot? If he wasn't so intent on finishing me off, I might have suggested he get checked for cataracts.

He pointed the gun at me, and I thought I was about to be a dead detective, crime lord, and Nunchuckery expert. But then the answer hit me. "Fredrico switched cases."

"What?"

"After he robbed the bank, he came back to the car and pretended to put the case in the backseat. In reality he stuffed it under his coat."

Marcino raised his eyebrows so high they looked like they might take off for another galaxy. "Really?"

"When he went to take a leak, he looked fat. He was obviously hiding the case."

"The man's fat 'cause he eats a ton of carbs. Last week he devoured three apple pies for his entre, then ordered dessert."

I rambled on. "He went to the tree, took the money out of the briefcase, and buried it. He threw away the case and came back to the car."

"If he threw it away, how did he give me the empty case?"

"Easy. He had previously put a duplicate in his vehicle."

Marcino rolled his eyes. "Even if I believed all that, what about the footprints in the snow leading to the cash? They look like they were made by someone wearing high heels." He looked down at my feet. "I'm guessing not too many people wear them when they go into a forest. So those prints have to be yours."

"I'm glad you mentioned that." Of course I wasn't really glad as the only answer I had was those weren't my prints and Big Foot had started wearing pumps. Then I figured that one out too. "Those aren't my prints. Notice how wobbly they look. If I walked in the snow the prints would be perfect."

"Show me."

"I'd prefer not..."

He moved the gun closer to my head, one of my favorite body parts which I'd hoped to keep where it was currently situated. Unfortunately, I wasn't sure I could unfreeze myself enough to move. But after a few seconds, I got into it. I sashayed along the snow like I was a supermodel in Milan Fashion Week even though I was wearing a blouse, skirt and jacket from Sal's Discount Emporium's, 'Everything for Five Dollars Sale.' "Do you see how perfect the prints are? That's because I've worn high heels all my life. On the other hand, someone who's wearing heels for the first time would have trouble with balance and the prints would be wobbly."

Marcino looked puzzled.

"I thought Fredrico had a gun in his pocket earlier, but now I realize the shape was wrong and that it was probably heels. He put them on to walk in the snow so the prints would look like they were from me. Have you noticed how he's been rubbing his feet lately? He's not used to wearing them."

It seemed to click in Marcino's brain, but then something else clicked. A double click is not usually good. "Why would Fredrico do such a thing?"

I had this. "He doesn't want any females in the crime family. So if it looked like I, a woman, had robbed you, you wouldn't hire any more of them."

I waited a moment for Marcino to make sense of it all. Then he lowered his gun. "I get it. That's why Fredrico told me Selma Hendricks stole the money from that other bank job. So I would get rid of her."

"I bet if you check Fredrico's pockets, you'll find the heels."

Marcino did check and found some pretty ugly shoes. The man had absolutely no fashion sense.

He did take Fredrico out, but only to Katz's Deli to do an intervention about his anti-feminist views, and to find out where he stashed the cash from the other job.

Marcino paid me a lot of money, more than I ever got from any royalties. Then he said he'd call again when I was required.

I wasn't exactly looking forward to that. But I had to get back to my writing. I'm working on a new book about the time I worked for the CIA.

BLUNT FORCE TRAUMA

DAVID BART

I'd been marinating in my own boredom outside Larry Chamber's palatial mansion, my mind beset with images of avoidable screwups from the past, though the sweating was contemporary; perspiring like a teenage girl at a Taylor Swift concert. This had been that way since I was a cop and got hit in the head with a length of rebar. Had to leave the APD.

So, there I was, on yet another stake out; this time as a P.I. It was a summer night in the desert; and here's a news flash: the air conditioner doesn't work unless the truck's running. Albuquerque claims to be a cool holiday destination, but it's not even close to cool. And they can spin that till they're dizzy, saying it's a dry heat: it's a hot heat and that's that.

My cell pinged. Rachel Tessay had sent a text. She was my partner in anti-crime.

Life was a Hollywood movie for me, and I had the lead role as a private detective with my own agency: *Gabriel Blunt Investigations*. I'm known all over the west; a legend. And at that very moment I was being texted by my beautiful associate. To further the film analogy: conflict's necessary in any good movie plot; in mine I wrestle with the fact that I'm a tad aggressive. Not whacko, but definitely have some self-control issues—tend to hit first and then hit again later. I'm not a nice guy by any standard; though I gots me *one* good quality: I'd give my life laughingly for anyone I care about. Admittedly a small group; consists of just me and one other human.

I looked at the phone screen. *Where you at?*

Rachel always texts first so as not to blow a stakeout gig by activating my ringtone: Queen's "Another One Bites the Dust." The heavy bass would certainly draw attention. Or even bullets. And who needs that crap?

I texted my location to her, mentioning how tedious it was to sit in my truck—a ten-year-old Acura SUV—out there all alone, in the middle of the night, without any booze or a warm, sexy sidekick to keep me—

Another text: *Paleface need cuddle? Kinda busy right now. Call me.*

Rachel was of the Jicarilla Apache persuasion. Looked like a young Cher, back when she was singing alongside Sonny; long black hair and a slightly bent, but interesting nose. Smarter than me. A lot prettier. Didn't drink, smoke or do drugs. Course, nobody's perfect.

I called her. "Did you forget that I'm a legendary investigator and can't be bothered with trivialities?"

Weird how you can tell, even over the phone, that someone's grinning; their mouth makes little clicks. I'd told her about my status as a legend a while back and when she stopped laughing she just shook her head, as though pitying me. Women can be cruel.

"Do you need something?" I asked in a polite tone. And if anyone buys the idea that I can be cordial, I have some New Mexico oceanfront property I'd like to sell them.

Rachel sighed. "Don't be so pissy. I'm calling from the office. There's a guy sitting across my desk from me with a gun pointing at me."

Now I'm really pissed. "Are you mental, Rachel? You should have opened with that, not just mention it now." I pushed the start button on the dash of my truck.

Rachel chuckled. "Scary, eh?"

She's sometimes a pain in the ass with all that fearless Indian crap. It's authentic, but still annoying.

"Let me talk to him," I said, but with difficulty due to my jaw being clenched.

The guy came on. "Hey, Blunt…'member me?"

Familiar voice; can't place it though. Course, I've known more than my share of dipshits, hard to keep them all straight, particularly when you can't see the face. And then you have all the political nonsense we have to watch on cable propaganda channels where idiots abound. "If my partner comes to any harm, I *will* find you, and I *will* kill you," I said.

"Wait, don't tell me…Liam Neeson in *Taken*. Am I right?" he said.

"I mean it, bubba, won't be enough left of you to moisten a stamp." I called him Bubba because he had a southern accent; Georgia or some such excessively humid place. He must've been holding his gun near the cell phone because I heard it being cocked—double-action revolver. Not pertinent, I suppose, what type of gun it was, but an interesting detail.

"You killed two of my brothers, Blunt—ya think threats will stop me from getting revenge?" I couldn't see him, but it sounded like he was gritting his teeth. Which were probably yellow, some of them missing.

And factually, I didn't kill his people, a bomb killed them. *His* bomb. I'd just "returned to sender," but on a short fuse, so to speak. His name's Billy Ray Bunker. To call him a lowlife would be demeaning to other lowlifes. He and his brothers were meaner than Tasmanian devils and dumber than a bag of wet hair. Well, Billy Ray was; his brothers weren't anything, being dead and all. Though there might be another brother. No doubt also a bag of hair.

"You got a fine-lookin' Injun for a partner, Blunt. Bet it'll hurt when she dies."

I bit my tongue, reminded him how *Taken*, the movie he'd accurately claimed I'd quoted, ends. "The bad guys die in great numbers, remember?" Asked him if it's true that folks in the South pick their feet; which was a rude characterization, probably untrue, but I was buying time. Because during the conversation I'd driven the mile and a half from my stakeout to the office. Dumped my Acura SUV on the street without looking for a parking space, put on the blinkers, took off my shoes and crept up the stairs—eased the door open and stepped up behind Bunker. The dumb cracker had his back to the door.

Rachel didn't look at me or give any indication of my presence. Kinda like at a surprise birthday gathering, only at this soirée the party favors were loaded guns.

Through the office window my truck's emergency lights provided a blinking red distraction to get his attention, but Bunker, the idiot, didn't notice. I couldn't shoot him because his gun was, you might remember, cocked and pointing at Rachel. The very someone I cared about.

So, here's a tip from an ex-cop and present-day PI: when you grab a gun, do so in a way that puts the fleshy web of your hand, the part that separates index finger and thumb, in between the frame of the pistol and the cocked hammer, so that if the trigger is pulled the gun can't fire a bullet at the most important person in your life. Well, second most important. Another tip: you should unhesitatingly strike the wannabe assailant on the side of the head with your gun—in my case a Sig Sauer compact nine-millimeter—or you could use something equally as unlikely to yield upon impact. In other words, a hard object.

"I think you might've killed him," Rachel said, her tone impassive as she gazed down at what's-his-name like he was an insignificant bit of lint on the carpet.

"These things happen," I said, uncocking Bunker's gun and setting it on Rachel's desk. Then I stepped over his possibly…probably…uh, pretty-sure-of-it, dead body.

"And I thought *I* was cold," she said, getting up to stretch out some of her tension, raising her arms and arching her back. Which I watched closely, to assess her well-being, something a trained investigator can establish by merely leering at the female body.

* * * *

Turned out Billy Ray Bunker wasn't dead, just severely injured. I told the cops I was sorry and some other lies and it pretty much went away. Might be a hearing—*wink, wink, nudge, nudge.*

The very next week Bunker's surviving brother—and no, his name's not Archie—came after me with a vengeance and a twelve-gauge shotgun. Not a welcome combination if you're the target.

Some of the pellets, first hitting my desk, continued on to hit me in the hip and leg—*"Stings like anything, Shane!"* I shouted. Admittedly an odd thing to say, but I was trying to throw him off by yelling before he could fire the other barrel, while I simultaneously pulled my gun from a clip holster at the small of my back. What I'd yelled was another movie quote—the best western of all time—and at the end of the movie Brandon deWilde also shouts "Mother wants you, Shane." Kinda racy for a Fifties flick.

Anyway, I shot Burt Bunker and that was that. He didn't die either. Maybe being wounded threw off my timing.

The cops gave me some trouble. *Who shot first? What's your problem, Blunt, always shooting people? Or hitting them over the head.* In the end they let the EMTs take me to the hospital. "Geez, dude," I'd told the cop. "I'm bleeding over here."

Rachel showed up in my room on the trauma floor bearing carne asada, beans and rice. Sat in a visitor's chair and started eating, or pretended to eat, looking out the window. Didn't offer a: *how are you, does that hurt,* or anything.

"You didn't bring me food?" I asked, trying to keep the hurt out of my voice because your average Apache views whining as weakness. I guess we all do.

She frowned. "They don't feed you in here?"

I gave her my legendary-investigator glare—very scary. "Well, yeah, but it's not carne asada from Gennaro's." Nodded toward the carry-out food.

My partner let out a big sigh. "Well, I'm full anyway," she said, dropping the Styrofoam container with all of the untouched food onto the little table-thingy they had for people who've been shot to shit.

After eating it all, down to the last grain of seasoned rice, spicy bean and marinated chunk of beef, I asked, "No beer?"

She snapped her fingers. "It's in the car, totally forgot."

That *really* hurt.

She chuckled, pulled a bottle of Dos Equis out of her butt pack and grinned.

"Smart aleck Indian," I said, taking the bottle from her and twisting off the cap—like a real man.

* * * *

Anyway…remember Larry Chambers from up at the beginning of the narrative? The rich guy's mansion I was watching while sweating like an

Arkansas razorback? Well, he was standing in my office looking pissed. And here's what he said: "I'm pissed."

"No kidding, what's the problem?" I asked in a tone that was obviously absent of sincerity. Hey, he's the kind of guy who brings out the worst in people. A low bar in my case.

Larry's mouth dropped open like a put-upon valley girl. "My wife's bonking somebody and you were supposed to get me evidence."

I pointed at my bandaged leg. "Shotgun wounds."

"Do I look like I give a shit?" he yelled.

It concerned me that his blood pressure had probably elevated dangerously. I'm kidding, I couldn't have cared less. "Well, Larry, if I'm being honest, you do *not* look like you give a shit. Want your money back?"

He stared at me so hard I almost pissed myself. Again, just kidding. Larry's rich, but still a twit; couldn't scare a mouse. And certainly could *not* intimidate a legendary…well, you know.

"Just find me some proof of that bitch's infidelity." And he stormed out of my office, the sound of my female partner's chuckles following him down the hall.

I asked her, "As a member of an American indigenous people, what do you think of Larry's accusation regarding his wife?"

"First of all," Rachel said, sighing, "we were here before there was an America. Second of all, I'm hungry. And third of all, if she's not screwing around, she should be—that little peanut's a real tool."

We ordered tacos and beer from Gennaro's, they deliver—or maybe they used Door Dash or something. Again, didn't care. The things I cared about could be counted on one finger. Guess which one.

"Does your leg hurt?" she asked, having finished her food, dabbing at her mouth with a paper napkin. I watched her do that until she rolled her eyes. She thinks I'm a horndog.

"They always forget the extra salsa," I said, looking inside the delivery sack.

My pretty partner just shook her head. "Poor baby."

* * * *

"His wife's dead," Rachel said, sitting behind her desk as I limped into our office, my clothes drenched in monsoon rain, and dripping like, uh… something that drips a lot.

"Who?"

"Chambers."

"Doesn't ring a bell," I said, exercising my right to be a smart ass.

Rachel sighed like many of my grade school teachers used to do and said, "He's one of our *three* clients."

"Larry's wife is dead?"

Rachel seemed tired of my feigned confusion. "No wonder people say you're slow on the uptake."

"Who says that?" I demanded. "I want names."

"Mrs. Chambers was found floating in their swimming pool. Face down."

"Difficult to breathe in that position," I said, nodding wisely as I sat down, wincing from the kind of pain a normal person would not be able to endure. But as stated, I'm a real man.

Rachel grinned, which made my day. Her smile always cheered me up. But then of course she spoke: "Our client is under arrest and wants to see us."

I raised both eyebrows; elevating just one was beyond me. "Why? *I* didn't kill his wife. Did *you* kill his wife?" I asked, squinting suspiciously at her.

"He's in county lockup. We can see him at noon."

"And miss lunch?" I can't *not* eat—blood sugar goes all to hell and I get dangerously irritable.

The interview room at the cop shop was decorated in moody shades of desperation: chipped everything, faded by age and despair. There were un-identifiable odors that should, and will, remain unidentified. Those might be mouse turds in the corner; didn't want to think about that. If an experience can have the potential to be gross, this one had real promise.

Larry sat hunched over the table, looking depressed; no doubt because the gaudy orange coveralls he was wearing clashed with his orangey-blond hair. His face had the haggard look of a badly executed expressionist sculp-ture. Reminded me of someone who'd been on TV a lot; but I couldn't place who that might be.

"So, Larry, how can we help?" I asked, noting he was not making eye contact with me or Rachel, just staring down at his own hands, which he'd folded on the table in front of him. A finger on his right hand was abusing a cuticle on a finger on his left hand. Looked painful. Again, didn't care.

But then his shoulders sagged into a defeated posture of profound sad-ness—I associated that body language with some of the veteran cops I'd known and so I dropped my usual glib manner to cut him some slack. "They have any evidence *you* did it?"

"It's on the security footage from one of the cameras at our home," he said.

I frowned. "What is?"

"A video of me holding Melanie underwater until she was dead."

Oh, boy. I just couldn't help myself; a chuckle erupted from my throat and I said, "Pretty good evidence there, Larry."

His eyes raised to look at me. "It's not *me* in the video. I've been framed."

"By who?" Rachel asked.

He shook his head. "Maybe whoever she was sleeping with…please help me."

I leaned back in the astoundingly uncomfortable chair. "Well, amigo, if we do the work, but you get convicted—how we gonna get paid?"

"I've set up an account that my lawyer will administer. You'll get ten grand upfront, as a retainer that you can keep no matter what. Beyond that you can charge expenses and fees to be paid weekly to you by the lawyer."

I grinned, nudged Rachel. She reacted with a scolding look.

"At first, Larry, I thought you were kind of an A-hole, but you're alright," I said. "Who's your lawyer?"

* * * *

"Darryl Flack," he said, holding out his hand.

He was wearing a three-piece suit of some extraterrestrial color that might be green on the home planet, with unfortunate pinstripes of maroon running through it. There was a button missing from his vest and his shoes were almost as white and shiny as his teeth.

I frowned. "*You're* Larry's lawyer?"

He sighed. "You don't seem all that sharp, Mr. Blunt. Why did he hire you?"

"Watch your mouth, Counselor," Rachel said.

He looked at her…swallowed. Might be a jerk, but he could recognize a dangerous person when one was giving him a cold stare.

I waved my hand to get his attention. "Let's keep this civil, eh, Darryl?"

"Here's your retainer, Mr. Blunt," he said handing me a check for ten grand.

I didn't look at it, just folded it and put it in my inside coat pocket. "Did you have the video of Larry drowning his wife examined for authenticity?"

"It was Larry," Flack said, with a dismissive gesture that knocked over a mug of coffee, brown liquid seeping into some papers on his desk.

Shrewd defense strategy for a lawyer: my client did it.

"He said it wasn't him," I said. "Says he pulled her out of the pool, not pushed her in."

Attorney Flack shrugged. Like lawyers do. A universal trait. Very annoying.

I thought about it. "Maybe that was copied from the original, then recopied in reverse, so it just looked like he had pushed her underwater."

Rachel leaned forward, nodding. "Then somebody put the copy in the server to be found by the cops."

"Who called them?" I asked.

Flack sighed. A big sigher. "It was the maid."

"Did she say she saw Larry do the deed?" Rachel asked.

The lawyer just shook his head. "Her English is untrustworthy, if you know what I mean."

A xenophobe, too. Larry sure can pick 'em.

"Can't see his face in the video, just that silly hair," Rachel said. "And he doesn't look very coordinated—didn't notice that Larry was the clumsy type."

* * * *

I racked my brain, wrestling with different theories. It looked open and shut alright. The only flaw in the DA's case was that Larry's face wasn't on the video. His orange hair was a bit damning, as evidence goes, but still…

My cell played "Another One Bites the Dust" and I looked at the screen. Possible spam.

I answered anyway and was greeted with cackling. "You're in deep doo-doo, Blunt," the caller said. And hung up.

The number had a local area code. I used a search engine I subscribed to—for licensed investigators—found that it belonged to a B. Bunker, which didn't narrow it down much, since the whole Bunker clan had names heavy on alliteration. Course some of them were dead and two were hospitalized. I wondered if it could be a prank call from one of those morons recovering from a gunshot.

An app I used for finding where a phone was located during a call came up with an address. I drove over there and knocked on the door of a marginally painted concrete-block house that looked like nobody loved it. Cracked windows. A door of some indefinable wood that the sun had punished for being so ugly.

No answer, but the back door slammed shut, indicating the hasty exit of an inhabitant of this Taj Mahal on Tijeras Avenue.

I sat down on the stoop and waited for Rachel, who'd gone around back to herd the guy up to where I was. "Why were you fleeing the interview?" I asked, glancing at Rachel with a wink.

"The what?" he said, his brow burdened with the weight of a ferocious frown.

Rachel shook her head. "That's Frances McDormand's line from *Fargo*, isn't it?" she demanded of me.

I shrugged.

"You been just waiting to use it, haven't you?" Glaring at me like I'd abused a houseplant.

I grinned at her; then looked at our prisoner and asked, "So, why'd you call me?"

His reply is one for the books…

* * * *

"There's a fifth Bunker brother?" Rachel asked, really overdoing it with a tone of incredulity. She's a real drama queen.

It's two days since Larry's release; she and I were at our office in Old Town, listening to the air conditioner in the window apparently give birth to a sick robot: rattling, groaning, coughing; dripping condensation on the carpet.

"Yeah, this Bunker's named Buford. Another genius. He thought he could get even with me for sending back their own bomb and then whacking Billy Ray on his thick skull, and shooting Burt Bunker after he shot me."

Rachel frowned. "How is that getting even with you?"

"Had the orange wig and some tanning makeup, put on some of Larry Chambers' clothes to wear while he drowned Mrs. Chambers. He's a gofer for a security outfit and, dumb as he is, still knew to locate the camera surveilling the pool area. Staged the murder to frame Larry."

"Still don't get it. That frames Larry, not you."

I grinned. "He figured that me having a guilty client would make me look bad and ruin my business and make me so despondent I'd commit suicide."

She raised just the one eyebrow. A physical attribute I envied. "The whole family is bonkers, eh?" Rachel asked.

"Certifiable."

She got to her feet. "Let's go to Gennaro's for lunch."

"I can't. Have to go see Buford Bunker."

"Why?"

"He hired me to get him off."

"After he confessed?"

I just nodded, cause if I started laughing, I'd never stop.

"Did he pay you?"

I tried to nod again, but didn't make it—burst out cackling like I was the idiot instead of any one of the many Bunkers.

Rachel stared at me, shaking her head in disbelief. "You have no conscience," she said. Turned and walked out.

She's a last word freak.

TEARS OF A CLOWN

J. JAMIE GROCE

I didn't want to go to begin with. When I was feeling particularly antisocial, as I was that morning, I would think that Edward was Marcus's kid, not mine. Why should I have to tag along to every birthday party in a fifteen-mile radius because I had shacked up with a guy with a ten-year-old?

Marcus wasn't making it any easier. "Sam's mom'll be there, you like her," he said, implying against experience and reason that a kid's birthday party is made bearable by the presence of a single palatable adult.

Pulling up to Sawyer's bland-but-nicer-than-our house, Marcus took my hand and squeezed it. He knew I didn't have to come, and I got to bask in that inner superiority that comes from being seen to sacrifice for the sake of one's partner. I didn't tell him that Paul and Alison's well-stocked bar the year before was what had ultimately tipped me into coming. The birthday boy's parents were such legendary lushes it made me confident that I could socially lubricate myself without causing much tongue-wagging.

And so it was that three hours into the party, when over-frosted white cake had been shoved into two dozen young mouths, and adults had gradually, even guiltily, stopped watching their children to talk, drink, and even flirt with one another, that a bulky balding man I didn't know approached me and asked if I would come with him into the house.

I won't lie. At that point I had downed about four gin and tonics, heavy pours I did myself. Marcus had promised to drive and so had switched to seltzer after a single glass of wine.

He came up to me as I was standing at the bar freshening my drink, by which I mean I was diluting the tonic to homeopathic proportions. I was taking my time with it. I'd escaped a conversation with four other parents who were debating the merits of their children's math textbook, and I might have wandered off with a serial killer just to get some more interesting dialogue.

I followed the stranger through an open sliding glass door and down the corridor past the guest bathroom—as far as I had ever ventured—before he turned and introduced himself. He was Dan, Paul's brother.

"Alison tells me you're in law enforcement."

"I was a cop once," I said, reverting to a professional instinct to say as little as possible. The Oregon Department of Public Standards said I was still an investigator, but I hadn't worked a case for over a year, and that was only to determine if a particular ex-husband had gotten a second dog, which he was honor-bound not to do since the border collie whose custody he shared with his ex supposedly didn't like other dogs. She had found the new dog's hairs on the old. Sad story, really. The ex-wife was right and got full custody of the dog, but I had watched the dogs together, and they were fast friends.

"What's wrong?" I asked.

"You'll see," Dan said, and at that we entered a bedroom that was larger than the upper floor of our house. I took it to be Paul and Alison's, but it was instantly clear what the problem was.

The birthday clown was lying on the bed. Dead. A large knife, maybe of the chef's knives I'd seen magnetically stuck to the wall in the kitchen, was plunged several inches into the clown's chest.

I had seen the clown when he arrived, but he didn't seem very interested in doing clown things—I never saw a balloon animal made or a bicycle horn get honked. But I couldn't blame him. Sawyer and the other kids were all ten, give or take, an age when clowns are decidedly lower on the cool scale. I even told Marcus that Paul and Alison must have hired him out of some kind of birthday tradition, but Marcus said he couldn't remember seeing a clown the year before. Just this guy's luck, get hired for a show no one appreciates, then wind up dead.

This clown was in the hobo tradition, a mashup of plaids and garish solids, his face the normal reds and blues, but with the thick black outlines of many clowns, or at least of what I remembered about clowns. It's fair to say it had been a number of years since I had seen one outside a *Simpsons* episode.

I realized we weren't alone. Alison was next to Dan, her hand frozen over her mouth in a stereotypical depiction of shock. I wondered where she had come from. She stepped forward and started to reach out towards the body, towards the knife, as if to grab the handle.

"Don't touch it," I said, and she jumped at the sound of my voice.

"But that's my best knife," she said, her voice trembling but firm, as if what she said was the best reason that could be given for tampering with evidence at a murder scene. True, I was more of a methodical detective than the instinct-driven kind, but I had the strong sense she was in shock. Most of us never have a clown stabbed on our bed, true.

"I assume you've called the police," I said, starting to regain some composure.

"About that," Dan started. "I know that's necessary, but I'm wondering if it's an immediate requirement."

"I guarantee you it is." I was feeling suddenly and dreadfully sober, and on top of that I was feeling sorry for a clown.

"Sure, but we just found him in here. If we hadn't discovered him for another half-hour, what would be the harm?"

I turned to Alison. "I assume you want the police called straight away?"

"I… I mean, really, what does thirty minutes really gain anybody? This poor man is dead at the business of my…my very best knife," she said, suddenly much more in control of her faculties than she had been seconds earlier.

"There are some rather delicate business arrangements taking place here today," Dan said. "That's why I'm here, other than to celebrate my nephew's birthday of course. Do you know the Schaefers?"

I shook my head. "Emma's parents," Alison said, which didn't help.

"They're selling their podiatry practice, which we plan to absorb into our family business." I nodded, finding it odd that he thought I knew or understood anything about his family business.

"Thirty minutes, even twenty," Dan continued, "would give us time to conclude those transactions, sign some papers, and the Schaefers to go on their way."

"Leave the scene of a crime?" If I had been drinking at the moment, I would have spit it out in a theatrical spray.

"If no one out there at the party knows a crime has been committed, what involvement do they have? Do all the children need to be detained?" he asked.

I wanted to say that's what the police were for, to decide that, but my neural functioning was still softened by alcohol, and so I just cut to my real question: "Why tell me at all, then?"

"Maddie," Alison said, suddenly warm and saying my name for what I was sure was the first time; nobody actually called me Maddie but I'm not one of those people who get worked up about that kind of thing, especially when a murder victim with painted-on freckles was a few feet away. "If you could do an initial investigation and verify that this…" She trailed off.

"Murder?"

She nodded. "That this thing doesn't put anybody else in danger, we could keep this world," she gestured to the bed, "from that world," gesturing out towards where the muffled sounds of children's shouts and tween rock could be heard.

I knew what I wanted to say. But they were right. Things were winding down, but the minute the police arrived nobody was going anywhere for hours. From this day forward, all the other parents would blame me for involving their precious Emma and Tyson in a murder investigation, and wrecking their Saturday for some clown who maybe just startled the wrong person in the kitchen and staggered all the way down the hall to expire in the master bedroom. I pictured Marcus no longer asking me to come with him to birthday parties, the other parents avoiding me.

"Make it fast," I said, feeling for a moment like a senior investigator in charge of a scene.

The two of them thanked me and began to rush out when I thought to ask where Paul was. Alison shook her head. "I don't know, and I don't really care. He moved out a couple of weeks ago. I told him he wasn't allowed back in the house, but I admit I thought he'd try to see his son on his birthday. Self-centered if you ask me."

So there was some gossip. The perfect couple were on the outs. Trouble beyond having a dead clown on their California king.

"Are you upset by that?" I asked.

"I was but I'm fine now. He knows what he did, and he'll either apologize or he won't." But she seemed more upset than she was letting on, as I could tell she'd been crying. A glob of mascara stood out under her left eye.

They hurried away, and I found myself very interested in the way he turned towards her as they departed. I wasn't generally interested in such gossip, but it seemed to be the coin of the realm in this neighborhood. I pictured myself as the life of the party after this. "Oh, Madeleine has an amazing story from Sawyer's birthday party. Yes, *that* party. Madeleine, tell it again from the very beginning."

I stepped to the window and pulled the deep blue curtains back, careful to make sure no small faces could see inside. The herd was beginning to thin, and I could see Marcus standing and appearing to enjoy himself in a crowd of other dads whose names wouldn't come to me.

Edward was playing with a few of the other boys, all crowding around Sawyer and looking at his toys. What do you get the boy who has everything? We certainly hadn't known and had gone with a baseball bat so expensive we could have bought a lathe and made a hundred for the price.

Sawyer, who had unwrapped dozens of expensive sporting goods and electronics, wasn't looking at any of that glittering booty, but was staring down at some paper in his hand. I watched him for a few seconds but couldn't make it out.

I called Marcus. I watched him pull out his phone and answer without hesitation—smart move. If he had rolled his eyes or obviously debated taking it, there would have been hell to pay. "Hey," he said. "Are you hiding somewhere?"

Without saying hello, I asked what Sawyer had in his hand. It took Marcus a second to understand what I meant. I saw him look over at the boy and say, "Oh, baseball tickets. Good seats, too, I heard. Why?"

But my attention was drawn to the unfortunate Harlequin on the bed, and I realized in a second what a fool I'd been. "Are you about ready to leave?" Marcus asked, but I hung up and was on the phone to 911 before he could finish.

I never mentioned that I had agreed to give the killers time to get away. Sure, I was tipsy and just trying to be agreeable, but there's agreeability and then there's accessory to homicide after the fact.

Of the parents who hadn't left by the time the cops showed up, a solid half of them blamed me for delaying their getting home. One even threatened to send me the bill for the overtime for their dogsitter.

But Dan and Alison were quickly caught. They hadn't even left the house, instead apparently arguing in the garage about whose car they were going to use to get away. An inauspicious start to their relationship free from her ex, his brother Paul.

"How did you know it was him?" Marcus asked as we were lying in bed that night, the commotion of the day still stirring in the air. Edward had asked me more questions that night than in the three years we'd lived in the same house and had only gone to bed under duress from his father. I felt lethargic as the adrenaline drained. I had already explained it all over and over to the detectives, so I gave Marcus the short version.

"He had regular shoes," I said. "Anyone can put on clown makeup, but you need real skills to walk in clown shoes."

"It's a shame he had to disguise himself just to see his own kid at his birthday."

"I wouldn't be surprised if he knew his life was in danger. Maybe he knew about the affair, knew that she was dangerous, or that he was, or both."

"Which one of them actually stabbed him?" he asked.

I didn't know. I knew that fingerprints would be lifted off the knife, but my money was on her. That she had recognized him after he gave their son the baseball tickets, that she had struck him in the face, leaving black makeup from his broad hobo face onto her hand, which she inadvertently smeared onto her cheek. But they would both pay for the crime.

"Sam's birthday is next weekend," Marcus started to say.

"No more birthdays. Edward's, yes, I'll be here, but other than his you're on your own." I rolled over and stared at the wall. Sam's mother had mentioned that he liked to ski. Maybe he'd like a new pair of gloves? Maybe I'd call one of the other mothers tomorrow and see what they were getting him.

THE ENERGY COFFEE
THAT CHANGES LIFE

REBECCA BRITTENHAM

Max Shapiro sat in the Trung Nguyễn Legend coffee shop, head bowed over the menu, itemizing his failures as chef, fiancée, son, brother, and human being. He had arrived in Vietnam two weeks ago determined to learn the inside workings of the cuisine before returning to New York to open his own restaurant. The plan had been straightforward: settle into Hanoi—the jewel of Vietnam's culinary crown, he'd been told— for three months, take cooking classes while exploring the restaurant scene, then offer his highly skilled services to two or three hand-picked restaurants.

Two whole weeks so far, and what did he have to show for it? Nothing!

Max slapped the table in anguish, realized he was attracting attention from the next table, and raised his menu even higher to mask the despair twisting his face. The menu read:

Trung Nguyễn Legend:
The Energy Coffee that Changes Life

Under that, it provided a series of affirmations that only mocked his plight: "The Learner's Mindset Leads to Riches" and "Great Aspiration Makes a Great Person." Or not! He'd certainly arrived with great aspirations and look what they'd come to. Two whole weeks and nothing except bills for overpriced, touristy cooking classes and dozens of restaurant meals massing ominously on his credit card. The ads for the various classes had sounded ideal: source ingredients in the greenmarkets in the old town of *Hoàn Kiếm*, then back to the chef's kitchen to cook and eat a meal. But each one had devolved into a performance piece designed to please a sweating cohort of Western tourists, more intent on being entertained and fed than actually learning to cook. Students would be given busywork chopping, mixing, then wrapping and frying spring rolls, with much attendant laughter at the overstuffed, leaking, rice-paper bundles they inevitably produced. Meanwhile the dipping sauces, the marinated meats, and the broth for *phở* would miraculously appear from under a counter, while the sources of those ingredients and their proportions remained a mystery.

Max had returned to his hotel every night in despair, his fingers itching to play with the ingredients he was seeing in the back-alley markets, longing to replicate and riff on the sublime flavors he was tasting in every little street stall or *bia hơi* open-air pub: swooningly tender chicken in delicate sauces, jellyfish salad, morning-glory greens sumptuously stir fried with garlic and (he suspected) pork fat.

And now the worst had happened, and he was through. He would have to head home and admit this was just another of his harebrained, badly planned, doomed-to-failure-from-the-start schemes.

"Excuse. Excuse. Excuse me, please."

Max lowered the menu. A young Vietnamese man in a crisp white shirt and tie had been trying to get his attention for some time.

"Sorry, I didn't realize you were speaking to me."

The young man nodded vigorously and scooted his chair a little closer. "You seem to be having a problem selecting a coffee." His English was precise, each word given deliberate care.

"Selecting a coffee?" Max smiled, tried to cover his despair with a joke. "Thanks, but I have problems no coffee would solve."

The young man brightened even more. "No matter the problem, Trung Nguyễn Legend coffee offers the energy and creativity to find a solution. I highly recommend that you choose a coffee. Once you drink it, we will find the solution. In the words of our Chairman and Founder, 'Together, nothing impossible!'"

Did he work here? But he was dressed in business clothes with perfectly creased pants and polished shoes, all exquisitely fresh despite the suffocating heat outside. He had a laptop open on the table next to a book bound in white leather and a tall glass of iced coffee. Clearly a customer—or maybe a shill? Max darted a hasty glance at the front counter, but the barista was dealing with a steady stream of customers and did not seem in the least interested in soliciting his order.

The man stuck out a hand. "I am called Sang. I come here most every afternoon—inspiring coffee, free wi-fi, good conversation—and I get more accomplished in two hours than in a full day at the office."

"How do you do? I'm Max."

"Pleased to meet you, Max." Sang's pleasure seemed genuine—a glow of goodwill radiated from him. "If I may recommend one approach—just close your eyes and let your finger fall where it may on the menu."

With an internal shrug (after all, he literally had nothing left to lose) Max followed the suggested protocol and found his finger resting on *Năng Lượng Tư Duy*, which meant nothing to him but was the cheapest thing on the menu at 25,000 *đồng*.

"The Energy for Thoughts—just the thing! No doubt this will help you concentrate on today's problem."

Max did a hasty calculation—about a dollar. He had 550,000 *đồng* or about twenty-two bucks to live on for the foreseeable future. He knew the precise amount, having spent an agonizing hour re-counting it while sitting in an empty hallway at the American Embassy waiting to speak to an official, only to be told he would need to make an appointment for the next day). He went to the counter, ordered by pointing at the menu, and returned to the table with a metal *phin* of coffee balanced atop a cup and saucer.

"The barista said I need to let this drip for a few minutes."

"Very important not to rush the process! In the meantime, perhaps you could describe your situation."

The despair from which he'd momentarily become distracted came rushing back, and the pit of Max's stomach opened into an abyss.

Where do I begin? The last straw is that my backpack was stolen this morning, and I was idiot enough to have stuck my wallet, phone, passport, and the printed copies of my passport and visa in there. I was supposed to be in Hanoi for ten more weeks, interning with chefs and learning the cuisine. I had planned to open a Vietnamese-influenced restaurant in the US, an upscale place, not just bánh mì and phở, but with big centerpiece dishes like *chả cá*. Every meal would be a whole event with a narrative arc built in, and New York diners would be fighting to spear the last bite."

"And with a coffee service in the afternoons, perhaps?" Sang nodded. "That sounds like an admirable plan."

"Well, I convinced my family it was a good idea in spite of all my past screw-ups. My mother plowed everything she and dad had saved for my college into a downpayment on the restaurant, my sister organized a Kickstarter campaign, and my uncle paid for my ticket to get here. And this is the worse part. I convinced a wonderful woman who deserves the best of everything to marry me and move all the way across the country to help me get the restaurant going. And now I have to go home with my tail between my legs. She… she thinks I'm wonderful and creative and enterprising when I'm really just a complete, utter, flipping failure." He groaned at the enormity of this and slapped the table again, nearly upsetting the *phin* balanced on his cup.

"Take care with the coffee. I believe it is time to drink now. No fear—all will be well."

"From your mouth to God's ears, as my mother would say." Max gloomily lifted the *phin*, tapped the last drops of liquid into his cup, raised it in mock salute, and took a careful sip. It was very bitter. He set it down hastily, then began to taste the subtle afternotes—the merest suggestions of chocolate, tobacco, butter, and pepper. He sipped again. Waited. Sipped. The palate-sharpening hit of each mouthful expanded on his tongue to a multitude of flavors, and he sat quietly for a moment, simply attending without trying to name them all, then sipped again until there was nothing left in his cup but a fine coating of silt.

Sang nodded. "I see you begin the journey into mind-nourishment—this is already an important step." He raised one finger as if testing the air. "Here I quote Article 68 from the *Philosophy of Coffee*: 'Mind-nourishing coffee helps people achieve 4K consciousness: knowing the flavor, knowing the savor, knowing the transcendence, knowing the immanence.'"

Max leaned back in his chair. His dire situation was still there, of course, but for the moment, he felt slightly removed from it, almost sympathetic to the sufferer. The room seemed brighter, Sang's features more defined, his shirt almost blazingly white.

"That was delicious, though you do seem to put a lot of faith in the power of one beverage."

"Not just me. Think of it! Artists through all time—Vincent Van Gogh, Wolfgang Amadeus Mozart, your Ernest Miller Hemingway. Philosophers and great thinkers—Ludwig Wittgenstein, Johann Wolfgang Von Goethe, Sigmund Freud, your Stephen Hawking. Great politicians and leaders from East and West—Sheik Abdul-Al-Kadir, Napoleon Bonaparte, Margaret Thatcher, and your Thomas Jefferson. Powerful entrepreneurs and business-men like your Napoleon Hill and our own Good and Righteous Mr. Dang Le Nguyễn Vu, Founder and Chairman of the Trung Nguyễn Legend Group— what is the one thing they had in common?" Sang paused as if waiting for the answer.

"Wait—Margaret Thatcher?"

"Coffee! That's what they all drank and knew as the source of their cre- ativity, inspiration, determination, and success. From Ethiopia, the Ottoman Empire, Colombia, Jamaica, Brazil, India, Korea, Spain, Italia, France, even Britain for a time, America, the United Arab Emirates, now Japan, each achieved a coffee culture which brought them to the peak of their global power. They understood coffee as the key to nation building and public unity. And the best coffee in the world is grown right here." Now it was Sang's turn to slap the table for emphasis. "Right here in Vietnam, in the Central Highlands, and exported from here all over the world. Only Brazil exports more, yet Vietnamese coffee is the better quality by far. We are a country on the move—you see the growth and energy all around you. And why is that?" This time he didn't pause for an answer. "Coffee. This is the vision of our Founder and Chairman, who wrote the 99 Articles of the *Philosophy of Coffee* and who has published the Life-Changing Foundational Bookcase, which he offers free for all who seek to share in his wisdom about coffee as the source of a new humanity and a new global order."

Max blinked. Was he about to be indoctrinated into a cult?

Sang patted the white leather book. "I have read every word of the foundational texts, you see. It has been my education and my great joy ever since I first discovered the Trung Nguyễn Legend cafés and realized that all this was freely available to me—pure opportunity between the covers of every book!" He gestured, and Max noticed for the first time a bookcase stacked with identical white volumes. Additional copies lay scattered liberally across many of the tables.

So, definitely a cult. Would he find himself on a street corner three weeks from now, in a toga with a shaved head, handing out leaflets? Yet he felt strangely suffused with energy, and a trickle of optimism ran through his veins.

"Excuse me for one minute, Sang. I think I'll have another cup of this coffee."

This time he went directly to the counter, closed his eyes, and stabbed the menu. His finger lighted on *Năng Lượng Khám Phá*, which was a little more expensive at 35,000 *đồng*, but translated as "the energy for discovery," which seemed appropriate.

When he returned bearing the new *phin* like a chalice, Sang said warningly, "Remember that the coffee here is very powerful. Now, let us work together and tackle the impossible until it becomes possible again. First, we analyze all your problems and what do we see?"

"The portrait of a first-class loser," Max said gloomily, but without his previous ferocious certainty. The trickle of optimism warmed into a generalized sense of wellbeing.

"We see a missing backpack! Find the backpack and you will stay in Vietnam, then go home successful to open your wonderful restaurant with your beautiful fiancée."

"But you don't understand. It's all a bureaucratic rabbit hole. The American Embassy requires a police report for me to request a replacement passport, and the police station wouldn't create the report without a copy of the passport, and they threatened to deport me tomorrow, and I can't replace my phone without money and a passport, and I can't report the missing credit card and license without a phone. I don't even have a hotel because I was planning to move to a different neighborhood, so I have nowhere to stay, and I just *can't bear* to ask my family to send me more money. For one thing, I'd have to admit to them that I'm not really learning the cuisine here. All the chefs I've talked to just keep putting me off because they don't really want a foreigner working in their restaurants. So, I'm limited to a tourist's experience of these dishes, and it's driving me *crazy*. Maybe I should just cut my losses and go home."

Even as he spoke, Max could hear how whiny he sounded. His memory flooded with all the exquisite dishes he had experienced in the last three weeks. Surely there was a way to unlock the secrets of those flavor combinations. Good fish sauce was certainly key, and maybe black vinegar, and certainly betel leaves in some cases. Garlic and lemongrass, of course, tons and tons of the fresh herbs he had seen bagged in the markets, heaped in restaurant kitchens, and piled on the sidewalk chopping-blocks where street cooks often prepared their wares. If he just tried harder to wangle a place in the kitchen where he could watch it go down and play with the proportions himself, surely this could still happen.

He looked wistfully at Sang, like a dog presenting a stick he knows will likely not get thrown.

"Finding you chefs to learn from is no problem. I am a fixer. I know many chefs and many of the families making even better than restaurant food who will take you in and teach you. I can introduce you to them all. We can find you a furnished apartment with a kitchen much cheaper than a hotel. The one problem is to find that backpack, so there is no more American Embassy tomorrow, no more police report, no more talk of deportation, and no more red tape." Sang nodded with satisfaction, as if half the battle were over.

"I'm pretty sure that backpack is gone forever, but I'm certainly willing to try." Max moved the *phin* aside, careful to tap every last drop into the cup, and took a sip. Closed his eyes. As he savored each warm mouthful, it felt as if a thick, protective helmet had gathered around him, cutting off external noises and filling his ears with the rushing sound of his own breath. Breath going in. Breath going out. So beautiful, this solitude. He existed alone on an island, cut free from space and time, invulnerable.

"My God, this coffee is good." He opened his eyes and returned to the contemplation of his problems, which now seemed very far away.

"Let us review every detail from the moment you filled and zipped the backpack this morning," Sang suggested.

"Okay. I checked out of the Golden Phoenix Hotel in *Trúc Bạch*, planning to attend the last cooking class I had scheduled for this trip, then find somewhere cheaper to live. I was jetlagged and already running late for the class. I stuffed some cash and my phone in the side pocket of my cargo shorts, and put my wallet and passport in the backpack, forgetting that I also had the only print copy of it *and* my visa tucked away in a zippered pocket of the same backpack. What kind of an idiot does that?" Max paused a second, waiting for the wave of cataclysmic despair and self-hatred to strike again, but instead a steady stream of wellbeing coursed through him, clearing his mind to look back at the events of the morning.

"I took a Grab to the restaurant where the cooking class was being held, *Chả Cá Tuyết* in *Hoàn Kiếm*. A total downpour hit just then, so the Grab driver had some trouble finding the place, and I was late arriving. The restaurant seemed a little off-putting, at first, a dark cavern of a place, but I knocked, and the teacher answered. Mrs. Ánh Tuyết—she was very nice and welcoming, and her English was great. The kitchen was good-sized, and the windows were all open. No air conditioning, so it got hot, especially later when we were cooking, but there were fans blowing. The last participants trickled in, and Mrs. Ánh served us iced coffee while we all exchanged names and small talk."

And you had the backpack with you at this point."

"Oh yes. We all put our bags in a big closet near the front of the restaurant. It was basically a cloakroom like they used to have in American restaurants. The shelves were loaded with our bags and luggage, and there were stands full of wet umbrellas and dripping plastic ponchos."

"And the door to that room was open."

"Yes—wide open, but the restaurant door locked automatically when you closed it."

"Good. Now, let us hear about the other participants."

"Right." Max pictured the group, gathered on stools around Mrs. Ánh's kitchen. He felt masterful now, confident in his ability to recall every detail.

"There was a Canadian couple in their sixties, recently retired. The husband, Tim, kept interrupting with questions all through the lesson, trying to get the techniques just right. His wife Donna transcribed every word like a court reporter. I started to wonder if they were secretly writing a cookbook. There were three young Australian women who had been on a dive team together and were traveling all over Southeast Asia—very athletic, and adventurous eaters, though they didn't seem terribly interested in learning to cook. There were two youngish Norwegian men who had just come from a cruise in *Hạ Long Bay*—one was a train engineer and the other was a plumber. They wanted us all to know why the Norwegian economic and mass-transit systems were better than anywhere else in the world. A newlywed couple from India seemed to be killing time until they could jump back in bed. Then there was a scary-looking Russian guy named Matvei, about my age, with huge muscles and neck tattoos, who was my partner for most of the cooking. I liked him a lot in the end—he was very funny, cynical, great knife skills—but he ducked any personal questions, and I couldn't help wondering if he was ex-military trying to escape reality for a while. Am I going into too much detail?"

"Not at all—very useful to know. Now we have our potential suspects, right?"

"That's just the thing… I can't even imagine any of them stealing my backpack. It was all so friendly and homey. Mrs. Ánh had her little boy there in his school uniform, helping to fetch things and doing his math homework at one of the restaurant tables. He must have been around eight or so—very sweet kid, and he seemed delighted to practice his English. He told me his

English name was Peter and drew me a picture of Batman. And the look on Mrs. Ánh 's face when we discovered my backpack had gone missing—she suddenly looked ten years older. It was horrible! She must have been imagining how bad it would be for her business, though I kept reassuring her that I wouldn't write a bad review."

"Yes—she would not want the negative attention on her business. When did the backpack leave your sight?"

"Well, after the coffee, we headed out to tour the *Long Biên* market—the one under the big bridge, I'm sure you know it—about a ten-minute walk away. We all got up to leave, and one of the Australian women—I think it was Isla—they were named Charley, Isla, and Olivia but I kept confusing one with the other—asked if they could leave their stuff. They were carrying big backpacks because they were catching a bus and heading off to do a motorbike tour in the North later that day. Mrs. Ánh said sure, the restaurant would be locked while we were gone. I thought it would be fun and less hot to walk without my backpack—I'd been to the *Long Biên* market before in the early morning, when it's packed and you're knocking against other people all the time. I thought I was being clever. What a fool! What a frickin' idiot!"

Even as he said this, Max felt a pleasant alienation from his own idiocy—a kindly sense of tolerance, even forgiveness, as if these were the foibles of a beloved friend.

"Just before we left, Mrs. Ánh handed out bottles of water for everyone. Then we all stood there and watched as she closed the cloakroom door and locked it with an ancient-looking key on her keyring. I literally heard the key click in the lock. She put the keyring in her purse—she had one that strapped across her body—gathered up some empty shopping bags, and we set out. She pulled the door of the restaurant shut to make sure that was locked, too. Peter walked with us for the first block or two, then headed to school."

"And did everyone leave something in the cupboard?"

"Let's see." Max closed his eyes, the memory spooling with cinemascope precision. "Everyone left umbrellas because the rain had stopped and the sun was blazing hot already. The Indian couple, Geetha and Rohan, had happened on an Indian grocery on the way there, so they had two grocery bags and a string bag. The Canadian guy, Tim, kept his fanny pack but his wife Donna left her bag—one of those quilted sacks. The Norwegians had hi-tech anti-theft packs, and one wore a fancy camera on a heavy strap. They left their packs, but it turned out afterward that they both had their valuables strapped into money belts. I don't think Matvei, my Russian friend, had a bag, so he must have carried his wallet and phone in his pockets."

"Interesting." Sang took another sip of coffee.

Vitality coursed through Max. It barely mattered that he was missing a backpack when he felt this flood of strength and determination.

"We walked through the market, which was *amazing*, and Mrs. Ánh seemed to know most of the vendors. I realized part way there that I didn't have my phone, but I had taken a ton of pictures last time through the market, so it didn't seem worth going back for it. All the others took pictures, and I mainly just gawked at all the stalls, with their heaps of pomelos, mangos, dragon fruit, jackfruit, rambutans, greens of every kind, long red peppers, buckets of fish, eels, snails—it was stupendous. Mrs. Ánh bought ingredients for lunch, and we all carried the bags for her while snacking on roasted sweet potatoes and wonderful grilled pancakes stuffed with chocolate or custard."

"Ah yes. But let us keep our eyes on the backpack."

"Right. Well, we got back from the market, and she started the class. It was one of the better ones I've taken. She taught us to make fried spring rolls, which I've done a few times now, but also *bánh cuốn* dumplings with pork and mushroom filling, and *bún bò nam bộ*." That was the beef noodle salad he couldn't get enough of. "I was disappointed that she wasn't doing *chả cá* and that she had prepped all the sauces beforehand, but she gave us the recipes with the proportions. The whole time, our stuff was in the cabinet, which was still locked. Lunch was delicious, except for the spring rolls, which fell apart and got too greasy, and everybody except Rohan and Geetha and Mrs. Ánh was drinking beer at that point, including me. It was nice."

Would this be his last cooking class before he got booted out of the country? No—he was determined now, fired up. He would stick it out no matter what.

"By the end of class everyone was friendly and stuffed. We showered compliments on Mrs. Ánh. It was suffocatingly hot at that point, and I think everyone was headed for afternoon naps. Mrs. Ánh pulled out her key. Her bag had been hanging on a hook near the front door where we had all left our shoes, so I guess it's just possible that someone broke in, took the key, and stole my backpack. In fact, that's the solution we all arrived at, but it just seems random and crazy."

"Who left the kitchen while you were cooking?"

"I think everyone did. We all took turns washing our hands before we started cooking, and with the beer and all the water we'd been drinking, I think everyone used the bathroom once or twice. But here's the thing. Say one of us took the key, opened the cabinet, and pilfered my backpack. They would have needed to hand it off to an accomplice or something because once the cloakroom was opened and I exclaimed that my backpack was missing, they all helped to search every inch of that closet, every shelf—we stripped it bare. Then we checked under the restaurant tables, under the stools in the kitchen, in the bathroom—everywhere it could possibly have been. Everyone was very kind—and I have to thank Matvei for that. He saw at once that we needed to rule out an accidental swap, since there were five backpacks among us. Everyone lined up their luggage and bags by the door so we could all verify that my backpack hadn't somehow been mistaken for someone else's."

"And no one else in the group was missing any items?"

"No. That's what's driving me crazy! Why take just my backpack and nothing else? The Australians were worried because they had their passports in with their luggage as well, and Geetha was freaked out because she had left her string bag behind with her passport and wallet inside, too. But it was all there. They tried to reassure me, and Tim offered to call the police, but Mrs. Ánh said she would take me to the American Embassy first on her motorbike. She really didn't want the police coming to her restaurant."

Sang sipped his coffee. "Hmmm. This is a difficult problem."

"It's impossible!"

"Oh no, not impossible. In fact, the difficulty lies in the many possibilities. While you all cooked, it would be perfectly possible to open the cabinet with the key provided by Mrs. Ánh's close-hanging purse. After all, if noticed someone could merely say they were getting something from their own luggage. Then they had only to take your backpack and secure it inside their own luggage. The Australians with their big backpacks, the Indian couple with their groceries and string bag, the Canadian woman with her quilted pouch, the Norwegians with their anti-theft packs—each had a bag large enough to contain a tightly rolled backpack. Or they could have handed it off to an accomplice, as you said, which they could have arranged while you were all in the market."

"But why focus on my stuff only?"

"You did provide the thief with an ideal combination for identity theft —passport, credit cards, driver's license, and visa."

"But if it was identity theft…oh my god, Matvei! He's the same height and age, and I bet he could pass himself off as me and get to the U.S. on my passport. He must have handed my backpack off to an accomplice while we were cooking! No wonder he was so helpful, making everyone check their stuff—it called attention to his own innocence." Max leapt to his feet, suffused with righteous anger. "I need to go to a police station and see if he can be stopped at the airport! Can you come with me to translate?"

Sang raised a restraining hand. "Please wait a moment. You have embraced the energy, but have we reached the true discovery? We have a solution, but is it the only solution? Is it the best solution?"

"But…"

"Let me propose to you one more possibility, simpler than all the others. What if the backpack was never stolen?"

"You think I hallucinated the whole thing?" Max cast a wild glance around. His vision was preternaturally sharp, throwing halos of light around every object. The ceiling, the bookcase with its white leather volumes, Sang's shirt, all seemed to radiate from within.

Sang drained the last of his coffee. "Mind nourishment," he murmured. "We have considered this problem from one angle only: the problem of a locked cloakroom. But what if the backpack never was in the cloakroom to begin with?"

"But that's impossible, I'd swear I put it in there."

"Yes—precisely. But before we rush to one conclusion, allow me to make just one phone call."

Max watched with growing impatience as Sang pulled out his phone, looked up a number, and began a lively conversation in Vietnamese. What could one phone call accomplish?

"Good news," Sang was more radiant than ever. "The lost backpack is found."

"Found?" Then it hit him. "I've got it! The little boy, Peter, must have worn my backpack to school by mistake! I bet you just called Mrs. Ánh."

"On the contrary. I just called your hotel, The Golden Phoenix. You left the backpack in the Grab this morning. The driver couldn't find you at the restaurant, so he sensibly returned to the hotel and left it with them." Sang smiled beneficently. "As our Founder and Chairman says so wisely, discover the flavor, experience the savor, find the transcendence, know the immanence of all things."

AUTHOR'S NOTE

Many of the places referenced in this story are real, including the Long Biên market and Trung Nguyễn Legend coffee, whose website is the source of the "philosophy of coffee" quoted here. All the characters and incidents in the story are entirely fictional.

ABOUT THE AUTHORS

DONNA ANDREWS

Donna Andrews is a bestselling mystery author best known for her humorous Meg Langslow series. Her work has earned multiple Agatha, Anthony, and Lefty Awards. A native of Virginia, Andrews blends witty dialogue with clever plots, creating lighthearted mysteries that have won her a loyal, worldwide readership.

GIGI PANDIAN

Gigi Pandian is a *USA Today* bestselling and multi-award-winning author who writes the Secret Staircase mysteries, Accidental Alchemist mysteries, and Jaya Jones Treasure Hunt mysteries. Gigi lives in northern California with her husband and a gargoyle who watches over the garden. Find bookish fun in her email newsletter at gigipandian.com.

MARCIA TALLEY

Marcia Talley is the Agatha and Anthony award-winning author of *Circles of Death* and nineteen previous novels featuring Maryland sleuth Hannah Ives. Her short stories are collected in *With Love, Marjorie Ann* and *Other Dangerous Stories* (Crippen & Landru, 2025). She divides her time between Annapolis, Maryland and a quaint, Loyalist-style cottage in the Bahamas.

Her story "Dead Man's Chest" is excerpted from *Hooked on Urban Legends—And Murder*, edited by Donna Andrews, Barb Goffman, and Marcia Talley, which will be published in 2026 by Wildside Press.

GREGORY MEECE

Following his career as an educator and head of school, Gregory Meece has rekindled his passion for creative writing. His stories have appeared in anthologies including Malice Domestic's *Mystery Most Traditional*, *Love Letters to Poe: Tales Torn from the Heart*, and *Larceny & Last Chances*, as well as magazines such as *Willows Wept Review*, *Black Cat Weekly*, *Bristol Noir*, *The Yard: Crime Blog*, *Kings River Life*, *Punk Noir*, *Flash Fiction Magazine*, and *Thriller Magazine*.

WILLIAM ADE

William Ade writes long and short stories, and humor often appears in both, sometimes consciously and often not. Level Best Books published his novel, *Big Scream in a Small Town*, written under the pseudonym Nic Knuckles, America's self-anointed premier private investigator. Ade has strong feelings for Nic, as the character has twice appeared in published short stories and once won Ade one hundred dollars in a humor contest.

KATHLEEN KALB (NIKKI KNIGHT)

Nikki Knight (Kathleen Marple Kalb) is an Author/Anchor/Mom… not in that order. An award-winning weekend anchor at New York City's 1010 WINS Radio, she's had stories published in *Alfred Hitchcock's Mystery Magazine*, *Mystery Magazine*, and more, and short-listed for Derringer and Black Orchid Novella Awards. She's a Co-VP of New York/Tri-State Sisters in Crime and past VP of the Short Mystery Fiction Society. She, her husband, and son live in a Connecticut house owned by their cat.

M.S. GREENE

M. S. Greene is a playwright, lyricist, screenwriter, novelist, and overall theatre nerd living the dream in New York City. Under his full name—Matthew Greene—his scripts have been produced on both coasts and several places in between. When he's not hunched over a keyboard, he can be found teaching, directing, and working to close the arts education gap with some of the city's most talented young people. He lives in Manhattan with his boyfriend and far too many books. His debut novel *There's No Murder Like Show Murder* is available now from Crooked Lane Books.

BECKY CLARK

Award-winning fiction and nonfiction author Becky Clark is seventh of eight kids, which explains both her insatiable need for attention and her atrocious table manners. She likes to read funny books, so it felt natural to write them. She writes several different cozy series, as well as some nonfiction. Visit BeckyClarkBooks.com for free series starters in the Mystery Writer's series (starring Charlee Russo) and the Sugar Mill Marketplace series, along with some short stories.

BRIAN COX

Brian Cox is a newspaper editor in Detroit. He was the managing editor of *Alfred Hitchcock's Mystery Magazine* in the late 1980s. His short story "The Surrogate Initiative" was selected for Houghton Mifflin's "The

Best American Mystery Stories 2020" anthology. He is a New York Times crossword constructor. His full-length play "Clutter" received the 2017 Wilde Award for Best New Script. His children's plays have been produced across the country and internationally.

MELINDA MULLET

Melinda is the author of the Whisky Business Mysteries, a lightly humorous series set in Scotland. A second traditionally published humorous cozy series will be released in Spring 2025. Melinda is happy to be known as a former lawyer, a travel junkie, and a lifelong advocate for children's literacy causes. When she's not in the U.K., Melinda lives just outside D.C., with her whisky-collecting husband, and two Covid canines named Bailey and Captain Jack.

NINA MANSFIELD

Nina Mansfield is an author and playwright. Her short mystery fiction has appeared in multiple anthologies and various publications including *Ellery Queen's Mystery Magazine* and *Alfred Hitchcock's Mystery Magazine*. Her ten-minute and one-act plays have had over 100 productions throughout the world. Nina's first novel, *Swimming Alone*, a YA Mystery was published by Fire & Ice YA. Nina is a co-President of the NY/Tri-State Chapter of Sisters in Crime.

SYLVIA MAULTASH WARSH

Sylvia is the author of the Dr. Rebecca Temple novels, one of which won an Edgar. The first book in the series was shortlisted for a Crime Writers of Canada award. Project Bookmark Canada chose her novel, *The Queen of Unforgetting*, for a plaque on their literary map. "Best Girl," a novella, is aimed at young adults. Her stories have been shortlisted for Derringers and CWC awards. Her new novel, *The Orphan*, was published in 2024.

SUZANNE FLAIG

Suzanne Flaig is the author of the Missy Jenkins musical mystery series, set in her hometown of Middletown, Pennsylvania. She is a former piano teacher and rollerskating coach who moved to Arizona and pursued her dream of becoming a published author and editor over twenty years ago. She is a past president of the Desert Sleuths chapter of Sisters in Crime, and a member of the Tucson and Triangle chapters of Sisters in Crime and the Pennwriters. She has also published short stories in various anthologies.

DONNA CLANCY

Donna Clancy (Donna Walo Clancy) lives on Cape Cod, Massachusetts in the U.S.A. She is a single mom of three grown children and happily divorced. Her favorite genre is cozy mysteries and she has several series on Amazon at the present time. The Jelly Shop Mysteries and The Shipwreck Café Mysteries are self published. The Braddock Mysteries are released by Level Best Books. Trash to Treasure Cozy Mysteries and Paint and Sip Cozy Mysteries are published by Summer Prescott Books.

SUSAN LOVE BROWN

Susan Love Brown is Professor Emerita at Florida Atlantic University. Her first short story, "In Kind" was published in *Mystery Most Devious* (Malice Domestic 18, 2024). She is an avid mystery reader and a poet as well.

ED RIDGLEY

Ed Ridgley (https://linktr.ee/edridgley) won a New Yorker Cartoon Caption Contest in 2010, the cartoon showing a bar scene with a bartender, a detective, and a ballerina. His caption (the bartender's words) said "The guy you're looking for waltzed out of here an hour ago." He won the *Alfred Hitchcock Mystery Magazine*'s Mysterious Photograph Contest, July/August 2023 edition. Ed hiked to Everest Base Camp in Nepal in 2018 crossing off number one on his bucket list.

ASHLEY-RUTH M. BERNIER

Ashley-Ruth M. Bernier's stories have appeared in *Ellery Queen's Mystery Magazine*, *Black Cat Weekly*, *Stone's Throw*, *Smoking Pen Press*, *Mystery Most Devious*, and *The Best American Mystery and Suspense 2023*. Originally from St. Thomas, U.S. Virgin Islands, Ashley-Ruth writes mysteries highlighting the vibrant culture of her home. She currently lives in North Carolina with her family, where she teaches first grade and searches for free time to write.

SARAH BEWLEY

Sarah Bewley is the author of the Eden County Mysteries published by Level Best Books. She's a former Private Investigator and an award winning playwright. She boxes and rock climbs.

HUGH LESSIG

Hugh Lessig's debut novel, *Fadeaway Joe*, was published in August 2023 by Crooked Lane Books. His short stories have appeared in numerous anthologies from Down & Out Books, including the Mickey Finn: 21st Century Noir series. His is a former newspaper reporter, having spent 34 years covering everything from small town government to the Navy's earthquake relief effort in Haiti, and currently works in communications for a major defense contractor in Virginia.

P. J. NELSON

P. J. Nelson (who also writes as Phillip DePoy, his real name) is the Edgar Award-winning author of 21 novels and 43 produced plays. He was writer in residence for the Georgia Council for the Arts for many years, awarded a Lifetime Achievement Award in 2015. Publications include five Flap Tucker mysteries (Shamus finalist), seven Fever Devilin novels, two Christopher Marlowe mysteries, and the Foggy Moscowitz series. He holds degrees in English literature and folklore, and a graduate degree in performance art.

MELISSA WESTEMEIER

Melissa Westemeier's fiction includes rom-com and a trilogy loosely based on her experience tending bar on the Wolf River in Wisconsin. She's thrilled to realize her childhood dream of writing murder mysteries. The first in her Nun the Wiser Mysteries, *Old Habits Die Hard*, appeared in April 2025.

PATRICIA GOUTHRO

Patricia Gouthro is an avid mystery reader and a professor in Graduate Studies in Lifelong Learning at Mount Saint Vincent University in Halifax, Nova Scotia, who has done research on fiction writing and Sisters in Crime, a women's mystery writing organization.

JEAN MACALUSO

The author is a long-time fan of Malice Domestic, all the way back to 1996, when her mystery made the finals in the competition for a first novel. More recently, she has focused on short stories, and was thrilled to have her "Home & Garden Gothic" included in Malice's previous *Mystery Most Traditional* anthology.

VICTORIA DOWD

Victoria is an award-winning bestseller, shortlisted for the CWA Dagger. Her novel, *The Smart Woman's Guide to Murder*, won The People's Book Prize for fiction and was In Search of the Classic Mystery Novel's Book of the Year. Her novel *Murder Most Cold* won the Grand Puzzly award. Victoria was awarded the Gothic Fiction prize for her short fiction. She is head of the London Crime Writers' Association and was a criminal defence barrister.

STEVE SHROTT

Steve Shrott's stories have appeared in numerous publications, including the Agatha-winning anthology, *This Time for Sure*. Steve also wrote the introduction and has a story in the humorous-mystery anthology, *Die Laughing*. He has written two comedic mystery novels, *Audition for Death*, and *Dead Men Don't Get Married*, and his comedy material has been used by well-known performers of stage and screen. Some of his jokes are in the Smithsonian Institution.

DAVID BART

David Bart has published over thirty short stories, appearing in many anthologies like the Mystery Writers of America Anthony award-winning anthology *Crime Hits Home*. His work has also appeared in *Alfred Hitchcock's Mystery Magazine*, *Ellery Queen Mystery Magazine*, *Mystery Magazine*, *Mystery Tribune* and *The Strand Magazine*.

J. JAMIE GROCE

J. Jamie Groce was a Michener Center for Writers fellow and writes fiction and screenplays in Seattle. His original script *Painkillers* was produced by Liberation Pictures in 2014.

REBECCA BRITTENHAM

Rebecca Brittenham is a mystery writer, a member of Mystery Writers of America and Sisters in Crime. She completed a psychological thriller, *Body in the Skylight*, and its sequel, *Body at the Cathedral*, which are currently in search of a publisher. Her current project, *The Uncooked American*, is a mystery set in modern-day Vietnam. By day, she is a Professor of English at Indiana University, South Bend, where she teaches Victorian Literature, Detective Fiction, Food Writing, and the Literature of Walking.

ABOUT THE EDITORS

JOHN BETANCOURT

John Betancourt runs Wildside Press, which takes up most of his time. He was a full-time science fiction writer in his misspent youth, hitting best-seller lists with his Star Trek novels and other series, though he's been writing mystery stories for years, too—winning the first Black Orchid Novella Award from *Alfred Hitchcock's Mystery Magazine* and the Nero Wolfe Society. His most recent novel (and his first in more than a decade) is *The Things from Another World* (2024), a sequel to the classic *Who Goes There?* by John W. Campbell, Jr. (filmed as *The Thing*, by John Carpenter).

MICHAEL BRACKEN

Michael Bracken (*CrimeFictionWriter.com*) is an Edgar- and Shamus-nominated author of almost 1,300 short stories published in *The Best American Mystery Stories*, *The Best Mystery Stories of the Year*, and elsewhere. He is the editor of *Black Cat Mystery Magazine* and several anthologies, including the Anthony Award-nominated *The Eyes of Texas*.

CARLA KAESSINGER COUPE

Carla Kaessinger Coupe became the editor of *Sherlock Holmes Mystery Magazine* in 2021. Her own short stories have appeared in several magazines, including *The Strand*, as well as many anthologies. Two of her short stories were nominated for Agatha Awards and another, "The Book of Tobit," was included in *The Best American Mystery Stories 2012*.